Beauty

TEMPTS THE

Beast

By Lorraine Heath

BEAUTY TEMPTS THE BEAST
THE EARL TAKES A FANCY
THE DUCHESS IN HIS BED
THE SCOUNDREL IN HER BED
TEXAS LEGACY (novella)
WHEN A DUKE LOVES A WOMAN
BEYOND SCANDAL AND DESIRE
GENTLEMEN PREFER HEIRESSES (novella)
AN AFFAIR WITH A NOTORIOUS HEIRESS
WHEN THE MARQUESS FALLS (novella)
THE VISCOUNT AND THE VIXEN
THE EARL TAKES ALL
FALLING INTO BED WITH A DUKE
THE DUKE AND THE LADY IN RED
THE LAST WICKED SCOUNDREL (novella)
ONCE MORE, MY DARLING ROGUE
THE GUNSLINGER (novella)
WHEN THE DUKE WAS WICKED
DECK THE HALLS WITH LOVE (novella)
LORD OF WICKED INTENTIONS
LORD OF TEMPTATION
SHE TEMPTS THE DUKE
WAKING UP WITH THE DUKE
PLEASURES OF A NOTORIOUS GENTLEMAN
PASSIONS OF A WICKED EARL
MIDNIGHT PLEASURES WITH A SCOUNDREL
SURRENDER TO THE DEVIL
BETWEEN THE DEVIL AND DESIRE
IN BED WITH THE DEVIL
JUST WICKED ENOUGH
A DUKE OF HER OWN
PROMISE ME FOREVER
A MATTER OF TEMPTATION
AS AN EARL DESIRES
AN INVITATION TO SEDUCTION
LOVE WITH A SCANDALOUS LORD
TO MARRY AN HEIRESS
THE OUTLAW AND THE LADY
NEVER MARRY A COWBOY
NEVER LOVE A COWBOY
A ROGUE IN TEXAS
TEXAS SPLENDOR
TEXAS GLORY
TEXAS DESTINY
ALWAYS TO REMEMBER
PARTING GIFTS
SWEET LULLABY

Lorraine Heath

Beauty
TEMPTS THE
Beast

A Sins for All Seasons Novel

AVONBOOKS

An Imprint of HarperCollinsPublishers

BEAUTY TEMPTS THE BEAST. Copyright © 2020 by Jan Nowasky. All rights reserved. Printed in the United States of America. No part of this book may be used or reproduced in any manner whatsoever without written permission except in the case of brief quotations embodied in critical articles and reviews. For information, address HarperCollins Publishers, 195 Broadway, New York, NY 10007.

First Avon Books mass market printing: October 2020
First Avon Books hardcover printing: September 2020

Print Edition ISBN: 978-0-06-303550-8
Digital Edition ISBN: 978-0-06-295193-9

Avon, Avon & logo, and Avon Books & logo are registered trademarks of HarperCollins Publishers in the United States of America and other countries.

HarperCollins is a registered trademark of HarperCollins Publishers in the United States of America and other countries.

FIRST EDITION

20 21 22 23 24 LSC 10 9 8 7 6 5 4 3 2 1

To Lenora Bell
For the friendship, conversations, brainstorming,
and stories that keep me reading late into the night

And to Chris Simmie
Who gave me an appreciation for all things Scottish

Beauty

TEMPTS THE

Beast

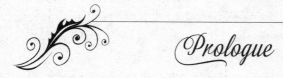

Prologue

The frantic knocking woke Ettie Trewlove from her first restful sleep in days. Her three lads, each only a few months old, were at various stages of teething, which made them a grumpy lot, but tonight for some inexplicable reason they were sleeping like angels.

The rapping continued. With no hope of it stopping unless answered, she tossed back the covers and climbed out of her bed. After turning up the flame in the lamp on the bedside table, she carried it with her to light the way as she passed by her dear boys, smiling at them snuggled against each other in the small crib. They'd soon be outgrowing it, and she'd have to make other accommodations for them.

Shuffling to the door, she opened it a crack and peered out, surprised to see a woman, a little younger than her own twenty years, standing there, a blanketed bundle cradled tightly in her arms. Until tonight, only men had made the deliveries.

"Are you Ettie Trewlove, the woman who takes in bairns born out of wedlock and sees them well cared for?" Hope and fear wove themselves through her thick Scottish brogue.

Ettie nodded. A baby farmer by trade, for a few pounds each, she took in by-blows no one wanted, sparing their mums the shame and challenges their presence would have brought them. "Aye."

"Will you take my lad? I've only a few shillings to leave with you, but you won't have to keep him long." With her wide, dark eyes, she glanced around quickly. "Just until it's safe. And then I'll be back for him."

A few shillings would see him fed for only a couple of weeks, and she had three others in need of food. Still, she set the lamp on the table beside the door, opened it wider, and held out her arms. "Aye, I'll take him."

The young woman eased aside the blanket and pressed a kiss to the sleeping babe's cheek.

"What the devil did you do to him?" Ettie asked in dismay.

The stranger jerked up her head, held her gaze. "Nothing. He was born this way. But he's a good boy, will give you no trouble a'tall. Please don't turn him away. You're my last hope for protecting him from those who wish him harm."

Ettie knew some people believed children born out of wedlock were born in sin and should be denied breath.

"I don't blame babes for things that aren't their fault." If she did, she wouldn't have found herself with three born on the wrong side of the blanket. Now four. She wiggled her fingers. "Hand him over."

Taking care not to wake him, the lass—the lamplight caught her fully, showing her to be more girl than grown—gently placed the lad in Ettie's waiting arms. "Promise me you'll love him like he was your own."

"'Tis the only way I know how to love a wee one."

With a tremulous smile, she pressed the coins into Ettie's palm. "Thank you."

Turning away, she took three steps before glancing back over her shoulder, tears now glistening in her eyes. "His name is Benedict. I *will* come back for him."

The words were spoken with fierce conviction, and Ettie wasn't certain who the lass was trying to convince: Ettie or herself.

The young woman darted into the thick fog and quickly disappeared into the shrouded darkness.

And Ettie Trewlove kept her promise. She raised the lad as though he were her own and loved him as only a mother could.

Chapter 1

Whitechapel
December 1873

The woman didn't belong here.

Not at the Mermaid and Unicorn, not serving spirits.

Sitting at a small table near the back of his sister's tavern, Benedict Trewlove—known throughout Whitechapel as Beast—knew that assessment to be true with absolute conviction, just as he knew he'd never planned to be a brothel owner.

But when he was seventeen, working the docks, with fists the size of ham hocks, sixteen-year-old Sally Greene had asked him to look out for her as she plied her wares on the streets. A gang boss was extorting protection money from her. She'd decided Beast wouldn't insist on taking most of her earnings like Three-Fingered Bill. She'd been correct.

Beast hadn't wanted any payment at all, but from time to time he'd found extra coins tucked here and there in his clothing. Sally was skilled not only at lifting her skirts but at picking pockets as well, often doing both at the same time. He suspected it had gone against the grain for her to be stuffing coins *into* pockets. But he never embarrassed her by confronting her about it. He accepted the copper and silver with grace.

When a few of her friends asked the same of him, he'd found it easier to watch them if they were in the same spot, so he'd let a few rooms. Doing so had the added benefit of keeping them warm in winter so they seldom took ill, which in turn increased their earnings. Eventually, he was leasing an entire building for his girls. Now he owned it.

God always rewards a man for doing good, his mum had often told him. But in his experience, rewards came when a man applied himself—even if what he applied himself to was sometimes frowned upon by those with a higher moral standard.

The woman he now observed would no doubt do quite a bit of frowning. She looked the type. Sounded the type. Her posh, distinct diction indicated nobility born, bred, and raised.

Her clothing, as well. The fabric, cut, and workmanship of her simple gray frock was exquisite, although he'd wager that she'd lost a little weight since it had been purchased. While the other serving maids bared a good bit of their cleavage in hopes the customers would leave a few extra coins, she was done up as tight as a drum, buttoned up to her chin, down to her wrists. Her hair, pale as moonbeams, gathered up in a rather untidy knot that had failed to keep several strands secure, so they now teased her delicate cheekbones, was the only thing about her that appeared inelegant. Her posture was perfect, her stride graceful as she made her way back to his table after asking what she could bring him a few minutes earlier.

Parting her lips slightly, releasing a quick gust of air that sent the rebellious strands of her hair flying, she set the tumbler in front of him. "Here you are, sir. The bartender indicated there'll be no charge."

While his sister wasn't here tonight, seldom worked within these walls any longer after becoming a duchess, Gillie didn't expect him to pay for food or drink, just as he didn't expect her to pay him for the transport on his ships of alcohol she'd purchased from beyond England's shores. Trewloves didn't charge Trewloves, nor did they keep an accounting of favors done.

The barmaid started to turn—

"What are you doing here?" he asked.

She swung back around, a tiny pleat forming between her delicate dark blond brows that framed the most unusual blue eyes he'd ever seen. A deep blue with the tiniest streaks of gray. "Bringing you your scotch."

Shaking his head, he waved his hand in an easy manner to encompass their surroundings. "I mean in Whitechapel, working, specifically in this tavern. Every aspect of you screams Mayfair."

"None o' yer bleedin' biz'ness," she retorted in perfect Cockney. "Is that better?" Perfect Mayfair.

Presenting him with her back, she marched off. Admiring the view as well as her huff of indignation, he took a long, slow swallow of scotch. She had spunk, he'd give her that. She was also correct. She was none of his business. Still, he was intrigued. She was too refined for the coarseness of this place. She'd look more at home in a ballroom, a garden, a stately manor house. She should be waited upon, not be the one doing the serving.

He liked for things to make sense. She didn't make sense. Until she did, he was going to be tempted to uncover, unravel, and solve the mystery of her.

ALTHEA STANWICK KNEW he was watching her, could feel the touch of his gaze as though he was walking beside her with his hand pressed against the small of her back.

She'd noticed him the moment he strode into the tavern. It was as though every molecule of air had shifted to accommodate not only his considerable height and the breadth of his shoulders, but his confidence and bearing as well. The man prowled about as though he feared nothing, possessed the power to topple empires at a whim.

She'd been both enthralled and unsettled. Then he'd taken a chair at a table near the back that was her responsibility, and she'd felt as though someone had given a hard yank on the lacings of her corset, crushing her ribs until she could barely breathe.

Servicing other customers, she'd put off approaching him as long as she could. Finally, she'd made her way to him, knowing he was taking in every aspect of her as she was him. His thick black hair brushed past his collar—lighting upon those broad shoulders as though the strands wished to eternally caress them—and was styled in such a way that a portion of the right side of his face was covered, which made him appear more mysterious, a man who possessed secrets and was extremely skilled at keeping them.

Something about him seemed familiar but she couldn't quite place how she might have come to know him. Perhaps she'd passed him on these streets that after three long months were finally becoming familiar, or he'd come in another night and not sat at her table. Although she couldn't imagine forgetting him if she'd ever seen him at the Mermaid. "What may I bring you, good sir?"

A barely perceptible widening of those onyx eyes that had steadfastly been studying her with an appreciation that had caused her to sound a bit breathy. "Scotch."

His voice had been a deep rumble that had shimmied through the entire length of her, like the warm and comforting sensations she experienced when she came in from the bitter cold and approached a blazing fire. She'd been disappointed that he'd uttered only a single word. But then when she'd returned with his drink, he'd shown an interest in her past, which was a secret she was skilled at keeping because if anyone learned the truth—

It did not bear thinking about.

As she now wended her way among the tables after leaving him, she decided *he* did not bear thinking about.

An arm suddenly whipped out, wrapped around her waist, and rudely jerked her off her feet so she landed hard on a sturdy lap comprised of thick thighs. His other hand going to places on her person it most certainly should not, pinching what she'd given him no permission to pinch, the young man grinned broadly, his eyes filled with mischief. "What 'ave we 'ere? Who ye be, me lovely?"

Reaching back, she grabbed a nearly full tankard resting near the hand of one of his mates and proceeded to dump its contents over his ginger head. With a curse and a yell, he abruptly released her. In all due haste, she scrambled off his lap and beyond his reach. "Pardon my clumsiness. I'll get you another."

She'd have rather conked him on the side of the head with the tankard but knew she was going to be in enough trouble as it was. The Mermaid prided itself on how well it treated its patrons, regardless of how many or how few coins lined their pockets. Striding quickly, she made her way to the bar and slammed the pewter tankard down on the polished woodgrain. "Guinness."

The bartender, who also managed the place, sighed as though she was the bane of his existence, probably because she was. "I've told you before, you can't be dumping beer over heads."

It was the third time she'd done it since she started working here ten days earlier. She considered defending her actions but had done so twice before already and received no sympathy whatsoever from him, just a stare that hardened with each word spoken, so she merely nodded in acknowledgment of the un-deserved scolding. Until recently, an admonishment had never been directed her way. She didn't much like being treated with so little consideration or having her opinion carry no weight, but then there was a good bit about her new life that she didn't favor. As a matter of fact, there was nothing at all about it that she did.

"I'll have to take this pint out of your weekly earnings."

Striving to reflect contrition so she wouldn't find herself dis-missed, she nodded again. At this rate, she was going to have no weekly earnings.

"Jimmy pinched her bum, Mac," Polly, another one of the serv-ing girls, said. "I saw it."

"How could you have seen it, Polly? You were standing right there."

"I've got good eyes."

"Not that good." He turned away and began filling the tankard.

Polly looked at her sympathetically. "They was just having a bit o' fun."

"But it's not any fun at all, is it?" She was certain Polly of the ample cleavage had endured her share of being dragged onto laps. Although she might not have minded. She was forever laughing and flirting with the chaps, seeming to have a grand time doing something that Althea disliked with every fiber of her being.

She was disappointed to see the large fellow she'd only just served leaning down to say something to the cackling Jimmy. Probably wanted to ask what her bottom felt like. But then Jimmy abruptly stopped laughing. She'd heard of people turning as white as a ghost but had never seen anyone actually do it. Until now. Jimmy looked as though the man had effectively and quickly leeched all the blood from his veins.

"Jimmy won't be touching you no more," Polly said with a bit of triumph, "now that Beast has had a quiet word with him."

"Beast?"

Polly looked surprised but nodded. "Yeah. The big bloke."

The big bloke who didn't even look back as he strode out through the door. She wondered how he'd come to have that moniker because to her eye he was anything but beastly. *Devil* would have served him better as he was devilishly handsome, his features strong and bold.

"Who is he when he's at home?" Althea asked.

Polly gave her a pointed look. "Someone you don't want to cross if you know what's good for you."

Althea rather wished she'd had that bit of advice before she'd had her previous encounter with him. She was relatively certain he hadn't been happy about her response to his question, so she doubted whatever had caused Jimmy to blanch had anything to do with her. Perhaps he owed the man money.

Mac placed the tankard on the counter. "Polly, why don't you take Jimmy his brew?"

"Would be better if Althea did."

She'd wanted to kiss Mac when he'd passed the task off to Polly, wanted to scowl at Polly for refusing, but knew it was unfair for the other barmaid to have to take on her chores. After picking up the tankard, she edged her way between the tables until she reached Jimmy's. He and his mates were staring at the surface as though they'd never seen wood before and were striving to decipher how it had come to be. Without uttering a word, she set down the tankard.

"I'm sorry," Jimmy blurted.

"I beg your pardon?"

With eyes big, wide, and fearful, he looked up at her. "I'm sorry. Shouldn't 'ave done it. Won't do it again."

She tried not to let her surprise show. "I very much appreciate that and your apology."

"You'll tell Beast, right, the next time 'e comes in, right, you'll tell 'im I said I was sorry, a'right. Don't need me fingers broke." His words tumbled out, one after another, no breath or pause between.

She suspected she had no success at all hiding her astonishment this time. He'd threatened to break the man's fingers? His chums were still not looking at her, had hunched their shoulders in an attempt to make themselves smaller, possibly hoping to avoid her scrutiny. "Yes, I'll let him know."

"Jolly good." Taking the tankard, he began gulping the contents.

She wasn't certain she blamed him. Nor was she certain why the stranger had stood up for her, but couldn't deny taking a great deal of pleasure in his efforts at being her champion. It had been far too long since anyone, other than her brothers, had taken a stand to defend her.

She made her way to the large gent's table to retrieve his empty glass. When she reached it, she saw the sovereign resting there. Picking up the glass, she started to walk away.

"That's for you."

She glanced back at Rob, who was wiping down a nearby table. Usually, the tall, slender young man collected everything off the tables and gave them a thorough wiping down, but since the customer hadn't been there long enough to make a mess, she'd thought to spare him the trouble. "I'm certain he meant it for you, for cleaning up after him." A more than generous donation for the service.

He walked over to her. "He gave me mine, said that one was for you."

"He gave us each a sovereign?" The coin's value of a pound was double the ten shillings—if she didn't subtract the upended beer—she normally earned for the six days she worked in a week.

The young man shrugged, the brown locks covering his forehead falling into his eyes. "Like all Trewloves, he's probably as rich as Croesus."

He was a Trewlove? That was no doubt why he looked familiar. She'd probably seen him at the spate of recent weddings when a number of Trewloves had married nobles. The owner of this establishment had married the Duke of Thornley. Would this Beast fellow tell his sister how rude she'd been to him? Would she lose her position? But then why would he have left her a little extra with which to line her pocket if he was going to take action to see her gone?

"Go on, take it," Rob said as he began running a damp rag over the table.

Very carefully, she picked up the coin and slipped it into her pocket. "Does he come here often?"

"Depends what you call *often*. The brothers all used to spend a good bit of their time here before they got married. He's the only one who's managed to escape the matrimonial shackles but doesn't come 'round as often now that the others are scarce."

When Mr. Trewlove returned she would not only let him know that Jimmy had apologized, but would also thank him for having a word with the rambunctious young man. She didn't think anyone at his table was going to be giving her bottom any attention in the near future.

Certainly no one troubled her the remainder of the night.

Still, she was grateful when the customers were ushered out at midnight and the front door was bolted. She and the other workers began placing chairs on tables, sweeping, mopping, tidying up. It was a little over half an hour later when they all stepped into the alley. Mac locked the back door behind them, said his farewells, and headed up to the rooms that came along with his position. As the others—Polly, Rob, the cook, another bartender, and another serving maid—wished her good-night and carried on, she wandered to the street that the tavern faced. Her brother was usually leaning against the front of the building, waiting to escort her home. He didn't like her walking alone about Whitechapel at night. *She* didn't like walking alone at night.

Once she reached the street, a fissure of dread speared her. Griffith wasn't there. He was always prompt, which at first had come as a shock to her. As the spare, he'd only ever been interested in play, had never taken responsibility for anything other than having a grand time.

The streetlamps dotting the area couldn't hold at bay all the shadows. Glancing around, she saw a couple of people walking in the distance, becoming smaller as they moved away from her, but he wouldn't have come from that direction anyway. Perhaps he was only running late.

Please, dear Lord, don't let anything have happened to him. While he was skilled at shooting at targets, had mastered fencing, and engaged in boxing for sport, she wasn't entirely convinced all of that translated well to dealing with the villainous scoundrels who made Whitechapel their home. He was no more accustomed to wandering these dangerous streets than she was.

Drawing her ermine-lined cloak more tightly around her, she began walking, hoping to meet up with him shortly and to be that much closer to their residence when she did. After ten hours at her labors, her feet, lower back, and shoulders ached. She wanted to be home. Even as she had the thought, she acknowledged they'd never go home again. It had been taken from them, and what they had now could barely be described as a residence.

Unexpectedly, the fine hairs on the back of her neck quivered as though someone had placed a warm hand against her nape. She swung around.

The people she'd seen earlier were farther away, weren't coming for her. While she didn't feel in danger, she couldn't shake off the sensation that she wasn't alone, that someone was near enough to hear her harsh breathing, that she was being watched.

But she saw only the shadows, heard only the occasional skitter of rats.

Reaching into her reticule, she pulled out the small dagger her older brother had given her and taught her how to wield, before he'd taken his leave to go God knew where. She doubted the four-inch blade would kill anyone, but it might at least give a miscreant pause, hold him at bay.

Besides, it could just be her imagination playing tricks on her. Until three months ago, she'd never gone anywhere alone. Her lady's maid, footmen, her mother, a friend—someone always accompanied her. She'd never had to be aware of her surroundings, never had to worry about being accosted. But now she'd become extremely vigilant and wary. She hated all the worry, the uncertainty, and tried not to recall all the years of security she'd taken for granted, assuming she would always be spoiled, well tended, without care. When every day had been filled with fun, laughter, and good cheer.

Turning back around, she came up short at the sight of Griffith a few steps away and very nearly screamed at his sudden appearance. Doing so would have angered her more. "Where the devil have you been?"

He ducked his blond head. "Apologies. I got caught up in something and lost track of the hour."

"In what, precisely?"

"It's not important. Let's get you home." He came nearer, put his hand protectively on her shoulder, and ushered her forward. Just like her, he was more aware of their surroundings, his head continually swiveling, as he searched for anything amiss.

Before the upheaval in their lives, he'd barely given her the time of day. She'd never been particularly close to her brothers. The heir, Marcus, was five years older than she. Griffith three. She'd had the impression they viewed her as a nuisance more than anything, avoiding her whenever possible, seldom engaging her in conversation when they weren't in a position to escape her company. They'd just sat in awkward silence. It seemed the only thing they had in common were their parents.

After taking several steps, she realized that warm sensation of being touched against her nape had melted away. She glanced over her shoulder. Had someone been watching her and backed off with Griffith's arrival?

"Did you see anyone about when you came up?" she asked.

"No one near, no one appearing to have any interest in you. Again, I apologize for my tardiness. I miss having the convenience of a bloody carriage whenever we damned well wanted one."

In all of her twenty-four years, she'd never heard him utter a profanity. Now his sentences were often peppered with words that shouldn't be spoken in the presence of a lady, but then she was no longer a lady. She, too, missed being able to call for a carriage, especially when she wasn't certain her legs could hold her upright much longer.

But they did their duty, kept moving forward until eventually they arrived at the shabby little residence they were leasing. It was two levels. They lived in the lower level. Someone with extremely heavy feet inhabited the second level, which was only accessible from stairs on the outside. Griffith unlocked the door, shoved it open, and waited until she'd preceded him inside. It was not a newer accommodation. No gas to make their situation a bit more convenient. An oil lamp rested on the oaken table near the empty hearth and her brother was quick to light it.

"Looks like Marcus has been here," Griffith said as he reached for a parcel wrapped in brown paper, secured with string. Opening it, he revealed a few pounds. "This will keep a roof over our heads for a bit longer."

"Why is he so mysterious? Why doesn't he visit with us, instead of just leaving little gifts when we're not here?" When they'd lost their standing within Society, lost everything really, he'd taken them under his wing, found them this residence. Once they were settled, he'd simply disappeared. She'd not seen him since.

"It's safer, for us, for him."

"Why won't you tell me precisely what he's doing?" She'd asked several times.

"I don't know the details of it." Always his answer, although she was beginning to suspect he was lying.

"But whatever it is, it is dangerous." Persisting with the topic, she was rather certain she should be worried about Marcus.

He rubbed his brow. "It's late, Althea, and I have to be at the docks early. I'm to bed."

"Let me see to your hands first."

"They're fine."

"Griff, if they get infected, you're going to lose them, and then where will we be?"

With a long-suffering dramatic sigh—she'd once heard a rumor that he'd had an affair with an actress, and she couldn't help but believe he'd adopted some of her theatrics—he nodded.

Not bothering to remove her cloak because the air was cold and they wouldn't have a fire tonight, she pumped water into a bowl, grabbed some linen and the salve. By the time she joined him at the table, he'd removed the bandages she'd wrapped around his hands that morning.

"They're looking better," he mused.

In spite of the fact he wore gloves, lifting and hauling crates had caused blisters, torn skin, and calluses. He winced as she saw to the raw places. She didn't know how he managed to continue at his labors. Until three months ago, the most laborious thing he'd ever done was lift a tankard or a card at a gaming table. And he'd certainly never arisen before dawn. He'd seldom moved about before noon.

"Oh, I forgot. A bit of good news. Someone left me a sovereign tonight."

"Why would he do that?" She heard the suspicion in his voice. They had learned to trust no one.

"My smile?"

He grinned. "It has been known to lay men flat."

Yes, once she'd been the darling of the *ton*, had been in no hurry to settle on anyone. Until finally, she'd decided on the Earl of Chadbourne. They were to have been married in January, a few weeks from now. "I'll give it to you when I'm done here."

"Keep it. You might have a need for it."

"I want to contribute." It was the reason she'd taken a position at the tavern. She'd begun feeling rather useless. Keeping things tidy, preparing meals—which had been a challenge in itself—and mending Griffith's clothing had not taken most of her day. She'd been left with nothing to do but sit and worry.

"Then simply hold it close. I'll let you know if we have need of it."

While she appreciated the protectiveness, she also wanted to be viewed as independent, wanted her brothers to understand she was as equal to the task of handling their change in circumstance as they were. She very much doubted if he should run into Marcus, Griffith was going to tell him to stop sneaking into the residence and leaving them money. But he refused to take her coins.

She patted his freshly covered hands. "There. Almost as good as new."

He gave her a crooked smile. "Not really." Shoving back the chair, he stood. "Will you carry the lamp?"

She didn't know why he asked. It was their nightly ritual. They journeyed across the small room to the hallway where he turned right and she went left. She always waited until he disappeared into his bedchamber at the front of the house. He claimed not to be bothered by the dark, that he could navigate his way through it. When he closed his door, she went into her chamber at the rear of the residence and fought against the melancholy that usually came over her at the sight of the unfurnished room, the pile of blankets on the floor that served as her bed.

She knew her life would never again be as it once was, but had to believe that in time, it would improve.

Setting the lamp on the floor, she divested herself of her clothing, changed into her nightdress, undid her hair, brushed it a
hundred times, and plaited it. She had just settled on the pile of
blankets, bringing her ermine-lined cloak over her, when she remembered the sovereign. She dug it out of the pocket of her frock,
closed her fingers around it, and snuggled back down. She didn't
know why she viewed it as a talisman of better things to come.

Nestling her closed fist against her breast, she was torn between hoping this Beast fellow would return and praying she'd
never see him again. He'd guessed correctly that she originally
hailed from Mayfair.

How long would it take him to determine that the change in
her circumstance had come about because she was the cursed
daughter of a traitorous duke?

AFTER STRIDING INTO the residence, Beast crossed the foyer and
peered into the front parlor. The madam, Jewel, was plying four
gents—who were no doubt awaiting their turn—with alcohol and
keeping them entertained with ribald stories and jests. It had been
years since she'd taken a man to her bed. Catching sight of him,
she gave him a little smile that signaled all was well, no trouble
was afoot.

Christ, but he hated this bloody business.

He headed for the stairs. On his way up, he crossed paths with
Lily escorting one of the gents down. The man looked so proud of
himself that Beast briefly wondered if it had been his first time. It
was none of his concern. He did not care. He was weary of the
gentlemen lounging about, the women entertaining them. The
need to protect them.

He finally reached the top floor that served as their main living
quarters. He and all the ladies who worked within these walls
had private rooms along this hallway. He went into the library,
poured himself a scotch, dropped into the comfortable wing-
backed chair near the roaring fire, and tried not to think of the

serving wench who was as fair as an angel, a beauty who would tempt a saint into sinning.

Just the memory of her was enough to cause his body to tighten with need as though she sat across from him.

Everything within him had gone on heightened alert when he'd seen the man approaching her after she'd left the tavern. It hadn't been his intent to spy on her but because she didn't appear to belong in Whitechapel, he'd wanted to assure himself that she wasn't fool enough to walk the streets alone late at night. But it seemed she had a protector—a husband or a beau—and once Beast had acknowledged that she was in no danger, he'd slipped farther into the shadows and headed home.

Home. A strange word for a place where women earned their keep on their backs. Over the years he'd managed to find other employment for many of them, until he had only half a dozen remaining. But they needed to learn other skills and to be buffed to a polish if they had any hope of leaving this life behind.

Until they left it behind, he couldn't leave it behind.

Because he wouldn't abandon the women who'd been under his care, wouldn't leave them at the mercy of men who had no fear of harming them. He owed it to Sally Greene. She'd put her faith in him, and in the end, he'd let her down.

After tossing back his drink, he set the glass aside and stared at the flames writhing on the hearth. The last of his charges needed to be as poised as the tavern maid who had served him tonight—although she was no doubt the product of a lifetime of refining that had begun the moment she was placed in the cradle. Every single aspect of her indicated that the minutest detail of her had warranted attention; no facet of her had been left to chance. If he had to guess, he'd say she'd had dozens of tutors. The elegant way she moved her hands, the calm with which she set down his glass, her hair—

Her hair had been a rather lopsided mess, no doubt because she'd not been tutored on how to style it. She'd had a maid to do it for her, and that maid was no longer about to ensure every strand remained where it needed to be. He'd like to remove the pins and watch the heavy tresses tumble around her shoulders.

He recalled the skewing of her mouth, the quick burst of air, as she tried to control the rebellious hair that had no desire to behave. He doubted she'd ever done that in Mayfair. It was pure Whitechapel, possibly the only thing about her that was.

Had she been embroiled in a scandal? Was there some handsome swain who stole her heart and then did wrong by her? Had she fallen in love with a commoner, cast aside the world for which she'd been prepared? Was he the man who'd come for her tonight, the one whose arrival had pleased her so damned much, brought her such relief?

Why was she even bombarding his thoughts? It wasn't as though she'd have any role in his life other than bringing him his favorite libation when he visited his sister's tavern.

Perhaps he should take one of the women with him the next time he went. Show the bawd how gracefully every aspect of her moved in tandem, how perfect her posture, how calm and steady her mien—

He'd have to explain mien and tandem. It wasn't enough for them to observe. They needed to be shown how it was done, how to acquire that level of inherent confidence. They needed a tutor. Where the devil was he going to find one of those in one of the poorest areas of London? It wasn't as though these streets were teeming with the posh.

Settling back, he picked up his glass and studied the way the flames created dancing light over the cut crystal. Whitechapel wasn't *teeming* with the posh. But it did have one.

And he knew exactly where to find her.

Chapter 2

*I*t was after ten when Althea felt him walk through the door. Her back was to it as she set two tankards on the table, and yet she knew with every fiber of her being that when she turned, he would be there. Tall, broad, bold, with his gaze homed in on her.

Still, she was surprised when she finally spun around to see that he hadn't moved beyond the entry, as though he'd been arrested by the sight of her. To say her gaze slammed into his was putting it mildly. What was it about him that made her feel as though he was brushing up against her, and not at all in the objectional way Jimmy had been touching her the night before, but in a manner that made her nipples pucker? Damned rebellious things.

She was the first to break eye contact, heading to the bar to collect the drinks for a table of four. *Don't sit at my table. Do sit at my table. Don't. Do.*

He did. He took the same table at the back that he'd had the night before, and it suddenly occurred to her that she'd never seen anyone else sit there. Was it a rule of the establishment that it was always to be open for him?

"Scotch," she said to Mac when he brought her the last tankard for the table of four. Quickly, she delivered the beer, returned to the bar, snatched up the tumbler, and headed to the table at the back.

It wasn't exactly a smile he gave her when she set the glass before him, but she detected a slight movement of his lips as though he was tempted to grin. It caused a funny sensation behind her ribs, as though a thousand butterflies had taken flight.

"You remembered my preference in drink."

"It wasn't that difficult. You were here only last night." Had she left her lungs with Mac? Why was she finding it a challenge to draw breath? "Jimmy apologized."

Leaning toward her, he cocked his head slightly, in the manner that many of the customers did, so an ear was more directly facing in her direction. As usual, the tavern was crowded, hardly an empty seat to be had. With the cacophony of all the various conversations, laughter, scraping of chairs, pounding of fists on tables, it was difficult to catch all the words when anyone spoke. She often engaged in the same maneuver.

"I beg your pardon?" he said.

She raised her voice to be heard over the din. "Jimmy apologized—quite profusely, actually."

"Good."

"He was rather insistent I let you know."

He merely nodded.

"Do you often threaten to break fingers?"

"I threaten to break a good many things. I don't tolerate men mistreating women."

"But you don't even know me."

"Acquaintanceship is not a requirement for my ensuring you're not harassed."

"I could be a right termagant."

The mouth wasn't smiling but the eyes were, and somehow that made him far more dangerous, more approachable, more charming.

"Wouldn't matter." He seemed to settle more comfortably into the straight-backed wooden chair as though it were the most plush cushioned armchair that existed in the world. "You don't speak as though you come from the streets."

"Neither do you." He spoke as though he'd been born to the aristocracy. She'd heard that the family of bastards, in spite of their humble upbringing and scandalous backgrounds, had educated themselves in all things important and proper so they could move about within the upper echelons of Society and not be found lacking. And it seemed of late, most of them were moving easily about in that world. Except him. She couldn't recall seeing him anywhere other than at a church for a wedding.

"I suspect we had a very different education. Did I have the right of it last night? You hail from Mayfair?"

"Why is it important that you know?"

"Why is it important that I not?"

She glanced around, made sure no one was signaling for her, wishing like the devil someone was, before bringing her attention back to him. If he was going to keep at it like water eroding stone, she might as well eliminate the mystery of it, so he'd leave her be. "I once lived in Mayfair, yes."

His eyes narrowed slightly as though he was striving to make sense of what that meant. "Then you're an aristocratic lady."

"No." Once, but no more. "You would be incorrect." *Three months ago you wouldn't have been, but today you are. But then three months ago I wouldn't have brought you scotch, we'd have never carried on a conversation, and I'd have been glad of it.* Although she'd have only been glad of it because she wouldn't have known how he had the power to look at her as though no one else existed in the world.

"It's not often that I am."

Was that his polite way of calling her a liar? "That's an arrogant statement, and yet you didn't sound particularly arrogant while saying it. As a matter of fact, you sounded rather humble."

Was she flirting? She didn't think so. She no longer flirted with men. It only led to heartache.

"The truth comes with confidence; it doesn't require arrogance."

"You're a philosopher, then."

He shrugged. "I'd wager you were trained to have a place in that aristocratic world, and not as a servant, but as one who is served."

"I won't take that wager. I've had some education, yes." The questions were becoming too pointed, too close to revealing the truth of her. "If you'll excuse me, I have other customers."

"I have a proposition for you."

Oh, she did wish he hadn't said that just as she was beginning to like him. "You and half the gentlemen here. I'm not interested."

As SHE THREW back those slender shoulders and marched away, he almost called out, "Who propositioned you?"

It seemed more words needed to be had with a few chaps.

With a sigh, taking a slow sip of his scotch, he admitted he could have handled that better. Probably should have eased into it a bit more, worded it a little differently. And how often were the blokes here referred to as *gentlemen*? Most were laborers, dockworkers, bricklayers—not that he found anything wrong with those occupations. He'd once been a dockworker himself.

But in Mayfair any man who crossed her path would have been a lord, a noble, a true *gentleman*. Referred to as such, treated as such. What the hell was she doing here?

It wasn't for a lark. When Gillie had first opened the place, on occasion he'd helped out. The work was demanding. He preferred the docks. At least there he hadn't been required to be polite to people upon whom he wanted to dump ale. Which might have been what prompted him to threaten Jimmy last night. Normally, he would have just told him to leave off and that would have been sufficient. But something about the quick flash of fear on her face when Jimmy had tumbled her onto his lap had set Beast's back teeth on edge. He didn't believe she was accustomed to the frequent roughness of this area of London. So his words had been accompanied with a warning.

After finishing off his scotch, he removed his watch from his waistcoat pocket, checked the time, and tucked it away. An hour before they closed. It was bloody cold out, and he intended to make sure the bloke who'd come for her last night came for her tonight.

As she appeared to be deliberately avoiding any reason to look in his direction, it took him a while to catch her attention and hold up his empty glass. While he'd been unable to stop looking at her.

Bloody hell, she was beautiful. But her attractiveness had little to do with her heart-shaped face, the sharp cut of her cheekbones, the delicate bridge of her small nose, or her kissable lips. Although when taken together they created a stunning creature.

It was the command she had over those features that intrigued him. They never revealed anger or irritation or impatience. No matter how long it took some people to tell her exactly what they wanted, asking questions about the offerings as though they'd never been in the tavern—or any tavern—before and didn't know what could be had. No matter how many times she had to return to the same table with additional drinks. No matter how often she had to replace a beverage because the person decided that what he'd ordered wasn't to his taste after all.

He suspected that on the nights he wasn't there she received swats on her backside. He saw one fellow reaching for her with the flat of his hand. His mate slapped his wrist and jerked his head toward Beast. The would-be offender's eyes widened before he gave a little nod of acknowledgment. Most people in the area were aware of the sort of behavior directed toward women that Trewloves didn't tolerate.

She offered the prettiest smile to her customers. But for him, no curling up of her lips, no sparkle in her eyes. Serving him was a chore, a duty, and an unpleasant one at that. He wished he didn't long to have her smile directed his way, wasn't certain why he did. He didn't know why she'd snagged his attention the night before and continued to hold it. Why she called to the loneliness in him.

When she finally made her way over to him and set the full glass of scotch down, he said, "You misunderstood regarding my proposition."

"I very much doubt it."

Her nose had gone up ever so slightly and in spite of her diminutive height, she'd managed to give the appearance of looking down on him from Mount Olympus.

When she immediately walked away, he didn't try to stop her. He'd had too many of those haughty gazes cast his way over the past couple of years, whenever he'd attended one of his siblings' blasted weddings. Each of them had married a noble and that had meant churches filled with the toffs. A couple of the *ladies* had even approached him, signaling their interest in experiencing a bit of the rough. Seemed they'd believed fucking—a word they'd used much to his astonishment as he'd thought proper ladies didn't even know, much less speak, the term—a commoner, especially a bastard one, would be distinctively different than fucking a noble.

Taking one against a wall, another bent over a vicar's desk, he'd probably proven them right, confirmed he was no better than the name they called him.

He'd felt tainted, sullied, and used afterward, had no desire to ever again be intimate with a blueblood.

If he'd had any doubts before regarding the new barmaid, he had none now. He didn't know why she was in Whitechapel but knew her blood was as blue as it came. And he'd be damned before he'd beg her to help him.

Staring at the two sovereigns, Althea gingerly picked up one.

"They're both for you," Rob said as he dropped the damp rag on the table and began scrubbing the surface.

"Why would he leave me two sovereigns?" To demonstrate the generosity he would bestow upon her if she accepted his proposition?

"Why would he give us any?" Rob asked.

"How many did he give you tonight?"

"Two."

He wasn't singling her out, which made her feel somewhat better. Tonight he'd remained until a couple of minutes before closing. She'd caught him checking his watch several times, as though he was anxious to be about his business. Why, then, had he remained as long as he had?

Why had his gaze remained steadfastly on her? He didn't leer or ogle but was rather subtle in the watching. She doubted anyone who observed him could have discerned exactly where his attentions resided, but since his arrival she'd felt as though the gentlest of fingers had been tenderly caressing her cheeks or freeing rebellious strands of her hair from the knot pinned at the back of her head.

When he'd signaled for a third scotch, she'd been certain he was going to broach the subject of his proposition once more, and she had a scathing retort waiting on the tip of her tongue that would make her other two rebuffs seem exceedingly polite. But he hadn't spoken a single word while she set his glass on the table or after. Had merely studied her as though he could see clear into her soul and had the ability to rummage about in it, seeking out and uncovering all of her secrets.

She was fairly certain her cheeks had gone crimson beneath his regard, and she regretted that she'd not had the opportunity to refuse him once more. With most gents, after they made the lurid suggestion of what they'd like to do with her, they didn't give up until the liquor put them under the table. His proposition was the first she'd received before a gentleman had even taken a sip of alcohol, and that had made it all the worse because she couldn't dismiss it as his merely imbibing too much and losing the ability to reason. He'd had all his wits about him. It had hurt that he'd viewed her as someone so undeserving of his respect.

What did it matter? Griffith had warned her that if she took a position here, she would have to deal with ribald comments and indecent proposals. She'd tried two other occupations before resorting to tavern maid. As a seamstress, her skill level was such that her stitches seldom met the standard of quality insisted upon for the small payment she was offered. Her time at the grocers had been equally disappointing. The owner was often brushing by her or placing his hand on her waist. When he'd "accidentally" grazed her breast, she'd found herself summarily dismissed because she'd "accidentally" slapped his face.

While she didn't care for the unwanted attentions here, at least the salary was better than she'd found elsewhere. Other occupations might have been more acceptable, and she was better suited to them, but no one in the aristocracy was going to hire her as a governess or a companion, not after her father's actions had made the members of her family all pariahs.

When all was tidied up, and the place was closed up tight for the night, she followed her usual routine and made her way to the street. Disappointment slammed into her because Griffith was nowhere to be seen . . . again. What the devil was he doing that was causing his tardiness? If it killed her, she would pry the answer from him when he showed.

Determining she was in as much danger waiting as walking, she removed the dagger from her reticule and began striding briskly home. She again had that warm sensation of someone wrapping a hand around the nape of her neck. Without stopping her strides, she swung about, walking backward as she squinted at the dark shadows. She couldn't see anyone but still had the sense of being watched.

Spinning back around, she quickened her pace and tightened her hold on the weapon. Surely, she would run into Griffith at any moment. Even a hansom cab would be welcomed. She could use a portion of the unexpected coins she'd received tonight to get herself home.

Glancing back over her shoulder, she saw nothing, heard nothing. It was probably just paranoia on her part after all the warnings Griffith had given her. He hadn't wanted her working at night, but it had been the only position—

Suddenly, a hand grabbed her wrist, biting into the tender flesh, and an arm snaked forcefully around her waist. Releasing a blood-curdling scream as she was yanked into the darkened alley, she struck out blindly with the dagger, shuddering when it hit its mark.

"Ye bitch! Ye sliced me!"

A brick wall slammed into the back of her head, and pain ricocheted through it. Flashes of bright light floated around her. Her legs lost their vibrancy, and she slowly slid down, down, down . . .

From a great distance, somewhere beyond where she existed, she heard a growl, followed by the echoing crunch of bone being crushed. A grunt. Footsteps.

A large hand gently cradled her head. "Stay with me, Beauty, stay with me."

His tone reflected a desperation and she dearly wanted to adhere to his demand, but oblivion beckoned, refusing to be denied.

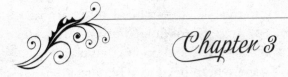

Chapter 3

*T*he first thing Althea noted was the warmth surrounding her, the absence of the cold that had been such a part of her for so long. Then she was hit by a powerful rose scent that made her eyes water. Someone was alternatingly patting the back of her hand and rubbing it.

"That's it, love, come on. Wake up." The feminine voice was a rough rasp, reminiscent of someone who spent a good bit of time coughing.

Opening her eyes, she was greeted by the countenance of a woman she judged to be a few years older than her own twenty-four years, her hair a fiery red. The woman's emerald eyes sparkled, and her smile revealed one front tooth overlapping another. Her kind expression was offering absolution, a shepherdess accustomed to taking in lost lambs.

"There, now, that's a good girl. You had him worried, you did." She jerked her head back slightly, and Althea looked past her to see Beast Trewlove standing with his right shoulder pressed against the dark green and burgundy patterned wall, near a window, his arms crossed over a massive chest that for some reason she thought she knew the feel of. Always before he'd been wearing a greatcoat and she'd thought it was partially responsible for his broadness. She was wrong. He was all brawn.

"What happened? How did I come to be here?"

Here being a dimly lit parlor rather garishly decorated with red fringed pillows as well as numerous statuettes and paintings revealing the taut buttocks and pert breasts of nude couples in various amorous positions. But it also contained the most comfortable sofa upon which she'd ever rested her weary body.

"Seems you swooned, love," the woman said.

"I don't swoon." She'd never swooned in her life.

"Call it what you like, he had to carry you here."

In those massive arms against that wide chest. Her mouth went dry with the thought.

"My name's Jewel, by the way. Here, let's sit you up, get a bit of warm tea into you."

Placing her arms around Althea until she was cushioned against her plump breasts, she helped her rise slightly and scoot back into the corner adorned with plush pillows. Althea grimaced as dizziness assailed her and pain shot through her skull. She pressed her hand to her forehead, but it didn't help.

"I've sent for a surgeon," he said quietly.

She met his gaze. "I'm not in need of a surgeon."

"The knot on the back of your head and the blood say otherwise."

All of a sudden the memories assailed her, and she remembered being dragged into an alley, the pain reverberating through her head. The growl, the crunching. *I threaten to break a good many things.* She had a feeling tonight he may have broken the man who attacked her. "You were following me."

"Not with any nefarious intent. I wanted only to ensure no harm came to you after your husband failed to show tonight."

"My husband?" She shook her head, nearly cried out at the agony, pushed her fingers against her temples. Not moving seemed to be her best course. "Not my husband. My brother." Then something else struck her. "How did you even know about him?"

He sported the look of a guilty man.

"You were following me last night as well." He was the warm feeling against her nape.

"Only until I knew you weren't alone. Then I went on my way."

She was torn between appreciating his attentions and resenting them. "My brother will be worried. I have to leave."

"Not until the surgeon gets here."

"A surgeon costs coins."

"I'll see to that matter."

"I don't want to be beholden."

"I imagine you already are, love," Jewel said, holding a cup and saucer in front of her face. She lifted the cup—

"I can do it." Taking the cup, she was surprised by how her fingers shook. She closed both hands around the delicate fine china, inhaled the rich aroma, took a sip, and nearly groaned from the delicious flavor of it. If she could get herself steady, she could leave before the surgeon arrived. But if she stood up now, she'd probably fall flat on her face, and she refused to display that weakness in front of him. Once again she glanced around. "Is this a . . . a brothel?"

Jewel's throaty laughter echoed around her. "It is indeed a bawdy house."

Narrowing her eyes in suspicion, she returned her attention to Beast, wondering if his earlier proposition had involved her working here rather than just tending to him personally. He may have been issuing a worse insult than she'd originally surmised. "You manage a brothel?"

"Jewel manages it. I simply live here."

She furrowed her brow in confusion. "You're a"—what would the word be?—"a male trollop?"

It still wasn't a smile he gave her, but the corners of his mouth eased up more than she'd ever seen them. "No."

"Not for want of ladies making offers," Jewel said. "I've told him he could earn handsomely if he'd make himself available."

"Jewel, why don't you see to the customers who are awaiting their turn?" His tone implied he was giving an order not offering a suggestion.

As the woman rose from her place on the sofa, Althea was surprised by how tall and substantial she was. Her red silk gown hugged her close, left little doubt she had ample attributes to offer a man. "You might want to move her upstairs. The gents aren't going to be happy standing about in the foyer for long. I think you terrified a couple of them when you shouted at them all to get out after you barged in here like a madman with her in your arms."

"Give them a free tumble. I'll cover the cost."

With a wink and a smile, she comfortingly patted Althea's shoulder. "Finish your tea. The brandy will do you some good."

Brandy. No wonder it tasted lovely and warmed so thoroughly. She took another sip, peering over the lip of the cup at Beast, who had yet to move so much as his little finger. She wished his nose would itch so he would engage in some movement instead of steadfastly watching each of hers. She'd never known anyone who could remain so still for so long.

Finally, he said, "We've never been properly introduced. They call me Beast."

"I know. Polly told me."

"Then you have me at a disadvantage, as I don't know your name."

She recalled how he'd referred to her in the alleyway, the desperation in his tone, the roughness of his voice. *Beauty.* "Althea Stanwick."

"What are you doing here, Miss Stanwick?"

"You brought me here."

He shook his head. "I'm asking the same question I asked last night. Why are you in Whitechapel, working at my sister's tavern, putting your life at risk wandering the streets alone at night?"

"I wasn't supposed to be alone." She set the teacup aside. "I have to leave. As I've already mentioned, my brother will be worried." Probably frantic by now. According to the clock on the mantel, it was past two.

"The surgeon—"

"I'm not seeing a surgeon." Gingerly, she rose to her feet, grateful when she didn't sway. "Where's my cloak?"

"This is unwise on your part."

"I don't see how it's really any of your concern. My cloak, please, sir. Now."

Uncrossing his arms, he strode over to a plush chair, snatched up her cloak, and what appeared to be his coat. "I'll accompany you home."

"That's not necessary."

His glare could have stopped an invading army in its tracks. "Did you learn nothing tonight?"

SHE WAS AN independent, stubborn little minx, the top of her head barely reaching the center of his chest. She projected such confidence at the tavern that it was easy to view her as taller. More challenging when she walked beside him. With the hood of her cloak covering her head, she gave the appearance of being huddled inside the velvet, her slender shoulders slightly hunched, not that he blamed her. It was cold enough to create fog when one breathed, and ice was forming in the dampness. He brought up the collar on his own woolen greatcoat.

She refused to hold on to his arm for support, but her steps were smaller, slower than they'd been earlier when he'd been following her.

Knowing she had a protector—refusing to acknowledge the relief he'd experienced to discover he was a brother and not a husband—he didn't understand why he'd lingered outside the Mermaid. Perhaps because her escort had been tardy the night before. Or perhaps because he'd had a sense that tonight trouble was afoot.

He'd learned to trust his instincts and be cautious when he was eighteen and a lass had lured him into an alley where Three-Fingered Bill had introduced him to the ease with which a knife could slide into flesh and the pain it wrought while doing so and afterward. It seemed Bill had not taken kindly to his loss in income. What he hadn't counted on was that Beast wouldn't go down easily. When Beast was done fighting for his life, Bill had lost his.

In spite of his victory, he had nearly died that night from the wound the gang boss and pimp so expertly delivered. Fortunately, a surgeon more skilled with a scalpel had seen him spared from dancing with the devil at such a tender age. Rapping on Death's door was not an experience he cared to repeat before his black hair turned silver. Some were still about who took exception to his prowling the streets to ensure none took advantage of those in need or preyed on the weak and disadvantaged. His fists had served many who hadn't the strength themselves to ward off the miscreants.

Tonight they'd served her. He'd never been more grateful that his size gave him the advantage in a fight, that he had the skills to protect, that he'd been there when she'd needed him.

He was relieved when he spotted a hansom cab and was able to hail it down because he hadn't wanted her trudging all the way back to her residence, had decided if her steps slowed any further, he'd carry her. Although she'd no doubt protest.

She didn't say anything as he assisted her inside the buggy, and he wondered if she needed all her energy to simply move. He should have insisted she wait for the surgeon. Instead, he'd directed a footman to inform the man his services weren't needed after sending one saying they were. He'd send a generous payment round to the surgeon in the morning for the inconvenience of disturbing his slumber. Knowing Dr. Graves as he did, he suspected he'd probably donate it to a charitable hospital.

He gave the driver her address. She'd shared it with him earlier, because she'd been unfamiliar with her surroundings. New to Whitechapel, she didn't know her way around all the warrens and alleyways that made up the rookeries. Whereas he was familiar with every nook and cranny, knew she lived in one of the less reputable areas. His mum's home was on the outskirts of Whitechapel, but as they'd grown up, he and his siblings had spent a good bit of time on these streets because they offered adventure. Often adventure fraught with danger, but excitement all the same.

He didn't think Althea was searching for adventure, didn't think she'd be here if she didn't have to be. She wasn't here because she'd married a commoner as he'd originally thought.

The cab drew to a halt in front of a residence that had seen better days. He handed up the fare through the opening in the roof. The driver took it and the locked doors sprung open. Beast leapt out and handed her down.

"Thank you." With a gasp, she widened her eyes, pointed toward the street. "There goes your cab. Why didn't you stop him? You're unlikely to find another near here."

"I'll walk, once I've seen you safely inside."

"That's not necessary."

"The windows are pitch-black. Allow me to go inside and light a lamp for you, ensure all is well."

With a sigh, no doubt too tired to argue with him, she walked to the door, removed a key from a hidden pocket at her waist, and inserted it into the lock. He heard the scrape, a little clank, before she shoved open the door.

Following her inside, with the dim light from the streetlamps easing in through the windows, he could make out the shape of a lamp on the table. Removing the match safe from his waistcoat pocket, he struck a match, lifted the glass covering, and lit the wick of the oil lamp. The light revealed the only furniture to be the square oaken table and two straight-backed wooden chairs. "It doesn't appear your brother is here."

"He could be asleep in his chamber. Thank you for escorting me home."

"I'll wait until you've checked."

With a sigh, she picked up the lamp. "You're quite irritating."

She wandered toward the hallway. He followed. It was short, hardly a hallway at all. She knocked on the door at one end. "Griffith?"

After another knock, she opened the door and lifted the lamp higher to reveal blankets and clothing strewn over the floor. No furniture at all. How did someone like her come to this?

Turning, she came up short at the sight of him standing there, the slight jerking of her head causing her to grimace with obvious discomfort. "He's not here. He's probably out searching for me. Unaware I've returned home, he could be gone for ages." She paled. "Unless something horrible has happened to him, and that's the reason he didn't come for me tonight."

In Whitechapel, something horrible happening was always a possibility, but her brother carried himself with the confidence of someone fully capable of taking care of himself. It was the reason he hadn't continued to follow her when the man had shown the night before. "I know you've taken a dislike to me, but if you'll let me tend to your wound, I'll go out and find him."

Her delicate brow pleated. "How will you manage that?"

"If he's searching for you, he'll be on the path between here and the tavern. I daresay he won't stray far from it, even if he decides to explore alleyways and mews. If another reason is preventing him from being here, I can enlist the help of others to locate him."

"Then go find him."

"After I've tended to you."

"It's not that bad. My head barely hurts."

"Against my better judgment I allowed you to leave without seeing the surgeon. I'm not going to dismiss my concerns when it comes to tending to your wound."

"Very well, but be quick about it." She marched into the kitchen with a little more vigor to her step, which relieved some of his worry.

When she started to pump water into a bowl, he took over. "Have you some scraps of linen about?"

While she went to fetch them, he finished with the task, set the bowl of icy water on the hearth, and crouched. Her footsteps signaled her return.

"What are you doing?" she asked.

"Preparing a fire."

"It's not that cold."

He twisted around on the balls of his feet and looked up at her, could see the small stack of folded linens she'd placed on the table. "Ice has formed outside."

She wrung her hands. "We save the coal for when it's truly needed."

"You might not be cold, but I am. In the morning I'll send over coal to replace what I use. Besides, I need to heat this water up a bit." He wasn't cold, but he wanted her warm and comfortable when he left. He took satisfaction from her moving a chair nearer to the hearth in anticipation of the warmth he was going to provide. Normally, he wanted no appreciation from those he assisted, didn't know why he wanted a grain of it from her. Perhaps because he saw it as a signal that she was coming down from Mount Olympus. He went to work.

"When we moved here, my brother didn't even know how to lay a fire," she said quietly. "We always had servants to do it."

Naturally, she'd had servants. "Laid my first fire when I was eight. It was my chore every fourth morning."

"You rotated it with your brothers."

He wasn't surprised she'd deduced that, or that she knew he had three brothers. Of late, the details of his family were on a good many gossips' tongues and taking up an unfathomable amount of ink in the gossip rags.

The fire began licking greedily at the coal. Simply wanting to get the chill off the water, he held the bowl as close to the flames as he could without burning himself. He was in no rush to leave, intended to take his time tending to her in order to reassure himself that she wasn't in need of the surgeon before he went in search of her brother.

"Did you kill him?" she asked with no emotion reflected in her voice. "The man in the alleyway."

"No. Smashed his jaw." Not that he hadn't considered inflicting far worse damage, but he'd needed to get to her as quickly as possible. He'd arrived in the alley in time to see the man fling her against the wall and to hear the thud of skull against brick. Knowing the damage an injury to the head could cause, he'd very nearly panicked. She might be a blueblood, but she didn't deserve death at such a tender age. She warranted having her hair turn silver and her face wrinkle.

"I *thought* I heard bone crunching."

"If a man with a broken jaw comes into the Mermaid, have Mac send for a constable. Then for me. I can identify him, ensure charges are brought."

"Do you think I might have served him at the tavern?"

"Possibly." The scapegrace had seen her at least one other night, knew her routine. Otherwise, he wouldn't have been there, ready to pounce. "I do think he was waiting for you."

"Like you were."

How could three small words bludgeon so effectively?

He touched a finger to the water. Warm enough. Unfolding his body, he set the bowl on the table, met and held her gaze. "Do you truly think I'm anything at all like him?"

SHE DIDN'T. NOT for a single minute. She didn't know why she'd implied she did, except that she wanted to keep distance between them. She hadn't taken a dislike to him. Far from it.

But the fact he'd thought so little of her as to make her a proposition that no doubt involved him having his way with her—it had hurt and never would have happened when her father was alive. She'd been treated with respect, admired simply by virtue of the fact she was the daughter of a duke. But of late, men were always seeking to take advantage of her.

"Can we get on with this? I'm worried about my brother."

He scraped the other chair over the floor, set it behind her, dropped into it, and began removing the pins from her untidy coiffure.

"Is that really necessary?"

"You have so much hair, it'll be easier to get to your wound if I'm not having to go through piles of it as I did before." His actions were slow, gentle. "I've never felt anything so soft."

He cleared his throat, and she wondered if he'd not meant to say the last aloud, or at least meant not to say it as though he were awed.

"Why no furniture?" Clipped. Crisp.

"We haven't lived here long and haven't gotten around to purchasing things." And they hadn't the coins for purchasing things. "Why a brothel?"

Equally clipped, equally crisp.

"It began as a favor to a friend. Grew from there."

Her hair began to tumble down and he caught it as though he feared the weight of it falling would cause her discomfort, would pull on her injury. Tenderly, he loosened it down her back.

"So you might not manage it, but you own it."

"I own the building. I take no payment from the women who work there, so I'm not a pimp if that's what you're thinking." He dipped the edge of a piece of linen into the water. "This might sting."

It did, even though his touch was light, tender, cautious. She sucked in her breath.

"I'm sorry. There are bits of debris embedded in the wound that need to be removed to lessen the chance of infection. I'll strive to be gentle."

"Serves me right. My brother's hands are raw from his work on the docks, and I insist upon tending them—even when he'd rather I didn't. He's probably grown weary of the sting, would like to avoid it occasionally. I placed the jar of healing salve by the linens if you want to use it."

"I do. I will. Have you any alcohol or whisky that I can use to torment you further once I've cleaned it?"

"I think my brother has a bottle of whisky in the pantry." She started to rise.

He lightly touched her shoulder. "I'll get it."

She was amazed by the grace and silence with which he moved. She suspected the fellow in the alley hadn't known of Beast Trewlove's arrival until he'd felt the pain of his jaw shattering. All the different distinctive sounds had come so quickly, one right after the other.

When he returned, he set not only a bottle on the table but also a glass holding a small portion of clear liquid. "Gin, not whisky, but you might find drinking a bit will lessen the hurt."

Taking a sip, staring at the fire, she was fully aware that she needed to distract herself, not so much from the discomfort, but from the touch of his large hands against her hair, her scalp, as he carefully worked to clean her wound. She couldn't seem to stop herself from envisioning those capable hands caressing and healing other aspects of her: her battered soul, her shattered heart.

"How did you come to be in Mrs. Trewlove's care?" That her children were others' by-blows whom she'd taken in and raised as her own had been frantically whispered behind gloved hands and elegant fans after Mick Trewlove had taken Lady Aslyn Hastings to wife.

"My mother left me with her shortly after I was born."

If he was upset or bothered by her question, his touch against her scalp certainly didn't betray him.

"You know who your mother is, then?"

"No. She didn't provide her name. Promised to return for me, but obviously . . ."

She hadn't.

He'd have been too young to remember her leaving him, so he would have had to have been told. "How old were you when you learned all that?"

"Six before I worked up the courage to ask. Mum doesn't hold back the truth. If you're not prepared to hear it, you'd best not ask the question."

Her heart went out to him. So young to face the reality of his past. How long might he have held out hope that it wasn't too late for her to come back for him? How old was he before he'd finally accepted that she wasn't going to return?

"That must have been terribly hard . . . to hear all that. I think

I might have lied to you to spare you the pain of knowing she'd not kept her promise."

"I've never known a lie, in the end, to have served anyone well. But one might have served me well at the time. Shortly after I learned the truth, I became afraid of the dark. I would scream unless a lamp was left lit to ward off the monsters who were coming for me. One night she gave me a match safe, so I would always have dry matches and the power to defeat the dark. After that the darkness became a choice. I had the means to chase it away, and I stopped being afraid of it. No longer needed the light so I could sleep."

"She was a wise woman."

"I think the oil for the lamps was becoming too costly."

She heard the lightness in his voice, imagined he was smiling, almost turned around to catch a glimpse of what she'd never seen. Although perhaps the slight tilting up of the corners of his mouth that she *had* seen was as broad as his smile went.

She wondered if he'd shared the story because he'd recognized that her questions were an attempt to distract herself from what he was doing. She nearly wept. It had been so long since anyone, other than her brothers, had shown her such kindness. Those upon whom she should have been able to rely had deserted her as though she was so much rubbish to be discarded. "You used a match from it to light the fire. May I see it?"

He stopped his ministrations and the silver container appeared over her shoulder.

As she took it, she felt a jolt as her fingers skimmed over the tops of his. His skin was rough, abrasive, and yet she thought it would feel marvelous scraping over hers. Swallowing hard, she directed her attention to the elaborate raised relief of intricate vines, leaves, and flowers that adorned both sides of the small metal box. At the top was a small hinged lid. She opened it to find the container stuffed with matches. "This is not an inexpensive gift. It's silver."

He was once more pricking her scalp to remove all the dirt and grime. Perhaps she should have waited about for the surgeon.

"It belonged to her husband. He died before I came to live with her, so I never knew him, knew only her memories of him. The day I moved out to make it on my own, I tried to give it back to her. But she wouldn't have it. 'Just because you consider yourself grown, it doesn't mean you won't have dark times. Keep it. It carries not only matches but also my love for you.'"

She felt the tears sting her eyes, blinked them back. She didn't know if it was the result of tonight's attack, her recent change in circumstances, or worry over Griffith, but her emotions were running an entire gamut tonight. "How old were you?"

"All of fifteen. Thought myself a man of the world, but still had a lot to learn. Probably still do."

As did she, it seemed. "As we get older, the lessons seem much harder, don't they?"

"They seem to come with more consequences, yes. I've gotten your wound as clean as I can. The gash isn't terribly deep. I don't think it's in need of stitches. But it does need the gin. It's not going to be pleasant, I'm afraid."

"I'm certain I've dealt with far worse unpleasantness." Not physically, but emotionally, and in some ways that was worse.

After handing the precious match safe back to him, she clasped her hands together in her lap. Out of the corner of her eye, she watched as he drenched one of the linens in gin.

To her amazement, he then gathered up her hair and draped it over her right shoulder. An odd thing to do when it hadn't been interfering with him getting to the wound.

She felt his knuckles land softly against the left side of her nape, slide up to her hairline, down to the collar of her frock. Up and down, gliding slightly forward with each stroke. As he neared her ear, she heard the rasp of rough skin over silky flesh. What was he doing?

She recalled reading somewhere that Anne Boleyn's executioner had distracted her by calling for his sword, even though he already had it in hand, so she relaxed before he lopped off her head. Was that what Beast Trewlove was attempting to do, to distract her?

When the gin-laced cloth landed against her wound, she couldn't stop the sharp intake of breath, but the sting was nowhere as harsh as she'd expected it to be. Perhaps because she was focused on the movement of his fingers, wondering where he was going.

He pressed the pad of his thumb to the spot just below her ear where her pulse thrummed, and she wondered if he was counting the beats of her heart. His fingers unfurled and the tips grazed along the sensitive underside of her jaw. She closed her eyes as warmth and a pleasant sensation flowed through her.

Suddenly the linen and his fingers were no longer there. He began gently applying the salve.

"While I'm out searching for your brother, don't go to sleep." His voice came out as rough and raw—and the warmth within her heated as a fire did when another lump of coal or log was added to it. She had to clear her throat and take a moment to gather herself in order to respond without giving away how his touch had affected her.

"I don't think that will be a problem. I'll be too anxious awaiting Griff's return." *And yours.* Although she didn't want to admit that to him or herself. "You won't be placing yourself in danger, will you?"

"If it comes to that, I can handle it."

She didn't doubt his capabilities for a minute. Still, she didn't like the thought of him encountering trouble on her behalf.

"The bleeding has stopped. It might be better to leave the wound open to fresh air. The knot is still there. Are you dizzy? Does your head hurt?"

"The room's not spinning. My headache is less. I think the tea earlier helped."

"Shall I brew you a cup before I leave?"

She twisted around in her chair. He was so close she could see the firelight dancing in his coal-black eyes. Stubble shadowed his jaw, made it appear stronger, more distinct. His features contained a nobleness that made it difficult to breathe. She wished she could blame it on her head, but it was him. All him. "Why are you doing all this?"

"Why should I not?"

Her smile was small, almost teasing. "Do you always respond to a question with a question?"

"Only when I don't know the answer."

Those words sobered her. "You strike me as a man who always knows the answer."

His dark eyes narrowing, he studied her for all of a heartbeat, and she wondered if he'd find whatever it was for which he was searching. If it was within her, did she want him to find it? She admired his honesty and openness but couldn't embrace the same traits, not when they could bring so much pain.

"Usually I am," he said. "But something about you—"

The front door burst open. "Althea!"

"Griff!" She leapt out of the chair too fast. If Beast hadn't quickly stood, wrapped an arm around her, and pulled her against his broad chest, she surely would have toppled to the floor.

"Easy, Beauty," he whispered.

The dark eyes drew her in. She'd never felt more protected, more treasured than she did at that moment. She had a strong urge to rise up on her toes, bury her face against the skin below his jaw, and inhale the masculine scent of him. Dark and forbidding, leather and scotch, and something so uniquely him—

"What the devil is going on here, Althea?" Griffith asked.

Having regained her balance, if not her equilibrium, she flattened her palm against the broad chest. "I'm all right now."

Never taking his intense gaze from her, gingerly, he slid his arm away, and she had to fight to remain steady, not to seek out the comfort of him.

"I got into a bit of a bother earlier. Beast—" She stopped, shook her head. "Your mother did not name you Beast, surely."

One corner of his mouth curled up ever so slightly. "Benedict. Sometimes my family will call me Ben."

"Benedict Trewlove, here, came to my assistance."

"Trewlove? Are you the Trewlove half of Whitechapel fears and the other half worships?"

"That description could apply to any Trewlove. You shouldn't leave your sister to walk home alone."

"I got held up tonight." He looked at her. "It won't happen again, Althea."

"Where were you?"

"Searching for you."

"Before that? Why were you late?"

"It's not important."

"It damned well better be bloody important if it puts her life at risk," Benedict stated succinctly in the same tone a king might use when proclaiming a decree.

Griffith blanched. "As I said, it won't happen again."

"Make sure it doesn't. And start taking different paths to the residence. You don't want to have a routine that footpads can expect and take advantage of." With long, purposeful strides, he headed for the door.

She started to rush after him, had to stop when her head protested. "Please, halt."

Her plea reached him just as he was closing the door. He paused.

The cold wind whipped through the narrow opening as she neared. "Thank you for everything you did tonight."

"Coal will be delivered in the morning."

"You don't have to do that. You didn't use that much."

"'Tis done."

She wondered if anyone ever won an argument with this man. "You were wrong earlier. What you said. I haven't taken a dislike to you."

His eyes darkened. Based on the visibility of his breath in the cold, his breathing had slowed. He lifted a bare hand, and she wondered if he was tempted to touch her face. He dropped his hand, began tugging on his gloves, stepped back. "Good night, Miss Stanwick."

As he strode away, she watched him hunch his shoulders against the cold. He cut such a lonely figure that she was tempted to call him back to make use of the fire as long as it burned. Instead, she closed the door, locked it.

Griffith was standing by the fireplace, staring at the flames. Not willing to let any of the heat go to waste, she joined him there. Now that they didn't have company, she thought he was more likely to answer. "What are you up to? Where were you last night and tonight?"

"With a woman." He slid his gaze to her. "I was only a few minutes late. Who was he?"

"I told you."

"His name, yes, but what is he to you? How did you come to be with him, with your hair undone? When I walked in, you looked as though you were on the verge of inviting him into your bedchamber."

"*Bedchamber* is a bit too elegant a word for the room in which I sleep. As for how I came to be with him . . ."

She explained all that had happened, and when she was done, he cursed soundly.

"I won't be late again. I swear to you."

"Was she someone I know?" She couldn't imagine he'd gone to a brothel. Their coins were too precious for something as selfish as that.

He turned his attention back to the fire. "Doesn't matter. She's to marry another."

Someone from their past, then, probably a lady of the nobility. She hadn't known he was courting anyone, but as she was discovering, there was a good deal about her brothers she hadn't known. "I'm sorry, Griff."

He shook his head. "How could it all go to hell like this? We had it all. Nothing was denied us. And now we've lost everything."

HE'D NEEDED TO get out of there before he jabbed his fist into her brother's perfect aristocratic nose. Entitlement had rolled off Griffith Stanwick in waves as forceful as those kicked up by a sea tempest. If they weren't bluebloods, Beast would sink every one of his ships.

Added to that, he'd miscalculated the impact that touching his fingers to her silken flesh would cause. He'd done it in an attempt to distract her from the bite of the gin. It was a trick he'd learned from his mum. Or at least a version of it. Hers had never been so intimate. She'd simply shaken some part of him—a hand, an arm, a leg—until he'd been so focused on what she was doing that he'd barely noticed the sting of anything she was pouring over a scrape in order to cleanse it.

He should have shaken her shoulder. Should have not touched her at all. Because now it felt as though her skin had married his. No matter how hard or briskly he rubbed his hand over his thigh, he couldn't rid himself of the sense he was still caressing her, that his fingertips were still pressed to the underside of her jaw.

She was not his concern, not his to worry over. He'd seen that she'd come to no harm tonight. All future nights were the responsibility of her brother. Would he see to it?

Two nights he'd put her at risk. Did he not understand the dangers that resided in Whitechapel? Did he not comprehend how precious she was?

Bugger it all. He was going to stop thinking about her. He had other matters to worry over. Finding a tutor for one. Perhaps he'd ask his sisters-by-marriage to assist him. If they each took a couple of hours a month—it would take forever. But still it would be a step toward ensuring the ladies no longer had to earn coins while on their backs.

He shouldn't have told her about his mother.

He released an obscene curse into the darkness surrounding him. He was thinking about her again. She'd been embarrassed that he'd seen the condition of her hovel—as though he'd judge her by it. Had someone judged her? Why did he have the sense she had no one else to come to her aid except for her unreliable brother?

Unreliability was something he avoided exhibiting at all costs, didn't tolerate well in others. His mother had been unreliable, had not kept her promise. When he was younger, that knowledge had created an unbearable pain, had confirmed she hadn't truly wanted him. He was fairly certain he knew why, and it had nothing to do with his being born out of wedlock. Parents liked for their children to be perfect, and he wasn't.

Telling her about his mother only served to remind him of things he tried to forget.

And now he needed to forget Althea Stanwick.

Chapter 4

*L*ying on the mound of blankets, she decided it had been long enough since her head had smashed against brick that she could safely go to sleep, and yet sleep eluded her, all because of him. Beast. Benedict. Ben.

It was an odd thing to find herself aching for his touch when he'd merely dabbed lightly at her scalp, skimmed a finger along her jaw, then held her briefly when she swayed, and yet she felt as though the length of his hard body had imprinted itself over hers. Or at least the part of him that had rested against her. He was comprised of substantially more than she. He stood at least a head and a half taller, and the breadth of him made her feel incredibly dainty.

If she still walked among the aristocracy, would their paths have ever crossed—other than a sighting at a wedding?

She was finally beginning to drift off when she heard the deep male voices outside her window. It had been a long night, and now that sleep was on the cusp of arriving, her neighbors had decided to have a harsh discussion.

"I don't understand why you won't let me help."

"It's too dangerous."

"I'm not a child."

The voices, the inflection of them, were familiar. Scrambling out from beneath the covers, she crawled to the window and lifted her head only enough to peer over the ledge and hopefully not be seen. The two men were shadows, but she'd recognize their silhouettes anywhere. The larger of the two was Marcus, the other Griffith. Why was her older brother visiting now, at this ridiculous hour? Why didn't he come inside out of the cold? Why not come inside so he could see her?

"Then don't act like one," Marcus said, disgust rife in his tone.

"Christ, you sound just like Father."

"I am nothing at all like him." Marcus's tone was hard, brittle, and she rather thought he'd uttered those words through clenched teeth.

"I misspoke. I apologize. I'm just frustrated. I hate living here, hate working the docks. Hate feeling so impotent. I want to assist with your endeavors. Are you getting any closer to discovering with whom Father was conspiring against the Crown?"

Althea's breath caught. Those were not the sort of people with whom Marcus should become involved.

"Possibly. I finally have some leads." He sighed. "What I said about you being a child. I know you're not, and I appreciate that you want to be involved with this undertaking, but it's important that you are here for Althea, that she is not left alone. Someone needs to look after her."

"But then who is there to watch your back?"

"Her back is more precious."

Horror was taking hold of her. All their backs were equally precious.

"Do you really believe that if you discover who all was involved in the conspiracy the Crown will return the titles and properties to you?"

"I care little for the titles or properties. I care only that we're not all viewed as traitors. Have you forgotten what it was like to be arrested, to sit in the bloody tower wondering if they were going to hang us as well?"

"I haven't forgotten. I'll never forget. I can hardly sleep without waking up in a cold sweat."

Her brother's confession tore at her heart. She'd had no idea he suffered so.

"I just want to regain our respectability, if not for us, then for Althea," Marcus said. "Who would marry her as long as this pall of doubt and suspicion hangs over us? She's the daughter of a duke. She should have her pick of suitors."

She backed into the corner and wrapped her arms around her drawn-up knees. They were placing themselves at risk in large part because of a desire to better her prospects? Although in bettering hers, they bettered themselves as well, but the risk was too great.

"She did. She chose Chadbourne."

"The scapegrace publicly turned his back on her. I should have done more than blacken his eye. I should have called him out."

"Not to disparage your skill with weaponry but if he'd somehow managed to kill you, he'd have been hailed a hero."

"There is that. Listen, you might see less of me. It's becoming a bit more . . ."

"Dangerous?"

"Risky. If it should be discovered that I've been less than honest in my desire to replace Father . . . I don't want anyone coming after you or Althea."

"I hate being a bloody nanny. I want to be in the thick of it. I want to help you."

"Then make certain you give me no cause to worry about Althea."

She was trembling by the time they went quiet, and she realized Marcus had left. She heard a distant door, the one that led into the garden, open and close, followed by the echo of footsteps. A pause in the hallway. Another door opening and closing.

She was vaguely aware of tears trailing down her cheeks, gathering in pools in the corners of her mouth. She'd never considered herself particularly close to her brothers, and yet here they were doing all in their power to protect her. As though she hadn't the means to protect herself, as though marriage was her only option. The thought of losing either of them created an acute pain in her chest.

Marcus was placing himself in danger. He needed someone to watch his back, needed Griffith far more than she did.

She certainly wasn't a child in need of a nanny. Although tonight, damn it, had proven she needed a protector. Except she had one, and it hadn't been Griffith. She could make do without him, and then perhaps Marcus wouldn't be in as much danger. Or if the danger didn't lessen, at least he wouldn't be facing it alone.

Benedict Trewlove had a proposition for her. Perhaps it would behoove her to at least discover the terms.

LATER THAT MORNING, after a restless sleep, Althea rapped on the servants' door of a house in Mayfair. A young footman opened it.

"Is Lady Kathryn about?"

He furrowed his brow. "Should you not be coming in through the front entry?"

Not any longer. "Will you please let her know Althea Stanwick has come to call?"

With a nod, he closed the door. She'd have preferred not to give her name, because it might ensure her friend was not at home to her, but it was doubtful she'd come to the servants' entrance without knowing who awaited her.

Looking out over the winter gardens, Althea fought against remembering all the times she'd taken tea with her friend among the greenery. How often they'd laughed. The gossip they'd shared. Kat had been the first she'd told when she developed affections for Chadbourne. Kat had been the only one at the last ball she'd attended not to turn her back on her. Or not turn it entirely. She had lowered her gaze and looked as though she wished to be anywhere other than where she was. But then Althea had wished the same.

When the door again opened, she swung around and forced a smile. "Hello, Kat."

"Althea, what a . . . surprise."

"I was wondering if I might have a word."

"Yes, of course. My parents aren't about, so they won't be objecting to your presence. Do come in." Once they were inside,

Kathryn glanced around nervously. "Would you mind if we met in the servants' dining hall? No one is there presently, and if my parents should return—"

"I can make a hasty and discreet exit."

"Oh, Althea."

"It's all right." She squeezed Kat's hand. "I'm just relieved you're willing to speak to me."

"Of course, dear friend." Kat squeezed back. "I think it's frightfully unfair that you have to suffer because of your father's lack of judgment. Follow me." As they made their way to the dining room, Kat called out to a maid to have tea brought.

Once they were settled at the oak table with tea and cakes in front of them, Kat said, "So what did you want to talk about?"

Best to get straight to the heart of the matter before her parents returned and she was forced to make a hasty—and undetected— exit. Oh, where to begin? She took a sip of her tea. "You're friends with the Duchess of Lushing."

"Former Duchess of Lushing. Selena prefers to be called Mrs. Trewlove now. I can't believe she married someone of illegitimate origins, but she's madly in love with him."

"Have you come to know the Trewlove family well?"

She knew they'd attended a few balls, when she still attended them, particularly earlier in the year when they were introducing their sister Fancy to Society. But Althea couldn't recall seeing Benedict at any of the affairs, other than the weddings. Although she did know he was a man of his word. The coal had been delivered that morning. More than a month's worth, longer if they didn't have a fire every day. It seemed the man was generous to a fault, having replaced far more than he used.

Kat shrugged. "Well enough to speak with them at balls."

"What of Benedict? Some people call him Beast. Have you had occasion to get to know him?"

Kat studied her for all of a minute before saying, "The Heathcliff-ish one?"

"Heathcliff-ish?"

"Tall, dark, brooding."

"Is he really the brooding sort?" Quiet. Observant. Unobtrusive. Not one for seeking attention, perhaps. "I readily admit he weighs his words carefully, but brooding?"

Planting her elbow on the table, Kat placed her chin in her palm and grinned like a cat that had lapped up all the cream. "You seem to know him better than I. How is that, I wonder?"

With a sigh, Althea was beginning to realize her foolishness in coming here. Odd, since her entire purpose in speaking with Kat had been to ensure she wasn't about to embark on something foolish. "I've taken employment at a tavern, and he comes in on occasion." It had hurt to admit she was working, even more so when Kat's eyes filled with pity. "I was just curious as to whether you had developed a sense of him during any encounters you might have had or if you'd heard anything untoward about him."

If she was going to accept his proposition, she wanted to ensure she wasn't stepping into a far worse situation than she was presently in. But if he was to become her protector then Griffith could join Marcus in the quest to reclaim the family honor. And Marcus had spoken true. Under their present circumstance no one would marry her. She was already four and twenty. By the time this matter was sorted—should it ever be sorted—she'd be so high on the shelf no gentleman would ever reach for her. She had no reason whatsoever to save herself for marriage. She might as well do what she could now to relieve her brothers of their worry over her so they could focus their efforts on ensuring no harm came to either of them as they pursued what she feared was a reckless venture.

Shoving her cup aside, Kat took Althea's hands as though to impart strength because she knew her dear friend was considering doing something rather scandalous. "I don't know anything about him specifically, but what I do know about the Trewloves is that, in spite of being born on the wrong side of the blanket, they possess a decency that is to be admired. It may be foolish of me, but I have often thought that if I needed to place my life in someone's hands, it would be theirs."

Althea found the words extremely comforting because since last night, she'd begun to believe the same thing regarding Benedict. Unintentionally, she had placed her life in his hands—and he had cared for her as though she was precious, even if she'd been somewhat of a termagant toward him.

How well might he treat her if she was more welcoming?

Chapter 5

*W*ithin his study, sitting at his desk, Beast repeatedly dipped his pen in the inkwell and scribbled frantically over the parchment, striving not to envision Althea peering at him through the narrow opening in her doorway, looking so delectable, so vulnerable, so beautiful with her blond hair cascading around her.

I haven't taken a dislike to you.

Better if she had.

Setting aside his pen, he read what he'd written, key phrases jumping out at him. *Moon-kissed tresses. Sapphire eyes. Heart-shaped face.* He realized he'd described Althea, made her the protagonist in this tale of murder and revenge that he'd only recently begun penning.

Bloody hell. He spread his palm, splayed his fingers over the foolscap, gathered it up, balled it tightly between his hands, and tossed it into the wicker bin that he'd been filling with the rubbish he'd written ever since he'd awoken at dawn.

He couldn't get her off his mind, how she'd been as light as a feather cradled within his arms, how right it had felt to have her pressed against his chest as he'd carried her from that filthy alleyway, terror at the thought of her dying in his embrace gripping him. Later in the parlor, he'd kept his arms crossed and his shoulder against the wall because he'd desperately wanted to curl himself around her and offer whatever comfort she'd required, even as he'd believed at the time that she wouldn't welcome his nearness, that she'd viewed him as beneath her. That she'd taken a dislike to him.

Only she hadn't. Or if she had, she'd changed her mind before seeing him to the door.

He was accustomed to people looking at him disparagingly. A bastard born and raised, he knew what it was to reside in darkness, searching for a sliver of light. When he'd finally found the courage to ask Ettie Trewlove about how he'd come to be on her doorstep, he'd learned how the sadness of being forsaken could eat at one's soul, how sometimes it could drag one under like being caught beneath a wave and unable to find the way back to the surface.

But he'd also learned from Ettie Trewlove and his siblings that love tempered the hurt. He understood the power of touch, of feeling a connection, of knowing someone was there for him, would always be there for him.

Still, he'd never *fallen* in love, had never trusted anyone outside his family to love him completely, flaws and all.

So he couldn't explain the ferocity with which he was drawn to Althea Stanwick, this irrational need he had to protect her. Lust was a big part of it, a physical attraction unlike any he'd ever experienced. When he'd finally gone to sleep, he'd dreamed of licking every inch of her, of her licking every blessed inch of him. He'd awoken aching with need and hard as granite, had been forced to take himself in hand.

That hadn't happened in a good long while.

As he seemed unable to forget about her, he would avoid her in the future. No more trips to the Mermaid. He would begin frequenting a nearby pub.

The rap sounded on his door. As usual, without waiting for him to bid entrance, Jewel opened it. "You have a visitor in the parlor."

He knew it wasn't any member of his family. They would have just come up and barged in without even bothering to knock.

Probably his publisher come to give him an update on the book that had been released two months earlier—his first. Although generally they just sent a message that they needed to see him, and he went to their office. They weren't particularly comfortable with his current living accommodations and were keen that no one found out about them. Bad publicity to own a building used as a brothel, apparently.

"I'll be down straightaway."

She disappeared from sight. Shoving back his chair, he stood, grabbed his jacket, and shrugged into it, buttoned his waistcoat, straightened his neck cloth. He headed into the hallway. Most of the women were abed. Although like him, Jewel seemed to require little sleep, enjoyed basking in the early-morning quiet.

Descending the stairs, he welcomed the distraction of having someone to take his mind off Althea. But when he strode into the parlor, he was bombarded with thoughts of her, because she was the one standing by the window with the rare winter sunlight streaming over her. She wore an emerald-green frock more suited to a ballroom than a parlor, the low neckline revealing the slender column of her throat and gentle swells of her breasts, the short sleeves displaying the delicate bones and creaminess of her arms.

"Good morning," she said softly, her smile uneasy, and he didn't want to consider how he would like to greet each day with her speaking those words to him, tucked beneath him as he slid into her.

"Did the coal not arrive?" He despised how gruff and rough his voice sounded.

Her smile seemed a bit more steady. "It did, yes, thank you."

Then why was she here? To thank him once more for his assistance last night? He didn't require her thanks. And why was she wearing something so alluring that it seemed a sin to take his eyes off her?

"Would you care for something to drink? Sherry, brandy—" He cut off the list. It wasn't yet noon. "Tea?"

"You don't strike me as someone who serves tea."

"I never serve tea. That was Jewel's doing last night. But I can have someone fetch some if you fancy a cup."

"No, thank you. I'm fine as I am."

He didn't want to contemplate the truth of those words, the smooth flawlessness of her skin. Her tiny waist. Surely, he could find some fault with her that would calm his body's need to be pressed up against her. "Then how may I be of service?"

"I've come to discuss your proposition."

He felt as though he'd been bludgeoned. It was the very last thing he'd expected after her lack of interest in even hearing him out the night before. Especially after deciding he wanted nothing further to do with her.

He should tell her the proposition was no longer available, but the reason behind it still existed. And he wasn't fool enough to cast aside the possibility of gaining what he wanted without at least having an earnest conversation on the matter.

Based on the personal nature of what she assumed the request involved, he strode across the room, leaned against the window casing, and crossed his arms over his chest so he wasn't tempted to touch her. The fragrance of gardenias welcomed him, and he imagined her bathing before coming to him. He'd never seen her in such bright light before. She had three freckles lining the curve of her left cheek. Only those three, no others. They fascinated him. Had she had more as a child, and these had been too stubborn to fade away? Or were they the only three daring enough to appear?

"I thought you had no interest in my proposition," he said, curious as to what had changed her mind.

"As you saw last night, my circumstances are quite dire. It occurred to me that I was being rather foolish to not at least hear you out."

"How did your circumstances become dire? You were not born into poverty. That much is clear by your clothing, your diction, the way you hold yourself as though you are above all others."

She looked out at the street, the passing carriages, rumbling wagons, people walking by. The children chasing each other. The occasional dog bounding after them. Taking a deep breath, she met and held his gaze. "My father was involved in a plot to assassinate the Queen."

Then she was once again studying the traffic, and he cursed himself, wishing he hadn't pushed, had been content to let her hold close her secrets. He should have guessed what had caused her fall from grace. He'd read about the arrest in the newspaper, but that had been months ago. The man had been a duke, but he couldn't recall his title. He did remember that the duchess had succumbed to illness shortly after his arrest and passed.

"Aren't you going to ask for the details?" Her voice sounded as though it came from far away.

"No." He wanted to take her in his arms, glide his large hands up and down her narrow back, and comfort her. But his insistence was the cause of her current pain.

"I don't know the particulars anyway. The plot was discovered before it could be carried out. They arrested him at someplace where he was meeting with the other conspirators. His partners, or whatever words are used to refer to treacherous comrades, escaped. He wasn't so fortunate. He was tried, found guilty, and hanged. The Crown confiscated his titles and properties. We were left with nothing, absolutely nothing. The heir, the spare, and I. You met the spare last night."

Everything was spoken as though it was rote, memorized, not a part of her. When she looked back at him, a vacantness had glazed over her eyes as if she'd returned to the moment when her world had crumbled around her. "So now that you know the truth of me, do you still have a desire for me to be your mistress?"

He didn't know the truth of her. He knew only the truth of her father. And while she may no longer be considered nobility by law, she was still nobility by birth.

"I don't want you as my mistress."

"I can't say as I blame you."

She started to walk past him. Reaching out, he wrapped his

fingers around her upper arm. Her skin was so bloody soft, like silk, velvet, and satin all woven together to uniquely create her. She was incredibly warm, comprised of secret places that would be warmer, hotter.

Her unusual blue-gray eyes were no longer vacant. They held heat, and he thought if a tankard were nearby that she'd be dumping its contents over his head. He almost laughed at that.

"My proposition never involved asking you to be my mistress." *More's the pity.*

Her delicate brow furrowed. Her eyes ignited with fury. "You want me to be one of your whores?"

"No, I want you to be a tutor."

ALTHEA COULD SAY with complete honesty that his words flummoxed her. "A tutor?"

He gave a brisk nod. "Allow me to call for some tea and I'll explain."

"Actually, I'd rather have the sherry you mentioned earlier."

He grinned fully, completely, and she realized all the little hints of his grin she'd seen before had failed to prepare her for the devastating reality of how it would transform him from handsome into achingly beautiful. He stole her breath, as stealthily as a pickpocket slipping a silk handkerchief from a pocket, a bracelet from around a wrist, a ring off a finger. So the object was gone before the wearer realized it was taken. One moment she was breathing, and the next she'd quite simply forgotten how.

His fingers slid away from her arm. Thank God, because that touch had also served to create havoc within her mind as she'd contemplated his roughened skin skimming over every inch of her. She was not about to admit that she was rather disappointed he didn't want her as his mistress.

"Make yourself comfortable," he said, indicating two winged chairs near the fireplace. "I'll fetch the sherry."

She watched as he walked to the opposite wall from where she stood to a corner table laden with various crystal decanters.

The smoothness of his movements, so calm, so deliberate, caused her own body to react with a warming of her skin, an itch of her fingers to reach out and skim over muscles that bunched and stretched. The jacket he wore couldn't disguise the ease with which his limbs adjusted to whatever chore he executed: grabbing the decanter, pouring the liquid, turning to face her—

Caught staring, she was rather certain her cheeks were now aflame. Trying not to appear to be scurrying to the chair by the fire, she feared her own movements were jerky and displayed her embarrassment. If he noticed, he gave no indication as he returned to her and handed her the small tulip-shaped glass. "Thank you."

She took a sip, surprised by the richness of the sweet flavor. "Excellent."

"As you're well aware, my sister owns a tavern. She'd have my head if I had anything inferior on hand."

"Well, this might be the best I've ever tasted."

They held each other's gaze for a long moment before she finally turned away and lowered herself to the chair. Its plumpness gave way and seemed to swallow her, creating a sensation of being hugged. She almost asked who was responsible for his taste in furniture. It, too, was excellent.

His chair groaned a bit as he settled into it, and she imagined she might make the same welcoming sound if he settled himself over her. Where had that thought come from?

She took another sip of the sherry, larger than the first, before tightening her fingers around the short stem, hoping to get her thoughts to behave. She'd come here with the expectation of becoming a seductress. Hence, the revealing gown she'd worn. And now she was to be a teacher.

He lifted a tumbler, probably containing his preferred scotch. He seemed much more relaxed than she felt.

With earnestness, he leaned forward, planted his elbows on his thighs, and clasped his glass between both his hands. "My proposition."

She waited. He cleared his throat.

"The women who work here—six remain, not counting Jewel—I want to help them find another occupation. Unfortunately, they aren't as genteel as might . . . be needed . . . elsewhere."

Her heart melted a little as he strove not to be unkind, as though the women were sitting there listening as he spoke.

"You, on the other hand. Every aspect of you has been buffed to a polish. It's the reason I knew you were from Mayfair or somewhere similar to it. I thought you could instruct the ladies on how to be . . . more elegant. How to dress with a bit more style. How to speak properly. Perhaps you could even instruct them on how to be a lady's maid, a governess, a companion. I'm well aware they will never find a position within a noble's household, but I know several men who have recently acquired wealth and they might convince their wives to be willing to give a few of these women a chance at a more respectable life if they have the ability to learn what you have the knowledge to teach them."

She hardly knew what to say.

"The bedchamber at your residence—is it like your brother's, lacking a bed?"

She hated to admit it, but honesty was called for when negotiating a transaction. "Yes."

"You could reside here, if you wished. A portion of this floor, this parlor in particular, is used for business. The floor above is where the women . . . entertain. The top one serves as our living accommodations. You would have your own bedchamber with a very comfortable bed, other furniture. A fire. We have no shortage of coal here. Your meals would be provided. Three a day. Naturally, you would also receive a salary. I'm willing to be quite generous."

"I would earn nearly twenty-five pounds per annum at the Mermaid."

"I'll pay you a hundred."

She knew her eyes had grown wide. "A hundred?"

Until three months ago, she'd had little idea what people earned, what constituted a good salary, what it cost to purchase food or lease a residence.

With a forefinger, he tapped the side of his glass. "What I'm offering you is only temporary. Once the ladies are placed elsewhere your services will no longer be required. I want to ensure you're not returning to a residence with no furniture and no fires. To that end, I will give you an additional stipend of a thousand pounds if you can teach them all they need to know within six months. Five hundred pounds if it takes you a year. If you can't teach them what they need to know in twelve months, I'll assume you're rubbish as a teacher and you'll be let go with only the hundred."

A hundred pounds. If it killed her, she'd see that they learned everything they needed to in six months to ensure she'd have the additional thousand. Her expenses would be minimal. She could save most of her earnings.

Moving to the edge of his chair, he leaned closer to her. "I'll be honest with you, Miss Stanwick. I hate this bloody business, and I want out. But I can't do it guilt-free without ensuring they have something better."

His tone held a desperation that gave her an advantage. "You've given me six months. I can accomplish the goal in three."

"Fifteen hundred if you do."

"Two thousand."

She could tell he wanted to smile again, but instead he flattened that lovely mouth and his jaw tightened. The victory was hers. He was simply striving to make it appear that he wasn't cratering into her demands without some contemplation.

"You drive a hard bargain, Miss Stanwick, but if you can see this business shut down in three months, I'll happily pay the two thousand."

It took everything within her not to gloat. But still it wasn't enough.

Three months. At the end of that time, what was she to do? She'd have money, yes, but it wasn't going to see her through the remainder of her life. And if Marcus and Griffith were still engaged in a dangerous enterprise, she couldn't have them worrying about her. She would still be in need of a protector and was unlikely to acquire a husband.

Clutching the sherry glass, she rose and began pacing, striding between the chair and the window, the window and the chair, passing by several statuettes of nude couples, their bodies scandalously entwined. Back and forth she went, giving thought to all he was offering, all she required.

She finally stopped in front of him. When she'd risen, he'd come to his feet, so now he towered over her. She should have been afraid of him, of the strength and power he projected with such ease. But she realized she'd never feared him. She hadn't needed to go to Kat to know that he would never harm her. She trusted him. For some reason she always had. "I need more."

"Name your price."

"I want you to teach me how to be a seductress."

Chapter 6

This encounter had certainly taken a drastic turn he'd not antici-pated. He'd assumed she'd ask for a few more pounds, a carriage for getting about, a new wardrobe. That she continued to hold his gaze indicated she was serious regarding her request.

"For what purpose?" he finally asked, crossing his arms over his chest.

She gave him a small, teasing smile. "To seduce."

"I'm deadly serious, Miss Stanwick. Why would you ask this of me?"

He saw a flicker of doubt in her eyes. She set her sherry glass on a low table near the chair in which she'd been sitting, and then lifted her chin defiantly. "Because it will give me the freedom and the means to be my own woman."

She took a step toward him. "You yearn to be free of your cur-rent circumstance. Help me gain what I desire." Another step.

Everything within him urged him to move away, but he held his ground as she came near enough that the silk covering her bosom brushed up against the satin of his waistcoat. His hands, once relaxed against his arms, now gripped them with such in-tensity that he was certain to discover bruises later.

"You could show me how men like to be kissed—"

He'd failed to notice before how full her bottom lip was, what a plump cushion it would be. If he rounded his shoulders, lowered his head, he could take that mouth gently, tenderly at first. Then once she'd become accustomed to him, he'd take complete possession, and deepen the kiss.

"—touched—"

The gown revealed the upper swells of her breasts. He could dip a finger or his tongue between the hollow where they met. Stroke one breast, then the other.

"—held."

Naked, on a bed. She couldn't reach all of him, but her head to his shoulder, her feet to just below his knee, would suffice. Her breasts flattened against his chest. His large hands cupping her buttocks.

Taking hold of one end of his neck cloth, she pulled until the knot he'd carefully created earlier was no more. She gave a little tug that brought him a fraction nearer to her. "You could turn me into a man's fantasy."

How could she not realize that she had already achieved that goal? The temptation of her was almost more than he could stand.

Never taking her gaze from his, she splayed a palm against his chest where his heart thudded, and no doubt vibrated against her fingers. "You. You could teach me how to bring exquisite pleasure."

But at what cost? Having had her, could he let her go?

ALTHEA COULDN'T BELIEVE she'd been so bold as to make such a demand of him. It amazed her that he could stand so still and give away nothing, not his thoughts nor his feelings. She wanted to be able to do that.

"I don't think you'd find it a hardship to teach me." She kept her voice low, a little raspy like Jewel's, and could have sworn she heard his breath hitch slightly.

He lowered his head, and her lips tingled in anticipation of his mouth claiming hers. "The first lesson"—his voice was equally low, equally raspy—"is not to give anything too easily."

When he stepped back, she stumbled forward, realizing too late that she'd been leaning into him, balancing herself against him. She'd been seeking to seduce him, and it seemed she'd been the one seduced. She might have been embarrassed if he'd gloated or given any indication that he knew the effect he'd had on her. But he merely studied her in that calm, assessing way he had.

Then his gaze went to her hand, still clutching one end of his neck cloth. She released it as though it had suddenly caught fire.

"I need more scotch for this discussion," he said. "More sherry?"

At least he wasn't dismissing her request completely out of hand. "Yes, please."

After snatching up her small glass, he headed for the decanters. She lowered herself into the chair, glanced over at the fire, thinking the flames were probably cooler than her skin right now. She did hope she hadn't turned a blotchy red beneath his studied stare.

He set her glass on the table beside her, and she wondered if he'd done so in order to avoid any risk of her touching him. His neck cloth was still dangling loose; he hadn't bothered to retie it. She liked the look of him a bit mussed but could hardly countenance that she'd begun disrobing him. Whatever had come over her?

She took a sip of the sherry. She'd never had a libation this early in the day. Perhaps it had influenced her.

"Other ways exist to gain means and freedom." He was settled back in the chair, keeping his distance from her, and she feared she'd destroyed whatever easy comradery they'd finally established.

"It's important I have a protector." Otherwise, her brothers would continue to feel responsible for her. She was striving to free them as much as herself. "If I am accomplished, skilled at pleasuring, I will have a choice in selecting the one lord I will welcome into my bed, and can be particular regarding the man whose favors I will accept. To that end, I need to be one of the most sought-after courtesans in all of England. Which means I must have mastered seduction."

"The occupation you are seeking is not an easy one. Why travel that path when you could be a governess, a lady's companion, something respectable?"

No one among the aristocracy was going to hire her except as a bedmate, but she realized she had more reasons than that.

"I don't want respectable. I had respectable. I had friends I loved, thought they loved me, but when I needed them the most, they turned their backs on me. Because of something that wasn't my fault. I want to return to Society on my terms. As the mistress of a lord, I will wield some semblance of power."

"Why do you need a protector?"

She rolled her eyes in frustration. "Why do you ask so many questions?"

He leaned forward again, and she was grateful less distance separated them. "If I'm to have a role in you acquiring this life you're seeking, I want to make damned sure you understand all the ramifications of it. You will be treated as though you are an object, property leased for a spell, to be used at the buyer's whim."

"Even in the most stately of homes, women are often treated as property. Are you not familiar with the laws that govern marriage, that apply to women?"

His sigh was long, drawn out. "Once you embark on this journey, doors that are now open to you will begin to close."

"They are closed now. Without my father's title, wealth, power, and influence behind me, no lord is going to marry me. I have no dowry. By the time I have earned your generous pounds, regardless of which deadline I meet, I shall be a quarter of a century old, gathering dust on the shelf."

"As I mentioned, I know a good many untitled men who have accumulated fortunes that rival those held among the aristocracy, in some cases even exceed them. They are finding themselves becoming accepted by the peerage, invited to their affairs. You could marry one of them. Return to Society as the wife of a gentleman who possibly wields more power than some of the noblemen surrounding him."

"This successful man who has worked so very hard to gain his elevated place in Society—how much will he loathe me when the rungs of the ladder are sawed out beneath his feet and he tumbles back to the ground because he demonstrated the bad judgment of marrying the daughter of a traitor? And our children? Do you think they will not suffer, that they will not be taunted and teased? Will servants take pride in serving our household? Do you not see how many people will be tainted by any association with me?"

His jaw was so tense that his back teeth had to be aching from the force with which he was biting down. "Do you not think a lord who takes you as his mistress will not suffer the same fate?"

"I will be his . . . My mother had a term for it—" She closed her eyes, envisioned her mother's face before illness had befallen her, illness Althea believed had been the result of her shame over her husband's actions. She opened her eyes. "A watercolor wife because I could be easily washed away. He may take me on occasion to the theater or a derby, but I'll never truly be part of his life. He may covet me, but he will not love me or sacrifice his position for me."

"Why would you want that?"

Now she was the one to lean forward. "I recently learned that my brothers are making decisions that place at least one of them in a dangerous situation. They are doing it in an effort to care for me, to increase my chances of finding a husband—as though marriage is all I should want from life. But I don't want to be dependent upon a husband. If I learned anything at all from my father, it was that a husband can let you down as easily as anyone.

"With the money you will pay me, I could lease a residence, determine who I entertain there. I could set the terms for what being in my company would cost the lord I take as my lover. Jewels, gowns, servants. Men lavish things on their mistresses. At least my father did. And if my lover disappoints or proves himself foolish, I can easily rid myself of him." She'd be exclusive, only one lover at a time and hopefully for an extended period. "Once I have established myself, my brother might end this dangerous quest he is on—if it doesn't come to an end before then. But if he continues, it won't be because he's seeking to make my life easier."

"You've given this a lot of thought." His tone held a bit of surprise, a tad of awe, and some admiration.

"To be honest, since I was twelve years old."

His eyes widened at that, and as though he was on the cusp of dropping his glass, he set it on a table beside his chair. "I thought noble ladies knew nothing of sex before their wedding night."

"Have you ever heard of Harriette Wilson?"

"No."

"She was a courtesan during the time that the prince regent ruled, was lover to some of the most famous and influential lords of her time. Lady Jocelyn, who was once my dearest friend, unearthed a copy of the scandalous courtesan's published memoirs. She refused to reveal how she had come to have it, although I always suspected she stole it from beneath her older brother's bed. We took turns reading each chapter aloud. Harriette Wilson described one lover as exhibiting 'ungovernable passion.' For some reason it stuck with me, and I thought that someday I would like to experience that level of hunger about something, anything. It has eluded me thus far.

"But another aspect of her story has also stayed with me: the power she wielded over men. They practically auditioned for the honor of being her lover. If they displeased her, she moved on. I know it won't happen overnight, but I do have a sense of the independence that awaits me if I follow this path. For the entirety of my life, I have been at the mercy of men's whims. Let them be at my mercy for a change. Teach me when to touch, where to touch, how to caress, how to drive a man mad with ecstasy."

Silence stretched between them until all she could hear was the *tick, tick, tick* of the clock on the mantel, the occasional hiss of the fire. Without taking his gaze from her, he reached back, grabbed his glass, tapped a finger against it, took a sip. How was it possible for the man to mask every thought, every emotion?

"If I were your brother, I'd break my jaw and nose before blackening my eye for good measure for even giving your proposal serious thought and not immediately dismissing it."

He was so incredibly somber, so serious. "I'm not going to tell Griff about this part of our arrangement. I'm going to tell him only that I'll be residing here, teaching etiquette. I'm not even going to reveal it's a brothel."

Another sip of the scotch. She longed for the sherry but didn't want to reveal that her fingers were trembling as she awaited his answer.

"I have a strict rule I adhere to, one I've never broken. The women under my protection are forbidden to me. I don't take advantage of them. I don't bed them. You'll be under my protection."

Disappointment slammed into her. "What if I didn't reside here?"

"I would still see myself as responsible for you."

Perhaps the ladies could teach her. Although how would she become comfortable with the touch of a man if a man wasn't touching her? She didn't want to admit that she was anticipating his caress, feeling the graze of his fingers along more than the underside of her jaw. "Surely, you could teach what I need to know without a full consummation. I should think that would be to my benefit. To be proficient but pure."

He studied her as though striving to envision it. A woman who was a contradiction, who knew how to pleasure but had never been pleasured fully.

"As much as you want out of this business," she said quietly, hoping her words could be heard over the thundering of her heart, "that is how badly I seek to master it."

His magnificent jaw tightened, and she wondered if seduction might involve scraping a razor over it, listening to the rasp of the bristles as they were removed, then kissing the smooth skin that remained.

Finally, he gave a long, slow nod. "I have the ability to instruct you on how to be a temptress without violating my principles."

HE WAS RATHER certain that with those words, he'd just condemned himself to an early grave. Because satisfying the temptation of touching her without possessing her fully was going to kill him.

When she released a shaky, shuddering breath, slumped back against the chair, and jerked her gaze to the fire as though she wanted to spare him the sight of the relief that filled her eyes with tears, he knew for certain he had the right of it: he was a dead man.

He shot to his feet and strode to the corner in desperate need of more scotch. He would probably spend the remainder of his life wondering why the devil he'd agreed to her terms. Maybe it was because he couldn't stand the thought of her seeking assistance elsewhere, and it had become increasingly clear that she was set on this path, and no argument he offered was going to sway her otherwise. Or perhaps it was simply that from the first moment his gaze had landed on her, he'd wanted her with a fierceness that defied all logic.

The irony was not lost on him. He wanted to get six women out of the business and to accomplish that, he had to introduce one more into it. At least she'd be more selective, more exclusive. He wondered if she'd change her mind if he paid her a salary of a thousand pounds. But then that would make him no different than the other men in her life, striving to control the direction she traveled.

He downed the scotch, poured some more, and turned back toward her. She'd returned to the window, the late-morning sunlight forming a halo around her. A delicate angel. That was what he'd thought the first time he saw her. But bloody hell, there was steel inside her, and a bit of a devilish nature as well.

"Would you like more sherry?"

"No, I have to report for work in a couple of hours."

He wandered over to the window, placed his shoulder against the casing, welcomed the bite of its hard edge. "I'll have my solicitor draw up the terms of our agreement."

She peered over at him. "How will you word the additional arrangement we made?"

"Innocuously. I'll give some thought to it. My main concern involves the financial arrangements so it's clear and we can't take advantage of each other."

"I trust your word."

He gave her an ironic twist of his lips. "Are you not the woman who just lamented that men are unreliable creatures when it comes to always doing good?"

She smiled, blushed, looked out the window. "I suppose I am. I'll have to work tonight. They're counting on me. But I'll give my notice to Mac. Hopefully, beginning tomorrow, he can have one of the other girls step in for me."

"I'll pay five pounds for any of your shifts worked by someone else until he can find a replacement for you."

Studying him, she bit her lower lip. "Could one of your ladies not take the position?"

"They earn more working here. That is one of the challenges you'll face. Few occupations for women pay as well, so you'll need to determine what each of them can be passionate about. Because if it's not going to bring them as much money, it must bring them joy."

"Perhaps I should have known that before I agreed to your terms."

"Until the contract is signed, you can walk away."

"I have no desire to walk away." She glanced over at the clock. "I have to leave. I could move in tomorrow if that's acceptable to you."

"More than acceptable. I'd like to get the ladies started as soon as possible."

"Good. Is there a particular time that would work best?"

"I could send a carriage round for you about ten."

"You have a carriage?"

"No, but my brother does. I can borrow it. It'll make it easier to transport your things."

"I have very little to transport. They literally tossed us out with little save the clothes on our backs and a few personal items. I'll take a hansom."

He nodded. "Did you want to see your chamber before you leave? In case the sight of it changes your mind?"

"As long as it has a bed, I won't change my mind."

He hated knowing how little had been left to her. A duke's daughter reduced to being content with scraps. She would discover within this residence there were no scraps. Anything she wanted, she would have. He would see to it.

In the foyer, he retrieved her cloak from the rack and draped it over her narrow shoulders. He shrugged into his own coat.

"You don't have to walk me home," she said.

"I don't intend to."

She looked both disappointed and pleased, as though craving independence but also a man to care enough to watch over her.

He did take satisfaction in her quick laugh when he hailed a cab. "I should have known you'd not let me walk home alone."

"I didn't think to ask. How is your head?"

"Better. The area is still tender, but the knot is not as large."

"Good." He gave the driver her address. "Wait for her to ready herself, then take her to the Mermaid and Unicorn. This should see your time well compensated." He handed up the coins.

The man gave them a quick look, doffed his hat. "Very good, sir."

"You don't have to do that," she said.

"We have an arrangement now. Besides, haven't you yet learned that when you tell me I don't have to do something, it doesn't stop me from doing it?"

"I do hope we won't be at cross-purposes for the next three months."

"I very much doubt we will be." Although his cock was going to disagree with a vengeance.

He assisted her into the cab. "Send word if there is anything you need."

"I require nothing more than what we agreed to."

As the driver sent the horse into a trot, Beast crossed his arms and watched until she disappeared from sight. He was quite looking forward to proving her wrong.

Chapter 7

*H*e didn't come into the Mermaid that night. Althea had barely been able to properly attend to her customers with all the minutes she'd become lost in watching the door, willing him to stride through it.

After catching Mac scowling at her several times, she was rather certain he was relieved she'd given her notice. With Benedict's generous offer, he'd had no trouble finding a couple of the other serving girls willing to take her shifts. One even had a friend who'd been looking for an opportunity to work at the Mermaid, so that eased her guilt at leaving so abruptly.

When they'd closed for the night, and everyone began tidying up, Mac called her over and pointed at some coins he'd set on the counter. "Your earnings for the nights you were here."

After counting it, she shook her head. "You didn't take out for the beers I dumped on heads."

"I never do. I just threaten to so a girl will think twice before drenching some bloke, but I figure if she still upends the tankard then he probably deserved it." He gave her a wink. "Probably pinched her bum."

She smiled at him. "I liked working for you. Thank you for hiring me when I had no experience."

"You gave the place a bit of class. Good luck with your new venture."

She hadn't told him what it was, only that she'd taken a position elsewhere. Slipping the coins into her pockets, she went to help the others, sweeping then mopping the floor. She wouldn't miss this.

When they were finally all in the alleyway, Mac gave her a gruff farewell. Perhaps he was going to miss her after all. Polly hugged her. Rob told her to come back for a pint sometime. The others just waved before they started off.

She walked to the street and smiled when she saw Griffith with his back to the wall, one leg bent, his foot pressed to the brick, his hands stuffed into the pockets of his coat, his head lowered. Hearing her steps, he glanced over, straightened, and returned her smile.

"Told you I wouldn't be late again."

She hadn't seen him since he'd left for the docks before dawn that morning. That was how their days always went, with a long absence from each other from dawn until midnight. She had so much to tell him.

"Miss Stanwick?"

Looking past Griffith, she saw the hansom cab and the driver sitting atop his high seat. She shouldn't have been surprised. "Yes?"

"I've been paid to see you home."

"Trewlove, I assume," Griffith said, not sounding particularly pleased.

"Probably." Absolutely. She'd wager the two thousand quid she had yet to earn.

"How did you know it was me?" she asked the driver as she strolled toward his conveyance.

"Gentleman told me to keep an eye out for the beauty coming from the alleyway."

That should not have pleased her, should not have made her cheeks warm. She had a feeling when all was said and done, she was going to resent that one rule he would cling to.

Griffith handed her up into the conveyance before settling in beside her. "Guess he didn't trust me to keep my word and not be late."

She suspected it had more to do with Benedict seeing himself as responsible for her now. As the driver set the horse into a trot, she sighed at the luxury of not having to walk home.

"His sister owns the tavern, doesn't she?" Griffith asked. "The Duchess of Thornley?"

"Yes."

"I'll get word to him through her that you're no longer in need of his assistance, that I'm fully capable of escorting you home."

Her brother had so much pride. Having to sometimes rely on the kindness of strangers had been one of the hardest things for any of them to accept. She thought about telling him that no missive was necessary but decided to wait until they were in the residence in the event he began voicing objections to her plans. She had no desire for the driver to overhear an argument.

Once they were inside the small dwelling, with the lamp lit, she walked to the fireplace and studied the bucket filled with coal and could not help but think she'd surprised Benedict by appearing in his parlor that morning. If he'd been expecting her, he'd have not sent so much coal. Oddly, the abundance served to not only reaffirm his generous nature and that the decision she'd made was the right one, but also to shore up her resolve for wading into what might become an unpleasant discussion.

"I'm to bed," her brother said, and she heard the weariness in his voice, but this could not wait. He'd be gone before dawn and matters needed to be settled.

She swung around. "Tonight was my last to work at the tavern."

He was standing near the table, no doubt waiting for her to pick up the lamp so they could go through their nightly ritual. "Thank goodness. I never liked you working there, especially so late into the night. I'll feel much better going about my day knowing you are simply locked in safely at the residence."

"Actually, Griff, this morning Mr. Trewlove offered me a position as a tutor. I've accepted it. Tomorrow—or I suppose really later today—I'll be moving into the residence where I'll be teaching."

"Teaching? You're not a teacher."

Neither was she a seamstress, a grocer's clerk, or a very accomplished tavern maid.

"I believe I'm well equipped to handle the subject matter. Mr. Trewlove is assisting some ladies in bettering their lives, and part of that assistance involves learning refinement. He's paying me a hundred pounds per annum, board, and lodgings. I could hardly refuse such a generous offer."

His brow furrowed so deeply she feared he might hurt himself. "That is an exorbitant proposal. Why would he make it? What does he want of you?"

"I explained. To teach refinement, finesse, and etiquette."

He shook his head. "No, he seeks to take advantage of you, to get you into his bed. I forbid this."

She could not have drawn her head back more if he'd slapped her. "I beg your pardon?"

"You're not to do it."

"I have already agreed to it."

"Send him a missive letting him know you have unagreed to it."

"I bloody well will not."

He looked as though she'd punched him. "I am your brother—"

"Yes, but not my father, not my husband, not my king. You do not reign over me. Besides, I want to do this. I'm excited by the prospect of it. I have the skills for it. I can make a difference."

Even as she spoke the words, she realized they were all true, truer than she'd fathomed. Having been so focused on securing her future, she hadn't truly taken the time to consider how she felt about what she'd be doing.

He appeared dumbfounded as he dropped into the chair at the table. "So you won't be here any longer?"

It occurred to her that he wasn't objecting so much to her position as he was to the fact that he would now be alone. He would awaken in the morning and return in the evening to an empty house. Joining him at the table, she lowered herself into the other chair and placed her hands over his. She needed to tend to his palms before they retired. After tonight, he'd have to tend to them himself. "I overheard you and Marcus talking last night. Griff, I don't need a nanny."

With a groan, he squeezed his eyes shut. "Althea, I didn't mean that the way it sounded."

"I know. Look at me."

He opened his eyes, as blue as hers, and she saw so much regret there.

"I don't know precisely what Marcus is doing, but I heard enough to know it's incredibly dangerous, and I know he needs you at his side, more than I do. With my new position, I'll be facing no peril whatsoever. No drunken gentlemen about to misbehave. No walking alone late at night. I'll be sleeping in a bed. I'll have a fire. I'll be safe. If you decide you are better needed elsewhere, you are free to go without battling any guilt." She squeezed his hands. "If you do decide to join Marcus in his endeavors, please, please, please take care. I cannot bear the thought of losing either one of you."

He gave her a crooked smile. "I think we both see you as that irritating little girl who wanted us to join her for tea parties with those tiny little cups that held no more than three drops of liquid."

They'd never accepted her invitations, although she'd always assumed it was the small table and the dolls occupying the chairs to which they'd objected. "I'm far removed from being interested in tea parties these days."

"Marcus probably won't like it. On the other hand, I think you're correct that this new position will create less worry for him . . . and me. It seems this Trewlove fellow has already taken it upon himself to shelter you, to ensure you are unharmed."

"From what I observed when he came into the Mermaid and what others have told me, it appears he's made it his life's work to see that people are not treated unfairly."

"No doubt comes from being born a by-blow. He can't have had it easy growing up. Although, I daresay the Trewlove name has more respect these days than ours. Imagine that."

It sounded as though imagining that left a sour taste in his mouth, and she wasn't certain if it was because Trewlove had become synonymous with *bastard* or because Stanwick had become synonymous with *traitor*, and that the majority of the population would choose an association with a Trewlove over one with a Stanwick. Which had not been the case not so long ago.

He glanced at the hearth. "He sent the coal, I assume."

"He insisted on having a fire last night, so he sent it to replace what he had used."

"With interest, it would appear. It does seem he will see you well cared for."

She decided against telling him about the additional money she would earn because she didn't want him realizing this was only temporary, three months at the most. The knowledge might prevent him from assisting Marcus and might force her to reveal her future plans. Not only would Marcus most definitely not approve of those, but neither would Griffith.

"I do feel I've made the right decision regarding my employment. He's expecting me to arrive at ten in the morning, so I'll see you off at dawn."

"I'll be going with you."

Her heart gave a little stutter. "I beg your pardon?"

"I'll see you to your new vocation, so I'll know where to find you."

"I can simply give you the address."

"I want to reassure myself that it is an acceptable, respectable abode."

"Dear God, Griff. Look where we live now." She flung her arm out in a wide arc. "A pigsty would be more acceptable than this."

He blanched as though she'd taken a gardening spade to his head. From the moment she had crossed the threshold into this sparse, cold, hideous dwelling with its faded and flaking paint, its chipped and scratched wood, its creaky water pump that tested her muscles every time she had to use the blasted thing, she had not revealed her desperation or despair that they had been brought so low.

"There are worse places, Althea. I expect Marcus is living in one right now—if he's living in anything at all. For all I know he's sleeping on the street."

She took a deep breath, and drew her cloak more securely around her, striving to regain some of the warmth she'd lost when she'd reacted as she had. In her new residence she would be able to hang up her cloak. She would no longer be forced to walk about inside as though still outside. "I didn't mean to sound ungrateful. It's not your fault or Marcus's that we are where we are. Escort me on the morrow if that is your wish, but know that no words you utter will deter me from the path I've chosen."

INTO THE LARGE bag made of carpet that she'd used when they'd stolen into the night three months ago after everything else was taken from them, she stuffed what clothing remained to her, her pearl-handled hairbrush and mirror, and her small bottle of gardenia-scented perfume that she used so sparingly she doubted anyone could actually smell it, but dabbing just a bit behind each ear always made her feel as though all was not lost. She left the blankets, folded neatly in the corner, because she was certain Griffith, possibly Marcus, could make use of them. On top of the stack she placed her earnings from the Mermaid, the three sovereigns Benedict Trewlove had given her, and the few pence that remained from her two earlier attempts at employment. She knew Griffith had too much pride to take the money outright but if she left the coins there, when he came to retrieve the blankets, he would have no choice except to add them to his coffers. She felt better knowing that perhaps they might serve her brothers well.

She didn't even consider pocketing a few coins for the hansom cab because she knew, simply knew, she wouldn't need them.

When she, with Griffith at her side, stepped out of the residence, she saw that she had the right of it.

"Good morning, Miss Stanwick," the hansom driver who'd brought them here last night called down from his seat.

"Good morning, sir."

Griffith helped her climb into the conveyance, then followed her in, holding her bag on his lap. They'd not spoken a word to each other since waking. She hated that things between them were so tense.

She studied his profile, striving to memorize it in case they never crossed paths again. This man had been in her life since she was born, and yet she could describe Benedict Trewlove in greater detail than she could her own brother. "What are you going to tell them at the docks regarding your absence this morning?"

"Nothing. I'm done working the docks. I'll pick up my wages this afternoon, and then I'll be moving on."

"Are you going to seek out Marcus?"

He finally slid his gaze over to her, offered a wry grin. "Yes. I feel guilty for being so relieved . . ."

"To be rid of me?"

He shook his head. "Never that. But to be able to assist him. I just hope this works out for you."

"It will. I left the blankets for you and"—she hadn't planned to tell him about the money but wanted to ensure he did return to the residence, did go into her room—"and all my earnings."

As she'd known he would, he looked less than pleased at that. "You might have need of them."

"I won't. I'll have him advance me this week's wages, and I'll be set."

"You've certainly placed a lot of trust in him."

"I've had no cause not to."

"You've misjudged a man before."

She knew he was referring to her betrothed. "That's unfair. And we all misjudged Father."

That seemed to take the wind from his sails. "Yes, we did."

The hansom cab slowed and came to a stop outside her new residence.

"I know this place," Griffith said. He jerked his gaze to her. "It's a brothel."

"Have you visited?"

"No." He swung his gaze to the building, then back to her. "Some of the chaps from work suggested it. You can't possibly think I'm going to let you walk in there."

She sighed. "Ah, Griff, I've already been in there twice. I'm going in there to teach, not to do the . . . other thing."

The doors of the vehicle sprung open and she clambered out. She wrapped her fingers around the handle of her bag. "Let go."

Holding tightly to her bag, he leapt out and placed it at her feet. "Althea—"

"I'm going to be all right. I promise."

"Shall I wait for you, sir?" the driver asked.

"No." Once the horse and carriage were on their way, Griffith gave her a wry grin. "I don't think Trewlove would have paid for my return home. If things don't work out here as you expect them to or if you should have need of us"—he pulled a scrap of paper from his pocket, placed it against her palm, closed her fingers around it—"go to that address, knock on the door, and tell the gent who answers that you have a package for Wolf that needs to be picked up straightaway. Word will get to Marcus and that night you should hear a tapping on your window. When you do, meet us outside. But only contact us if it's crucial."

It was as if she'd stepped into a world of criminals and spies and intrigue. If not for their father's actions, Marcus would have become the Duke of Wolfford. She wondered if that was the reason behind the moniker he'd chosen to use. Wolf. "That's how you got in touch with Marcus."

"Only a couple of times. It's better for him if they believe he's turned his back on all he once held dear."

She did what she'd never done before. She hugged him close, hugged him as though she'd never again have the opportunity. When his arms tentatively came around her, she nearly wept. "Please take care. And if you need *me*, you know where to find me."

He stepped out of her embrace and nodded toward the building. "Go on with you."

Picking up her satchel, she made her way to the steps, hurried up them, placed her hand on the door handle, and glanced back to give him a final wave of farewell.

He'd already dissolved into the crowd of passersby on their way to work, home, the shops, and appointments. She had the unsettling thought that there were a good many aspects to Griffith of which she was unaware.

The door opened and before she could even react, the satchel was taken from her grip.

"He didn't seem particularly happy," Benedict Trewlove said. She imagined him with his nose pressed to the window, awaiting her arrival, watching as she said farewell to her brother.

She shouldn't have been pleased with the thought that he'd been anxious for her return. Nothing of any serious nature could develop between them. He wasn't to be part of her permanent plans, her future. He was simply the means to an end, just as she was for him. They would assist each other in achieving their goals and then they would amicably part ways and get on with their lives.

He moved back and she stepped over the threshold. "I doubt his disgruntlement over recognizing this place as a brothel some mates had told him about will last long. He's rid of me now, free to do as he wishes."

"His loss is my gain. Let's get you settled in your bedchamber. Then we'll leave for our appointment with the solicitor to sign the agreement." He escorted her across the large foyer, past the parlor, to the stairs. "The ladies are all abed. We close the business at six. They're usually ravenous by then so breakfast is served before they retire. If you're not an early riser, I can instruct the cook to prepare another meal later for you."

"As I've been getting up long before dawn in order to prepare food for Griff before he left for the docks, I suspect I'll find myself continuing to awaken at an ungodly hour."

"You cook?"

"I wouldn't go that far in describing my skill. We ate mostly cheese, bread, and boiled eggs, anything that required little preparation."

"You'll have better selections here. I could have enticed you with that."

"You offered more than adequate inducements."

He started up the stairs. "Beginning tomorrow, your mornings will be yours to do with as you please. The others sleep until half twelve or so. Luncheon is served at one. You'll begin your lessons at two. I thought a couple of hours a day would suffice, although you're welcome to adjust the schedule to suit you. We dine at half six. The women prepare for the night. The doors are open to customers at eight."

She wondered if all brothels ran with such efficiency or if this one was simply more of a reflection of its owner.

At the landing she glanced quickly—and guiltily—down the ordinary corridor at the row of doors, behind which naughtiness occurred. Did the chambers contain large beds, mirrors, scarlet satin sheets, silk-covered chairs?

"You can explore if you like," he said, humor lacing his voice, making her realize she'd stopped walking while he had continued on and was now leaning on the balustrade several steps up. "They won't bite."

Mortification warmed her skin. "No, I just . . . I'd rather see my room."

She breathed a little easier when they reached the next level.

"My study." He pointed to a closed door at the nearer end of the hallway. "You can usually find me there."

He crossed over to an open doorway. "The library. You'll tutor the ladies in here."

Peering inside, she felt a contentment settle over her at the familiar musty scent and the shelves of books, so many books. "I hadn't expected a library in a brothel."

"This floor isn't considered part of the brothel. It's considered our residence." He glanced around. "And I like books."

"Are these all yours, then?"

"Every single one."

They must have cost him a fortune. She couldn't stop herself from walking over to the wide, tall bookcase that lined one wall. It contained an astonishing assortment of leather-bound volumes. She was surprised by the variety and number and how unworn so many of them appeared. "Is anyone welcome to read them?"

"They are."

She crossed back over to him and smiled softly. "You probably could have gotten me for half the cost if you'd shown me this."

"You enjoy reading?"

"I do, very much."

Her answer seemed to please him. "Meet me here tonight at ten. It's where we'll begin your lessons."

Her lessons. On seduction. She'd expected them to take place in a bed or at least near one, but she refrained from questioning him on it because she'd suddenly become unbearably warm.

"We should move on," he said quietly. "We haven't much time before we need to be at the solicitor's."

"Yes, of course."

He led her to a door at the end of the long hallway, swung it open, and indicated she should go in first. Throwing back her shoulders, she swept by him and was immediately hit with the scent of him. Sandalwood and cinnamon and something darker, richer, more enticing, a scent uniquely him. A scent that would fill her lungs if she breathed in his skin. In the library. In a bed.

Perhaps the library was to be merely the starting point and they'd end up in here. On the four-poster bed, with the pale lilac counterpane and deep purple pillows.

As though it was a sin to look at the bed, to consider what might transpire there, she jerked her gaze away from it and gave the remainder of the room an intense scrutiny. The walls were papered in lavender. A winged chair of mauve brocade with violets embroidered in violet, of course, rested near the fireplace. A dark mahogany wardrobe dominated one wall. A mahogany escritoire and a wooden straight-backed chair with a padded purple cushion rested near the window. She imagined sitting there, writing letters as the morning sunlight dappled the room. If any friends or relatives remained to her who would welcome receiving word from her. But not only had all friends abandoned her and her brothers—except for Kat, who hovered on the precipice—so had every relation.

"Are you all right?" he asked.

Something regarding the reminder of her loss must have shown in her suddenly stiffening stance. Fighting it back, regaining herself, she glanced over her shoulder. He waited on the other side of the threshold, although he had set her bag on the floor inside the room. "Absolutely. The bedchamber is quite wonderful. To be honest, I'd expected little more than a bed."

His eyes darkened, his nostrils flared, and she couldn't help but wonder if his viewing her with the bed behind her had him regretting his rule.

"You're welcome to add any personal touches, hang anything on the walls."

She wasn't going to be here that long. It was unwise to do anything to make the room a place that she would miss. Still, she wanted to be gracious. "Thank you."

"We have two maids-of-all-work who will keep your room tidy. A footman who can haul anything up for you—packages, the copper tub, hot water for a bath. A laundress. As you can imagine, we have a lot of linens to be seen to. But she'll also tend to your clothing. I'll introduce them all later."

"You seem to have thought of everything."

"I very much doubt it. If there's anything you need regarding your accommodations, you can speak with Jewel. As I mentioned before, she manages things, including the staff. Anything else you require, you may ask of me. If you've no questions at this point, I'll leave you to get settled in. We'll need to depart in no more than twenty minutes."

Suddenly, a bout of nervousness hit her with the realization of all that she was doing. "That's more than sufficient time. As you can see, I haven't all that much."

Something flashed across his face that she couldn't quite identify: sadness, anger, disappointment, sorrow—dear God, she hoped it wasn't pity. She couldn't stand it if he pitied her.

"Meet me in the parlor when you're ready."

Then he was gone, and she could breathe again. After retrieving her bag, she set it on the counterpane. The room was nowhere near as elegant or posh as the ones in which she'd slept beneath her father's roof at the estates or in London. But it did make her feel as though she was regaining her footing.

GAZING OUT THE window in the parlor, his half-finished scotch in hand, Beast fought to distract his thoughts away from images of her with the bed looming in the background. How easy it would have been to tumble her onto it. How satisfying to begin her lessons with one she'd never forget.

He'd hovered at the doorway, not daring to step into the room, because he'd feared giving in to the temptation of her. He wondered how many times his rule would come perilously close to being broken. He couldn't recall a single time in his life when he'd yearned for a woman more.

Like a besotted lad still in short pants, he'd stood at this very window awaiting her arrival, and when the hansom had finally appeared, he'd had to stop himself from rushing out to welcome her. Which had turned out to be in his best interest if her brother's balled fists were any indication of how Beast might have been greeted.

He wasn't convinced she understood exactly how much Griffith Stanwick did not want her in this dwelling. That she was now upstairs was a testament to her ability to cajole, or perhaps her brother's faith in her judgment, or the extent of his desire to see her happy, or the strength of his own need to be free to do what mattered most to him.

What mattered most to Beast was to keep his promise not to

bed her. In three months—he had little doubt she would meet that first goal—with money in hand, she might change her mind regarding her desire to be a mistress. She might realize marriage was still an option for her and he didn't want to lessen her chances of finding happiness by taking from her something many men coveted on their wedding night. He wasn't going to ruin her.

He heard the quiet footfalls. Something felt different about the residence now that she was here. It seemed not quite so . . . tawdry.

Turning, he watched as she glided into the parlor, anticipation in her eyes, color in her cheeks. He set aside his glass. "Let's go make this agreement between us official."

After which, there would be no turning back.

Chapter 8

$\mathscr{A}$s they waited in the receiving room for their audience with the solicitor, Althea struggled to calm her fraying nerves. It was one thing to negotiate scandalous terms, conditions, and outcomes with Benedict Trewlove in the privacy of his front parlor. Quite another to have them put in writing by a decent man whose job it was to uphold the law, to know he would bear witness to her not only signing her signature but also condemning her soul to the eternal fires of damnation. But then according to the *ton*, her father's actions had already secured that end for her simply by virtue of her being a product of his loins. Ever since yesterday, she'd begun to see the advantage to embracing the freedom his sins afforded her. She might as well embrace her own.

"Mr. Beckwith will see you now," the secretary said, holding open the oaken door that loomed like a great maw threatening to swallow her whole.

Her legs weren't quite as steady as she would have liked when she rose in tandem with Benedict, but then his hand landed on the small of her back with a surety and a strength that coursed through her and calmed all quivers.

She preceded him into the office where a much smaller man, slender of stature, stood behind his desk. He bowed his silver head. "Miss Stanwick, Mr. Trewlove."

It remained a bit incongruous to be addressed in such a manner, rather than as Lady Althea.

"Mr. Beckwith, you have the agreement ready?" Benedict asked.

"I do, sir. Please have a seat." He indicated two leather chairs set before his desk.

Benedict directed her to the one on the left while he took the other. If the solicitor thought anything at all regarding her relationship with the man beside her, he kept his thoughts closely guarded. She suspected Benedict paid him a good deal for his ability not to disclose his judgment on matters.

He looked at them through piercing blue eyes that appeared all the larger because of the spectacles resting on the bridge of his patrician nose. "I have a copy for each of you, and one that I shall keep on file. If you'll read them, ensure all is to your satisfaction."

She did hope neither man noticed the slight tremor in her fingers as she took the sheaf that he offered her and began reading. It was all so formal, so precisely spelled out just as they'd discussed the day before.

Her salary of one hundred pounds per annum to be paid out weekly, the balance to be paid in full should she leave his employ for any reason before the full fifty-two weeks had occurred. If he dismissed her or she decided to leave of her own accord, she was guaranteed that one hundred pounds even if the fault for her departure rested with her. They'd not discussed the little detail regarding how they would handle an acrimonious parting of the ways; she hadn't even considered that they might have one, that a reason might arise that would see her leaving before she'd anticipated. It seemed Benedict had more experience at drawing up contracts than she, leaving nothing to chance. She found no fault with the terms favoring her.

The payments for reaching the three-month, six-month, and twelve-month goal were spelled out. Succinct and to the point.

But it was the wording of her addendum to their negotiations that had her heart pounding so hard she was fairly certain the solicitor could hear it.

Mr. Trewlove shall provide to Miss Stanwick lessons in being an accomplished temptress. When their association comes to an end, should Miss Stanwick deem Mr. Trewlove failed in his endeavors, the only proof required being her opinion on the matter, Mr. Trewlove shall immediately hand over the sum of one thousand pounds.

She looked to her right where he sat so calmly in the chair beside hers, his sheaf already returned to the desk to indicate he'd read it. "This last part regarding my deeming your efforts a failure . . ."

He shrugged one large shoulder. "If I'm going to penalize you for not meeting my expectations, it seemed I should be penalized if unable to meet yours."

"You're trusting I won't lie simply to acquire that thousand pounds."

"Will you lie?"

"Well, no."

"Then I don't see the problem."

"The terms don't seem equitable. They favor me more than they do you."

"You know what I want. It can't be measured in coin."

For the briefest of moments, she imagined he wasn't talking about getting out of the brothel business but was talking instead of having her. What would it be like to be wanted that desperately, that badly? To be a need, an ache that overrode all good sense?

"If you are looking at the amounts referred to in this document," he continued, "and believe you are getting the better deal, I assure you, you are not. I'm ready to sign. Are you?"

Never in her life had she signed a legal document; never had she placed her signature on something that tied her to another. She had always assumed the first time she did would be the day she married and signed her life over to her husband. Yet, she would secure freedom in signing this document with this man, something marriage would not have granted her. With a deep breath, she calmed her nerves. "Yes."

Three times she dipped the gold nub of the pen in the inkwell.

Three times she signed her name. Three times she watched him do the same. Then the solicitor as witness.

When they were finished, Benedict Trewlove looked at her with satisfaction reflected in his onyx eyes. "'Tis done."

"Indeed it is," Mr. Beckwith said as he neatly folded two of the sheaves, once, twice, and handed them each one.

She placed hers in her reticule. Benedict placed his in the inside of his jacket and stood. She followed his example, which resulted in Mr. Beckwith also coming to his feet.

"Before you take your leave, Mr. Trewlove, as you're here, and if you would not consider it an imposition, I wondered if you'd be good enough"—he opened a drawer, withdrew a book, and set it on the desk—"to sign your novel for the wife. She enjoyed it immensely."

Stunned, Althea wondered if he was talking to someone who had wandered into the room unobserved. Although Mr. Beckwith had addressed him by name, she couldn't fathom that he was implying Benedict Trewlove was an author.

But Benedict picked up the book and the pen with which he'd signed their agreement only moments earlier. "Is there anything in particular you'd like me to say?"

"I shall leave it to the discretion of the wordsmith. Her name is Anne, with an E at the end."

In fascination, she watched as Benedict turned back the cover, dipped the pen in the inkwell, and scrawled inside the book. Not closing it, he handed it back to Mr. Beckwith.

"'To Anne, a woman of mystery. Yours sincerely, Benedict Trewlove.' Ha. She'll love that." He smiled. "I very much appreciate it. She did want me to inquire as to when the next one might be published."

"Sometime late next year."

"I shall so inform her. Do you require anything else of me?"

"Not at the moment. We appreciate your discretion on this matter."

"By all means. It is one of the things for which you pay me so handsomely."

He shook Mr. Beckwith's hand. "Good day to you, then."

Mr. Beckwith smiled at her. "It was a pleasure, Miss Stanwick."

"Thank you, sir."

With his fingers splayed over her lower back, Benedict urged her toward the door, and she wondered if it was with that hand that he penned novels.

It seemed while he'd asked many questions of her, her shame over her answers had numbed her to the need to make inquiries of him as well. Quite suddenly, she realized she knew very little about him and wanted to know everything.

"WHY DIDN'T YOU tell me you were an author?"

She'd waited until they were settled in a hansom cab and were on their way to ask her question of him.

"It's not something that easily comes up in conversation." Beast sighed. "And to be honest, I'm not quite comfortable with it yet. I don't know that it'll last. The one I'm writing now is not . . . cooperating. Which makes me sound like a madman, as though a novel is a living thing that determines where it goes."

"But it is, isn't it? A living thing? Even when it's finished, it breathes life into people as they read it. Or they breathe life into it. The reason I love books is because it's as though I'm traveling with a friend."

He didn't know what to say to that. Mostly because he felt much the same way, and for him, books had always provided an escape from a reality that had not always been kind.

"How many have you published?"

"My first was published about two months ago."

"Is it in bookshops?"

Her flurry of questions and her excitement made him even more self-conscious. He lifted a shoulder, dropped it. "In many of them. I don't know if it's in all of them." His sister Fancy, the Countess of

Rosemont, owned a bookshop, the Fancy Book Emporium. She'd ordered in about a thousand copies. Or so it had seemed.

"What is the title?"

"Murder at Ten Bells." The proprietor of the pub in White-chapel hadn't minded his use of the establishment for the setting of the murder. Apparently, the notoriety had brought an increase in business to his door.

Her smile of delight tightened his chest. "That's the reason you wrote to Mrs. Beckwith what you did. A woman of mystery. Because you write mysteries."

He viewed what he wrote as more of a detective story than anything.

"I want you to tell me everything."

What more was there to tell? As he realized where they were, he shifted his focus to something of a more urgent nature that required his attention. He'd meant to inform her after they'd climbed into the cab that they'd soon be parting ways, but then she'd begun her inquisition. "I appreciate your interest. However, it will have to wait. It's not often that I get to this area of London, and I need to make a stop elsewhere. If you've no objection, I'll have the driver drop me off and carry you on to the residence."

A flash of disappointment lit her eyes like lightning during a bleak winter storm. Appearing quickly and gone, leaving him to wonder if it had ever been. "No, none at all. Do what you must."

Leaning back, he called up through the small opening in the roof to the driver. "Deliver me to Abingdon Park. Stop at a flower shop on the way."

WHEN THEY ARRIVED at the garden cemetery, with his arm cra-dling an abundance of colorful blossoms that could only exist this time of year in a hothouse and had no doubt cost him a small fortune, he promised to return to the residence before Althea was to give her first lesson. With the grace and agility that she'd come to expect of him, he leapt out of the conveyance.

After paying the driver additional coins, Benedict told him where to deliver her. As they started off, she glanced back to see him trudging through the gated entrance, his gait slower than she'd ever seen it, and she was struck—as she'd been the night she watched him walk away from her shabby little residence—by the loneliness of him, but something had been added to deepen it. A forlornness hovered around him. And why shouldn't it? He hadn't passed through the gates in order to enjoy a spot of tea.

They barely reached the next street when she ordered the driver to circle around to where they'd been. After instructing him to wait, she clambered out of the vehicle and stood on the precipice of indecision. Should she simply wait for his return or join him in order to offer whatever support he might welcome as he visited whoever it was now lost to him? Would he be glad to see her or angry at the intrusion?

In the end, she decided it was worth the risk of garnering his anger on the off chance that he needed her solace.

As she walked along the path, she couldn't deny the area contained a peacefulness, a quietness, a calmness. A rustling sounded as the slight breeze toyed with the last of the tenacious leaves clinging to the trees. A briskness on the air made her breath visible.

Passing by a statue of a huge stone angel, she noted the words carved at its base indicated it watched over the Duke of Lushing. His widow had married a Trewlove.

Rounding a corner along the path, she spotted Benedict with his dark head bent, kneeling on one knee at the foot of a grave marked with a small, simple headstone, his beautiful bouquet of fresh flowers resting against the black marble with its gilded lettering.

SALLY GREENE
JUNE 15, 1841
AUGUST 5, 1866
WALTZING NOW WITH THE ANGELS

Stopping far enough away so as not to intrude, but near enough to read the words, she felt a sharp pang of sorrow, wondering who the young woman was and what exactly she'd once meant to him. She wondered at the shade of her hair, the gentleness of her soul. Although she couldn't quite imagine him with someone who wasn't as strong, bold, and daring as he.

It was several long minutes before he finally stood, settled his beaver hat on his head, and turned to face her.

"I apologize if I disturbed you," she uttered with all sincerity.

"You didn't, but you were supposed to take the cab back to the residence."

"This area isn't exactly teeming with cabs. I decided it would be better to return here and have the driver wait for us in order to ensure you're there when I meet the ladies. I'm a bit anxious about my first encounter with them, to be honest."

He studied her for a full minute before nodding. "You have such confidence it hadn't occurred to me you might be experiencing a spat of nerves. You were right to bring the cab back. We should be off."

"Did you love her?" The words were out before she could stop them, before he could leave, and she realized she already knew the answer. It resided in the flowers, the manner in which he'd been kneeling, the somberness, the sadness that now clung to him like a well-worn cloak.

Shoving his gloved hands into the large pockets of his greatcoat, he looked up at the graying sky. "It was hard not to love Sally. She often complained that her mouth was too wide and her teeth too crooked, but when she smiled, her dark eyes sparkled, and it was like a thousand tapers had been lit to brighten the world."

Such profound, poetic words. Her throat tightened, and she wondered how she might explain the tears stinging her eyes. She was rather certain that the Earl of Chadbourne had never spoken so passionately about her or held her in such tender regard, for if he had, surely, he wouldn't have broken things off after her father's fall from grace. Surely, he would have stood by her. "Sally was a fortunate woman indeed to have such devotion. But she died so young. Had you plans to marry her?"

He met her gaze. "My affections toward her never ventured beyond friendship."

"Friends seldom leave such an abundance of flowers." Costly ones at that.

"Ah, those . . . My attempt at easing my guilt. I'm the one responsible for her death."

Before the words had fully settled like an anvil on her chest, he removed his watch from his pocket, flipped open the cover with a practiced flick of his thumb, studied the time, and tucked it back into place. He jerked his head toward the path down which she'd traveled to arrive here. "We've lingered long enough."

A tenseness threaded through his voice, as though he dreaded her response to his earlier confession, regretted making it, was hoping by moving on to another topic he'd never learn her thoughts on the subject.

"I don't believe for a single moment you killed her."

"Not directly but I may as well have."

He started to move past her, and she stopped him easily with a hand on his arm, an arm thick with firm muscle, the strength of it clear even through his greatcoat. "You can't possibly believe you can say something like that and not clarify."

He studied her intently. "Do you remember my saying that the brothel came about as a favor to a friend?"

She nodded.

"She was the friend, in need of a place where she could safely ply her wares, so I provided it."

"She was a fallen woman?"

He gave a little scoff. "More girl than woman. Fifteen when she started working. Sixteen when she approached me to see if I'd provide her with a sanctuary. She had a way about her that made it impossible to refuse her. In that one regard, at times you remind me of her.

"Anyway, some years later, one night I heard her scream. I don't know what the blighter did to her before I got to the bedchamber, but by the time I burst through the door he was straddling her and banging her head against the floor. I dragged him off her, beat him bloody, and tossed him out into the street. By the time I returned to her, she was sitting on the edge of the bed. She said her head hurt a little, and she was going to retire for the night. I wished her pleasant dreams. On the way out, she patted my shoulder. 'Always my hero.' She was dead by morning. A true hero would have known to fetch a physician."

Her heart was breaking for him. How could he believe any of that was his fault? "That's the reason you sent for a surgeon the night I was hurt, the reason you watched me so closely."

"I couldn't have borne it if you'd died."

HE'D NOT MEANT to be so fervent in his declaration, hoped she understood it was the guilt of another death on his conscience and not some ardent affection toward her that was responsible for what would have been better left unsaid. Because whatever he was beginning to feel for her was also better left unfelt. She had her plans, her goals, and they certainly didn't include him.

Neither spoke as they made their way back to the waiting cab. He was torn between being grateful she'd not left without him and desperately wishing she had.

As though she'd actually come up and tapped him on the shoulder, he'd been acutely aware of her arrival as he knelt before Sally's grave. Damnation, as if he hadn't been telling Sally about her, and his words had conjured her.

The two women would have liked each other, he was rather certain of that. Althea possessed a strength he wasn't certain she realized she owned. But life had battered it, left it bruised, as circumstances had brought her to a part of London where she didn't belong.

When they reached the cab, he handed her up and then settled in beside her. It was beginning to feel almost natural to be so near to her, to have his thigh pressed up against hers, to have the scent of gardenia wafting around him, to glance to his left and see her pink-tinged cheeks chafed by the cold.

As they made their way relatively swiftly through the crowded streets, he felt as though he should say something—thank her for not leaving, explain the last words he'd spoken were simply the result of the cornucopia of emotions that always bombarded him when he came here, mention the brittleness of the weather— anything that would dispel the awkwardness that had settled between them. He shouldn't have gone to the cemetery with her in tow, shouldn't have burdened her with his regrets. All these years and still they lashed at him. They were the reason he continued to reside in a bloody brothel, wouldn't abandon the women who relied on his reputation—and occasionally his fists—to keep them safe.

She must have felt his gaze on her, because she glanced over at him with sympathy and understanding in her eyes, and he remembered she'd only recently lost her mother. Perhaps she was struggling with her own grief and regret.

"Tell me about the women I'll be teaching," she said so softly that he almost didn't hear her over the plodding of hooves, whirring of wheels, creaking of springs, shouts, and yells that comprised the cacophony of people going about their day. "What should I expect of them?"

He was grateful she was willing to not dwell on what he'd shared. But then what more was there to say on the matter?

"Lottie is flirtatious, likes to tease, and hardly takes anything seriously. I think she'll present the greatest challenge to you because she thoroughly enjoys men, so is likely to be let go from one position after another for being generous with her favors. Lily is the shyest of the lot but has a heart of gold, is always mothering. I've often thought she'd make an excellent companion to a wealthy widow. Pearl and Ruby are fast friends, and I suspect where one of them goes, the other would like to follow. Hester has an interest in being a lady's maid—again not in a noble household, but the wives of successful men have a need to be properly put together. You might consider allowing her to wait on you and teach her what a lady requires of a maid who serves her personally."

"That's a simple enough thing to do, although it would benefit me."

"She'd no doubt be delighted with the practice. As I understand it, she often treats the others as if they are dolls, fiddling with their hair, telling them what they should wear."

"I'll talk with her about it, then."

"Good. The last is Flora. She spends a good bit of her time tending the garden."

As he'd spoken, her brow had begun to furrow, deeper and deeper, with each word. Her lips were parted slightly, and he considered lowering his mouth to hers and introducing their tongues. He hadn't determined exactly what his lessons to her would entail. Any physical intimacy, even if it was only a mere touch, could lead to other things and test his resolve not to take advantage of her. Which was the reason he'd added the thousand-pounds payment should she be disappointed by his efforts. He didn't plan to intentionally not honor his agreement to teach her what she wished to know, but he also knew the fulfillment of it could create problems. He probably should have included in the terms that at any time, if unwanted emotions began to surface, either of them could bring a halt to the lessons without any forfeit.

"You seem troubled," he finally managed once he was able to stop thinking about her mouth.

"I didn't expect them to be . . . so normal. Tending gardens, pinning up hair . . . I expected them to be tawdry."

"Oh, there's a little bit of that. It's the reason I need you to make these diamonds in the rough sparkle a bit. They're open in their discussions. The topic is often sex rather than weather. They share crude jokes. They walk about scantily clad, but beneath it all, like everyone else they have things beyond their job that they enjoy. They have dreams."

"And smiles that light tapers."

"For some, yes. Don't judge them by their covers."

"I immediately liked Jewel the night I met her. She was kind, concerned, and teased you. I guess I thought her the exception."

"In my experience, I have found her to be more the rule."

Chapter 9

By the time they'd arrived back at the residence, luncheon had already been served and finished, the ladies of the night having returned upstairs to ready themselves for lessons.

So it was only Althea and Benedict being served at the large table that seated a dozen. She was surprised by the simple yet elegant style of the dining room. It was equal in taste to any found in the poshest of houses in Mayfair.

"You have a most excellent cook," she said.

"Growing up in the rookeries, with so many siblings, I was always hungry. It was a situation I intended to correct as soon as I had the means."

She thought of the coins he left on tables, the hansom cabs he so easily hired, the residence, its fine furnishings, the well-tailored clothing that accentuated his remarkably fit and tempting physique. "Now you have the means."

"I do."

"I'd have not thought being a writer was so lucrative." Especially after only one book.

"It's not, but my ships are."

Another bit of information about Benedict Trewlove she didn't know. Not that it would have made any difference in her decision to accept his proposition, but she'd been right that first night to think he was a man adept at keeping secrets. "You have ships?"

"A man must have a livelihood."

He said it so simply as though it was of no importance. Yet, of all the ships she'd watched come and go, all the adventures she'd imagined the crews encountering, she'd never known anyone who actually owned a vessel that traveled the seas. "How many have you?"

"Four."

"How did you come to have them?"

He swirled the glass of white wine a footman had poured for him. "When I was younger, about fourteen, I began working on the docks."

Dear God. At fourteen. She knew the toll the dock work had taken on Griffith. She couldn't imagine the challenge it would have presented to a fourteen-year-old boy.

"As I loaded and unloaded cargo, I would speak with the merchants who came to claim their wares, and ask questions of the captains and crews. I knew money was to be had in the shipping business. So I saved my earnings until I could purchase a ship. Took several years, of course, as ships are not without significant cost. With all my inquiries, I was able to determine a profitable route for acquiring merchandise for a host of merchants who liked that I was willing to charge less than my competitors in order to acquire their business. Soon, I had so many contracts that I needed another ship. And then another . . . and another. I'm thinking a fifth might be in order soon."

"Have you traveled the world, then?"

He studied his wine. "When I acquired my first ship, I thought I might. Got as far as the cliffs at Dover. Ferguson—he was the first captain I hired—told me to take a good look because soon we'd be far out at sea with no land in sight." He scoffed and gave her a wry grin. "I made him return to port. I didn't want to be beyond sight of land, beyond sight of England. I'm not certain why it didn't occur to me before that eventually I'd be surrounded by nothing except water. Have you ever left England?"

"I've been to Paris for gowns."

"Was the green you wore yesterday from Paris?"

She nodded. "Did you like it?"

Rather than answer, he glanced at his timepiece. "The ladies should be ready for you now."

LOTTIE, LILY, HESTER, Pearl, Ruby, and Flora.

They were lounging around the library in various stages of undress, corsets pushing up breasts, silk wraps tied loosely, revealing cleavage and bared thighs. In one instance hinting at a shadowed area, indicating the woman didn't bother with drawers. Some feet were naked, others slippered. Some of the women pinned up their hair, while the others left the strands to hang loose. One woman's hair was styled with combs and curls that would have served her well at a ball.

Althea decided she was Hester. She looked so damned young that she couldn't have seen more than two decades.

"Straighten yourselves, ladies," Jewel ordered, standing to Althea's left.

They did so with a sinewy roll of their bodies that had her thinking she should ask them to teach her about seduction. Although they studied her as though not quite sure what to make of her, she also saw a measure of hope and excitement in their expressions, tentative smiles welcoming her.

"As I mentioned yesterday," Benedict said, "Miss Stanwick is here to teach you refinement and some skills that will help you find a position elsewhere. You're to show her respect and follow her instructions without complaining about them. Any questions?"

A hand shot up. The woman appeared short of stature. Althea fought not to envy her ample bosom.

"Lottie?" he said.

"Is she a toff? She looks like a toff."

"She is familiar with the world that can offer you more than this one."

"If she's not looking down on you, love, don't you be looking down on her," Jewel added.

"Ain't lookin' down on 'er, Jewel. Want to be like 'er. Bet she could get a fancy bloke with deep pockets to take 'er to the altar. That's the kind of permanent position I'm lookin' fer. One beneath a rich bloke."

Althea couldn't help it. Laughing, she had a feeling she was going to have conversations with these women unlike any she'd ever had in the posh parlors of London's elite.

He sighed deeply. "Lottie—"

"It's fine," Althea assured him. "Even the toffs dream of that."

She was delighted by the ruddy hue that unexpectedly stained his cheeks. The women were suddenly out of their chairs and circling her. She suspected they'd been testing her, and she'd somehow earned good marks.

"Ladies, before we get started with today's exercise," she said, "I'd like you to tell me what you might want to do if you can't be beneath a rich bloke."

They started laughing and talking all at once.

"I'll leave you to it," he said near her ear before walking from the room.

"Ladies," she said, "I can't hear anyone if you're all talking at the same time. Why don't we move the chairs into a circle and get to know one another a bit better?"

Once they were all gathered, Lottie asked, "Do you like your bedchamber?"

Althea was surprised the young woman would care. "I do, yes. I find the colors very calming."

Lottie grinned. "That's what I was 'oping fer when I chose the wallpaper and counterpane."

"You're the one who designed it?"

"Lottie does all the rooms," Pearl said.

She did? Well, that was interesting. It was also a possible alternative to her current occupation. "This room?"

Lottie grinned, lifted her shoulders. "All the rooms."

"I find the parlor an interesting contrast to this room."

The woman just blinked at her.

"Why did you decorate the parlor as you did?"

"Oh, that was for the blokes. They like to see naughty bits. Makes 'em think they're bein' just as naughty."

She leaned forward slightly. "If it wasn't a receiving room for a brothel, how would you decorate it?"

With her brow so deeply furrowed, she appeared incredibly serious as though she'd been asked if Parliament should pass a particular piece of legislation. "In blues and yellows, I think, 'cuz of the way sun comes in through the windows in the mornin'."

Althea could envision it. The woman had the right of it. The colors would be perfect.

As she grilled the other ladies for the next half hour, she began to get a sense of their interests and how she might guide them toward other avenues. Once that was established, she moved on.

"I'd like to discuss your attire for these lessons. Since I'm striving to teach you how to be a lady, it might help if you didn't see yourself as someone comfortable revealing . . . quite so much. You must have proper attire that you wear when you go shopping."

They all nodded. Good. She'd encourage them to wear that.

"Then there's our leaving frocks that Beast had a seamstress make for us," Lily said.

"Your leaving frocks he had made for you?" She shook her head.

Lily nodded enthusiastically. "For interviews and for leaving. He's had one made for every strumpet who ever worked here. To hang our dreams on in the wardrobe, he said. So whenever we open it, we remember something better is coming."

"Every"—she could not say *strumpet*—"woman who's worked here? There have been others?"

"Caw, yeah. We're just what's left."

The ones who needed a bit more refinement.

"Lottie's been here the longest. Lottie, how many do you think?"

"Blimey, I don't know. Two dozen or so. I ain't been here as long as Jewel. She'd know, for certain."

Althea was stunned to learn there had been so many, and yet after their visit to the cemetery, she understood his need to help them and wanted to do all in her power to assist in their transition to a different life. "Perhaps your leaving frock is what you should wear for your lessons, as a sort of motivation."

Lily appeared horrified. "It's only for when we're leaving and ain't comin' back."

"Well, then, perhaps wear something a little more proper to-morrow, so you're reminded of what you're aspiring to be rather than how you are currently engaged."

"Blimey, ye talk so fancy," Lottie said.

She smiled. "And soon, so will you. But first, I'm going to teach you how to walk like a lady."

SHE EASED THE *loneliness that marred his soul.*

It was the only sentence he'd written during the past hour since he'd left Althea to her lessons. It could apply to him and her as much as it did to his detective and the woman he suspected of murdering her husband.

He'd intended for the recent widow to be the culprit, but now saw the potential for her to soften his no-nonsense inspector. Did he need softening? Would it make him vulnerable?

With a groan, he dropped his head back and plowed his fingers through his long hair. He felt as though he were examining him-self more than he was the character he'd created.

But then it seemed he was constantly analyzing his reactions to Althea. He enjoyed talking with her. Liked that she wasn't afraid of him, hadn't been from the first. Liked that she knew her own mind. Most of the time it didn't bother him that she wouldn't let him sway her from her decisions—but when it wasn't in her best interest, it irritated the devil out of him.

Funny thing was, he even enjoyed that.

He'd been tempted to stay and observe the lessons but needed to work. He wasn't certain eight words counted as achieving his goal.

He heard a bang, something falling. One of the ladies tripping over furniture?

Bang.

What the devil were they doing?

Bang.

He walked out of his study and crossed over to the library that was right next to it. The women were walking through the room with one of his precious books balanced on each of their heads—or trying to. One step, maybe two, and the thing toppled off and hit the floor. *Bang.*

Except for one. Except for the one sitting atop Althea's head as she demonstrated how it was to be done, gliding along the length of the room with the book barely moving. So poised, so elegant, so in control. She wouldn't tolerate it slipping from its perch.

How many hours had she practiced that stroll? How diligently had she worked to perfect that one small component so that particular facet of herself would not be found lacking? So she wouldn't be looked down upon, so no fault would be found with her, so she could acquire a husband worthy of her? He couldn't imagine that she'd given any less attention to fewer than a hundred other characteristics that defined her as a woman of the nobility.

Yet, for all her training, her father's actions had made it all unnecessary.

Four and twenty. Why had she not already married?

She pivoted about and her gaze immediately landed on him, and the touch of her eyes might as well have been the touch of her hands on his skin, so forceful was the impact. That did not bode well for him remaining indifferent when it came to tutoring her in the art of seduction.

Turning on his heel, he headed down the stairs at a near gallop, needing to put distance between them, needing this warm, electrifying sensation to dissipate. He finally reached Jewel's office near the kitchen. The door was open. Unlike him, she never shut it, didn't mind being disturbed when she was at her labors.

"Why aren't you upstairs taking the lessons?"

Sitting behind her desk where she'd been writing in a ledger, Jewel glanced up. "What need have I for them?"

She poured scotch into two glasses and scooted one toward

the edge of the desk. "I did stay long enough to ensure the girls would behave. Althea rather quickly charmed them."

He wasn't surprised. Even when she'd been irritated with him for asking questions that first night at the Mermaid, he'd been charmed. Dropping into the chair before Jewel's desk, he took the glass, lifted it in a salute, and sipped the amber liquid. It went down smoothly, heating his chest. "I need you to teach her the precautions she should take so she doesn't get with child."

Jewel paused with her glass nearly to her lips. He seldom knew precisely what she was thinking. The best doxies—and Jewel had been one of the best—were skilled actresses. But her guard was down, and he could see that he'd stunned her.

"I've never known you to dip your wick within these walls, but I could sense from the beginning that something about her was different."

He tapped his glass. "I have no plans to do any dipping, but she's asked me to teach her how to seduce men."

Eventually, someone else would do the dipping. His jaw clenched as he fought not to envision it; his stomach tightened as fury threatened. He didn't want anyone else bloody touching her. But what he wanted was not the issue, was not how the terms had been laid out.

With a Cheshire cat-like grin, Jewel leaned back in her chair. "That should prove interesting. Are you going to do it?"

"I haven't a choice. It was a condition of hers in order to tutor the ladies."

"You don't sound pleased. Do you fear falling for her? Being unable to resist the temptation of her?"

Yes. Yes. "No. It's simply that I hesitate to set her on a path fraught with dangers."

"The path she decides to travel should be her choice to make—just as Sally's was. You're not responsible for her dying. If anyone is, it's the blackguard who attacked her that night. That they wouldn't even consider arresting him because she was a doxy still eats at me."

"If I hadn't agreed to protect her—"

"Sally still would have engaged in her trade, Beast, and she'd have had a harder time of it, filled with more slaps, punches, and men who treated her unkindly. I speak from experience. Before you took me in, I cursed men on a nightly basis but saw no way out. Now look at me. You taught me how to manage things and keep ledgers. How to be a hostess. I daresay when the last of the girls is gone, we could turn this place into a proper boarding-house and make a tidy profit."

"Is that what you want to do?"

"I think I'm well suited to it."

He nodded. She would do well with that plan, had lots of time to implement it and enjoy the fruits of it. She was only four years younger than his thirty-three years.

"Why does Althea have a need for this skill you're to teach her?" she asked quietly.

"She plans to be some man's—some lord's—mistress."

"Ah. I know a couple of girls who went that route. It hasn't been a bad life for them. Fancy house, fancy clothes, fancy food. Makes it a bit rough, though, when they fall in love with their keeper."

He couldn't imagine Althea being content to be *kept* as though she were a pet. He often wondered if his own mother had been kept. His brother Aiden knew his mother had been his father's mistress. During the past year Aiden had come to know his mother, and Beast fought not to envy his sibling for the closeness he was developing with the woman who'd given birth to him. At the time Aiden was born, she'd had no choice but to give him up.

Based upon what Beast knew of his own mother's words when she'd handed him over to Ettie Trewlove, she'd had no choice, either. She'd promised to come back for him, but perhaps that had been said only to ease her conscience. He didn't like to consider that some misfortune had befallen her, preventing her return. He'd rather imagine her healthy, happy, and well cared for. He could forgive her for not wanting him. Life wasn't easy when a woman had a bastard in tow. "You'll teach her how to avoid pregnancy?"

"Who? Althea?"

"No, my mum." He gave her a frustrated glare. "Yes, Althea. That's who we've been discussing."

"For someone you have no interest in knowing carnally, you certainly are worrying about her."

After tossing back his scotch, he set the glass on the desk with a little more force than was necessary, taking satisfaction in the loud *thunk,* and stood. "We have a responsibility to ensure she avoids all the pitfalls."

He just wasn't certain that where she was concerned, he had the wherewithal to avoid them.

Chapter 10

$\mathcal{A}$lthea stood before the cheval glass in her bedchamber, studying her reflection, wondering if she should change into the green rather than wear the gray that had serviced her all day, from arrival through dinner.

She'd been startled to appear for the evening meal and discover the ladies wearing what they'd worn in the library—not a stitch more.

Sitting at the head of the table, fully dressed in a black jacket, gray waistcoat, white shirt, and a perfectly knotted neck cloth, indicating he saw these women of the night as worthy of his attiring himself properly when dining with them, Benedict immediately came to his feet when she entered the dining room.

Clutching her hands in front of her, suddenly self-conscious, she said, "You don't have to stand for me."

"He stands for everyone, love. Don't think you're special," Jewel said, sitting at the other end of the table.

Yet, for him she wanted to be.

Then he indicated the chair to the side, immediately on his left, and she had felt she was special. During the entire meal, they'd not spoken. Not because she hadn't wanted to but because the other ladies had dominated the conversation, talking over each other, revealing their excitement as they illuminated their successes and others' failures during their lessons. While she was gratified by their enthusiasm, tomorrow she would begin tutoring them on proper dining etiquette.

Afterward, they'd all adjourned to their rooms and she had listened to the minutes tick. She had heard their laughter and footsteps when they'd traipsed down to start entertaining customers. And still she'd waited.

She'd pinned and unpinned her hair three times. To wear it up, to wear it down. She'd finally decided on up.

She had considered penning her impressions of the women, a sort of journal for her own edification, or maybe an article for others. The afternoon had been a revelation. They were so very different from the ladies with whom she'd previously spent her time. She was no longer certain it was to the benefit of the aristocracy to be so dictatorial regarding with whom they should associate. As a result, she'd acquired a rather limited view of the world.

But then so had these ladies, begrudgingly referring to her as a toff, a bit suspicious until they'd come to know her a little better. Eventually, they might even become friends. Wouldn't Society have a laugh at that?

When the clock finally struck ten, she quietly padded down the hallway papered in green decorated with tiny pink flowers, giving it a homelike feel. This residence ran the gamut from sensual to masculine to feminine, which made it easier to determine the purpose of each area. As she neared the library, she noticed the door was opened wide.

When she peered inside, she saw Benedict sitting before the fireplace in one of two wing chairs upholstered in a plum-shaded velvet. She thought she'd been quiet but he either heard her arrival or felt her presence because he immediately put aside his book and stood.

"You don't have to stand for me," she said again.

"It's the way I was taught."

By the woman who had given him a treasured silver match safe. Taking a step over the threshold, she wandered in, wondering if the ladies had been as nervous about their lessons as she was about hers. Then she spotted the glass of sherry resting on the table beside the empty chair and smiled.

"If you prefer something else—" he began.

"No, sherry is good." Standing before the chair, she folded her hands in front of her. "As I'll have a few hours to myself each day, I should like to spend the time reading. Somewhere within this room must be at least one copy of *Murder at Ten Bells*. Are you going to make me search for it?"

She took the opportunity to appreciate the smoothness of his long strides as he made his way to a bookcase with glass doors near the entry into the room. A click sounded as he pulled open one of the doors, and when he closed it. As he neared her, he extended a book. Reverently, she took it and skimmed her fingers over the wavy grain of the violet hard cover. Then she turned it in order to admire the spine where the title and his name were etched in gold. She wanted to caress the man as much as she did the book. She lifted her gaze to his. "Will you mind if I read it?"

"You may have it, do with it as you will."

"I don't want to take your copy—"

"I have another. Several, in fact." He returned to his chair but remained standing.

She edged around hers, eased onto the plush cushion, and took a sip of the sherry, waiting while he settled.

Studying her, he took a long swallow of what she was fairly certain was scotch. "During dinner, each of the ladies shared their account of the afternoon, but you held silent. So now tell me the truth of it."

She was grateful they weren't going to immediately leap into her lessons. "It went fairly well, even if they are a bit unruly at times. I'm given to understand you had a very nice frock made for each of them. I need them to wear it during lessons."

"Then have them do so."

"When I suggested it, I learned you told them the frocks may only be worn on the day they leave—and they see your word as sacrosanct. However, if they are to have any success, they need to view themselves differently, as ladies. And they can't do that if they are flaunting their attributes."

"I'll talk with them."

"Thank you."

His gaze traveled the length of her in an assessing way that had her wishing she was dressed in something similar to what the ladies had been wearing that afternoon.

"Tomorrow I'll take you to a seamstress to have some frocks made for you."

"That's very generous of you, but not necessary."

"You have the gray, a blue"—that she'd worn the second night he'd seen her at the pub—"the green. Have you anything else?"

A flannel nightdress and undergarments, although she didn't think he really had any interest in those items. She didn't want to acknowledge how worn the gray and the blue were becoming. "I find them to be sufficient."

"You just successfully argued that a person's clothing should reflect who they are and what they want from life. Shouldn't the same apply to you? Shouldn't you have clothing worthy of a seductress?"

With her own words, he'd trapped her into doing what he wanted. It annoyed her that he should be so clever.

She looked toward the fire, remembering a time when she would have stalked from the room in a fit of temper, would have rained down oaths, would have seen servants sacked, for an irritation much less potent than the anger roiling through her for having fallen into his snare. But that was back when she had options, relied on no one's mercy, because her father had wielded such power that the tentacles of it reached out and cradled her, so she mirrored that power. But she no longer had the luxury of showing her annoyance, or the authority to insist those surrounding her work diligently to make matters right. As a mistress, her future would be determined by the whims of a man and her ability not to show her upset with him. She feared she wouldn't be up to the task, that she didn't possess the acting skills necessary to disguise her displeasure.

She turned her attention back to him. "You're quite right. I thank you for your kind consideration. A trip to the dressmaker would be welcome."

If he gloated with his success, she would call it a night. Only he didn't. He simply continued to study her.

"I forgot to mention, and I don't know if you discerned it this afternoon, but all the ladies read. If there are any books that would help you in achieving your goal, give me the titles and I'll see them delivered here."

"I'm surprised. I would have thought not knowing one's letters would have been a factor in leading them to this occupation."

"Women turn to this life for all sorts of reasons. Some have the ability to read, some don't. My sister Fancy offers free reading lessons for adults a couple of nights a week. I took the ones who couldn't read to her classes so at least they'd have that advantage."

She recalled that the youngest Trewlove had recently married the Earl of Rosemont. For a while Althea had been obsessed, striving to keep up with the happenings within the aristocracy, each marriage, birth, and scandal bringing home how much she was no longer a part of it all. But finding gossip sheets lying about was always a challenge. She no longer had any friends willing to gossip with her.

She'd once hoarded the most inconsequential of rumors, the ones that didn't make it into the gossip rags, as though they were the rarest of sweets to be savored. But then she'd lost her taste for them after her family had dominated everyone's tongue in a most unflattering and unsavory manner.

"You're very keen to see women educated."

"My mum believed knowledge was key to achieving a better life. She insisted we attend the ragged schools, wouldn't allow us to miss a single day. When we all began working, we pooled our coins to purchase a yearly subscription to a lending library. It only allowed us to borrow one book at a time, so we rotated who had the honor of selecting the book. Even if we weren't interested in the one chosen, we had to read it so we could gather to discuss it.

I suspect some are surprised by how much we know, how much we comprehend, how easily we can carry on a conversation regarding the most complicated of topics. How we can back up our stances and arguments with facts. As a result, I *am* keen to see women educated. They should have as much opportunity as men to better their lives. I've never understood a man wanting a wife with whom he couldn't have a rousing debate."

"As I won't be anyone's wife, I won't be debating. I imagine my paramour will be of the mind that I should be seen and not heard."

"More fool he. A woman's words can seduce me more effectively than the sway of her hips."

She couldn't deny that *his* words were more seductive than the breadth of his shoulders. Not that she wouldn't mind skimming her fingers over those shoulders.

"Are there particular words you find more seductive than others?" she asked.

He took a sip of his scotch, and she wanted to gather from his lips whatever dampness remained. Chadbourne's lips had been thin, the upper one barely visible, but Benedict's mouth was like the rest of him—broad, full, and tempting.

"Honest ones, perhaps even painful ones," he finally answered. "I recall reading about your father in minute detail, all he endured as a traitor to the Crown, but nothing about you. Yesterday you told me that I knew the truth of you. Only I don't. Tell me the truth of you."

She gave her attention back to the fire. "I was so enjoying our conversation."

He drew back his legs, leaned forward, placed his elbows on his thighs, and cradled his glass in both hands as though it was a tiny bird in need of protection. "Althea, I've shared a good bit of my life with you—personal bits, successful bits. I told you the truth of Sally, my role in her death, the guilt I feel because of it. You comforted me and now that secret is no longer between us. Why do you hide so much of yourself from me?"

"There's shame in my past."

"Do you think being born a bastard, that I know naught of shame? That I would ridicule you for hardships suffered or judge you for circumstances over which you had no control?"

"I told you I don't know the details."

"I don't want the details of him. I want the details of you."

If he hadn't gone so quiet, so still, merely waiting for her to come around, to confess all, she might have been able to ignore him. But she'd never been able to speak of the matter with anyone, to unburden herself. Her family had suffered as well, but by tacit agreement, they'd all refused to hash out the matter, to give voice to their feelings of betrayal. It seemed to express any of it aloud would serve to make matters worse. So they'd all pretended it hadn't happened as it had. They'd simply woken up one morning to find themselves commoners and paupered.

It might have been easier if she'd kept her gaze on the blue, red, and orange flames dancing wildly on the hearth, but for some reason she sought out the dark depths of his eyes, the square cut of his jaw, the sharp, knife-like edge of his nose, the high bones of his cheeks, all the contours of his face that had become so achingly familiar she could have drawn him from memory. The intensity with which he studied her as though he truly cared about the answer frightened her as much as it comforted her. Scared her because she shouldn't long for his attentions, cherish his presence. He was a temporary part of her life, as so many had been. She had learned through heartbreak and disappointment that devotion could be snuffed out with a mere word or gesture.

"It was eight minutes past two in the wee hours of the morning when the loud knocking at the front door woke me," she croaked, her throat knotting as though to prevent the hideous words from being uttered. "I don't know why I thought to look at the clock on the mantelpiece. The window of my bedchamber looked out over the drive. Otherwise, I probably wouldn't have heard the commotion. When I looked out . . . the entirety of Scotland Yard must have been there. I suppose the butler, maybe a footman, opened the door to them and then the corridors were filled with the echo of stomping boots and yells. The door to my bedchamber burst open—"

She gulped some sherry. Its sweetness seemed contrary to the bitter words she was uttering.

"The inspector, or whatever he was, gave me a quick look and returned to the hallway. As though in a trance I followed as far as the threshold. My mother was shrieking, her maid striving to calm her. So many men were moving about I couldn't cross over to her. They were dragging my brothers down the hallway—I suppose they'd dragged them out of bed as well—and all I could think was that they weren't civilized enough to wear nightshirts. How curious. Then Marcus shouted, 'For God's sake, man, allow us to make ourselves presentable.'

"You've not met Marcus, but he can be quite intimidating. Probably comes from being the heir, as they did let them dress themselves. I remember as they marched him past, he caught my eye and said, 'It'll all be all right.' And I believed him. Only it wasn't, of course."

Chapter 11

$\mathcal{A}$s much as he hated hearing the details of what had happened to her, he welcomed the opportunity to know her better, to understand her.

Her fingers were visibly shaking as she took hold of her glass and tossed back the sherry as though it would provide her with additional stamina. He considered getting her more but that would involve too much activity, and it seemed wrong all of a sudden to have any sort of movement other than the hands on the mantel clock ticking off the minutes and the writhing flames creating a soft crackling as they turned coal into ash.

Very slowly, as though she were a baby hare that would dash off if startled, he extended his glass toward her. "Here."

Taking it, she stared into the amber. "Scotch?"

"Yes."

"I've never tasted scotch."

"Then take a small sip." Such mundane words after her devastating description of what was no doubt the worst night of her young life.

Briefly the rim of the tumbler touched her lips. He very much doubted she'd swallowed a thimbleful. She tapped her fingers one after the other in a rhythmic movement against the cut crystal. "They thought my brothers were involved, knew something. Only they weren't, they didn't. It was two weeks before they released them.

"A week after my father and brothers were arrested, my mother decided we should attend a ball to which we'd been invited. She argued that we should carry on as though all was normal, and that our appearance would signal that we were not involved in this conspiracy, we did not support it, and our loyalty to the Queen was above our loyalty to her husband, my father, the Duke of Wolfford."

As she had yesterday, she spoke as though all this had happened to someone unknown to her, not to herself. Her voice was distant and flat. But he couldn't help but believe that inside, a maelstrom of emotions bombarded her.

"I tried to convince her we would be better served to wait until all was settled. I had not yet accepted the notion that my father could possibly be involved in so traitorous an undertaking. I was certain matters would soon be set right, and he would be vindicated. All would return to what it had been. In addition, I was betrothed, you see, to the Earl of Chadbourne, and he had not visited to determine how I fared, and it gave me pause. None of my friends called upon us, and when I called upon them, they were not home. But my mother was insistent, and I couldn't let her go alone. Only later did I realize the stress was affecting her judgment. She had begun to live in a world where her husband was not accused of treason. But I did not know it at the time, and so I went with her.

"After we were announced, as we descended the stairs, Chadbourne made his way to the foot of them. Gossipmongers—even the articles in the society sheets—made a point of recounting the joy that wreathed my face, describing my expression as that of a princess who believed a knight had ridden up to defend her honor. To my utter chagrin later, at the time I did very much feel that way. He would save me. Only when I reached him, he turned his back on me, which resulted in everyone else doing the same. He felt the need to make a public statement regarding his loyalty to the Crown and England and my unsuitability as the daughter of a traitor to become his wife."

An immediate loathing for the man ratcheted through him. He would seek him out, he would find him, he would destroy him.

"Mother swooned, and it was left to the servants to haul her out, rather unceremoniously, I'm afraid. She never recovered, never again spoke, never left her bed, simply withered away like a flower plucked from the soil and left without water. A few hours after they hanged Father, she passed. Couldn't bear the mortification, I suppose. Which was all for the good because the following day they came and took everything from us. That alone would have killed her."

She met his gaze, and he could see that it had cost her to reveal so much, and yet so much more remained to be divulged. "Tell me about Chadbourne."

Her smile was self-deprecating. "He caught my attention during my first Season when I was all of nineteen and in no hurry to be spoken for. I enjoyed the dancing, the flirtation, the being sought after. He didn't court me seriously until my second. During my third Season he asked for my hand."

"And you hope to regain his attentions by becoming a courtesan?"

Her laugh was caustic, reflected the pain she still harbored. "Good God, no. But I wouldn't mind being so sought after that he *would* want me, and I could rebuff him. I'd find some satisfaction in that." She tossed back the scotch, wheezed, coughed as her eyes watered. "It's suddenly so frightfully cold in here."

Setting aside the glass, she stood, wrapped her arms around herself, and walked to the hearth. Cautiously, he joined her there and rested his forearm against the mantel.

"I used to take fires for granted," she said softly. "They were simply always lit, always burning. I barely paid any heed to the servants who saw to the task."

"We seldom appreciate what we have until we no longer have it."

She looked so bloody miserable standing there, and he despised himself because he'd forced her to dredge up the memories, because his curiosity wanted to turn over every stone of her life in order to fully understand her, even as he knew he had no right to know anything at all. "Did you love him?"

Her nod was shallow, barely perceptible, but he felt it like a punch to the gut.

"More fool I," she said flatly, and he knew the blackguard's betrayal had cut her more deeply than her father's, had stolen more from her than her father, Society, or the Crown. He'd stripped her of hopes and dreams. His actions may have driven her to Beast when she'd thought his proposition involved becoming his mistress.

"He was the fool."

Before he could consider all the ramifications, before he could remind himself of the tenet he'd always held sacred, never broken, he lowered his mouth to hers.

It was a mistake. In the same manner that eating too much cake was a mistake. There was certain to be an ache in his gut and regret later, but while the sugary goodness existed, he longed for nothing else.

Her lips were as warm, soft, and plump as he'd known they would be. He might have left off, then and there, after the initial touch, but she made a little mewling sound that sounded like desperation to his ears, and her arms entwined around his neck like vines clinging to a solid surface for support. He circled one arm around her waist and brought her in nearer as he enticed her lips into parting for him and deepened the kiss.

The heady flavors of sherry and scotch coated her tongue, but it was she and she alone who was responsible for the lightheadedness that assailed him. He was no stranger to women, but he'd never experienced such an overwhelming need to take what was being offered and to beg for more. An innocence marked her movements, a tentativeness as she greeted his eagerness, and he was relatively certain it wasn't because she was wary of him but because she was unfamiliar with the journey upon which they'd embarked.

Good Lord. Had her betrothed never taken possession of her mouth? What sort of saint had he been that he could resist the temptation of her? Beast had been right to call him a fool. He himself was neither saint nor fool, but sinner.

When it came to what passed between men and women, he held nothing back, was open to exploring all possibilities. Nothing was off-limits. She wanted him to teach her how to be seductive. He could show her how to destroy a man's will, how to conquer, how to entice, how to manipulate, how to master.

Not that she required lessons. Here he was doing what he had sworn he wouldn't do: inhaling her fragrance of gardenia heated with passion, feeling the outline of her body against his, memorizing all of her dips and swells and noting where they pressed so convincingly against the hard contours of his chest, his stomach . . . his groin. Her frock was simple, lacked an abundance of petticoats. She had to be aware of the effect she was having on him. Or was she so lost to the sensations they created together that they dominated her to such an extent she was cognizant of nothing beyond herself?

Her fingers scraped up the back of his head along his scalp, came around—

Grabbing her wrists, he carried her arms behind her back, which only served to lift her breasts more firmly against his chest. She was a duke's daughter, and although she may have fallen from grace, it didn't change the fact that she was born on the right side of the blanket while he was born on the wrong side of it.

No reason existed for her to be abandoned by her parents. A reason existed for him to be.

Tearing his mouth from hers, staring down at her lovely features, he wondered whatever had possessed him to think he had the right to touch so much as her little finger, let alone her mouth and every other part of her that was presently pressed up against him. Those lovely lips were damp and swollen, little gasps of breath escaping between them. In her blue eyes were the dying embers of desire.

She didn't want *him*. She wanted only the lessons. His earlier assessment had been incorrect. He *was* a fool.

Releasing his hold on her as though she'd suddenly ignited, he stepped back. "We leave for the dressmaker at ten tomorrow morning."

He headed for the hallway.

"Benedict?"

Increasing his tempo, he loped down the stairs, jerked open the front door, and stalked out into the night.

Iᴅɪᴏᴛ.

He'd kissed her. He enjoyed kissing her. He wanted to kiss her again.

As he was a colossal idiot, he'd also left without his greatcoat. Being too stubborn to go back to retrieve it, he hunched his shoulders against the cold, which no doubt made him appear more beastly, and strode on. He had a strong urge to strike something: a brick wall, a jaw, a gut. If he ran across someone causing havoc, he'd be only too happy to add to the mayhem.

In spite of his size, he'd never been in favor of violence except as a last resort. He meted out punishment. Tonight he had a strong need to be on the receiving end of it. He'd made a fool of himself.

She'd kissed him back.

Had she enjoyed it? Did she want to kiss him again? Or had she merely thought, "Ah, here is lesson one."

Bugger it. Women didn't generally get under his skin, but from the moment she'd told him she was none of his bleedin' business with a Cockney accent, her acerbic tone had embedded itself in his mind and grown tentacles to reach every aspect of him that responded to womanly wiles.

That she had the most beautiful eyes he'd ever seen and dainty features that reminded him of the princesses in the fairy tales he'd read to his sister Fancy—fourteen years his junior—when she was a wee lass did not mean that Thea saw him as deserving of her or thought of him as a prince riding in on a white steed to save the day.

Thea. Thea seemed to suit her better, at least in his mind.

Althea was for the lady she'd once been. Thea was the woman she was now.

Presently, she was under his roof, under his care. And his care should not include kisses that even now, in spite of the cold, managed to keep his lips warm. When he was daft enough to run his tongue over them, he could still taste her. Not the sherry she'd sipped or the scotch she'd gulped, but beneath it all a mixture of cinnamon, butter, and sugar, all things sweet, a flavor that was unique to her, that he would recall and savor until his last breath.

At the end of their time together, he was going to be a thousand pounds poorer, because he'd be damned if he'd teach her how to seduce another man into her bed.

Chapter 12

*I*t was only a kiss. She'd carried a litany of those words into her slumber, and upon awakening discovered they still mocked her. It had been only a kiss in the same manner a feast was merely one dish or a storm a single raindrop or a blizzard a solitary snowflake.

It had been everything, all consuming, the brightest sun, the largest moon, a thousand upon thousand stars. It had been more than pliant lips moving in tandem, testing, gliding, settling in. It had been tongues and teeth, sighs and moans. It had reached beyond mouths to include limbs and breasts and that very sensitive spot between her legs that had been straining toward him, had tingled and pulsed, and seemed nearly ecstatic when she'd felt the hard evidence of his desire pressed up against her belly. It had warmed. It had been the spark that ignited passion. It had been like nothing she'd ever before experienced while at the same time it contained a familiarity, as though every aspect of her recognized that with him, she somehow belonged.

Which was absolutely absurd, especially as it was apparent he'd experienced none of the mind-numbing pull she had. It was obvious he'd not been able to get away from her fast enough, had recognized their encounter as a mistake. Strange how his escape had hurt far worse than Chadbourne's turning his back on her when she'd believed he was stepping up to show Society that her father's actions changed nothing between them.

As she went through her morning ablutions, washing her face, unplaiting, brushing, and plaiting her hair, and changing into her simple blue frock, she fought not to remember the devastation that had hit her mother when all of Society had literally and figuratively turned their backs on them, left them to make their own way without any assistance or support. Her mother's decline had begun that night and she blamed the *ton* as much as her father for destroying such a proud, kind woman.

When she cast off those musings, she found herself anticipating seeing Benedict at breakfast, hoped a chair next to him had been reserved for her—in spite of his hasty retreat. She would find a way to laugh it off, to give the impression she saw it as merely the first of several lessons, so he would realize she wouldn't take seriously whatever emotions might rise to the fore with his nearness, his touch, his tutoring.

But when she made her way to the dining room, it was to find the chair at the head of the table vacant, and it struck her almost like a physical blow. "Is Benedict"—the women all stared at her—"Beast not joining us for breakfast?"

"He was out until the wee hours," Jewel said. "I 'spect he's having a lie-in."

She imagined him sprawled over a bed, one larger than normal, one especially designed and built to accommodate his size. Did he wear a nightshirt? She very much doubted it. At the thought of him quite possibly not wearing anything at all, her mouth went dry. She didn't want to see him wearing nothing. Well, maybe not wearing a shirt. Would his arms be as ropy and sinewy as they felt? Would his chest be an assortment of contours? She rather envisioned him modeling for a sculptor who was creating statues of Greek gods.

Although she had little appetite, she filled a plate with the offerings from the sideboard, took her seat, and forced herself to eat as though her stomach wasn't knotted up with misgivings and doubts.

"You look troubled, lass."

She jerked her gaze over to Jewel and wondered if she'd ever known anyone who gave the impression of truly caring as much as this lady of the night did. She needed to master that technique but had been raised to never show exactly what she felt, especially when it involved extreme emotions. Even during the reception she'd received at her last ball, she'd kept her chin up, had refused to crumple beneath the weight of their rejection. "Benedict mentioned going to the dressmaker at ten. I wasn't certain if perhaps he'd changed his mind."

"Oh," Hester said on an excited breath. "Is he getting you a frock to hang your dreams on?"

What she was pursuing wasn't her dream. It was simply an alternative to a nightmare. But she didn't want to go into all that, didn't want them to know anything about her past. They might be sinners, but it didn't mean they wouldn't be horrified if they learned the truth of her father. She forced herself to smile. "I suppose so, yes."

"Can't wait to see what it looks like."

It would be provocative, sensual, and no doubt comprised of very little fabric.

"What is your dream?" Hester's brow furrowed. "What is it you're wanting to do if you're not doing it now?"

Before she could answer, Jewel said, "I suspect Beast is merely showing his appreciation to Althea for having to deal with you lot."

Seeing the compassion in her eyes, Althea knew he'd confided in the madam regarding her ambitions.

"After we're finished with breakfast, Althea, I wondered if you might give me a few minutes in my office. And, yes, pet, if he told you he'd take you to the dressmaker at ten, then that's what he'll do. He's not one to break his word."

WHEN SHE DESCENDED the stairs later that morning, it was to find him waiting in the foyer for her, and she wasn't particularly happy with the gladness that swept through her at the sight of him. It was imperative that she remember they had a *business* arrangement. Nothing good would come of developing any deep affection for him. He had a use for her. She had one for him. Only their signatures on parchment bound them. In three months they'd each go their own way and probably never cross paths again.

As he was wont to do, he studied her intently and she was grateful that her cheeks—which had fairly ignited during her candid discussion with Jewel—had finally cooled. At his behest, the madam had instructed her on various methods she could use to avoid getting with child. She was grateful for the information, but it had also brought home the reality of what she was doing.

Without a word, he opened the door for her, and she stepped out beneath the eaves. Rain was splattering the pavement. A hansom waited at the end of the walk. She suspected he'd gone in search of it to spare her having to stroll through the cold and wet.

Bringing up the hood on her cloak, she dashed to the hansom with his hand on the small of her back the entire way. She didn't even have to stop before he was swinging her up and inside the carriage and settling in beside her.

Althea was beginning to look forward to the moments when they traveled in a hansom cab together. Benedict took up so much room that she had little choice except to be snuggled against him. While she had her cloak and he had his greatcoat, she could still feel the warmth radiating from him into her. She kept her attention forward, to the unbarred view of the scenery that the rain painted dark and gray. Because he hadn't even bothered with a proper greeting, had said not one word to her, she decided to poke the beast. "I rather enjoyed last night's lesson."

"It wasn't a bloody lesson."

She glanced over to see him looking at her, his jaw so tense that

his back teeth had to be aching from the force with which he was
biting down.

"But you taught me to kiss." To feel, to melt, to want, to need.

"It shouldn't have happened."

"At some point it was on your lesson plan, surely."

"You think I have planned out exactly what I'm going to
show you?"

"I would have thought so, yes. It'll save us wasting time. I've
planned out my lessons for your ladies."

He seemed both stunned and disgruntled. "I told you. I find a
lady's words seductive."

She scoffed. "You can't have found anything seductive about
last night's tale of horror."

"You confided in me more than you ever have. It was more than
your words. You let me feel your pain."

"You find my pain an aphrodisiac?"

Shaking his head, he squeezed his eyes shut. "No."

When he opened them, she saw true remorse reflected there.
"I wish you didn't know what it was to feel pain of any kind, but
you trusted me with it, not to abuse it, not to take advantage. I
took advantage."

"Did I give the impression I didn't welcome it?"

"You were vulnerable."

"You were comforting me." Perhaps that was the reason it was
wrong. What had passed between them hadn't been based on seduction, lust, or attraction. He'd seen someone hurting and sought
to ease the hurt. Perhaps in the morning light, despite how little
there was of it, he'd realized she wasn't a temptation.

"It won't happen again."

"What will these lessons entail then?" *If not kisses, caresses, and
embraces?*

"Althea, is being some man's mistress truly the life you want?"

"I can't have the life I want."

"What you have mapped out for yourself is not the life you deserve, and if it's not the life you want but you accept it as your due, then you're giving all those judgmental toffs power and a victory they have not earned."

"You know nothing at all about it."

"You might feel differently if you knew why I go by Beast."

PERHAPS SHE WOULD have asked, perhaps he would have told her if the cab hadn't at that precise moment come to a smooth halt on a street lined with shops, if he hadn't handed the money up through the tiny opening to the driver, the doors hadn't sprung open, and he hadn't leapt out and immediately handed her down. If the pavement hadn't been crowded, the rain increased its tempo, and they'd had to rush toward shelter beneath the eaves. Or she'd thought they'd sought an escape from the rain until he shoved open the door, and she noted Dressmaker in elaborate script painted in gold on a sign over the threshold.

He waited for her to precede him into the shop and suddenly it was the last place she wanted to be. She wanted to be at the Mermaid talking, wanted to be on a park bench beneath a shared umbrella as he confided something as intimate as she had last night.

She was unacquainted with this dressmaker but welcomed the familiarity of bolts of fabrics, the scent of dye, the sight of pattern books, and the din of women discussing various styles. A woman who appeared slightly older than Althea excused herself from a small group of three other ladies and approached them.

"Mr. Trewlove, what a pleasure to see you again."

"Beth. Business seems to be flourishing."

"It doesn't hurt to have a duchess as a client."

He turned to Althea. "Beth has been my sister Gillie's seamstress for years now. This is her establishment. Beth, I'd like to introduce Miss Stanwick."

"It's lovely to meet you," the shop owner said.

"You as well." She'd not been to a seamstress since her world unraveled, had never had one not address her as Lady Althea or go out of her way to ensure the duke's daughter had the very best needleworkers at her disposal.

"She's in need of a few frocks," Benedict said. "A couple for everyday wear. One appropriate for a ball. And one designed for seduction. That one should be in red."

He spoke the word *seduction* so easily, as though it was appropriate to announce she was in need of something to accomplish that objective. She had no doubt her cheeks flamed as red as the outfit he'd ordered be made for her.

"I don't know that I need one for a ball." She kept her voice low, hoping not to be overheard.

"It can be used for seduction as well, possibly more effectively."

He provided attire appropriate for the ultimate goal of the ladies under his care. But Althea's lover would provide her with a gown. She wouldn't attend a ball without him, so acquiring his attention came first. But she didn't want to discuss any of that here, and if he wanted to waste his coins, they were his to waste. So she merely said as graciously as possible, "You're extremely generous. Thank you."

"If you'll give me a few minutes to finish up with Mrs. Welch," Beth said, "I'll be available to see to you personally."

She remembered a time when a seamstress wouldn't have finished up with anyone. Althea had garnered all the attention once she entered a shop, and she'd gloried in the singular devotion. Looking back on it from where she stood these days made her feel as though she'd been unjustifiably spoiled. Whatever had she done to deserve special treatment, other than having the good fortune of being born into a particular family? A good fortune that had not lasted, as it turned out.

"We're in no hurry, so take your time," Benedict said. "I do have some other matters to attend to. Will an hour be sufficient?"

"More than enough," Beth said before hastening over to assist Mrs. Welch.

"You're not leaving me," Althea said, not at all happy with the thought of being abandoned.

"I assumed you'd be comfortable here, would know your way around a dressmaker's shop."

Of course she was. She'd had a wardrobe stuffed with satin, silk, and lace. One of her favorite gowns had looked as though the skirt had been created from peacock feathers, the embroidery so exquisite it never failed to snag attention whenever she wore it. "Do you suppose she thinks I'm . . . your paramour?"

"What does it matter how she perceives you? Do you believe once you've achieved your objective that you'll be looked upon favorably anywhere?"

Not favorably perhaps, but she would surround herself with so much haughtiness that no one would dare turn their back on her. She would gain the attention of a prince who was known for enjoying wicked widows, and once she curried his favor, she would have power. "You sound cross."

"What reason have I to be cross? And Beth doesn't judge. I'll return for you when I've completed my affairs."

She watched as he strode out into what had morphed into a downpour that threatened to flood streets. Did he find getting drenched preferable to her company? How was it that everything had changed so drastically from the comfortable visit in the library last night to the awkwardness that seemed to latch on to them with the steadfastness of a harness to a horse? Was it because he'd rethought what she'd revealed about her family and discovered the truth of it left a nasty taste in his mouth? Or was it the kiss he'd found distasteful?

"Miss Stanwick?"

She swung around to face the seamstress whose eyes were filled with understanding, as though she recognized the look of the lovelorn when she saw it. Although Althea wasn't in love. At the moment she wasn't even certain she was in like. "Miss Beth."

"Beth will suffice. For the day dresses, I have some fabrics, the shade of which I think will complement your complexion nicely. Shall we have a look?"

"The gown. I'd like it to be red as well, a bright red that is impossible to miss, with a low neckline that leaves no doubt regarding my endowments." She was hoping for an evening when she might assess its allure before ever attending a ball by testing it on Benedict Trewlove.

Chapter 13

He was cross. Cross that she thought herself deserving of being a lightskirt. Because of something her dunderhead of a father, her idiot of a betrothed, and a host of unappreciative friends, had done. He'd never suffered a cut direct but knew what it was to be made to feel less—less than deserving of breath or kindness or acceptance. It all came with the circumstances of his birth, something over which he'd had not one iota of control just as she'd had no power over her sire's decision to become embroiled in a plot to change who sat upon a throne.

But in both cases innocents were made to suffer.

It angered him that he was angry. In his youth he'd fought inner demons to ensure he maintained control of his emotions. He'd always been big but hadn't grown elegantly into his size. He'd seemed out of proportion with legs too long, arms too short and beefy. Hands three times too big. His torso had been bulky, stout, rotund. Eventually, he'd evened out, grown into a mighty oak that could move without clumsiness. But he'd often struck out at those who'd laughed at him, mocked him, called him unflattering names.

Whenever his mum had tended to his cuts and scrapes, she would admonish him to ignore the cruel barbs slung at him—"One cannot throw horse dung without getting his own hands covered in muck."—to exercise patience, which in the end would elevate him above those who thought making sport of others somehow made them better. Eventually, he'd sought out Gillie to see to his hurts because, like him, she'd been abandoned, having been left in a wicker basket on Ettie Trewlove's doorstep. Also, like him, she hadn't an inkling as to who might be her parents. So their common ignorance regarding why they'd been given away and by whom had formed a strong bond between them.

He wasn't even certain the woman who'd handed him over was, in fact, his mother. She'd never claimed to be. He suspected she'd told Ettie Trewlove she'd return for him because she hadn't sufficient coins to pay her required fee, and had given a lie so he wouldn't be turned away. Perhaps that meant she'd cared for him a bit. But even caring didn't prove she was his mother.

Not that it mattered, not any longer. Having recently turned thirty-three, he'd accepted what he didn't know wasn't nearly as important as what he did. He knew his temper could be a frightful thing, which was the reason he kept it on a tight leash, but he might untether it if he ever encountered Chadbourne. He most certainly would have given it free rein should his path have crossed Thea's father's. Especially as it seemed a hanged duke could continue to do damage. Could make his daughter feel unworthy of the dreams she'd once held.

By the time he reached his destination, rainwater flowed off the brim of his beaver hat, flowed in rivulets down the length of his heavy greatcoat. He jerked open the door and strode into the foyer where most gents were escorted right back out of the exclusive club for ladies, but then he wasn't most gents. "Aiden about?"

"You'll find him in the garret, Mr. Trewlove," the young woman behind the counter said as she held out her hands expectantly to receive his hat and greatcoat. It always unsettled him when someone referred to him as mister, as though he was a civilized bloke, and hadn't banged a few heads in his day. He was nearly grown before he'd recognized the wisdom of his mum's admonishments and had begun working to curb his temper, but it easily flared when needed, and his fists were always ready to deliver justice in order to douse the flames.

With reluctance, he removed his hat and shrugged out of his coat. "They're quite wet."

Taking them from him, she smiled. "As we have few clientele about at the moment who are in need of me, I'll see what I can do to remedy that before you go out again."

It wasn't only the fact that it was late morning, but also the time of year that resulted in the dearth of customers. Most of the women who visited the club were aristocratic and presently in the country. But Aiden and his family resided in rooms on a floor above, so he was usually found here. "I'll just head up."

He took the stairs two at a time, following the familiar path up a few flights until he reached the floor where a narrower set of stairs led to the attic. At the top of them, he discovered the door was ajar, no doubt because the rain prevented the window from being opened in order to let some of the fumes from the paint escape the small area where his brother worked. Pressing a shoulder to the jamb, he studied what Aiden was committing to oils. "Do you paint only your wife these days?"

His brother didn't seem startled by his words, but then the stairs had echoed Beast's footsteps and he'd been told on more than one occasion that his presence stirred the air in a room so he couldn't go unnoticed. On the other hand, when necessary, he could sneak up on a bloke and not be detected until it was too late.

"Why would I bother with anything else?" Aiden asked, stepping back to study his own work, which Beast always found ethereal in nature, as though the subject was being viewed through gossamer. In this instance it was a mother holding her infant son. "One should paint what brings joy."

Swinging around, Aiden tilted his head toward the canvas. "These two bring me joy. It's to be my gift to Lena for Christmas so if you see my wife before then, please don't mention it."

"Your secret is safe with me."

Aiden walked over to a small table, lifted a decanter, and poured scotch into two tumblers. He handed one to Beast. "If you were out in this mess, you could use warming."

"Indeed. Cheers." He took a healthy swallow, welcoming the heat that burned his throat and seeped into his chest and limbs.

"I'm accustomed to seeing you more often during the late hours of the night rather than during the day."

They both thrived at night, a trait they shared in common. "I had some business to tend to that could only be done during the day, so I was in the area and needed to have a word. I wanted to know if a Lord Chadbourne makes use of the Cerberus Club."

In addition to this one, the Elysium Club, that catered to ladies' fantasies, Aiden owned a gaming hell where fortunes were won and lost—mostly lost—each night. His brother had always had a fascination with mythology, which might account for his wife appearing to be a goddess in every portrait he created of her.

"Only within the past year or so." While the club had once held a reputation of being a last resort for the nobility who couldn't get credit elsewhere, its reputation had gained a bit more respectability since Aiden had married a widowed duchess. "Why?"

"Does he owe you? Do you have any of his chits that can be called in?"

"No. He has astoundingly good luck at the tables. I've considered that he's cheating but if he is, I've been unable to determine how."

"Do you know if he's still in London?"

"He was as of a couple of nights ago."

"What game does he favor?"

"Four-card brag."

Beast wasn't surprised that Aiden knew the answer. People often underestimated his brother, didn't realize he remembered the smallest of details when it came to the people who frequented his clubs. "Would you inform your club manager to send word to me the next time he comes in to play?"

After slowly sipping his scotch, Aiden traced a finger around the rim of the glass. "What's her name?"

The question shouldn't have come as a shock. Aiden had been in his life from the moment Beast had been dropped off at Ettie Trewlove's door. While none of them had known precisely when they'd been born, their mum had been able to determine based on when their first teeth appeared that only a few months separated them in ages. He thought about ignoring the question but trusted no one more than he did the members of his family. "Althea."

"I assume he did wrong by her."

"Not in the manner you're thinking." He and his brothers had come to the defense of many a woman whom some man had taken physical advantage of. Their own mum being the first. Beth, the seamstress, being another. "But he hurt her all the same."

Aiden nodded. "Word will be sent."

Beast felt the tight band he hadn't realized was around his chest loosen, even as the hand not holding the tumbler began to flex in readiness for delivering a blow. "I don't love her."

He didn't know why he'd blurted that. If he could go back in time three seconds, he'd bite his tongue.

"I didn't say you did."

"She's just someone I'm helping out."

"Lena was someone I was simply helping out, so take care, brother, or you might find yourself writing poetry instead of novels."

BETH WAS A talker, extremely adept at carrying on a separate conversation in between measurements, displaying fabric choices, and suggesting changes to patterns. So it was that Althea learned a good deal more about not only Benedict but the Trewloves overall. She was looking forward to presenting her newfound knowledge on the way home—not home. The residence was not her home, in spite of the fact that she felt incredibly comfortable within its walls. It was merely a temporary abode. None of its inhabitants would remain in her life, Benedict wouldn't remain in her life. Eventually, he would become merely a memory.

She didn't much like the joy that swept through her when he came in through the door. It had been so encompassing that she'd failed to notice the woman who'd glided in ahead of him—with a young servant girl in her wake—until the termagant spoke.

"Beth, I was not aware you catered to traitors. I shall have to take my business elsewhere if you inform me this chit is indeed one of your clients." Lady Jocelyn stood before her appearing offended and righteous at the same time, her nose tipped up so high and haughtily that Althea wouldn't have been surprised to discover she caused a crick in her neck.

Before Beth could respond, Althea said, "You look well, Lady Jocelyn."

As impossible as she'd thought it to be, the nose went up a tad higher. "I do not as a rule address traitors, but I am rather certain I am glowing as a result of my recent betrothal and upcoming nuptials. Perhaps you've heard. I'm to marry Chadbourne."

She hadn't. Although she'd expected that eventually he would marry if for no other reason than to gain an heir and that it would hurt when she caught wind of it. Surprisingly, the blow was not as powerful as she'd anticipated. Yet, she knew not one iota of what she was feeling showed upon her face. "My condolences. It cannot be an easy thing to take to husband a man who has not the strength of character to honor his word or his commitments. When life throws him a challenge, it seems he is quick to run."

Lady Jocelyn was not as skilled at hiding her emotions. If the fire in her eyes was any indication, she was livid. "He is quick to realize he deserves a woman of the highest caliber, not one who comes from a line of treasonous scapegraces."

"You have always tended to exaggerate. A *line*? There was only one."

"Who is to say you will not produce another?" She held up her hand with such speed, it created a breeze. "Enough. I will engage with you no further. It is beneath me to speak to a person of such low character. Beth, if you intend to outfit her, the trousseau you are creating for me will go unpurchased."

Althea was familiar with the cost of a trousseau. She had been planning her own before her father spoiled things. She couldn't have Beth sacrifice those coins. "No, actually—"

"Yes," Beth interrupted. "I am creating magnificent frocks and gowns for her." She turned to Althea. "We shall have the fitting Friday, and everything will be ready next week."

"Beth—"

"'Tis done." She gave her attention back to Lady Jocelyn. "Do not worry yourself needlessly about your beautiful trousseau, Lady Jocelyn. I shall donate it to a mission that caters to the poor. I'm certain there are women aplenty who can make use of the items my ladies and I spent hours stitching. I wish you all the best. Good day."

Flabbergasted. That was how Lady Jocelyn appeared, and Althea was relatively certain her once-dear friend had never had someone below her in station speak to her as though she were above her in station. She wanted to hug Beth.

"I'm certain the Duchess of Thornley will not be at all happy to hear of this development as I came to you based upon her recommendation." Lady Jocelyn turned on her heel and went for the door, only to find it blocked by Benedict, his arms crossed over his chest. Althea was quite familiar with that implacable stance.

"You owe Miss Stanwick an apology. Her father was treasonous, not her."

"I don't see that it's any of your business."

"I'm making *her* my business."

While she couldn't see Lady Jocelyn's face, Althea was rather certain she was bestowing upon Benedict a hard stare capable of shooting daggers because she'd seen it many times in her past. The woman didn't like being challenged. "You look familiar." She lifted a finger, wagged it at him. "You're one of those Trewlove *bastards.*"

She spat *bastards* as though it left a foul taste in her mouth and might cause her to cast up her accounts. Apparently, it had yet to register with her that the Duchess of Thornley, whose name she'd tossed out imperiously as though she were related to the Queen, was a Trewlove as well and considered this man her brother. But it wasn't the reason Althea stepped forward. She did it because she didn't want to see him hurt for a kindness he'd shown her.

Although it took everything within her not to grab the woman's hair and yank her back. "Jocelyn, you have no call to insult him."

"It's Lady Jocelyn to you."

"No insult," he said evenly. "'Tis true. I am a bastard, born on the wrong side of the blanket, with no earthly idea who my parents might be, but my manners far exceed yours, Lady Jocelyn. Apologize."

"Or you'll do what, precisely?"

He leaned back against the door. "I can stand here all day barring your way. While you need to hasten to another dressmaker in order to get work started on your new trousseau. A simple 'I'm sorry' will suffice."

Lady Jocelyn glanced back over her shoulder. The fury distorting her lovely features should have ignited Althea on the spot. Her mouth went askew, flat, tight, pinched. She squeezed her eyes shut, opened them. "I apologize."

"As do I. I wish you nothing but happiness with Chadbourne."

For a moment the woman was blinking so much that Althea thought she might be fighting tears. But when Benedict opened the door, she was through it in a blur, her faithful servant trailing quickly after her.

Ignoring the stares of the few remaining customers and staff in the shop, Althea turned to Beth. "I'm so sorry. Let me know the value of her trousseau and when I have the means in three months, I'll pay you for it." She was rather certain it would take at least a quarter of the extra she was going to earn by meeting his deadline.

"Don't worry yourself. The clothing will be put to better use. I doubt she would have worn anything more than once." She took Althea's hand, squeezed it. "To be honest, I'm glad to be rid of her. She kept changing her mind about what she wanted, but only after we'd finished making what she'd asked for. It was becoming tiresome." She looked over Althea's shoulder and clapped her hands. "All right, ladies, back to work. The entertainment is over."

Now it was Althea blinking back tears at the simple kindness.

Once she'd taken so much for granted, and she no doubt wouldn't have appreciated the manner in which a hardworking seamstress—who was dependent on the goodwill of others to earn her living—had stood up for her.

"Hopefully, everything went better before I returned here," Benedict said, having moved closer, distracting Althea with his presence. For which she was grateful. She'd never shed a tear in public and certainly didn't want to begin now.

"Everything was lovely," she assured him. "I'm quite looking forward to seeing all the frocks completed."

His assessing gaze held a touch of sorrow. "I recall you telling me that a Lady Jocelyn had once been your dearest friend. That particular Lady Jocelyn?"

She merely nodded, for what more was there to say?

"Now she's to marry the man who threw you over."

"So it would appear."

She was grateful he left it at that. They bid their farewells and headed out into the rain. Or would have if an elaborate blue coach with red trim hadn't been waiting and a footman hadn't immediately opened a door when they emerged. Benedict's hand came to rest against the small of her back as he urged her forward. "Is that for us?"

"Yes. Inside. Quickly."

The footman assisted her up, and she settled against the plush interior. The vehicle rocked as Benedict joined her, sitting opposite her.

"How did you come to have this?" she asked as it launched forward.

"It belongs to my brother Aiden. I was visiting with him and asked to borrow it to spare you getting soaked."

"I appreciate your thoughtfulness as well as your insistence that Lady Jocelyn apologize." She looked out the window at the sheets of rain, listened as it pattered the roof of the carriage, lulling her into a place of calm and quietness, completely opposite to the tenseness she'd felt in the shop.

"You are extremely skilled at displaying haughtiness," he said quietly as though he, too, found the atmosphere peaceful and was loath to disturb it. "I must admit I very nearly clapped when you offered her your condolences."

She gave her head a little shake. "I was already fuming because she'd threatened to deny Beth payment. I was going to skulk out after announcing that Beth would be making nothing for me, but then the sweet woman stood up for me and the lady I'd once been came to the fore and I couldn't let Lady Jocelyn go unchallenged."

"Beth will be paid for that trousseau."

"It shouldn't come out of your coffers."

"It won't. Lady Jocelyn's family will pay, one way or another. I simply need to know who her father is. Or her eldest brother. Whoever sees to her care." He shrugged. "Or perhaps I'll have Chadbourne pay." A bit of malice and glee wreathed his smile. "I like that idea better."

She looked at his large gloved hands folded over his thighs. "When you say one way or another . . ."

"Perhaps they'll lose more than normal at the gaming tables or something they wish to remain hidden might come to light if they don't pay for work that's been done."

"You're not going to actually hurt them."

He heaved a heavy sigh and glanced out the window as though disappointed that she'd asked. "Let's just say they'll see the advantage to paying a seamstress who has put in hours sewing clothing for spoiled Lady Jocelyn."

"If they should fail to see the advantage?"

The smile was gone when he turned his attention back to her. "I can be quite persuasive. And if not me, then one of my brothers. Mick, in particular, has the ear of a good many aristocrats these days, and they want to stay in his good graces. But they won't feel the weight of my fist, if that's what's worrying you."

She feared she might have hurt his feelings, so she gave him an impish smile. "I probably wouldn't mind if Chadbourne felt it once."

His laughter, deep and rich, rang through the confines of the carriage. "I'll have to keep in mind that you're a vindictive wench."

With a long exhale, she studied her hands covered in worn gloves, knotted in her lap. "A woman scorned and all that." She looked up. "Beth told me that you and your brothers helped her out of a difficult situation with her landlord." *Difficult* being a paltry word for the situation in which he'd been extracting payment with sexual favors from the sweet seamstress.

"That was Gillie's doing."

"She said you confronted him."

"Because Gillie asked us to."

"Did he feel the weight of your fists?"

"Several times."

"Is that the reason they call you Beast?"

"Part of it."

"And the rest?"

He merely shook his head. She wasn't in the mood to push. He'd stood up for her today. He could keep his secrets.

"How was your visit with your brother?" She missed her own brothers, but wouldn't put them at risk by sending word she wanted to see them.

"Successful. It got us a comfortable ride back to the residence."

Chapter 14

*L*ater that evening, as the clock chimed ten, clutching *Murder at Ten Bells,* she strolled into the library. If he wasn't in the mood to give her a lesson, she would read. When she spotted the small tulip-shaped glass of sherry resting on the small table beside the chair in which she'd sat the night before, something melted inside her chest, near the area where her heart beat.

As always, Benedict came to his feet. She shouldn't be so glad to see him. Only a few hours had passed since dinner, and yet it had seemed an eternity.

Gracefully, she lowered herself into the chair, just as she'd taught the ladies that afternoon to lower themselves. She didn't know when he'd done it, but at some point he'd spoken with the women because they all arrived in simple but elegant frocks that revealed not so much as a quarter of an inch of cleavage.

"Thank you for speaking with the ladies regarding their clothing. I noticed a decided difference—a positive one—in how they responded to the lesson this afternoon. Then, of course, it was nice to enjoy dinner without so much skin on display."

"I noticed they were less . . . rambunctious than usual during the meal."

"Today we focused on sitting and dining etiquette. They're sharp, anxious to learn. I thought of a couple of books that might prove helpful to them." Reaching into the pocket of her dark blue frock, she removed a scrap of paper upon which she'd written the titles. Leaning forward she extended it to him. Leaning forward he reached for it. As he took it, his fingers skimming over hers, she felt as though the rain from that morning had returned with lightning in full force, striking her. How could so simple a touch in such a small area be felt throughout her entire body?

She settled back so quickly she might have created a breeze that stirred the flames on the hearth to dance more wildly, while he merely leaned back as though he'd felt nothing at all. Except that he, too, was watching the flames as though they'd become the most fascinating thing on earth. "I'll have Fancy order copies for each of the ladies."

He looked to be a man battling demons, a man pulled taut who could snap at any moment. If he snapped, she wondered if his lips might land on hers. She was tempted to find out.

He'd told her that words seduced him. Was it the same with all men or with only him? She'd thought being a temptress involved peering through lowered lashes, revealing bits of forbidden flesh. What if she'd had the wrong of it all along, and it merely involved being only herself?

Last night he'd sought her secrets. Tonight she wanted his.

"After dinner I had time to curl up with your book. I suspect after we are done here, I shall be up the remainder of the night turning the pages."

He'd abandoned the fire to look at her, and she was grateful to have a clear view of his eyes, his features, as she continued on. "Your depiction of the city at night is so vivid I felt as though I were actually walking through it. How do you manage it?"

"It's the world I know."

"Why do you write about murder? Why not write about fairies or ship captains or young ladies searching for a prince?"

"I know nothing of ladies searching for a prince."

"But you know of murder?" She knew it was a silly question. People could write about things of which they had very little knowledge. Yet a tiny part of her, no bigger than a grain of salt surely, wondered why he'd not told her how his name, Beast, had come to be.

After taking his drink in hand, he crossed the ankle of one foot over his other knee. He looked to be a man settling in to tell a saga that would take most of the night. And she didn't care if he spoke until dawn, didn't care that it was dangerous to her heart to know so much about him. To see him as anything other than an impartial tutor. Unfortunately, when it came to him, none of her feelings sought impartiality.

"When I was a lad of about eight, I spied a man, in clothing finer than anything I'd ever seen, strolling about Whitechapel. He so fascinated me that I followed him for a time. Periodically, he would stop, remove a golden timepiece from his waistcoat pocket, look at it, tuck it back into place, and carry on. I wanted that time-piece with a fervor that to this day I don't think I've ever known since. So I stole it."

Her eyes widened at that because every timepiece she'd ever seen a gentleman carry had been accompanied by a fob that se-cured the watch to a buttonhole in his waistcoat. It would take remarkable skill to free it without being snatched up by the scruff of his collar, and only one sort of person would have that skill. One with a great deal of experience at lifting things. "You were a pickpocket?"

He merely shrugged. "It's not an aspect of my life about which I'm particularly proud or tend to boast. However, a lot of lads and lasses in the rookeries are. Some blighter is always willing to teach you how to nick things without getting caught as long as you give him a large portion of what you pilfered. But I saw the timepiece as my way out. I knew if my mum ever realized what I did, she'd be ashamed. At the end of the day, I gave everything I'd stolen, except for the watch, which I'd hidden in my shoe, to Three-Fingered Bill and told him I was done, wouldn't be working for him any longer. He was not pleased with my announcement, and that evening I returned home with two broken arms."

"My God, no." When she reached for her sherry, she realized her hand was shaking.

Again, he simply shrugged. "He gave me the choice. One broken arm for the arrogance of believing I could just walk away. Two if I wanted his permission to walk away. I chose the latter. Never regretted it."

"He let you go?"

"He might have been a criminal, but Bill was a man of his word. Sometimes I think about how he might have used me once I grew into myself because at the time, I was naught but gangly legs and arms, large for my age but not particularly graceful. I paid a small price to be free of him. And I had the timepiece, so I went to work as a knocker-upper."

Until three months ago, she'd not known what one was because they'd had servants to wake them. "Griff hired a man for three-pence a week to rap on his window at half five every morning so he could get to the docks on time. Is that what you did?"

"I did."

"Who woke *you*?"

He gave her a smile that caused warmth to sluice through her as though she'd taken another sip of sherry. "I slept during the day, which actually worked well because my brothers and I had only one bed between us. At night I would haunt Whitechapel, walking the streets, mews, and alleyways until it was time to begin waking people."

"That's the reason you can paint such a vivid picture of it."

He nodded. "I saw the doxies, the drunkards, the sly ones who meant harm, and those who did good. I saw a part of life that some people never see. And about a year later, one night, shortly after I'd begun waking my customers, I stumbled across a woman slumped in an alleyway. I thought perhaps she was foxed and had fallen asleep. I went to wake her."

He took a long swallow of his scotch as though he needed the fortification, and she had a horrible feeling regarding where this story was going. "She was dead."

His gaze was focused on the tumbler, the way the flames from the fire reflected off the cut crystal, and she wondered if he was envisioning the woman there.

"Her blue frock was drenched in blood. The coppery stench of it hit me as I crouched before her. Based on the slashes in her clothing and on her hands and neck, I assumed someone had taken a knife to her. Her eyes were open but no life was in them, and I wondered if the last thing on this earth she'd looked at had been her killer."

The fire crackled and hissed. The mantel clock ticked. Her own blood rushed through her ears with the pounding of her heart. How impressionable he would have been at that tender age. How horrific what he had seen.

After another swallow of the amber liquid, he met her gaze. "I went to find a constable. I was clutching the willowy bamboo stick of my trade. He patted me on the shoulder, told me to get on about my business of waking people because they needed to get to work. I did as he ordered, but it seemed wrong somehow to carry on, ignoring that something horrible had transpired. After I knocked on my last window, I went back to where she'd been, but she was no longer there. I imagined that I'd been wrong, and she'd stirred herself to her feet and walked home. But deep down, I knew the truth of it. She was never going to walk home again."

He downed the last of his scotch. Without even thinking, as though in a trance, she took his glass, went to the sideboard, and refilled it. When she returned to his side, she handed him the glass. "I'm sorry I asked. The memories can't be easy to live through again."

"But they helped to shape me, I think."

She sank down onto the plush cushion of her chair. "How so?"

Leaning forward, he planted his elbows on his sturdy thighs, clasping both hands around his glass. "Before that, I saw my bulk as an inconvenient thing. It made me stand out when I didn't want to." He seemed to be struggling to find the correct words. She didn't push. She merely waited. "It made children call me a beast.

But I was convinced had I been about when the woman was attacked, I'd have been able to save her. My logical self, my grown self, knows that's not true. But I began to pay more attention when I was on my routes, and a few times I was able to chase off someone who meant harm. I began to gain a reputation: the Beast of Whitechapel. But I also became fascinated with murder."

"You're not the only one obsessed. I can't believe the amount of ink the newspapers devote to describing the crimes and the trials of murderers in such lurid details."

He gave her a self-deprecating grin. "Which provided me with fodder for my stories. In addition, I spoke to the constables, detectives, and inspectors. I went to the courts, observed the trials. I even paid a shilling to go on tours of some of the murder sites."

A cold shiver ran down her spine. "That's a bit macabre."

"I can't argue with you there. Murder tourism was popular for a while. I wasn't looking for the blood. I was striving to understand the provocation. Often, everything about the place seemed so normal. Crockery on the shelves. Quilt on the bed. A chair before the fire. I came to realize that was one of the horrors of murder. It can happen anywhere with no hint that it's lurking about. In a quiet village. On a noisy street. In a verdant park. I devoured detective novels. I began writing my own. They were rubbish." He tipped his head toward her lap where his book rested. "Until finally one wasn't. Or at least I was led to believe it wasn't."

She gave him an encouraging smile. "It's not. I could hardly put it down once I started reading it."

He settled back, took a sip of the scotch, and turned his attention to the fire. "Apologies. I don't usually go on like that."

"I'm glad you did. Your passion for your endeavors is evident."

His gaze slid unerringly back to her. "What is your passion?"

She ran her finger over the spine of the book, over the gold-embossed title. Over his name. Learning about him had become a sort of passion. She wanted to know everything, all the large and small moments of his life, the exciting ones and the mundane. She wanted him to kiss her again, wanted to kiss him back.

She'd thought by becoming some lord's mistress, she could free her brothers from worrying about her care, thought she could free herself. But she was beginning to wonder if she wasn't in truth simply exchanging one sort of prison for another.

She wasn't quite certain what she might have answered, what she would have confessed, because Jewel suddenly swept into the room, and he immediately came to his feet.

"A missive was just delivered for you."

He took the letter she extended toward him, unfolded it, and read whatever had been written. When he was done, he refolded it and tucked it inside his jacket before turning to her. "I'm sorry but I have a matter to which I need to attend."

She thought she detected a measure of disappointment in his expression, in his voice, although it might have been only wishful thinking on her part. "I'll bid you good-night, then."

He began striding toward the doorway. Halfway there he came to an abrupt halt. She was fairly certain she heard him growl, darkly and roughly, a crass reference to testicles.

He swung around. "I'm going to my brother's gaming hell. Women are welcomed there. Would you care to join me?"

Chapter 15

*H*er excitement was palpable. Beast could feel her fairly bouncing on the squab opposite him, the aftermath of each movement creating tiny tremors along the floor of Aiden's carriage. His brother had ensured that not only a missive was delivered but a comfortable conveyance as well. A footwarmer and fur blanket had been waiting inside, which confounded him a bit. Surely, Aiden didn't think he was delicate and needed to be pampered, although he was grateful they were available for Thea's use.

He was still having a hell of a time believing how he'd rambled on in response to such a simple question. One sentence would have sufficed. "I came across a murdered woman once and it fired my imagination."

Only it hadn't—not at the time. The sight of her bleached of color, her limbs cold and stiff, had numbed him, made it difficult to think. As he ran off to find help, it had felt as though ice were slushing through his veins, causing his frantic strides to be ungainly and cumbersome. When he'd finally located a copper, he'd stammered almost incoherently until he'd managed to slow his racing heart with deep breaths and regain a sense of calm.

For a time he'd considered that when he was of the proper age, he would join the Metropolitan Police Force but had feared he'd become as inured to empathy as the constable who had absently patted his back and sent him on his way without giving any thought to the notion that a nine-year-old lad had just seen something that would give him nightmares for months.

He was grateful the missive had come, and he wouldn't spend the remainder of the night contemplating the past. He did wish it had arrived a bit later, preferably after she'd revealed her passion. That her gaze had been focused on his lips as she sought her answer had made it nearly impossible for him to draw breath as he anticipated her response. And now he needed a distraction from that path of thought. "Are you familiar with four-card brag?"

"No."

"It's quite popular at Aiden's gaming tables, so it would behoove me to teach you the rules, how to determine which card to discard, so the three remaining are more likely to see you with a win."

"Oh, I shan't be gambling. I haven't the coins for it. I'm simply curious. I've never been to a gaming hell before. I'm quite looking forward to the experience of seeing everything, absorbing the atmosphere."

He was willing to wager two of his ships that once they arrived, she would indeed sit at a table in order to try her hand at winning.

"Will the matter you have to deal with take long?" she asked.

"Not long."

"Perhaps I'll have the opportunity to observe you at the gaming tables."

"Then let me explain things so you'll be able to fully appreciate how very skilled and clever I am at card play."

Even within the dark confines of the carriage, he could sense her gaze homed in on him as though she'd reached out and touched him with her gloved fingers. "I realize I've not known you that long, but I've seen you as more modest than braggart."

He'd boasted about a skill at which he didn't excel in order to entice her into having an interest in learning how to play. After she'd bid him good-night and he'd headed for the door, he'd realized it was important for her to be with him at the club. "Indulge me."

Her laughter was soft, and yet it inhabited his soul. "All right."

He explained how cards in the same suit beat those in a sequence, how three matching cards beat cards in the same suit or a sequence, how a sequence of the same suit beat everything.

"It's not a very complicated game," she said.

"No, but it is responsible for fortunes being won and lost."

It was a dangerous thing to have her within the dark confines of a carriage, with her gardenia scent wafting around him, teasing his nostrils.

With a shake of his head and a long sigh, he pressed his back farther into the cushion, stretched out his legs, and crossed his arms over his chest. Now was not the time to reach for her, pull her onto his lap, and take possession of that mouth that taunted him still, to sample once more a kiss that haunted him. He chided himself. There would never be a time for doing that.

The carriage came to a stop. A footman opened the door, and Beast leapt out. Reaching back, he handed her down.

Her eyes widened slightly. "I'd expected something like White's."

The building was brick, stone, and sturdy but was half the size of the well-known gentleman's club. "Not in this area of London. Stick close so it's understood you're with me."

He offered his arm, and when she wrapped hers around it, he experienced a sense of satisfaction and pride that were not his to own. He led her up the steps. A footman opened the door.

Beast ushered Thea inside and despite the dimly lit interior, he noticed Aiden standing at the end of the short entryway, gazing into the first of several large rooms where various games of chance were being played. After handing the woman at the small desk his greatcoat and Thea's cloak, he approached his brother. "I wasn't expecting to see you here."

Aiden glanced over his shoulder, opened his mouth to speak, stopped, his eyes widening slightly—no doubt at the sight of Thea—and faced him fully. Although in truth he didn't seem particularly surprised by her appearance. Rather, he seemed pleased, as though he'd guessed correctly that a footwarmer and blanket would be needed in the carriage. "I had my man send word to me when he sent word to you. You didn't think I was going to miss whatever you had in mind, did you?"

Aiden had always loved nothing more than witnessing or participating in a well-executed reprisal or swindle.

"Thea, meet my brother Aiden. Aiden, allow me the honor of introducing Miss Stanwick."

Aiden bestowed upon her one of the devilish grins for which he was so famous, took her hand, and placed a kiss against her knuckles. In spite of the fact she wore gloves so his brother couldn't feel the silkiness of her skin, Beast still had a strong urge to punch him. Which was a patently ridiculous inclination because Aiden was madly in love with his wife. "A pleasure, Miss Stanwick."

"It's lovely to make your acquaintance."

"So how is it that you know my brother?" He was still holding her hand, blast him.

"That's unimportant at the moment," Beast interjected. "We need to get to business. Where is he?"

Aiden's eyes were twinkling when he returned his attention to Beast. Of all his siblings, Aiden was the one who laughed the most and saw life as a grand jest. Except when it came to his wife and son. Then he was as serious as a mute who accompanied a funeral procession. He cocked his head in the direction Beast should look. "At the table set halfway along that wall. The fair-haired chap whose face is most visible to us."

The man was of a slight build, smaller than he'd expected. Standing, he couldn't have been taller than five feet eight, if that. His clothing was exceptionally well tailored. His hair looked as though his valet had a few minutes earlier taken a brush to it and styled it. His movements were refined and elegant. She'd chosen a peacock to love, to marry. Now she stood beside a proper bear.

Out of the corner of his eye, he could see her straining forward slightly, no doubt striving to determine who the *he* might be. Beast knew the moment she saw the scapegrace because she gave a little audible gasp, released her hold on him, and pressed both hands to her mouth.

"It's Chadbourne." She jerked her gaze up to him, betrayal written clearly across her features. "You knew he would be here?"

He nodded. "The missive informed me." It had merely said, *He's here.* It was all he'd needed.

She swiveled her head back toward the card room, then back to him. "He's the matter you needed to attend to?"

"Yes."

"What are you going to do?"

"Ensure that he loses every farthing he brought with him tonight."

It was subtle, but he saw the lessening of the alarm in her eyes as though she'd feared he'd intended to kill him. That realization hurt, and he knew the hurt to be irrational. Yes, he was a beast, had killed once, had no desire to repeat the experience.

"How many pounds in chips do you want to start?" Aiden asked.

Beast didn't look away from those beautiful blue eyes that he feared might be damning him. "A thousand."

Aiden left to retrieve the wooden disks.

"You're going to wager and risk losing a thousand pounds?" she asked, clearly horrified.

"No. You are."

THE AIR LEFT her lungs as though he'd punched her. "Have you gone mad?"

"I don't think so. Why do you think I taught you the rules of the game in the carriage?"

"Because you're a braggart." She would have been so much happier if that was the reason.

"Thea." Firmly, he held her gaze. "I had originally planned to play him, but as I was leaving the library, I realized it's not my fight to win. I'm not the one he publicly mortified. I'm not the one he turned his back on. I'm not the one he abandoned."

"Taking the money he brought with him tonight will not change any of that."

"No. His humiliation at losing will not compare to what you suffered, but it is *something*. And sometimes that's all we get. Once you return to Aiden the thousand quid he's loaning you, the remainder of what you win will be yours. A little nest egg to do with as you please."

She didn't like at all the hope that filled her with that possibility. A little more to squirrel away, perhaps enough so she could immediately pay Beth for the trousseau. "And if I lose?"

"You won't. I'll sit beside you and if you need help determining which card to toss away, you can ask me."

She would indeed experience some satisfaction in besting Chadbourne. "He very well might leave when he sees me. As you saw with Lady Jocelyn, I'd be more welcomed if I had the plague."

"I doubt he's going to leave. But I don't want you to feel as though you have no choice here. If you don't wish to play him, I will. But make no mistake. He is my purpose in coming here tonight, and I shall see to that purpose. Aiden can have one of his men accompany you back to the residence. You can stay and watch. Or you can play and deliver the drubbing he deserves."

At that moment she realized she wasn't a very nice person. She not only wanted to see Chadbourne lose but also wanted to be the one responsible for his losing. Making up her mind, she nodded quickly, decisively. "No, I'll play him."

"Good. When all is said and done, I think you'll be ever so glad you did."

"Here you are," Aiden said, handing a small tray filled with wooden disks to Benedict, not showing any surprise at all when the tray was passed off to her. "Each of those is worth ten quid. Good luck."

"I'll try not to lose them."

He shrugged as though it was no large matter. "I'm not worried." He touched Benedict's arm. "The bloke in the red shirt sitting opposite Chadbourne—just tap his shoulder and he'll move to another table."

"We'll need your special dealer."

"Danny's already there, ensuring Chadbourne's winning enough hands that he should be fairly cocky and full of himself by the time you arrive. Now entertain me by putting him in his place."

Benedict shook his head, and she suspected if he was the rolling-his-eyes sort, he'd have done that as well. As it was, he turned to her. "Are you ready?"

"As I'll ever be."

Placing his hand on the small of her back reassuringly, he guided her around the tables, through the crush of people. It was an odd mixture of the well attired and the coarsely dressed. She doubted a single woman she spotted was of the nobility. Their woolen frocks were simple and plain, their hair pinned up but not nearly as tidy as it might be. The pipes and cigars made the room smoky enough to sting her eyes. Even some of the women were puffing on slender cheroots. It seemed everyone was indulging in spirits. Footmen were dashing around refilling glasses.

People were so absorbed in their play that no one was paying attention as they wended their way through the room. If any other lords were here, anyone who might recognize her, she thought it unlikely they would notice her. After all, she no longer dressed as an aristocrat but as a commoner, and nobles seldom gazed into the faces of commoners unless they were standing right in front of them, as she'd been with Lady Jocelyn that afternoon. Therefore, she didn't feel as though she was walking a gauntlet fraught with any danger of being called out by another.

"Does your brother loan this much so easily to everyone?"

"It's not a loan, Thea. If you should happen to lose it all, you won't be paying it back."

She stopped abruptly to look up at him. "You can't be serious. He's just giving it to me?"

He gave her an indulgent smile. "Eventually, if he stays at the tables long enough, whoever you lose it to will lose it to the house and it'll go back into Aiden's coffers. It's one of the reasons gambling hells are so profitable."

"He doesn't give money to everyone."

"No, everyone else has to pay him back with interest. Only family gets to play without any investment."

"But I'm not family."

He sighed. "You're with me tonight and I arranged this little endeavor, and so the chips are a favor to me. Now come along, before Chadbourne grows weary of playing."

She knew the moment Chadbourne spied her. His eyes grew as round as a barn owl's, and she regretted that her new frocks weren't yet ready, the frocks with the unfaded cloth, the untattered cuffs, the unfrayed collar, the unscratched buttons. The frocks that would fit her perfectly rather than hang slightly loosely because she was no longer the stout girl she'd been when food had been abundant and she'd spent every afternoon enjoying an entire box of chocolate-coated bonbons while lounging on a burgundy velvet-covered divan with a book in hand. Her hair was another matter entirely. As her first lady's maid lesson, Hester had spent over an hour before dinner arranging it in an elegant coiffure.

He didn't come to his feet as she neared but remained seated and she hoped rather wickedly it was because the sight of her had weakened his knees. Although she suspected the truth was a bit more disheartening: he simply no longer thought her deserving of the small courtesy.

His lack of movement made her appreciate more that Benedict not only came to his feet whenever she entered a room but also extended the same respect to the women in his residence who earned their coins by performing intimate services. She wondered if he looked down upon anyone. When she glanced quickly up at him, she saw in his dark eyes that Chadbourne apparently occupied that position. She found the realization fortifying.

Oddly, all activity at the table had stopped, and she suspected it was more a result of Benedict's presence than her own, that wherever he appeared, people went still until they determined what he wanted. Or perhaps it was simply that the "special dealer"—she had no idea what made him special—had been awaiting their arrival.

She stopped just shy of the table, her gaze locked on the blue eyes that had until recently held hers so tenderly, made her feel precious. "Lord Chadbourne."

"Lady Alth—" He stopped, disgruntlement sweeping over features she'd once deemed incredibly handsome. Interesting how betrayal made him look far less attractive. "Althea, what the devil are you doing here?"

"It's Miss Stanwick to you, and I'm here to take all your money."

Chapter 16

*B*loody hell. She'd delivered that pronouncement with such confidence that a few mouths—including Chadbourne's—had dropped open, and one gent was still blinking in wonder. A couple of them might have even fallen instantly in love with her. Not that he had. Not that his chest hadn't swelled with pride because she wasn't intimidated by this lordly buffoon.

"You can't . . . You can't play here," Chadbourne stuttered. He looked to the dealer, who was quietly shuffling the cards with slender hands that matched the rest of him. "Her father was a traitor to England. She shouldn't be allowed in here."

"Mr. Trewlove's only requirement for entry is that a person has money to lose." He narrowed his dark eyes at the tray Thea held. "I'd say she has about a thousand quid in chips there, so she is welcome at this table." He gave her a little nod.

Beast touched the red-clad shoulder and the chap slipped away like smoke. He pulled the chair out farther, and she lowered herself into it with the elegance of a queen taking her place upon the throne.

"I can't play with the daughter of a treasonous bastard," Chadbourne announced and began gathering up his chips, their clattering loud as he tossed them into his palm, no doubt expecting Danny to fall into line and oust Thea so the entitled lord could continue to play.

"Embarrassed to lose to a woman?" Beast taunted, understanding fully the foolishness of men's pride and how to take advantage of it.

The earl gave him a long, thorough study, not bothering to disguise his detestation for someone he recognized as not being part of the aristocracy. "What concern is any of this of yours?"

"*She* is my concern." He wondered if he should have the words etched on his forehead so he wouldn't have to keep repeating them to every idiotic aristocrat they happened upon.

The clacking stopped, his hands went still, his eyes narrowed. "Who the devil are you?"

"They call me Beast." Turning slightly, he grabbed an empty chair from a nearby table, swung it around, set it between Thea and Danny so the back of it faced the table, dropped into it, and folded his arms across the top.

"You intend to play?"

"Watch." He gave a careless shrug. "As well as offer advice to the lady when needed since she's never before played."

"That sounds as though it has the potential for cheating."

"How can I cheat if my hands never go near the cards? Besides, I've heard that Lady Fortune has been smiling on you tonight. Would be foolish on your part to move to another table and risk that she wouldn't follow. She certainly won't follow if you walk out of here completely."

The man studied Beast as though he was striving to determine if he was being goaded into a trap. He knew the exact moment the earl decided Beast was no danger to him. Many a man had made the same mistake.

"You make a good point." Chadbourne began neatly restacking his chips. Dear God, but the arrogant were easily manipulated.

"If the discussion is over," Danny said, "we'll get started." He gave the cards one more shuffle, then straightened them. "The ante is ten quid."

"May I have your hand for a moment?" Beast asked Thea in a hushed tone that spoke of intimacy. He was fairly certain he heard Chadbourne's spine snap when he straightened so quickly, with almost military precision. The earl no doubt had used the same tone a time or two and understood fully what it portended.

She didn't question him, simply held her hand out to him, and that gave him as much satisfaction as he would have had if, in fact, he had been pleasuring her. Well, not quite. But it meant she trusted him, and gratification surged through him with that knowledge. Very slowly, he peeled off her glove. It was the first time he'd touched her hand when it wasn't covered in kidskin, and he wished he'd done this service for her when they were in the carriage, in the dark, and alone. When he could have pressed his lips to the heart of her palm, could have traced the lines that some claimed predicted one's future. Her palm contained a slight roughness, one callus, all of which he suspected had been absent before the maggot sitting at this table had turned his back on her.

And yet that palm told a far more interesting tale than it might have if it had been as smooth as silk, and he valued it more because it wasn't.

After folding the glove over his thigh, he loosened the three buttons on her cuff and began rolling up the fabric along her forearm. "We don't want anyone to think you're hiding a card up your sleeve and accuse you of cheating."

"Oh." The single word came out on a breathy sigh, and he wondered if she was becoming as wet as he was becoming hard. He really should have done this elsewhere, where it might have led to a kiss . . . or more. Another mistake. A worse mistake.

The silence at the table was nearly deafening, and he could sense the other men were absorbed in observing his ministrations, no doubt each of them experiencing at least a modicum of envy. Therefore, he went even slower when he removed her other glove and rolled up her sleeve. When he was done, he lifted his eyes to her face and discovered she was studying her hands as though they were suddenly foreign to her, as though she was striving to determine how they had come to be hers.

Finally, she met his gaze, and he saw a woman dearly in want of ravishing, a woman he dearly wanted to ravish.

A harsh clearing of a throat had her jerking slightly and turning her attention to the dealer.

"As I said, everyone ante up."

Beast didn't fail to notice that Danny's voice was a little rough at the edges, slightly hoarse, and he wondered if he might be seeking a woman's arms when he was done here.

The five other players at the table—which included the dealer—tossed in their chip. Thea looked at him, and he saw an infinitesimal amount of doubt in her eyes. With a smile for encouragement, he gave her a nod. She carefully selected a chip as though the one chosen made a difference, and scooted it across the baize-covered table to join the others. He wasn't the only one who watched the journey of that slender, elegant hand.

Danny began dealing the cards. Beast signaled to a passing footman. When the young lad arrived, Beast said, "A sherry for Miss Stanwick and a scotch for me."

"Right away, sir."

"You know what she likes to drink?" Chadbourne asked, surliness woven between the syllables.

Beast held silent for all of a minute before bestowing upon him the grin that men had been displaying for centuries when they knew they possessed what another man coveted. "I know everything she likes."

ALTHEA HAD THE distinct impression two games were being played at this table.

One involved cards and was being played between her and Chadbourne. The other involved . . . Well, to be honest, she thought it quite possibly involved her and was being played between Chadbourne and Benedict. Based on the frequency with which the muscles in the earl's cheeks jumped, she was rather certain Benedict was winning. Especially as he appeared to be so frightfully relaxed and enjoying himself, rather like a panther that had just pounced upon a gazelle and feasted. It was an unfair match. The gazelle had never stood a chance.

She wasn't certain the odds of her winning when it came to Benedict were much better. Her plan had seemed so uncomplicated when it had taken shape in her mind, mostly because at the time she'd thought her heart dead, naught but ashes scattered on the wind. Her mind hadn't been much better. Three months after the destruction of her world, her ability to handle complicated matters was nowhere to be found. She'd still been numb at ending up where she had, so far from where she'd envisioned life to take her. The numbness had been a blessing, stopped her from going stark raving mad.

She'd reasoned that her absent heart and numbed mind would make it easier to do what needed to be done because her heart wasn't there to make her long for things, and her mind had no desire to think about things. Except the winds had shifted and blown her heart back into her chest, and her mind was analyzing decisions made and calling her every sort of fool. All because of the man sitting beside her, who somehow had the power to not only make her feel again, but also to think again.

The card game was incredibly easy to play, didn't require a lot of concentration on her part. Still, she always experienced a sharp thrill when she won the hand. After a winner was revealed, the discarded cards were tucked against the bottom of the deck. The deck was only shuffled if one of the revealed hands had three cards of the same rank.

Because concentration wasn't required on her part, she found herself focusing on Chadbourne and noticed something about him she'd completely overlooked before: he had a weak chin. As though shy, it made a small appearance, the tiniest bit of a jut, and then disappeared behind his perfectly knotted neck cloth.

Nothing about Benedict was weak. Although he wasn't playing, he managed to give the impression that he owned the table. Perhaps it was because of the intensity with which he watched the card play. Even though the only cards revealed at the end of each session were those held by the final two players—because they went around the table as many times as necessary with players betting or folding until only two remained—she was left with the impression he knew what cards were being dealt during each turn.

After deciding which card to discard, she would glance over at him. Usually, he would give a slight nod, and she would be pleased to have chosen correctly. But every now and then, he would give a subtle shake and when it was her turn to either toss money into the pot or fold, she would fold. And always, when the cards were revealed, she realized she would have lost no matter which card she tossed out.

His arms never moved from the back of the chair upon which they were folded. Just one hand ever unclamped from his upper arm and it happened only when he wanted to enjoy a bit of scotch. He wasn't manipulating the cards, but she was willing to wager all the tokens now stacked before her that somehow he was helping her cheat.

And she didn't care.

It almost always came down to her and Chadbourne as the final two players, and she almost always bested him. It felt so deliciously sweet to watch the various emotions flicker over his face: disbelief, disappointment, anger, resolve. He *would* win the next hand.

Only he rarely did. Sometimes his cards were so atrocious that even she, a novice, could have predicted he was bidding his chips farewell as he tossed them onto the heap in the center of the table.

Over the course of the evening, their group of six players dwindled to three, so more frequently now she and the earl paired off. Her confidence was growing, and because the lord's stack of chips had diminished to such a degree that he would not remain at the table for much longer, she determined it was time to add a third game to the night. She decided to call it, "Irritating the Devil out of Chadbourne."

"I crossed paths with Lady Jocelyn earlier today," she said evenly as though the words no longer had the power to punch her in the gut.

His gaze snapped up from his cards to land solidly on her, and she faintly recalled a time when his attention devoted to her had made her fairly light-headed with giddiness. What a silly chit she'd been. She'd considered him elegant, refined, polished. But he was neither gold nor silver, merely brass.

"Where?" His delivery was curt. She suspected if he discovered the meeting had been intentional, he'd be having a sharp word with his betrothed.

She smiled sweetly. "Quite by accident, I assure you. It seems we're using the services of the same dressmaker, if you can believe it."

Based on the furrowing of his brow, it was likely he didn't.

"Or we were," she amended. "She decided to take her business elsewhere, without paying the seamstress for the work she'd already done on her behalf. The cheek of her. I suppose it shall fall to you as her future husband to make matters right. Knowing her preference in clothing, I should think her trousseau's value rests at somewhere near five hundred pounds. If you would like to give me the amount before you leave here tonight, I'll be more than happy to deliver it to Beth—the seamstress—when I go in for my fitting on Friday." She tossed two chips into the pile. She'd gotten good at flicking her wrist just so in order to make them land on top of the others, so they made that lovely little clacking.

He was staring at her as though he didn't know her any longer. And she realized with both a bit of satisfaction and sadness that he didn't. "I'm certain her father will sort it."

His two disks clattered.

"I do hope you're correct. We wouldn't want to see her cheated out of what she has rightfully earned." She looked to Danny. One corner of his mouth quirked up slyly as he flicked his bet into the pile. As long as he stayed in the game, it would continue as would the new game she was playing. She picked up two wooden tokens and tapped them on the table. "When is the wedding to take place?"

"January. St. George's, naturally."

Naturally. The same church they'd chosen. The same month. It was surprising that the hurt had the same impact as the sting of a bee, which was hardly anything at all. Perhaps because while Benedict kept his hands locked around his upper arms so he couldn't be accused of slipping her cards, he had slid his booted foot across the floor until it was nestled against hers, announcing secretly to her his solidarity and support as though they had been heralded with banners waving and trumpets blaring. Her knee knocked accidentally against his, and then returned to rest there, to absorb more fully the comfort he was offering. He fortified her with the simplest of gestures. "To be honest, I was surprised you went with her."

Toss.

"I've always liked her."

Clatter.

Danny's tokens hit the pile.

"You certainly didn't waste any time in asking her."

Flick.

"After having chosen poorly the first time, I decided it would behoove me to quickly move on so my misjudgment could be soon forgotten."

As the growl sounded, his hand froze in midair and his gaze shifted ever so slightly and ever so slowly to the man sitting beside her, whose hands had balled into fists. They still remained against his arms, but it was evident he was straining to keep them there. "You'd be wise to choose very carefully what you say next," Benedict advised in a silky voice that she suspected resembled the one used by Satan when he welcomed someone into hell.

She gave him a gentle smile. "He can say nothing that will hurt me. To be hurt, I would have to care what he thought, and I no longer do."

It was with a bit of wonder that she realized she'd spoken true. A weight she'd been carrying for months suddenly fell away. What did his opinion matter?

"You're different," Chadbourne said.

She turned her attention back to him, but for him she had no smile. "Yes, I quite imagine I am."

He leaned forward, elbows on the table, hands outstretched. "Althea, where you are concerned, I had no choice but to do what I did. You can see that, surely. My family, our children, they would have been ostracized had we gone forward with our marriage."

Our children. The ones they would have created together—only now never would.

"We always have a choice, even when it seems we don't." She had chosen to follow a path that would make her scandalous but would lessen her brothers' worry over her and reduce their sense of responsibility toward her.

"Fine." He finally added his chips to the pile. "I chose to uphold my family honor."

"More like family dishonor." Most people would have muttered the words under their breath, but then Benedict Trewlove was not like most people. In truth, he was unlike anyone else she'd ever met. He made no excuses for any of his decisions, his choices. Even though she suspected a good many people questioned his wisdom in being associated with a brothel.

"I think I know who you are," Chadbourne said, his eyes narrowed on Benedict in an attempt to appear threatening that only served to make his squinting look as though he was in want of spectacles in order to see properly.

"*Think?* I told you who I am."

"You told me part of who you are. I recall now seeing you at a few weddings of late. You're a Trewlove, which means you're a bastard."

"You spit that word out as though it's something of which to be ashamed."

"You're unlawful. A nonperson. Nothing you do will change the circumstances of your birth."

"'Tis true. I am a bastard by birth. You, on the other hand, are a bastard by choice."

Chadbourne fairly quivered with indignation. "How dare you!"

"Would you rather I call you an arse?"

"I am an earl. You will give me the respect I deserve."

"I give no one respect unless he's earned it, and you've not."

"I. Am. A. Lord."

"You're not in Mayfair, mate," Danny said cheerily as though he was accustomed to breaking up squabbles at the tables before they broke out into fisticuffs. "You're in Whitechapel. Here the Trewloves are royalty. Ask anyone." He tossed his chips onto the pile and looked at her. "Miss Stanwick, do you wish to bet or fold?"

It seemed he was growing impatient for the game to end. Chadbourne had only four tokens left. He might win the chips in the center of the table, but it wouldn't be because he'd beaten her. She laid down her cards. "I fold."

Danny looked at the earl. "Lord Chadbourne, do you wish to see my cards?"

"You're bloody right I do." He gathered up his four remaining chips because to see an opponent's cards, he had to pay double what the individual players had been betting. One by one he dropped them on top of the pile.

Danny turned over his cards. Three jacks. Hearts, clubs, diamonds.

People walking outside the club no doubt heard Chadbourne's deep groans of dismay. He had the option of showing his cards, but his reaction made it unnecessary. He couldn't best the dealer's hand.

Danny scooped up the wooden disks. "It's been a pleasure. Hope you'll join us another evening."

"Not Lord Chadbourne," a deep voice stated with authority. "He won't be returning."

Althea glanced to her left to see Aiden standing there with his arms crossed over his chest in a familiar stance, and she wondered if it was a habit shared by all the Trewlove men. She also wondered how long he'd been there. As he'd wanted to be entertained, he'd no doubt been around for a good bit of what had transpired, although he'd been discreet about it. Another thing the brothers seemed to share: they preferred the shadows.

"My lord, you're no longer welcome at the Cerberus Club. My brother has always been more tolerant of those who disparage bastards than I. And lest you think otherwise, I can assure you that within these walls, you will never again win. Not so much as a farthing."

Chadbourne squeezed his eyes shut and, with his thumb and forefinger, pinched the bridge of his nose. She'd forgotten how he always did that when he was disappointed or frustrated. Once she'd found it to be a charming little quirk. Now she found it somewhat irritating.

He opened his eyes, and she suspected he'd been using that time to try to soften his glare. "Congratulations, Althea. Not only have you seen me lose all the money I allotted for the evening as you claimed I would, but you have seen to it that I have lost access to my favorite club. I suppose now we are even."

"You *are* an arse, Chadbourne, to think for one single second that the loss of access to a gaming hell can even begin to compare to the loss of everything, to the extent that I no longer even knew who I was."

Chapter 17

*U*ntil she'd spoken the words, she hadn't recognized the truth of them. When her father had been arrested, she'd become unmoored, had difficulty thinking of herself as his daughter. But she'd had Chadbourne, was betrothed, would become a wife and mother. When he'd turned his back on her, another thread that had comprised the fabric of her being had unraveled, and she'd stood on those stairs no longer certain of who she was. Then the Crown had taken everything, and she was no longer a lady, had no home. She had known and understood every aspect of Lady Althea Stanwick. But who the devil was Althea Stanwick?

It was half two when she and Benedict walked out of the Cerberus Club to find the carriage waiting for them.

"I know it's frightfully cold and the air is scented with fresh rain, but could we just drive around for a while?"

"Anywhere in particular?" Benedict asked as though her request at this time of night wasn't absurd, inconvenient, and an imposition.

"No, I just want the darkness and the absence of anyone about save you."

Even when she was alone in her bedchamber, she could sense the presence of the residents and the strangers who called upon them, could often hear the odd little bumps scrapes, and cries that accompanied their actions.

Now the curtains at the windows were drawn, the fur blanket

was tucked about her, the foot warmer had been reheated, her toes were cozy, and Benedict sat opposite her, his long legs stretched out, his booted feet on either side of hers. When he'd positioned them like that, she'd lifted the blanket and draped it over his calves so he could enjoy the warmth with her.

"I don't know what I ever saw in him." When silence was his answer, she added, "Lord Chadbourne. I don't know why I thought I loved him."

"Thought? You didn't know you loved him?"

"At the time I was convinced I did. I've reminisced about him often, longed for him on occasion, but my memories of him were far too kind. I didn't much like the man I beat tonight. Did I cheat to do so?"

"A little."

She'd known he'd answer honestly, even if his response cast him in the role of villain. But she couldn't envision that he'd ever been the villain, not even when he was a lad of eight and nicked a timepiece.

As much as she craved the darkness, she wished a lantern was burning so she could see his features clearly, judge his expressions, and gaze into his eyes. She was rather certain she'd see a tiny smile of satisfaction. "Whenever you indicated I should fold, the winning hand always would have beaten what I was holding. You're able to keep track of the cards that are played."

"To an extent. The ones that are shown, at least. Then I can make other assumptions based upon how quickly hands are folded. It's not an infallible method, but it does increase the chances of winning more often than losing."

"What makes Danny a *special* dealer?"

"His ability to keep track of the cards and his mastery of sleight of hand. He doesn't always deal the top card, but rather the one below it. Although when I gave him a few quid for his assistance tonight, he claimed only to have dealt from the top."

"Do you believe him?"

"He had no reason to lie. Aiden told him to do what needed to be done to ensure the outcome we wanted. However, I suspect he was manipulating the order in which he added the cards to the bottom of the deck. Does it make you feel less victorious to know you might have had some assistance?"

"No." She didn't hesitate with her answer. "I was just glad to see the earl lose. I didn't care how it happened. Which I suppose says more about me than him." She grew silent, thought about how the night had gone. "The other three gents at the table. Do you know them? I'd like to see their losses returned to them from my winnings." After Aiden had taken back his stake—as he referred to the chips he'd originally given her—she walked away with a little over twelve hundred pounds. A rather astonishing amount for a couple of hours' entertainment. She could hardly countenance that people allotted so much money to wagering.

"Aiden can sort it and let you know how much he'll need to cover it. He won't let them know any possible cheating was involved. He'll probably tell them it has to do with the lady's remarkable generosity."

"I suppose any rumors of cheating in his establishment wouldn't go over well."

"It would not. For the most part, he runs an honest establishment. But on rare occasions when a certain outcome is needed, he's not averse to doing what must be done to attain it. You don't have to give any of your take back to the other gents. As I mentioned earlier, anyone who spends any time at a card table eventually loses. It's understood, expected, accepted."

"I'll feel better about it. Their clothing indicated they were laborers of some sort. I suspect Chadbourne's boots cost more than they earn collectively in a year." A time existed when she wouldn't have known that, hadn't known how hard people worked for so little pay. She'd cared only about gowns, new dance steps, and the latest gossip. She'd cared about her appearance: her hair, the glow of her skin, her frocks, her hats, her shoes, her gloves. She most certainly never would have gone out in public in a frock with little worn spots here and there or a glove with a tiny hole on the palm side slightly below the spot where her middle finger was attached.

"Why did you do it?" she asked softly. "Why have them send you a message? Why go there to confront him?"

The silence stretched out between them, growing thick and heavy.

Finally, he spoke, his voice a tender caress in the night. "Because you deserved better of the man you were going to honor by becoming his wife."

Tears stung the backs of her eyes. Benedict deserved better than the scorn he'd no doubt received for most of his life. "I'm sorry for the unkind words he said to you. About your birth."

"My skin is thick. I've had worse said about me."

"But you shouldn't have had. I don't know if I've ever known anyone who cares about the welfare of others as much as you." In spite of the cold, she removed her gloves and set them beside her on the bench. With her winnings, she could purchase a new pair but would never rid herself of the ones she'd worn tonight. She would put them away in a box so she could more easily hold on to the memory of him taking them off her hands. For the short time it had required for him to do so, no one else had existed in that smoke-filled room that had carried the din of winners' cheers and losers' grumbles.

It was the most effective lesson in seduction he'd given her thus far, although she suspected he'd argue he'd not intended it to be a lesson.

Very slowly, she swept aside the fur blanket and fought to keep her balance as she swung inelegantly over to his side of the carriage. Because his outstretched legs had caged her in, she'd had very little choice except to land on his lap, which would have caused a proper lady—sitting on his thigh, so close to his crotch, her feet dangling between his legs—to blush profusely in mortification.

Other than his arm coming around her back to brace her so she didn't tumble to the floor, she detected no other movement on his part, wasn't even certain he continued breathing. With her hand, she cupped the left side of his face, so his strong jaw rested against the edge of her palm, the thick stubble coating his chin prickling her skin, sending delicious spikes of pleasure through her. With her thumb, she lightly stroked his full bottom lip. It was soft, smooth, and warm. He was comprised of so many different textures, and she wanted to explore every one of them.

"Earlier, when you were removing my gloves, I was wondering if you took off all of a woman's clothing so slowly." Her voice was a hushed, intimate whisper.

"Not always."

His voice was a rasp that for some reason caused her nipples to pucker and ache. His hot breath wafting over the curve of her thumb made her stomach tighten.

"I know you claimed it was a mistake, but have you thought at all today about the kiss we shared?"

"Not a single second has passed that I haven't thought of it."

Heat pooled between her thighs, coursed through her veins.

In spite of the darkness that made them little more than shadowy outlines and silhouettes, she unerringly pressed her lips to the corner of his mouth that always quirked up when he wasn't quite ready to give her a full grin. "Do you want to kiss me now?"

Some sort of jerky movement occurred behind her back, and when his free hand came up and cradled her cheek, the glove that had been keeping it warm was gone. With his long, thick fingers threaded through her hair, he guided her nearer. "More than I want to draw breath."

Then he took possession of her mouth as though he intended to own it for all eternity.

The kiss in no way resembled his removal of her gloves. It wasn't slow, disciplined, or civilized. It was frenzied, accompanied by his guttural groans as he licked the raised bow of her upper lip before journeying into the interior where their tongues clashed with fervor. It wasn't only a kiss. It was a feast as each lick created a heated sensation that traveled all the way through her. How was it possible that his occupation with a portion of her could cause the rest of her to feel as though little bolts of lightning were dancing over every inch of her skin? Why did each aspect of her coil and twist into a weave that created a tapestry of sensations?

In an attempt to steady herself, she clasped his shoulder with the free hand, dug her fingers into him, resenting the thickness of his coat. She lifted her hand to cup his head. He grabbed her wrist, turned his mouth from hers to plant a kiss in the center of her palm, and then carried her hand inside his greatcoat, inside his jacket, and slipped it beneath his waistcoat.

"Relish the warmth I can offer you," he rasped, placing her hand at his shoulder over his linen shirt where her fingers clamped hard as he reclaimed her mouth.

She couldn't imagine any other man devouring her thusly or her allowing any other man to do so. Not even Chadbourne when she had fancied herself in love with him. She couldn't envision his arms enveloping her, his mouth engaged in such wickedly wonderful deeds, coaxing her tongue to pass through his parted lips where he suckled it with an enthusiasm that she suspected Chadbourne had never exhibited about anything in his life. Certainly not her. Their relationship had always been a quiet, cool, calm sort of thing. It had never created a storm of desire. Had never made her think, "Without this, I would wither away."

It was a revelation at that moment to realize she was incredibly grateful she'd not married him, had not been denied the opportunity to know such wild abandonment.

Benedict bracketed her hips with his large hands, tearing his mouth from hers, his breaths coming in rushed, greedy gasps for air. "Straddle me."

He could have commanded anything of her, and she would have obeyed. Such was his power over her at that moment. A power held because of the vow for more pleasure he offered and the promises of delivering exquisite sensations that he now kept, promises he'd made with smoldering stares and earnest conversations and alluring smiles. He knew what he was about. He'd made sure she knew it as well.

With his assistance, in spite of the rocking of the carriage, she easily scrambled onto the seat, resting on one knee while she swung her other leg over his and settled the slender cavern between her thighs against the hard ridge between his. They both groaned as though nothing had ever felt as sublime, then released a quick huff of laughter that they should be so attuned to each other. Then each reclaimed the other's mouth.

This was better, so much better, facing him squarely. She slipped her hands inside his jacket, clutched both his shoulders, dropped her head back as he trailed that heated mouth along the column of her throat even as his fingers went to work loosening the buttons that ran along the front of her frock. When he reached the last one, he pulled back, and she felt his gaze homed in on her. For a second she resented the shadows that prevented her from seeing the obsidian depth of his eyes and what she might discover revealed in them.

More slowly than he'd removed her gloves, he glided the edges of his hands along the parted cloth, up the front of her corset, his fingers taking the time to outline each of the steel hooks. The absence of a lady's maid had made it necessary for her to acquire a corset that fastened in the front so she could more easily dress herself. She couldn't help but believe that it was on the verge of becoming handier than she'd ever anticipated.

When he reached the top, his thumbs came together and traveled up to her collarbone and then across it to the edge of her chemise, back to the hollow at her throat. His breath stuttered as he once more neared her corset. Just as she had so easily flicked a wooden token onto a pile, he flicked a hook free of its post.

"Stop me if you object." Another flick.

"I was actually considering offering to assist so the task is completed faster."

"Ah, Christ." His arms came swiftly around her, pressing her forward so where the upper swells of her breasts met landed against his open mouth, his heated breath forming dew at the tight hollow between them.

His hands returned to their earlier endeavor. Flick. Flick. Flick.

Her corset fell open, and if she wasn't still wearing her frock, it would have fallen to the floor instead of merely against the cloth.

"I can't imagine how many lovers you've had in order to be accomplished enough to do this so unerringly in the dark." She squeezed her eyes shut, bit her bottom lip. Why the deuce had she said that? Even worse, why had she said it in such a waspish tone? She didn't want him to answer, didn't want to know the number of women with whom he'd lain.

"I can remember the sequence of the cards placed in an ever-changing order within the deck. I need see something only once to recall how it goes."

She didn't believe for a single second that he'd only ever been with one woman, but deeply appreciated his attempt to reassure her. How many men would have boasted, would have exaggerated the number, in order to demonstrate their virility or to prove how irresistible they were? But Benedict Trewlove never felt a need to prove anything to anyone. He made no excuses for who he was, was content with who he was.

Leaning in, she took possession of the mouth that so often seemed to utter the words she dearly needed to hear. She didn't linger, but soon straightened, took his hands, and placed them against her chemise.

He loosened the ribbon at the top and set the buttons free of their moorings. Which in turn freed her breasts of all constraints.

His hands replaced the cloth, felt so much lovelier than the cotton and muslin that her reduced circumstances had necessitated. In spite of the shadows, she saw the flash of his teeth as he grinned.

"I knew they would fill my hands. Perfectly. Your skin feels as though silk, satin, and velvet were all woven together to create a texture that would drive men mad."

Men. A courtesan would have a parade of men in her life. Was that what she truly wanted? Lovers constantly changing? The habits of one so very different from those of another? Suddenly, it seemed it would be enough to drive only one man mad. This one.

Lowering his head, he peppered each breast with kisses, a dozen, two. She didn't want him to stop. But when he did, it was to circle his tongue around her nipple, and the heat that sluiced through her threatened to scald her. When he drew it into his mouth and suckled, every part of her body wanted to stretch and contract at the same time. Her fingers dug into his shoulders in an attempt to keep her tethered when she felt as though she could float. While his mouth gave attention to one breast, his thumb and forefinger were devoted to the other, rubbing the hardened pearl between them. She was the one being driven mad. Or if not mad, then wild.

Nothing had prepared her for this, for the sensations ricocheting through her, for that secretive, sensitive place between her legs begging to be touched next.

And perhaps it would have been, if the carriage hadn't begun to slow.

He cursed harshly and began buttoning her bodice. "I instructed the driver to give us an hour before returning to the residence. You were right. I should have undone those fastenings more quickly."

She couldn't help it. She laughed. His mouth slamming against hers stole her laughter and her breath.

When the coach rumbled to a stop, he quickly but gently moved her off his lap and drew her cloak snuggly around her. "Just clutch it so it stays closed."

Before the footman could arrive, he was opening the door and disembarking. He reached back in for her, and she placed her hand in his. Once her feet hit the pavement, without waiting for him, she dashed up the steps, her unfastened corset bouncing against her back. She should have brought up the hood on her cloak. If anyone caught sight of her face, which was no doubt a fiery red, they'd know she'd been up to no good. She rushed into the foyer and headed for the stairs.

Jewel was standing in the doorway that led into the front parlor. "How was your adventure to the gaming hell?"

She didn't even slow down. "Interesting."

"If you can believe it, I've never been to a gaming hell. I want to hear all about it."

"Tomorrow." She darted up the flights, not stopping until she was safely ensconced in her room, her back flattened against the closed door. She pressed her hands to her cheeks. They were incredibly hot. Her breasts felt heavy as though they were straining for his touch, his mouth. She was also relatively certain they were slightly abraded from his whiskers moving over them. The prickling should not feel so welcome and delightful.

It was one thing to lose herself in the throes of passion while in the dark, but how the devil was she going to meet Benedict's eyes when they were engulfed in lamplight or worse—bright daylight? Her thoughts were absurd. She wanted him to teach her about seduction, passion, and pleasure. Had she thought their paths wouldn't cross except during lessons?

She couldn't engage with him outside of lessons. She'd sought him out for a purpose, had plans, and becoming involved with him would derail them.

The rap on her door nearly had her leaping out of her skin. Reaching into her still-unbuttoned frock, she grabbed hold of her corset, tugged, tugged, tugged it out, and tossed it toward the bed. It fell short and landed with a plunk on the floor.

"It's Beast."

"One moment." It was ridiculous to require any modesty at this point. Still, she rapidly buttoned up her frock before opening the door a crack and peering out. Why couldn't he look as though he, too, had been ravished? She should have untidied him a bit. How did the ladies here ever act normal around a man with whom they'd been intimate? She needed to make inquiries on the morrow.

He seemed to be searching for evidence that he had indeed caressed her, tasted her, suckled various areas. "You left these in the coach."

She dropped her gaze to his hand, a hand terribly skilled at eliciting pleasure, that presently had a pair of cream-colored gloves draped over it. Very carefully, without touching him, she slid them from his grasp. "Thank you. And thank you for the lesson in the coach."

"It wasn't a bloody lesson."

She licked her lips. "Then what happened in the carriage was a mistake. It would be best if our activities were limited to lessons only."

She didn't know how it was possible to describe him as going any quieter, but it seemed that somehow he had.

"I'm a firm believer in doing what's best," he finally said without a single trace of irony. Reaching into his pocket, he brought out a packet wrapped in brown paper secured with string. "Your winnings."

Good Lord, she'd almost forgotten about that. Because she hadn't brought a reticule with her, he'd offered to carry it for her. She took it, clutched it, along with her gloves, to her breast. "As I now have this, I'll purchase the frocks and other items Beth is sewing for me."

"You don't think it would be wiser to save it for a rainy day?"

"Today was a rainy day." At her little quip, she'd hoped for a brief smile or a half smile or at least a quirk of his lips.

With a nod, he reached out and trailed his forefinger along her jaw. She should have stepped back and closed the door. Instead, she fell into the depth of his gaze as he tracked the movement of his finger along her flesh. His thumb joined in to hold her chin as he lowered his mouth to hers. Unlike the others, this kiss was tender, sweet, slow like the first buds of spring unfurling. It communicated sorrow, regret, apology . . . desire, yearning, need.

When he pulled away, he pressed his thumb to her dampened

lips. "I've found I learn more from my mistakes than I do from my successes."

Leaving her there, battling not to call him back, he strode into his study at the far end of the hallway and closed the door with a bit more force than he normally did, and she wondered if he was going to spend his time in there murdering someone on foolscap.

Chapter 18

*O*nce more he failed to show at breakfast. Another lie-in supposedly, although she didn't accept that explanation. More likely he was avoiding her, or the temptation of her.

To her astonishment, none of the ladies had ever been to a gaming hell. They plied her with questions, their eyes dancing with excitement as they gave her their rapt attention while she described the decor, the atmosphere, the customers.

"We should all take a night off and go," Lily announced, her voice brimming with enthusiasm at the potential for mischief.

It was agreed they would do so during the evening of Boxing Day.

At some point during the morning, he slipped out of the residence without her noticing. In order to "see to some business," Jewel told her.

Perhaps he needed to meet with merchants who were waiting on cargo or one of his ships had returned from its voyage. She would like to be at the docks to watch one of his ships arrive, stroll along its deck, stand at the helm with him at her side. It was a dangerous thing to imagine him beside her, regardless of what she did or where she went. He was not to be involved in so much of her life. He was not to make it difficult for her to walk away from this residence without looking back, without misgivings.

He didn't join them for dinner.

Nor was he in the library when she arrived at ten. She poured her own sherry and a glass of scotch for him. But his remained untouched.

Why had he not told her he wouldn't be available that evening? Where the devil was he? What was he doing?

Perhaps he'd gotten lost in his writing. She certainly never liked to leave a letter unfinished. Maybe he felt the same about a scene or a chapter.

When the clock struck eleven, she went to his study and knocked. No answer. She opened the door. No Benedict.

Some urgent matter must have arisen that required his undivided attention. Surely, he would explain himself on the morrow.

Only he was as noticeably absent, not joining them for any of the meals. Jewel assured her that he'd slept in the residence but had left that morning to attend to some matters.

But that evening, once again, he didn't join her in the library. She was beginning to suspect he was never going to join her, that he was making himself scarce for a reason, and the reason was her.

The following morning, she was in the library when she heard his heavy footsteps on the stairs and the closing of the door to his study. But he failed to join them for the midday meal. If his behavior of the past couple of days wasn't avoidance, she didn't know what was. And she wasn't having it.

She didn't bother knocking. She simply opened the door to his study and strode in.

Wearing only shirtsleeves and trousers, he was standing at the window, arms raised, hands braced on either side of the window casing, reminding her of the stance of a prisoner chained to a wall in a dungeon that she'd seen depicted somewhere.

Lowering one arm, he glanced back at her without fully turning. "I'm not to be disturbed when I'm working unless fire or blood is involved. Which is it?"

Well, he was in a right mood, which suited her just fine because so was she.

"What work are you engaged in? Holding up a wall?"

With a huge sigh, he faced her and flung his hand toward his desk. "I'm trying to write."

"I would think you'd have more success if you were dipping your pen into the inkwell."

His eyes darkened with heat. He squeezed them shut, opened them. "You don't understand the process. What do you want?"

She marched over until she was halfway between him and the door. "The lessons we agreed to, the ones you promised."

He couldn't have looked more stunned or irritated if she'd smacked him. "Speaking of lessons, aren't you supposed to be teaching the ladies at this moment?"

"I've given them the afternoon off."

"Why the bloody hell would you do that?"

"Because I think you're avoiding me. You're not joining us for meals and for two nights now, you failed to join me in the library at our agreed-upon time for a lesson."

"I have work to do."

"I think it's more than that." Was afraid it was more than that. "When you kissed me, you said it wasn't a bloody lesson. The other night in the carriage, what happened, you said it wasn't a bloody lesson. I don't think you ever intended to give me any lessons. I think that's the reason you had the agreement state that you'd pay a thousand pounds if I determined you hadn't upheld your end of the bargain. You planned to take only what you needed from me without giving me what I needed from you."

"That's not true."

"Then when are you going to give me a proper lesson?"

His hands fisted at his sides, and she didn't want to think about the power he could unleash. A muscle ticked in his jaw. His eyes were fairly smoldering. "You want a bloody lesson?"

"It's what we agreed to."

"Close and lock the door."

Those words effectively doused her irritation with him. "Pardon?"

"Like you, Jewel is wont to barge in. The last thing you're going to want is to be interrupted. Lock the door."

She licked her lips. "You're going to give me a proper lesson now?"

He didn't respond with words, but the answer was evident in his intense focus, and she wondered if he'd looked at her like that in the carriage after they'd left Aiden's club. She might have burst into flames if she'd seen him more clearly, had known the fire those eyes were capable of igniting.

A tremor of anticipation coursed through her. Swallowing hard, she spun on her heel, fought to calm her steps as she made her way to the door, closed it, and turned the lock.

When she swung around, it was to find him already there. How could a man of his size and sturdy muscle move so silently? But then from the beginning his elegance had been incomparable, like a large ship gracefully slicing through water.

Taking her slender wrists, he clamped one large hand around both of them, lifted them over her head, and held them securely, yet tenderly against the door. She felt no discomfort, knew he would leave behind no bruising.

"Do you remember the day you first came to me that I told you not to give anything too easily?"

He'd lowered himself slightly, so she didn't have to tip her head back too far in order to meet his gaze. She nodded.

"Never give anything too quickly. Make him want. Make him beg. Make him believe if he can't have you, he will die."

"How do I do that?" She sounded breathless, could barely hear herself for the blood rushing through her ears.

Again, he used no words, but within his dark eyes, she saw the answer. He was going to make her want, make her beg, make her believe she'd die if she couldn't have him.

IT WAS SO dangerous to trail his fingers along the soft skin beneath her chin. Each stroke made him want. Made it harder not to beg. Convinced him that he'd die if he couldn't have her.

But he couldn't have her.

Since Sally Greene had asked for his protection, two maybe three dozen women had been under his care. An assortment that would rival a sweetshop when it came to choices. Strikingly beautiful. Plain. Voluptuous. Slender. Stocky. Tall. Short. Funny. Kind. Sweet. Coarse.

Not once had he ever been tempted by any of them. He'd easily adhered to his personal code of conduct. They lived under his roof. They were not available to him. He effectively built a wall between himself and them that lust couldn't climb or shatter. He enjoyed engaging them in conversations, spending time in their company. But every action, activity, and moment had been platonic. He'd been able to hug them in celebration, embrace them in sorrow.

He couldn't even look at Althea without his cock wanting, and that was becoming a problem. Therefore, this lesson was for him as much as it was for her. A reminder, a reaffirmation of his vow.

But if she touched him, he'd be lost. Just as he'd been in the carriage when he'd had more than a taste of her, just as he'd been the night in the library when he'd kissed her.

Therefore, he held her wrists, cushioned against his palm so the wood of the door bit into his knuckles rather than her sensitive skin. He took his time caressing only the flesh that was naturally exposed by the cut of her frock. Another lesson. Yearning did not require nudity.

She was a fast learner. Her lips parted, her breaths shuddered as they sawed in and out of her lungs. The blue in her eyes darkened, the gray turned silver. Her long, golden eyelashes fluttered, and then she opened her eyes wide as though determined to hold his gaze, to be defiant, to not beg.

But eventually she would.

He turned his hand so now his knuckles, rougher than his fingertips, skimmed along the silken expanse. How could she be so damned soft?

How was it that she smelled of freshly cut gardenias? Surely, she hadn't bathed after finishing her luncheon. He squeezed his eyes shut. He didn't need the image of her soaking in a tub filling his head. Water sluicing over those lovely breasts he'd caressed, kissed, suckled. Ah, to see them in light now. To know if those nipples were dusky or pink. To know all the various shades of her.

But that was not where this lesson needed to go. Not where it could go if he was to maintain control.

He opened his eyes, grateful to see that hers were still open so he could fall into the depths of them. It was a dangerous surrender, but he could limit the length of his captivity. He lowered his mouth to her cheek. "Are you aware you have three freckles?"

"I hate them."

"Don't. They have the ability to mesmerize. Did you have more when you were a child?"

"Yes."

He would have liked to have seen her then. Probably would have teased her unmercifully and hated himself later for doing it. Young lads could be such idiots, not appreciating what would eventually lead a girl to becoming a beautiful woman.

He pressed a kiss to the corner of her mouth. She turned her head to take possession of his. He pulled back. "No. We're not going to kiss."

"Why not?"

Because he would be lost, would lose control. "Because seduction doesn't require it."

He trailed his lips along her throat, and she released a sigh mingled with a moan. His trousers became far too tight. The temptation to press up against her was strong, but he tethered it, kept his lower body away from her, even as it nearly killed him to do so.

He felt the pressure on his hand as she sought to break free of his grip, as though she needed to touch him as much as he did her. It was wrong to feel such a surge of satisfaction, but he kept her shackled, knowing her physical strength was no match for his.

Yet, she was not weak. A weak woman couldn't have brought him to his knees, and she'd held that power from the moment she'd brought him his first scotch.

With a smile, she could bring him low. With a laugh, undo him. With a glance through half-lowered eyelashes, steal his ability to think or reason. With the stroke of a finger, conquer him.

Her body writhed and strained as he licked, nipped, and grazed his teeth along her throat, as his broad hand skimmed the length of her narrow torso, over a breast, dipping at her waist, flaring at her hips. Curving over one rounded butt cheek, sliding down her thigh until he could hook her knee over his forearm, lift her leg to circle his waist, opening her to him.

IF SHE DIDN'T touch him, she would die. But he seemed intent upon her death.

How was it possible for such desperation to ensue with so little of him touching so little of her?

When he'd begun trailing his fingers over her skin, she'd expected a repeat of last night with buttons undone, flesh exposed to air, his questing tongue, and his exploring hands. But he was leaving her clothing intact and in doing so was forcing her to become frantic with need.

With her leg resting at his waist, draped over his hip, she rose up on her toes, striving to create enough slack in her body that she could press an aching and needy secretive spot against him, but he held himself just beyond her reach. Her groan was nearly a whimper of despair.

While still touching her, he somehow managed to fluff out her skirt, his hand slipping beneath the fabric until his agile fingers closed around her ankle.

She was aware of him going still, like a deer caught in the sight of the hunter. Perhaps he'd not expected to encounter the bare flesh that skirts always kept hidden. Because she'd had no plans to go outdoors, she'd not bothered with stockings or shoes but wore only her slippers.

Triumph at surprising him surged through her. His mouth pressed more firmly against her throat. His breaths came in shortened gasps as though the need for a more thorough touching that embraced her had reached out to encompass him as well.

His fingers danced slowly, provocatively, along her calf, before creating small circles over the back of her knee. His tongue slowly traced the shell of her ear. "Do you *want*?"

In his rasp, she heard hunger and need.

"Yes." Her low sigh echoed the same.

"Do you want me to touch you?"

He was already touching her, but instinctually she knew he was referring to a different sort of touch, the kind for which he might make her beg.

"Yes." The word was a stutter, a cry, a plea.

"Where?"

"Don't make me say it." *Don't make me beg.*

His mouth left her ear and she nearly wept that he would deny her that small part of him.

"Open your eyes, Beauty. Let me see in the blue and silver where you want me to touch you."

She did as he bade. In his taut features she saw reflected the same need she felt. Raw and primal. The need to possess, to be possessed. The need to devour, to be devoured.

"Please," she whispered.

His growl was one of pain as his mouth landed on hers, taking what he'd told her he wouldn't. She opened to him, welcomed him, met the thrust of his tongue with one of her own.

His fingers journeyed up her thigh, stroked up and down. He adjusted the position of her leg, spread her wider. His fingers slipped unerringly through the slit in her drawers, fluttered over her soft curls, before going deeper. Parting the folds, he stroked the length of her before pressing his thumb against the swollen nub. She whimpered, gave a little jerk.

"You're so damned wet, so hot," he said against her mouth. He slid a finger inside her. "So tight."

He sounded like a man in torment, but his torment could be no worse than hers. She was on the verge of begging when he reclaimed her mouth and began stroking in earnest where she needed to be stroked, circling, applying pressure, gliding over slick wetness.

Pleasure tripped through her, wave upon wave, each expanding farther, each growing more powerful until no part of her didn't feel the magic of his touch. Sensations of pure ecstasy burst through her, tore a scream from her throat that he silenced by pressing her mouth against the corded tendons of his neck. She bit down as the bliss continued to undulate through her, as her released wrists landed hard on his broad shoulders, as the leg upon which she stood threatened to give way, would have if he hadn't circled one arm around her and held her tight.

When it all passed, when the tremors began to subside, when she came back into herself, she realized she was breathing as harshly as he.

Slowly, gently, he lowered the leg he'd lifted back to the floor and eased away from her until no part of her was touching any part of him.

"That's it. That's the lessons. We're done."

HE HADN'T MEANT for it to go that far, had meant only to carry her to the brink and then send her to her room so she could finish herself off. He'd never planned to slip his hand beneath her skirt, to know her so intimately.

But he hadn't the strength to deny her what he could give. Didn't want her finding her surcease with her own hand rather than his.

She was flushed with pleasure, and he wanted nothing more than to take her back in his arms. But from this moment on, every aspect of her was going to be denied to him. Because with a single touch he lost all will to resist her.

He watched as she blinked, blinked, blinked. As the import of his words began to sink in.

"Lessons. Plural." She shook her head. "This was only the first one."

"The first, the last. We're done," he repeated with emphasis. "I'll acknowledge to being rubbish as a tutor and go ahead and pay you the thousand. I'll have the funds to you tomorrow."

"But you're not rubbish. You're anything but rubbish. Why will you not give me more lessons? Is it the way I responded? You found my reaction repulsive?"

"You're jesting, correct?"

Except no humor lit her eyes. Only worry, embarrassment, a shyness. This woman who had never been shy in his presence looked as though she wanted to retreat, and he hated himself for the doubts he caused her. "Do you know how many men would surrender their souls to the devil to have a woman respond like that in his arms?"

Of course she didn't. She was an innocent.

She shook her head, the hurt in her eyes tearing him apart. "I don't understand what I've done wrong."

He cursed every blasted person who had ever made her question her value, herself. "You did nothing wrong."

"Then why won't you tutor me?"

Frustration seized him, the same frustration he'd been fighting since he met her. "Because I can't keep my bloody mouth off you. I can't keep my bloody hands off you. And it's getting harder to keep my bloody cock away from you."

The sadness in her eyes morphed into astonishment. "Oh."

"You don't need to be tutored, Thea. You don't need lessons. You're a natural temptress. You need but be yourself. For me not to acknowledge that, to continue to tutor you, would be to take advantage of you. I gave you my word I wouldn't do that."

"But I'm not complaining. I don't mind."

With a deep sigh, he shook his head. "But I do. It's not right."

"What about the rest of the agreement?"

"That's entirely up to you. If what has passed between us has made you uncomfortable, we'll visit Beckwith tomorrow, see the agreement properly terminated and you paid. I'll honor the yearly salary and the three-month achievement. With that and what you won last night, you should be able to set yourself up nicely, so you can be selective in choosing your lover."

"I'd rather continue to teach the ladies." She gave him a tentative smile. "I've determined an occupation for each of them that I think they'll find very fulfilling. To be honest, I want to help them move beyond here. I would find satisfaction in it, fulfillment. And I should think I would be hard to replace."

He almost confessed she'd be impossible to replace.

If he didn't have to tutor her, he could put some distance between them, perhaps ignore this constant undercurrent of want and need. "No sitting on my lap in carriages, that sort of thing."

She nodded. "You and I would simply strive not to tempt each other. Because you're a natural temptress as well."

His deep laughter echoed between them. "I can honestly say I've never been called that."

She smiled. "But we can be friends, can't we?"

"We can certainly try."

Chapter 19

$\mathscr{B}$efore she'd left his study, he mentioned he'd be dining with his mum that night, so she didn't expect him at dinner, yet still, she missed him. In her bedchamber, she thought about what he'd taught her that afternoon, what he probably hadn't meant to teach her: he wanted her as much as she wanted him. But she understood his struggles with their attraction to each other, his need to be honorable. She admired him for them. She was going to strive very hard not to be a temptress, to develop a deep and abiding friendship with him. Perhaps when the ladies all left, things could go further between them.

As he was no longer giving her lessons, she had no reason to go to the library at ten, yet still she went, carrying his book with her. If he wasn't there, she would read.

Only he was there, as was her glass of sherry.

As he came to his feet, she was relatively certain she saw a measure of relief cross over his features for the briefest of moments. Or perhaps it was simply a reflection of what she felt, the joy that spiraled through her because he was here, quite possibly anticipating her arrival if the offering was any indication. "You knew I'd come."

"I'd *hoped* you'd come."

In this particular circumstance, she thought *hoping* was a good deal better than *knowing*. Hope involved wishes, desires, and wants. In some cases, even dreams.

She wandered over to her chair, sat, took pleasure from watching him fold his large body into the cushioned chair. It was rather relaxing knowing there would be no lesson, not wondering when it might begin or what it would entail. "How was your visit with your mother?"

"Enjoyable, as always. Too much food."

"Were your siblings there?"

"No. We all gather to be with her one Sunday a month and strive to ensure at least one of us has dinner with her during the week."

"It's good that you appreciate her, spend time with her. It's hard when they're no longer with us."

"I'm sorry you lost your mother."

She nodded, fought not to miss her, not to travel down a path of melancholy.

He shifted in his chair. "As I've been distracted of late, I've failed to let you know that Lady Jocelyn's father will pay Beth for her work."

"How did you manage that?"

He lifted a shoulder, tilted his head. "We had a little chat and he agreed it wouldn't do for word to get around London that he didn't honor his debts, especially as he's interested in investing in one of Mick's ventures."

"I'm so glad to hear that. Thank you for ensuring Beth didn't pay a price for her kindness."

"It was a simple enough matter to take care of."

She rather doubted that. She reached for her sherry. It was only then that she noticed the long, slender box secured with string resting beside it. Her gaze jumped to his.

"It's for you." His outstretched legs, his hands folded over his stomach, gave the impression he was relaxed, unconcerned. Yet, she also sensed a bit of tension in him, as though he feared her disappointment.

"I'll set it aside for Christmas, shall I?"

"It's not for Christmas. It's for now. Open it."

Her breath was a bit shaky when she reached for it, set it on her lap, and pulled on the string, watching as the bow disappeared. Lifting the lid, she smiled at the ivory kidskin gloves with exquisite stitching nestled inside the box. "They're gorgeous."

"I noticed your pair had a small hole."

Of course he'd noticed. He noticed everything. Purchasing her gloves had been another matter that had added to his recent absences. Taking out one, she drew it onto her hand, not at all surprised to find it fit perfectly, encasing her hand snugly. Once more she raised her gaze to his and found he now appeared completely at ease, and she wondered if he'd been worried she wouldn't like his gift. "Thank you."

His shrug was slight, barely enough movement to be noticed, as though he didn't know what to do with the appreciation cast his way. After removing the glove, she tucked it into the box, set it on the table, and wrapped her fingers around the stem of her sherry glass.

"I thought when I go in for my fitting tomorrow I would do some additional shopping, pick up a few other items my wardrobe is lacking." Gloves had been at the top of the list. "I want to take Hester with me, teach her how a maid accompanies her mistress."

"She'll enjoy that. I'll see about having Aiden's carriage made available to you, so it'll be easier to get about with all your packages."

"I appreciate it."

"Tell me what you think the other ladies would enjoy as an occupation."

"Flora, obviously gardening, since she already putters about here. I thought you could have your gardener teach her. Lottie has incredible taste in decor." She waved her hand to encompass the room. "These people who are gaining wealth could use someone to give their homes style. You could help her set up her business. Lily, Ruby, and Pearl would make excellent companions. I can teach them how to manage that."

"How long will that take?"

"No more than three months." She grinned. "You're going to pay that two thousand pounds."

"Money well spent."

She liked the easy camaraderie that had returned to them, halfway wished she had never asked him to teach her how to be a seductress. Before she came here, life had seemed so despairing, and she'd seen little hope for the future. Now it suddenly seemed filled with promise. "What will you do when the ladies are no longer . . . entertaining?"

"Jewel wants to turn this place into a boardinghouse, let rooms." His lips spread slowly into a smile, and she thought of other things he did slowly. "We'll have to hire Lottie to make all the rooms on the floor below more suitable to a permanent resident."

She imagined everything within them would need to be replaced. "The front parlor must be redone."

"It is rather gaudy."

"Risqué."

They settled into a comfortable silence. Deciding they'd exhausted all topics of conversation for now, she opened the book he'd written.

"My family will be gathering for Christmas."

Lifting her gaze, she gave him a soft smile. It was difficult to believe that Christmas would arrive the following Thursday. "How lovely for you."

"I'd like you to join us Christmas Eve."

Staring at him, she couldn't have been more stunned if he'd suddenly discarded all his clothing. "Half your family is now of the nobility. You can't possibly think the nobles would welcome me."

"For the ladies who reside here, Christmas Eve and into Christmas is the busiest time of the year. Men without families or sweethearts are lonely and seek comforting arms. Jewel provides a very welcoming atmosphere, more so than usual. Liquor flows. The women chat, dance, and flirt. And yes, they take men to bed. Seldom quietly. Do you really want to be upstairs, alone, listening to all the festivities?"

"I am scandalous, the daughter of a treasonous—"

"My siblings and I are all unlawful, no doubt the product of scandal. Those who married them created scandal by doing so. Thea, I doubt there is a drawing room in all of London where you would be more welcomed or feel more at home."

"Who all will be there?"

"Gillie and Thorne as the gathering is at their residence. Then Mick and Aslyn. Mick was the first of us our mum took in, so he's always been seen as the eldest and he's not shy about flaunting that role. Aiden and Selena, Finn and Lavinia, Fancy and Rosemont. Then there are the children. Mick, Finn, and Gillie each have a daughter. Aiden has a son. Gillie's babe is the eldest, close to eighteen months now, I think. Then there's an orphan lad named Robin whom we've all taken in. We don't know his actual age, but I'd put him at about ten. Loves anything to do with animals. He lives with Finn and Lavinia at their horse farm. Our mum will be there, of course."

"What if you're wrong and my presence brings you shame?"

"I would not have asked if I didn't want you there, if I didn't know of a certainty you'd be welcomed."

Everything about him was dark: his hair, his eyes, his skin burnished by the sun. And yet looking at him, she felt the light of hope. She nodded. "I would be honored to accompany you."

Chapter 20

*D*uring the nights that followed, when she stepped into the library, he was always there as was her glass of sherry, waiting for her. While they each held a book—a mere prop so they could pretend they'd come to read rather than spend time in the company of the other—the covers were never turned back, the pages never glanced at. Instead, they talked and shared stories and laughed.

She told him about her first pony. He told her about a mangy dog he'd had as a boy. The first time her father took her to the theater. The night he and his brothers had gone to a penny gaff. The naughty books she and Lady Jocelyn had read aloud to each other. The naughty ones he'd read silently to himself.

She could tell him anything and everything. And if they sometimes gazed into each other's eyes for a little too long, if want, need, and desire threatened to make themselves known, he was adept at breaking the spell by stirring the fire, or pouring more libations, or moving to stand by the fireplace. A couple of times he'd excused himself, claiming his unfinished manuscript was calling to him. But she'd known he hadn't trusted himself to honor his commitment not to take advantage, which only served to make her trust him all the more. She found herself desperately wishing he would gift her with a kiss, a caress, or a whispered endearment.

She had her fitting, impressed with the excellent work Beth had done. She and Hester went shopping, although she refrained from purchasing everything she wanted. Money was a commodity she no longer took for granted. She intended to hold on to as much of her winnings as possible.

Her frocks arrived on Tuesday, and on Wednesday, Hester spent a good part of the early afternoon assisting Althea in readying herself for spending Christmas Eve with Benedict. And his family. Of course, his family. They would be there. But they weren't the reason she was looking forward to the evening. He was.

She wanted to tempt him into breaking his blasted rule.

It was one of the reasons she'd bathed using the gardenia-scented French milled soap she'd purchased. The reason her new undergarments were made of satin, silk, and lace. The reason she'd rolled the stockings up her legs and placed her feet in the satin slippers for the first time.

Standing before the mirror in the red velvet gown, she hadn't realized how unflattering her daily frocks had been, not only because of the frays and mended tatters, but because they no longer hugged her curves as closely as she was hoping Benedict's hands might when they returned home tonight from his sister's.

Pressing her fingers to the hollow at her throat, she did wish she had a necklace to wear. Not having the jewelry to break things up, it was quite an open expanse of skin from her chin to the swell of her breasts. While she missed having pearl combs for her hair, she couldn't fault the fine job Hester had done with the red ribbons Althea had purchased, turning them into little bows that covered the pins holding back the strands of her hair from her face, leaving them to flow in curls down her back.

"Caw, he's going to fall in love with you tonight, and what a fine Christmas present that would be."

She wasn't quite certain how to respond to Hester's declaration, hoped her increasing feelings for Benedict weren't written all over her face. Perhaps the *he* she was referring to wasn't even Benedict. "I'm certain I have no notion as to what you're talking about."

Hester laughed, a light tinkling. "I'm certain you do."

Althea gave the perfect imitation of a haughty duchess. "A maid does not contradict her lady."

"Oops. I forgot that rule."

Althea could see the young woman's smile reflected in the cheval glass. She hadn't forgotten anything. "Don't be cheeky."

But her tone lacked any sort of admonishment.

A light rap sounded on the door. Benedict had come for her. While Hester went off to answer it, Althea picked up her reticule in which she was carrying the gifts she'd made for the members of his family. She'd worked on them diligently every morning and late at night after she and Benedict parted ways in the library. She could seldom sleep until her skin stopped tingling from the gazes he gave her.

"Oh, he's not going to half fall in love with you tonight."

Not Benedict. Jewel.

"I told her almost the same thing," Hester said, plopping down in the chair as though her work was done. For all practical purposes, it was.

She decided against responding to Jewel's comment because if she couldn't fool Hester, she most certainly couldn't fool Jewel. "Do you know if he's ready?"

"He's waiting in the foyer."

"Then I should probably be off." She took a step.

"Before you go . . ."

Althea stopped, met the gaze of a woman Lady Althea never would have given a passing glance. She arched a brow.

"These were my mum's pearls." She held out her hand, unfolded her fingers to reveal a necklace. "I've never worn them when I'm working. I only bring them out on special occasions. I thought tonight you might like to wear them. They'd look awfully nice with that gown."

"Oh, Jewel." She was so deeply touched. "What if I lose or break them?"

"You're not going to do that, pet. It would mean a lot to me if you would wear them." Her smile was a bit impish. "Then I can boast that they've been inside a duke's residence."

Her throat had grown so tight she wasn't certain she could speak, so she merely nodded and turned to face the mirror. Jewel draped the necklace around her neck, secured it, patted her shoulder. "There."

"It's beautiful, Jewel. It really sets off the gown."

"It'll draw his gaze to that fine cleavage you're displaying so enticingly."

She squeezed her eyes shut, even as she laughed and shook her head. The madam was too forthright with her comments, even if there was truth to them. She gave her a hard hug. "Thank you, Jewel, for so much."

"Anytime, pet."

"Hester, if you'll help me with my cloak."

"Oh, no," Jewel said. "You need to descend those stairs wearing naught but what you have on now. Hester, you carry her wrap and put it on her in the foyer after he's gotten a good eyeful."

She had no reason to be nervous as she descended the stairs. She was simply going out for a nice evening with a gentleman she liked very much. So many people would be there, they'd probably have very little time to actually be together. She'd once had no trouble at all carrying on conversations with strangers. If his family didn't welcome her, she would adapt.

She was halfway down the final flight of stairs when she came to an abrupt halt as his gaze slammed into hers. It wasn't so much the heat in his eyes as it was every aspect of him. She'd given so much thought to how she wanted to look for him tonight that she'd given no thought at all to how he might look for her.

Gorgeous was too paltry a word. As were *striking* and *magnificent*, but still they all ran through her mind in rapid succession.

He'd trimmed his hair. Half an inch. Strange that she knew him so well she could discern the slightest changes in him. He was wearing proper evening attire: his black trousers fitted, his black double-breasted tailcoat unbuttoned, hanging open to reveal the white silk waistcoat. His snowy shirt was pristine. His light gray neck cloth was perfectly knotted. His outercoat was draped over one arm, his hand holding his black hat. It was obvious he had an incredibly skilled tailor. He could stride into any aristocratic ballroom, and no one would question his right to be there.

"Breathe," Jewel whispered behind her, and only then did she realize she'd ceased doing so.

She continued down until she was standing before him, basking in the appreciation warming his eyes.

"You take my breath," he said quietly.

"That's only fair. You took mine."

She smiled. He grinned.

"Thorne sent a carriage," he told her, "so we should be off."

IN THE CARRIAGE, she sat opposite Beast, a fur blanket draped over her lap, her slippered feet resting near the footwarmer. She'd offered to share the warmth with him, invited him to sit beside her, but his skin already felt like it was on fire, a fire that could only be doused by tumbling her. On a bed, on a settee, in a carriage.

Why he continued to put the temptation of her within easy reach was beyond him.

When he'd first caught sight of her, he'd been able to easily envision her descending stairs at a fancy ball. Everything about her screamed nobility. It wasn't the exquisite gown or the styled hair. It was something deeper, something inside her, something that had been passed down through the centuries. They might have taken her father's titles, but they couldn't take from her what she was destined to be: a lady of the highest caliber.

And for tonight at least, she was on his arm.

She'd already mastered seduction with the ease with which one mastered waking up. It came to her naturally. With the soft smile she bestowed upon him whenever she first saw him, the warm welcome that sparkled in her eyes, the light blush that washed over her cheeks as though she was remembering what it felt like to have his hands cupping her breasts.

The evenings they shared in the library were both bliss and hell. To have her presence, her scent, her voice telling tales. But to not touch those lips, caress her skin, have her pressed against his throbbing cock . . . to know that eventually her plans would lead her away from him—

He didn't inhabit the world from which she wanted to select a lover. Unlike his brothers, he'd never had a desire to move about in it, to be accepted by it. He wouldn't be welcomed into it now.

Each night after they parted ways, as he lay in his bed alone staring at the shadows dancing over the ceiling, he was tempted to return to her. *You want to be some man's mistress? Be mine.*

He had the means to purchase her a residence, more gowns than she'd have occasion to wear, jewelry that would dazzle. He could provide her with servants, a carriage, anything else she wanted. His shipping business had given him a foundation upon which he'd begun building an empire. He'd amassed a modest fortune. If he never earned another farthing, the interest alone would see him in good stead into his dotage. Presently, he used it to support good works but could use it to acquire her—but if she had him, she couldn't have the prestige of having a lord as her protector. Would she give it up for him? Was it fair of him to ask her to? To settle for a commoner, a bastard, when she could have a man of rank and privilege?

"I assume they know I'm coming." The tiniest thread of doubt, perhaps even nervousness, laced itself through her voice.

"They do."

"Do they know the truth of me?"

"They know the truth of your father. I saw no reason to keep it secret when those who have married into the family might have recognized your name or you. I thought it best to avoid any awkwardness that might come about if they were taken by surprise."

She was lost in the shadows, but he suspected if he reached across, he'd find her gloved hands knotted in her lap.

"Thea, it'll be just a couple of hours of trimming a tree, drinking some really good wine and scotch, enjoying a delicious dinner, and then we'll leave. If you enjoy yourself tonight, you're welcome to join me tomorrow when I go over for a few hours to exchange gifts and have another fine meal."

"The only other gown I have is the red one designed for seduction, although I'm not really certain there is enough of it to qualify it as a gown. If I join you tomorrow, I'd have to wear it."

He could tell a part of her was teasing, and another part was striving to come up with an acceptable excuse not to join him on the morrow. He didn't want to contemplate how much less he'd enjoy the day without her there. "When are you going to show it to me?"

"I don't know that I am. Truly, she could have used a bit more fabric. Although it is quite lovely."

He'd like to see her in it. But then he'd also like to see her out of it. "It might not be what you want to wear tomorrow. One of the other frocks will suffice."

"It's so nice to have choices again. Thank you for providing the clothes."

I could provide you with everything hung on the tip of his tongue. But now was not the time. It might never be.

"We're in Mayfair," she said quietly, gazing out the window. "I know which residence belongs to the Duke of Thornley but have never been inside."

"Where did you reside when you lived in the area?"

"If I tell you, you might be tempted to take us by it. I don't want to see it. Returning is harder than I thought it would be."

"We can go back to the residence if you like."

"That would be unfair to your family. I'm certain they're looking forward to having your presence this evening. I'll push forward. Tonight will be a test to see if I'm ready to face the demons of my past."

AS THEY ENTERED the residence, the scent of evergreen hung heavy in the air, no doubt because of all the boughs and garlands that decorated the wide sweeping stairway.

"The duke and duchess are in the parlor," a liveried footman announced as he took Benedict's hat and coat and her cloak.

When Benedict offered his arm, she didn't hesitate to take it before they made their way to the huge room just off the marbled foyer. Once they entered, they stopped and simply absorbed it all. Sprigs of evergreen decorated various tables, garlands draped the mantelpiece. At the far end, on a small table, stood a fir tree.

Throughout the room, people were gathered in little groups talking. His family. Some held babies, jostling them in their arms. While she'd known how many to expect, it was a bit overwhelming to see them all. Or perhaps it was the memories of the cool and distant gatherings in her family's parlor flooding her mind that had her feeling as though she was drowning and had her tightening her hold on his arm. Or maybe it was her fear that he'd been wrong, and they would indeed all turn their backs on her—or at least the ones who had known her father, her mother, her brothers, herself.

He rubbed his gloved hand over hers, where it rested on his arm. "All will be well."

Looking up at him, she forced herself to smile. How many times might he have experienced the same trepidation, all because of his birth?

"You've arrived!" a tall, slender woman announced, quickly crossing over to them. Her red hair, cut shorter than Benedict's, framed her face. "Just in time to help us trim the tree."

Althea didn't know if she'd ever seen a more welcoming smile. She had to release her hold on Benedict as the Duchess of Thornley's arms went around him, his around her.

When they separated, she immediately took Althea's hands, squeezed. "Althea, we're so glad you could join us. I'm Gillie."

"I'm very honored to have been invited, Your Grace."

She smiled once again. "We don't stand on formality here. I believe you know Thorne."

The duke had come up to stand behind his wife, and without even turning, she'd known he was there. Just as anytime when Althea walked into the room, no matter how engrossed Benedict was in his book, he seemed to sense her presence and come to his feet.

"Hello, Althea. You're looking well," Thorne said.

She had to admit that since moving into the brothel, she was feeling better. Abundant food, warmth, and shelter had benefits, although she suspected she could attribute more of her well-being to the man standing beside her. "Thank you. You as well."

"How do your brothers fare?"

"Well, as far as I know. I haven't heard from them recently."

"Well, we're glad you're here."

"And to that end"—Gillie entwined her arm around Althea's—"let me introduce you around."

With Benedict following, she led her over to where Aiden stood with his wife, the former Duchess of Lushing.

"We've met," Aiden said before Gillie could speak.

"Oh?" Selena said. "At the Elysium?"

He grinned. "No, the Cerberus. She made out like a highwayman."

Her cheeks warmed. "I had a little help I think."

"Nothing wrong with a little help when it serves a greater good."

Selena reached out and squeezed her hand. "I'm glad you could join us."

Finn and Lavinia were next. She couldn't help but think that in some ways Finn and Aiden resembled each other.

Once introductions were made and greetings exchanged, Lavinia smiled at Benedict. "Thank you for all the dolls and wooden soldiers you sent. Tomorrow morning two hundred children are going to be overjoyed."

"Two hundred children?" Althea asked.

"They have a children's home at their horse farm," Benedict said quietly.

And he'd provided the children with toys. She'd have never

known if she'd not come here tonight, and she wondered what else he did for which he neither sought nor received any credit.

"This is Robin," Finn said, placing his hand on top of the dark head of a lad with mischievous brown eyes, who looked as though he was holding secrets he was dying to share.

"Hello, Robin," she said. "I hear you like animals."

"I love animals. Have you been to the zoological gardens?"

"It's been a while, but, yes, I have."

"It's my favorite place in the whole world."

"That makes it very special, then, doesn't it?"

He bobbed his head.

After introducing Althea to Mick and Aslyn, as well as Fancy and Rosemont, Gillie excused herself, and Benedict escorted Althea to a chair where a small woman with dark hair streaked with silver sat, a sleeping child nestled in her arms. When they arrived, he bent and kissed the cheek the woman had tilted up toward him. "Hello, Mum."

"Hello, lad. Sorry I can't stand, but I don't want to wake the little one. She was having a time of it earlier."

"That's all right. Better to have Gillie's babe sleeping than crying. I'd like to introduce you to Thea."

Her smile was a wreath of happiness. "What a joy it is to meet you."

"I'm honored to make your acquaintance, Mrs. Trewlove. Your son is a remarkable man."

"I can't argue with you there. But then they all make me proud." Looking up at Benedict, she gave her chin a little jerk. "Move that chair a bit closer so your lass can sit, and we can have a nice chat."

"She's not my lass."

"I'm not his lass."

They'd spoken at the same time, their eyes clashed, and she could see that his cheeks had gone a ruddy hue. If the heat scoring her face was any indication, hers had as well.

"The chair, lad," his mother insisted.

He shoved a chair nearer, and Althea sat.

"Off with you," Mrs. Trewlove ordered her son.

She could tell he was hesitant to leave her. "I'll be fine."

"You don't have to answer any questions you don't want to." Reluctantly, he walked away.

"Now, tell me everything about yourself," Mrs. Trewlove urged.

A QUEUE OF nannies arrived to take the babes to the nursery. The tree-trimming was well underway. Beast had assisted at first, but eventually, when he'd realized his proximity to the tree didn't allow him to overhear whatever his mum and Thea were discussing, he'd excused himself, sought out some scotch, and took a strategic location near the fireplace. He still couldn't hear them, but from his new vantage point, he could at least see Thea's face clearly, watch her expressions, and discern if or when he needed to step in to stop the interrogation. Thus far, she'd laughed three times, smiled eight, nodded repeatedly, revealed two things at length—based on how long she'd spoken without interruption. Her shoulders, a good bit of them bared, were relaxed, her hands covered in the gloves he'd given her floated through the air when she spoke, twice seeming to be emphasizing some important point she was making.

"Kissed her yet, guv?"

With a quick exhale, he glanced down at Robin. A time had existed when he would have crouched in order not to lord himself over the boy. But he'd gained some inches and now reached the center of his chest. He wondered if he was older than they'd assumed. "Can you keep a secret, young Robin?"

The lad bobbed his head. "Aye."

"I have indeed kissed her."

Robin's eyes widened as though it was the first time anyone had ever made such a confession in response to his oft-asked question. "What was it like?"

He turned his attention back to Thea. With delight, she was listening intently to whatever tale his mum was spouting. How to do justice to a description of her kiss? All the words in his vocabulary seemed inadequate, incapable of fully revealing the power of it, the way it had made him feel. "It was as vast as the oceans, as infinite as the stars."

Silence greeted his declaration. He looked down. Robin's brow was deeply furrowed, his brown eyes troubled, his mouth twisted.

"What does that mean?" the lad finally asked.

"It means I had a jolly good time doing it."

His eyes brightened and his grin was broad enough to guide seafarers to shore. "Caw. That makes her the best, then, don't it?"

"*Doesn't* it," he corrected. "And, yes, she is the best." He didn't need a qualifier to identify what she was best at. *The best,* all by itself, applied to her.

"Robin," Gillie called out, "time to put the star on top of the tree."

The lad dashed off, gangly arms and legs flying. He was going to be a tall one when everything evened out. But he wasn't yet tall enough to reach the top of the tree resting upon the table. After setting his tumbler on the mantel, Beast ambled over to where Robin was hopping foot to foot. "Ready?" he asked him.

The boy nodded with enthusiasm. Beast placed his hands at Robin's waist and lifted him onto his shoulders. Gillie offered the star. Robin took it, leaned forward, and placed it on the top of the tree. Beast set him back on the floor. As Gillie began lighting the candles resting on branches, he wandered over to where Thea stood at the back of the gathering, a little away from it, not part of it.

"Did you enjoy your visit with my mum?"

"I did. She's full of love, your mum. It just spills out and you can feel it touching you. If your mother had to leave you in someone's keeping, I think she chose well."

ONCE ALL THE candles were lit, *ah*s and claps sounded. The married men lowered their heads and brushed light kisses over their wives' mouths. Althea wondered if she should have lifted hers to Benedict. If he'd been looking at her, she might have but he seemed to find the star of more interest.

Gillie gave her hands two quick pats, the clap echoing around them. "We have about an hour before dinner, and Aiden has some sort of project he wants us to participate in. Aiden?"

He stepped forward. "It'll take a bit of time to accomplish, so fetch a lovely libation and make yourselves comfortable while I set up things."

She and Benedict wandered over to a corner where a footman poured a sherry for her and a scotch for him. With glasses in hand, they'd taken only a few steps away when Fancy and the Earl of Rosemont stopped them.

"I meant to tell you," Fancy said to her brother, "the books you wanted arrived. We brought them with us in case you want to take them."

"I will. Thank you."

"What is the name of your bookshop?" Althea asked.

The young woman smiled. "The Fancy Book Emporium."

"A play on your name. How clever."

With a light laugh she affectionately patted her husband's arm. "Everyone understood that except him. He declared I'd forgotten the apostrophe and S."

"It's where we met," Rosemont explained. "In my defense, I wasn't quite myself at the time. I didn't want her to be clever."

"He was taking a sabbatical from women, didn't want to be intrigued by me."

Althea smiled at Rosemont. Had danced with him on occasion. "But you were."

"I was indeed. Sometimes when life puts us on a path we don't necessarily want to travel, we discover it was a journey we needed to take in order to secure happiness. Perhaps like me, you'll find yourself richer because of the rough road you're now on. Mine led me to the love of my life."

Fancy snuggled against his side, and his arm went protectively around her. "He can be so poetic at times. It's only one of the reasons I love him."

A shrill whistle rent the air. "We're about to get started," Aiden yelled.

"Oops! We'd better go." Fancy took her husband's hand and began leading him toward a sofa.

Benedict placed his hand on the small of her back. "They've not been married long. Still in the first blush of love."

She looked up at him. "Do you think it'll fade?"

He shook his head. "No."

His answer, his belief in the sustainability of love, made her chest tighten as they made their way to a settee and settled into place beside each other. But then how could he not believe when each husband was either holding his wife's hand or had his arm protectively around her shoulders, when each wife was nestled against her husband?

The furniture was arranged in a horseshoe shape, with Aiden standing in front of what appeared to be an easel. Only its legs were visible because a cloth covered whatever was on it.

"All right," he announced, "we are to begin." With a great flourish, he whipped off the draping to reveal a large canvas upon which was written TREWLOVE in what appeared to be pencil, possibly charcoal.

"Not one of your better pieces of artwork," Benedict said.

"Because it is not yet finished. We have the canvas"—he pointed to it—"the palette with assorted colors"—he held it up—"and the brush." The last he swiped dashingly through the air as though it was a sword and he upon a stage battling pirates.

"He's always enjoyed performing," Benedict said sotto voce, and she wished he was whispering other things, more romantic things, in her ear. He wasn't holding her hand, but his arm was resting along the back of the settee, a finger lazily tracing a small circle over the flesh just below the sleeve of her gown, and she wondered if he was even aware of the action.

"No disrespect to those who have married into the family," Aiden continued, "but only those originally named Trewlove will be participating. Each of you, in turn, will come up and paint one of the letters. We shall create a nice display of our name. Mum, you're up first. Come paint the T."

"Oh my. I didn't know I was going to start." She pushed herself out of her chair and walked over to him. "What if I mess it up?"

"I'll guide you. If we make a mess, I can fix it."

"All right, then."

"What color?"

"My favorite. Blue."

He dabbed the brush at the palette before handing it to his mother. Then he stepped behind her, wrapped his hand around hers, and helped her to slowly trace the letter. "Perfect," he said when they were finished.

Mrs. Trewlove was beaming when she returned to the winged chair.

"Now we go in the order in which we arrived. Mick."

"Orange," he announced as he crossed over to his brother.

He was done in a tick and headed back to his place beside Aslyn, who smiled at him as though he'd just conquered the world.

"I'm next," Aiden said. "I'm going with purple because that's the color of the gown my lovely wife was wearing when I first met her." He moved his arm as though he was stroking a violin.

By the time he was finished, Finn was already standing there. The brothers exchanged a few quiet words and a grin.

"They resemble each other so much," she whispered.

"They have the same father."

She jerked her gaze to him, a question in her eyes.

"The Earl of Elverton," he said quietly.

She'd never liked the man. It was no secret that his unfaithfulness to his wife included multiple affairs at the same time.

"Beast, L is yours."

He shoved himself to his feet, and she found herself desperately missing his touch. She watched his graceful, powerful strides. How was it that so simple a movement, a movement common to most, seemed extraordinary when performed by him? It had the ability to addle her mind, still her breath, cause her heart to drum a little faster. At that moment she knew if Father Christmas existed and was to grant her one gift for Christmas, she would ask for a waltz with Benedict Trewlove.

Slowly, he outlined the L in red, and she wondered if the shade of her gown had influenced him at all.

Once he was headed back, Gillie stood. "This is taking too long. Come along, Fancy."

With arms locked, the sisters marched forward, took their turns with the O and the V, and returned to their husbands' sides with no fanfare. Trust a woman to get on with things. Only the final E remained unpainted.

Aiden eyed them all as though each was responsible for some nefarious act. Then he looked back at his canvas. "Well, I didn't plan that very well now, did I? You can't have Trewlove without an e at the end and we've run out of original Trewloves to paint it."

"It seems to me," Mick said, "that what we need to do is find someone who has only one name. I just don't know who—"

"I have only one name," Robin piped up. He was sitting on the floor, nestled between Gillie's and Lavinia's feet.

"Are you sure about that, lad?" Aiden asked.

"I should hope I know my own name. It's just Robin, nothing else."

"Well, isn't that a lucky coincidence," Gillie said.

Finn slid off the sofa and knelt, making himself nearly eye level with the boy. Althea realized she'd made a dreadful mistake when shopping for her wardrobe. She'd failed to purchase a handkerchief and feared during the next few minutes she was going to be in desperate need of one.

"Would you like to be a Trewlove, lad?" Finn asked gently.

The boy nodded with so much force that his hair flopped against his forehead. "Caw! Would I? It's the best name ever."

"Shall we make him a Trewlove?" Aiden asked. "Everyone in favor raise a hand."

Not only the original Trewloves voted, but so did everyone

who sat beside them. Althea shot her hand up so fast she likely hurt her shoulder.

"Well, Robin Trewlove, come give us our final E," Aiden announced.

The boy jumped up and dashed over to the easel. As he painstakingly painted the E, a different color for each line, Althea turned to Benedict, who was little more than a blur through the veil of tears she'd been unable to blink into submission. "Did you know that's where this *project* was headed?"

As he handed her his linen handkerchief, he slowly nodded. "Finn and Lavinia wanted to give Robin our name, asked our permission, and since we were all in agreement, we wanted to do it in a way that let him know he was part of all of us."

She dabbed at her eyes, at the tears. Such a simple gesture and yet its impact couldn't be measured, would change the manner in which the boy viewed himself. She might possibly never have another moment like this, of sharing in the giving of a gift that had not cost a single penny but was still more valuable than gold.

As she sat there clutching the linen of a remarkably generous man, surrounded by the members of his incredibly kind and thoughtful family, she didn't know why happiness rested in returning to Society, why she had put such value on its embrace.

If she became another man's mistress, she would likely never see Benedict again, would most certainly never be alone with him again. She would have no more evenings of sitting in a library and talking. No more moments of discovering yet another facet of this layered, complicated man.

"Well done," Aiden announced, and she glanced over to see that Robin had finished painting the E and was wearing a broad smile that had to be causing his jaw to ache. "When the canvas is dry, we'll frame it and you can hang it in your bedchamber, so you don't forget you're a Trewlove now."

"I won't forget," Robin said with such earnestness that Althea had to use the linen once again. "Ever."

As Robin strutted back to his place, she couldn't help but believe that any woman Benedict took to wife would emanate the
same sort of pride at sharing his name.

"Oh, look, it's snowing," Gillie suddenly announced.

"Coming down quite heavily as a matter of fact," Thorne added.

"Mum, Finn, and Lavinia were already planning to stay the
night. Everyone else must stay as well. We have ample room."

"Gillie, we didn't bring any clothes with us," Fancy said.

"Wear tomorrow what you're wearing tonight. Your safety is
more important than changing your frock. When you retire, you
can borrow one of my nightdresses. I have plenty to go around.
Think of the poor horses, drivers, and footmen going out in this.
And what if it's so thick on the streets tomorrow that you can't
join us?"

Althea paid no heed to the myriad voices over her shoulder
as the others discussed the consequences of their options. Her
gaze had returned to Benedict's as though she needed confirmation that he'd not melted away, but was real, had never been only
a dream.

"Do you want to remain or leave?" he asked quietly.

"They're your family. The choice should be yours."

"Are you comfortable being among them?"

They were like being wrapped in a warm blanket on a cold
day. "Yes."

"We'll stay then, shall we?"

Chapter 21

*A*lthea lay in the bed, in a nightdress that fairly swallowed her since her hostess was several inches taller than she was, staring at the window where distant streetlamps or garden lamps provided just enough light to reveal that big fat snowflakes continued to fall as the wind whistled eerily beyond the glass.

Everyone had decided to stay, and the remainder of the night had seen a good bit of alcohol consumed following a sumptuous dinner. Robin Trewlove had eaten with them, but afterward he and Mrs. Trewlove had gone up to bed. Althea had been concerned that an awkwardness between her and the ladies might settle in when the gentlemen went off to have their port, but this family apparently didn't follow the tradition of giving men their time alone. Everyone had headed to the billiards room where Selena had soundly beaten Aiden three times.

At one point, when Althea was sitting on a sofa with Benedict, watching Aiden's thrashing, Thorne had wandered over and crouched before them. "I was wondering if you might have any ships heading to South America in the near future."

"What do you need from South America?"

"A toucan."

"What the deuce is a toucan?"

"Colorful bird with a large beak."

"What the devil is Robin going to do with a toucan?"

"What the devil does he do with the massive tortoise I gave him?"

Benedict had sighed, but it had lacked any true irritation for what was certain to be an inconvenience for one of his captains. "I can probably arrange something."

Thorne had winked at her. "It pays to have a brother-by-marriage with ships."

After Thorne walked away, she'd asked, "How did you know the toucan was for Robin?"

"Because he's always giving Robin animals. Tomorrow morning it will be a spaniel."

The camaraderie among the siblings was unlike anything she'd ever known. They knew so much about each other. They'd exchanged stories, laughed, teased each other. They'd included the spouses. They'd included her.

What she had enjoyed most was watching Benedict's interactions with the others. Mrs. Trewlove had told her that Finn had always been the most sensitive, Beast the most contemplative. All the times in the beginning when he'd merely watched her, she now realized was simply his way. While his siblings argued and debated, he merely listened, sorting things. When he did finally contribute, his words were usually met with, "Knew you'd have the answer." Or, "Knew you could make them see sense."

Observing their exchanges, she understood they'd shared secrets, sorrows, hurts, successes, and failures. They didn't judge each other. They accepted each other as they were.

She kept running the entire evening through her mind, recounting conversations, reexamining moments that had made her laugh or smile or tear up. As long as she focused on the past, even if it was only a few hours past, she wasn't reminded that Benedict was presently in the bedchamber adjoining hers.

"I saw a flash of panic on your face when I suggested everyone stay the night," Gillie had told her, "so I thought you would be more comfortable sleeping in the bedchamber adjoining Beast's. You can always ring for a servant, naturally, if you're in need of anything, but I wanted you to have reassurance he's near."

In her parents' home, bachelors slept in a wing separate from the one in which unmarried ladies slept. Never would they have been within easy reach of each other. Her mother would be appalled to know Althea had counted the steps from the bed to the door that led into his room, that she was now listening for any sound, any indication he was still awake. That she was hoping he might be on the other side straining to hear any sounds coming from her.

Perhaps it was all the wine now coursing through her veins or the love this family showered on each other or simply a need not to be alone on Christmas Eve—

She nearly laughed aloud at the realization she might be no different than the men who would be spending their night with Jewel, Hester, Lottie . . . men without families, men without someone to love them. Tonight she'd experienced something finer than what she'd always dreamed her future would hold. But she knew it could contain so much more.

If she was willing to take those eleven steps, knock on a door, and make a complicated mistake.

WITH HIS HANDS shoved beneath his head, Beast stared at the ceiling and cursed Gillie for the hundredth time.

Every time his errant gaze fell on the door, he thought, *Three steps, four; that's all it would take to be there.*

It wasn't as though each night, at some point before he finally managed to force sleep upon himself, he didn't consider knocking on her door. But it was easier to resist the temptation when her bedchamber wasn't right next to his, when he didn't think he could smell the scent of gardenia—surely it was his imagination. Her fragrance couldn't be slipping in beneath the door.

It had been a mistake to bring her here, to see how easily she fit in with his family, how *right* she looked sitting with his mum, how much he had enjoyed having her near, how much more special the moment when they'd given Robin their name had been because she'd shared it with him. Years from now when they looked back on it, when he recalled the tears in her eyes—

Except years from now *they* wouldn't look back on it, they wouldn't reminisce. It would be only him, alone. Because he couldn't imagine another woman coming into his life whom he would want more than he wanted her—and if a person couldn't have what he wanted most in the world, could he find happiness with less?

She didn't want marriage. She wanted Society on her terms, notoriously, scandalously, infamously. Oh, certainly he could take her to Gillie's balls and Fancy's, but that wouldn't be what she wanted most in the world. Could she find happiness with the *less* he could offer her?

Why was he even debating this? Because it stopped him from thinking of her lying in the bed—

The rap on the door was soft, but it caused everything within him to immediately freeze as though he was the prey realizing he was in danger of being spotted by the hunter. Maybe it was wishful thinking on his part, because surely she would not—

The rap came again, a trifle louder. Something had to be wrong. She wouldn't seek him out otherwise. Perhaps her room had caught fire.

Rolling out of bed, he snatched up his trousers from the chair, drew them on, and buttoned them up. On bare feet, he padded to the door and quietly opened it only a sliver in case he'd misheard.

Only he hadn't. She was standing there, appearing vulnerable, with Gillie's nightdress billowing around her, the hem pooled at her feet. Her hair had been plaited and hung over her shoulder. He had a strong urge to unravel it.

"My fire has gone out," she whispered.

"Ah." Nothing on fire in her bedchamber, no fire at all. The disappointment that she'd come to him to help with a chore was stronger than he would have liked. "I'll stir it back to life for you."

"No." She gripped his forearm, her fingers digging in with a firmness that signaled something akin to desperation. "I thought I could share yours."

"My fire?" he asked cautiously. Did she mean to curl up in the chair before it?

"And your bed, beneath the blankets where it's warm and snuggly."

His heart thudded against his chest with such force he was surprised the residence didn't shake. "Thea, I have the ability to resist temptation only so far. If you come in here, if you're nestled in my bed, it's going to result in a rather large mistake being made."

"I know. But I'm not under your roof tonight, not yours to protect."

He slammed his eyes closed. She understood the ramifications, what would happen between them, and still she was here. And if her fire had really gone out, why were shadows dancing around her room?

"As you've pointed out, something can always be learned from a mistake."

He heard the uncertainty edging her voice, the embarrassment that she had come to his door and he might deny her entry. But doing so would be the equivalent of turning his back on her, causing her hurt, giving her doubts. He could no more do that than he could stop the sun from coming over the horizon.

Yes, it would be a mistake, but he could limit the damage done, ensure it wasn't as great a blunder as it had the potential to be. He could leave her virginity intact, so she didn't pay too high a price for coming to him, so she would still have the option of becoming a wife instead of a courtesan. He opened the door farther.

To avoid the possibility of tripping, she began gathering up the flannel. "Your sister is taller than I." Was that nervousness that made her voice warble just a bit?

"She's taller than most women." Than some men.

When her toes were visible, she stepped over the threshold. He closed the door with a quiet *snick* and approached her, where she had come to a stop near the foot of the bed. "We can solve the problem of the cumbersomely large nightdress easily enough."

She was still clutching the folds of cloth. Gently, he brushed her hands aside and began gathering the material, his large hands more effective than hers had been. When he had enough of it, he drew it up over her head and tossed it onto the nearby chair.

His breath hitched at the sight of her revealed. She was beautiful. From head to toe. Delicate. Slender. Like blown glass. Yet, she possessed a steeliness that reassured him he wouldn't break her.

The drapes were drawn, no lamp was lit. The fire provided the only light. At the mercy of the writhing flames, the shadows ebbed and flowed over her pale skin. While he longed for more light—from a lamp, the gaslight, the sun—he wanted the near darkness that muted flaws and added mystery to what was about to transpire.

He took her plaited hair in hand, held her gaze, and slowly began unraveling it.

Her hands came to rest against his chest, a tentative touch. "I've wondered what you look like beneath your clothing." She trailed her fingers over his ribs slowly as though counting each one. "I assume working the docks was responsible for shaping a good bit of you. You're so firm, so taut."

His task done, he combed his fingers through the long, silken strands he'd set free. "You're so soft."

Bringing his hands around, he cradled the underside of her jaw against the edge of his palms, tilted up her face, and claimed her mouth for his own.

THE KISS WAS not a gentle thing. It was wild and hungry from too many nights of abstinence. The fever of it grew when his hands glided over her back, pushing her forward so her bare breasts flattened against his bare chest. She moaned low at the silkiness, the heat, the intimacy. How many women knew the glorious sensation of their skin touching his?

He towered over her. She should have felt small, a shrub in the shadow of a mighty oak. Instead, she felt powerful, more in control than she'd ever been. They were giving and taking in equal measure. While his experience far exceeded hers, he gave her no cause to believe he found her any less pleasing than she found him.

While his mouth moved provocatively over hers, she glided her hands up over his shoulders, kneading the hard muscles that bunched and relaxed as his hands swept down the length of her back to finally close over her buttocks and squeeze. She rose up on her toes and took her hands higher, up the tense cords of his neck—

His fingers closed over one of her hands and he carried it down to the front of his trousers, cupping it against the hard bulge that was an aphrodisiac to her senses. If size was any indication, he wanted her badly. Groaning low, never taking his mouth from hers, he guided her hand up the lengthy shaft and down.

"Unbutton me," he rasped against her lips before reclaiming the mouth he'd temporarily deserted.

Her other hand joining the first, she set herself to the task. Her fingers trembled not from fear, but from excitement. When his cock sprang free, the heat of it surprised her, as did the silkiness. She glided both hands along its length, his groan nearly feral in its intensity.

"Halt." He sounded as though he were on the cusp of dying.

She did as he bade. He shoved down his trousers, kicked them off to the side, reached for her—

"Halt," she ordered.

He did, his breathing harsh and heavy. The firelight was at his back, giving her a view of him that was largely lost to shadows. "I want to see you more clearly."

Taking his hand, she turned them, so they traded places, and he was more fully revealed to her. The orange light danced over his skin, highlighting the contours of muscle, the flatness of his stomach, a hideous raised welt at his side. She touched her fingers to the mottled scar. "How did you come to have this?"

"Knife."

Which told her very little. "Did someone attack you?"

"It was a long time ago. It doesn't hurt."

But it had at one time. It was three or four inches long. It looked angry, and her own anger ignited with the knowledge that someone had wished him harm, that he might have been taken from her before she'd ever even had an opportunity to know him. "Why?"

"It's not important, and it's certainly not conducive to seduction."

Determined to know the answer, she lifted her gaze to his. "Why would someone want to hurt you like this?"

He released a long, drawn-out sigh, obviously coming to the conclusion that she wasn't going to let this matter go. "I'd taken from him his doxies, let rooms for them so they could work in relative safety, and kept watch over them. He took exception to my meddling."

She had little doubt one of those doxies had been Sally Greene. "I hope you saw to it that he regretted hurting you."

"I believe it's safe to assume he did come to regret it."

Lowering herself to a crouch, she kissed one end of the ragged line where a knife had torn into his flesh, the center of it, the other end. With each touch of her lips, she felt a quiver go through him, saw the tight muscles in his stomach jump. "I hate that anyone ever hurt you."

He cradled the back of her head. "Wounds of the flesh heal much easier than wounds of the heart. If it was possible, I would take upon myself the pain others have inflicted on you."

She didn't know if anyone had ever uttered sweeter words to her, but she wouldn't wish upon him what she had suffered—and if it was possible he could take her pain, she wouldn't allow it because it would bring her greater agony to know he endured any sort of torment.

Now she wondered if what had destroyed her mother wasn't the pain of her father's betrayal but a greater pain of knowing what her children would suffer and realizing she could do nothing to lessen it.

His large hand closed around the back of her slender neck, and he urged her to her feet, so he could once more blanket her mouth. Here, she thought, was the danger of being intimate with a man. Clothing provided a sort of armor, and when it was removed, things were revealed that one might never guess at. She now knew things about him that few people probably did. That his body was a sculpted marvel, like a living statue. That his impressive cock throbbed when pressed against a belly. That he had a scar, and she knew its story. He'd have never told her the tale if she'd not seen the scar. Because of all this, she felt closer to him than she ever had.

His mouth still clinging to hers, he lifted her up, cradled her in his arms, and carried her the two steps to the bed. It was a silly thing to be delighted by, when she could have gotten there easily on her own, but something in the action spoke of tenderness, of wanting to ensure she felt special. Just as he continued to stand when she walked into a room.

He laid her on the rumpled bed where he'd no doubt been when she'd knocked on his door. "Did I wake you?" she thought to ask now.

"No." He followed her down, skimmed his forefinger around her breast. "I couldn't sleep for thinking of you, knowing you were so damned near."

Threading his fingers through hers, he spread her arms wide, held her there, and closed his mouth over her breast, taking as much into his mouth as he could. Licking the sensitive flesh, suckling on it. Her body felt as though he was touching all of her, every inch, inside and out. That somehow he was reshaping her, so she would never again be the same. She wanted to provide him with the same gift, to leave him as changed.

She struggled to break free of his hold.

"Still yourself. Tonight is for you."

"I want it to be for us."

"Then let me guide you."

When she relaxed, he released his hold, pushed himself up, and straddled her hips. Beginning at her wrists, he glided his hands along her arms, down her sides, up over her stomach, and around her breasts.

"Spread your legs for me."

She didn't know if it was the low, sultry tenor of his voice or the directness of his words, but such molten heat coursed through her veins that she was surprised her blood didn't turn to lava. The fire only intensified when he stretched out on his stomach, nestled himself between her thighs, and blew softly on the curls at the juncture. She wished for more light so she could see him clearly, was grateful there was so little he couldn't see her in detail. She had no scars to hide, but no man had ever viewed her exposed thusly, placed her in such a vulnerable position. Yet, embarrassment made no appearance because the manner in which he tenderly trailed his fingers and lips over her made her feel treasured.

Biting her lip, she watched the firelight play over his muscled back and firm buttocks. He was magnificently built. So long, so broad.

He kissed the inside of one thigh, then the other. Slid his hands beneath her knees, lifted them, bent them, until her hips tilted upward, strained toward him. Then he licked her most intimate private place as though he'd discovered a dollop of cream that had been begging to be lapped up.

Just as she was now begging. She could not stop the little mewls from escaping her, and they seemed to incite his enthusiasm for the task at hand. She had known an intimacy was to be experienced when a man and woman came together, but hadn't known it would delve so deep, would consume her until the world around her faded away and there remained only him, his body, his hands, his fingers, his tongue, his mouth. Kissing, stroking, sucking, tugging, conquering.

That was how it felt. As though she was on the verge of being laid waste before him, yet she would be the one victorious. She scraped her fingers through his hair, and once more he laced his through hers and held them tight. The restriction only added to the pleasure building inside her. As the sensations intensified, her thighs began to tremble and shake. Still, he continued to plunder.

"Ben?"

"Give in to it, Thea."

Her breaths turned into shortened gasps, her chest tightened, her skin felt as though it was shrinking. Her head thrashed from side to side. She no longer had any control over it, no longer had any control over anything. Her fingers clutched his. *Don't let go. Don't let go. Don't let go.*

Suddenly, an ecstasy so intense, so incredible, burst through her, burst out of her. As her back arched, she swallowed her scream, and it somehow made the release all the more powerful.

While she trembled and shook in the wake of the cataclysm, he lapped at her, once, twice, thrice. Finally releasing her hands, he shoved himself up the length of her body, and cocooned her within his embrace, murmuring in her ear. *Shh, sweetheart. Shh, darling.*

Some minutes later she noticed a dampness on his chest, her cheek. Surely, she'd not wept. Yet, the intimacy of what he'd done had left her reeling, feeling incredibly raw, while at the same time treasured. How could tears have not been a response?

Only when her quivering lessened, did she manage to rasp, "You?"

Lifting himself up slightly, he held her gaze. "I found my pleasure pleasuring you."

As touched as she was by his words, she shook her head. He'd done that once before, in his study, and she'd been too overwhelmed to consider what he'd not taken for himself. "It's not fair that I should"—she didn't know exactly how to identify it—"should . . . come undone"—yes, that described it: an unraveling, a coming apart, a piecing back together—"and not you." Tonight it made her feel vulnerable and somehow . . . "It makes me melancholy. Show me what to do. Aren't you supposed to be inside me?"

"I'm not taking your virginity."

"Why ever not?"

"You might have a need for it."

If she kept to her plan. But how could she after experiencing him?

"There must be another way for you. Please, don't leave me alone in this, not this time."

Never taking his gaze from hers, he reached for her hand, brought it up, and placed an openmouthed kiss against her palm, coating it in dew. She watched his throat muscles work as he swallowed hard. Slowly, slowly, he lowered her hand and pressed it against his hard, throbbing cock, groaning roughly when she wrapped her fingers around him.

Keeping his hand covering hers, he guided her in stroking the hot, glorious length of him. Down, up. At the top, he steered her thumb over the silky dome, spreading the moisture gathered there before directing her back to the long caresses.

Because their gazes were locked, because neither looked away, it seemed more sensual, more intimate . . . simply more.

She gloried in watching the shifting of his features, the tightening of his jaw, the manner in which his eyes would briefly squeeze shut as though he'd experienced almost unbearable pleasure, the intensity with which his eyes smoldered when they were again open. Releasing her hand, he began kneading her breast.

"God, I love your breasts."

She was discovering she loved his cock. She felt naughty calling it such, but no other word she could think of would suffice. Every so often, when she skimmed her thumb over the head of it, gathering the dampness there, he would groan so deeply she'd feel the shuddering in his chest. It made her feel powerful to know she had such an impact on him. The melancholy drifted away. This was what she wanted: to feel equal.

"Harder, faster," he rasped.

She obeyed, tightening her hold, pumping more quickly.

Satisfaction swept through her as his breaths began to stutter because hers had when she'd neared the height of sensations, so he had to be close. He growled a harsh curse—or perhaps it was a benediction—as he buried his face in the curve of her neck and closed his mouth over her shoulder. His body jerked, trembled. His hot seed poured against her hip, over her hand.

Gently, he stilled her actions, and she wrapped her arms around him, held him tight, not certain she ever wanted to let him go.

FORTUNATELY, A WASH basin and pitcher were in the chamber, so Beast was able to clean up the mess he'd made over her and himself. He was now stretched out on the bed with her nestled against his left side—where she could no doubt hear the thudding of his heart—his arm around her, while he held the hand she'd placed on his stomach, the hand that had caused him to spill his seed with such force that he'd nearly lost consciousness. Periodically, he brought it to his lips and planted a kiss on her knuckles, her palm, her fingertips, her wrist.

He couldn't remember the last time he'd experienced such satisfaction after sex. It was an odd thing, especially considering the manner in which he'd gained his release. He hadn't been buried deep inside her. He hadn't felt her muscles throbbing around his cock when she found her own release. He regretted that, wanted to know the tightness of her, wanted no part of her to go untouched. But he wouldn't ruin her for a moment's satisfaction that might cause her a lifetime of remorse.

"As far as mistakes go," she said quietly, "I do believe it's one of the better ones I've made."

Chuckling low, he kissed the top of her head, loving the way her hair fanned out over the pillow, across his chest.

"I used to feel sorry for prostitutes but if they experience that—"

"I doubt they seldom do. Talk to Jewel. She'll tell you honestly."

"Do mistresses, do you think?"

"Depends on the selfishness of her lover, I should imagine." He skimmed his fingers up and down her arm. He didn't want to think about her taking a lover and yet the possibility of it hung heavy over his heart.

She began rubbing her instep over his calf, up, down, around. "I lied. My fire didn't go out."

"I know. I saw the firelight dancing over the wall." Against his chest, he felt her smile form, and somehow it seemed as intimate as everything else they'd done.

"Do you think your sister was encouraging us to do this by putting us in chambers with a door between?"

"Gillie isn't usually duplicitous, but there's an entire other wing she could have put me in." He shook his head. "I don't know. It doesn't matter."

"This wasn't a lesson, was it?"

He brought her hand up, whispered, "No," against her knuckles. Kissed them.

"Where do we go from here?"

"I don't know." It was humbling to realize he was not as strong-willed as he'd always thought himself to be, at least not where she was concerned. "Not a single night has passed that I haven't wanted to follow you into your bedchamber."

"Not a single night has passed that I haven't wanted you to."

He groaned low. "Thea—"

Rising up onto her elbows, she met and held his gaze. "You're not taking advantage if it's what I want. If we can pleasure each other without my losing my virginity, where's the harm?"

Could he resist the temptation of possessing her fully? She knew not what she asked of him. But neither could he turn away the pleasure of having her naked in his arms. "You have to promise you won't open your door to me unless it is what you want."

"I promise."

Cupping her head, he settled her back into the crook of his shoulder. Silence eased in between them. He didn't mind it. It contained a comfortableness. He could hear her breathing, and that sound he especially liked.

"I probably shouldn't linger much longer," she said. "The maids will be coming in soon to relight the fires."

On the hearth here only embers remained, dying out one by one. "I didn't realize they did that. I've never stayed overnight in a noble's house before."

He'd visited his sisters several times in their grand residences—

was pleased that they had such fine living accommodations—but had never seen any reason not to return to his own place at the end of the visit. While he had servants at his residence, they saw to the needs of the women more than his. They certainly didn't go about lighting any fire he might want.

"I assumed as much when you offered to stir my fire. You should have said, 'I'll ring for a servant.'"

"Why would I do that when I can see to the matter myself?"

"Because that's the way it's done."

Quickly, he rolled over onto her. She gave a little squeak, slapped her hand over her mouth, her eyes wide as they took him in. He had a clear view of her face because he'd hemmed her in between his arms and was resting on his elbows. "Besides, I thought you enjoyed the way I stirred *your fire*. Shall I stir it once more before you take your leave?"

Chapter 22

*A*lthea feared—as she sat beside Benedict on the sofa in the parlor while gifts were being exchanged—that anyone looking at her would be able to discern the wicked things she'd gotten up to during the night.

Before she'd left him, he had indeed stirred her fire and she had stirred his, at the same time, because he'd used his fingers instead of his tongue. Each method had its own advantages, and whenever she thought about him, warmth flushed her cheeks, and she was relatively certain they were as red as if she'd just come in out of the snow.

The babes were too young to really appreciate that they were being given a gift. Robin was striving to teach his wriggling pup to sit, but the rambunctious thing was more interested in exploring his new environs. After a rather spirited discussion in which everyone contributed names, Robin had decided to name the spaniel "Lucky" after declaring "the luckiest thing in the world is finding a home with the Trewloves."

She was glad she'd brought gifts for the Trewloves because they were giving her things. She'd received a fine bottle of sherry from Thorne and Gillie, an ivory fan from Mick and Aslyn, hair ribbons from Finn and Lavinia, a knitted shawl from Mrs. Trewlove, and a rare first edition copy of *A Christmas Carol* signed by Charles Dickens from Fancy and Rosemont.

"Happy Christmas," Aiden said, holding out both hands upon which rested two small boxes.

She took the one nearest to her while Benedict took the other. Usually after handing someone a gift the person moved on, but Aiden stood there rocking back and forth on his heels.

"Are you just going to stand there and watch us?" Benedict asked.

"Yes, as a matter of fact, I am."

While Benedict glared at Aiden, she opened her box. Her breath caught. Gingerly, she took out the miniature portrait of Benedict. It was done in oils, had an ethereal quality to it as though she was looking at it through angel wings. She lifted her gaze to Aiden. "Did you do this?"

"I did."

"You're so talented."

"Do you like the one I did of you?"

"Of me?"

He tipped his head toward Benedict. When she glanced over at him, it was to see him studying a miniature resting in the palm of his hand. A perfect likeness of her.

"How did you manage that? From memory?"

"I sketched you while watching you best Chadbourne."

"Why?"

"Thought I'd be seeing you again, and might have a need for it."

Only he hadn't given it to her; he'd given it to Benedict. "Did we take the wrong boxes?"

He gave her a warm smile. "No." He walked off.

"I don't know why Aiden thought you'd want a portrait of me," Benedict said, a bit of irritation lacing his voice. "We can exchange if you like."

She studied him, the seriousness in his dark eyes. The shadow of doubt flickered. "Thank you, but I'd rather keep this one."

And with her winnings, she was going to purchase a locket in which to keep it.

HE DIDN'T REALIZE he'd been holding his breath until she gave him the answer he'd been wanting to hear. Not that he thought she was keeping his miniature for any sentimental reason, but he didn't want to give up hers. If he was very careful with it, he could trim enough off so he could insert it inside the cover of his timepiece and then he'd always be carrying it around. Whenever he checked the time, he would see her face.

Although he was a bit irritated with Aiden for too closely reading his feelings where she was concerned.

"I have something for you," she said. Gingerly, as though it was the most precious thing in the world and should be pampered, she placed the box in her reticule and removed a stack of . . . something. She extended one toward him.

It was a long, narrow strip of light blue linen upon which she'd embroidered in red his name and a ship with sails capturing the wind.

"You use it to mark your place in a book. I made one for each of your family members."

"I'm touched, Thea, that you went to so much bother. They will be as well."

Her cheeks turned a lovely shade of pink, and he wondered if they'd been the same hue when he'd been nestled between her thighs. So much he didn't know for certain, so much he wished he did. A room lost to shadows lacked color.

"I'll go pass them around, shall I?"

After he nodded, he watched as she first approached his mum, and he saw the delight illuminate his mum's face. It seemed the perfect way to honor their love of reading.

Aiden was suddenly crouching before him. "I forgot to mention . . . you might let Gillie know there may be a mouse in the room in which you were sleeping. I heard a squeak coming from it near dawn."

He clamped down on his back teeth. "No need to bother Gillie with it. I took care of it myself."

Aiden grinned an all-too-knowing grin. "I'm sure you did."

"Say another word and you'll feel the weight of my fist."

"I like her."

He sighed heavily. His brother couldn't *not* say another word but at least he'd chosen words that lessened Beast's irritation with him. "She has plans, Aiden. They don't include me. She'll only be about for a little while longer."

Aiden twisted around on the balls of his feet and his gaze swept over the room. "I'm sorry to hear that. You seemed well matched."

"As though you know what constitutes *well matched.*"

Once again Aiden was facing him. "Not being able to take your eyes off her for one thing. Spending the night in a grand residence when you hate grand residences. To arrange for her to give an arse a drubbing."

"Originally, I was going to do the drubbing."

"But you gave up the satisfaction you'd feel so she could have it."

"I remember a time when you didn't spout such wisdom."

"Love changes a man." Putting his hands on his knees, he straightened. "The snow didn't fall as thickly as we thought it might. Traveling might be slow going but not treacherous. Lena and I will be heading off soon to spend the remainder of the day with her family. Take care of the little mouse."

As his brother strode away, Beast wasn't certain he knew how to take care of Thea, how to determine exactly what she needed to be happy.

She was kneeling beside Robin, talking with him, petting Lucky. He wondered if she'd ever had a dog. So many things about her that he didn't know.

A clapping drew his attention to Fancy, who was standing in the center of the room with her husband. "We wanted to be last, after everyone else had given out their gifts. Our gift requires a bit of patience on your part—and ours—as it won't arrive for several more months."

Rosemont threaded their fingers together and brought her hand to his mouth for a kiss.

"We're going to give you a new person to love," Fancy announced.

Cheers followed, with the ladies rushing to surround Fancy, and the gents shaking Rosemont's hand as though he'd done something truly miraculous when all he'd done was make love to his wife.

"That's a wonderful gift, isn't it?"

He glanced up at Thea beaming down at him. Time spent with her was turning out to be a wonderful gift. He rose to his feet. "I have something for you."

Her smile softened. Damn it all. He'd spent hours striving to determine what to get her. Something meaningful but not too personal. Something that would be appropriate for her to accept. "It's a silly thing, really."

She waited expectantly. Reaching into his pocket, he withdrew the small box and handed it to her.

Gingerly, she removed the lid. "A match safe. Very much like yours."

Except hers had roses circling her name etched in the silver.

"No matter how dark things get, you'll always have light."

A fine sheen of dampness was in her eyes when she lifted them to him. "I'll always treasure it."

He would always treasure his memories of her.

Chapter 23

*T*he winds of change did not blow in gently. Sitting in the library, in a reflective mood, Althea was amazed by the difference three weeks could make in a life. She shouldn't have been surprised. After all, at twenty-four her life had changed overnight. She'd felt powerless, like a leaf caught up in a whirlwind that had no say in the direction it traveled or where it eventually landed.

But now she was in control, and as other lives began to take different shapes, she began to carefully consider and mold hers into what she wanted, discovering she wanted something very different than what she'd originally thought she wanted when Benedict had first come into her life.

Although it wasn't only him. It was everything happening around her that was causing her to look at things slightly differently. Nothing stayed as it was. Which was clearly evident as she occasionally sipped her sherry.

On Boxing Day, the ladies had gone to the Cerberus Club, where they'd discovered that Pearl and Ruby were quite skillful at dealing cards. They'd left the establishment with not only a substantial amount of winnings but an offer of employment as well, which they each accepted.

Shortly after one of Benedict's ships arrived at port, one of the shipmates had shown up at the residence and declared his love for Flora. Apparently, they had been seeing each other on the sly for quite some time, and the tendre he'd developed for her had tormented him while he'd been away, and he could no longer bear to be without her. They were married within the week.

Lily became a companion to Captain Ferguson's wife, to ease her loneliness when he was at sea.

Hester had stopped entertaining gentlemen because a lady's maid didn't "do that sort of thing," and she was now tending to Althea's needs exclusively and being paid handsomely for her services.

A brothel with only one lady, Lottie, seeing to gentlemen, was no brothel at all. The decision was made to begin converting the building with its many rooms into a boardinghouse.

Lottie oversaw the conversion that began the first week in January. All the risqué paintings and statuettes were carted away. Walls were redone, draperies replaced. Althea fully expected the former doxy would hire out her services to decorate the homes of those coming into wealth—once she was finished with the current project.

The challenge was alerting the clients. Jewel greeted the men when they arrived, poured them a glass of scotch, and explained that the purpose of the establishment would be changing. Lottie took her favorites to her bed for one last hurrah. Those she didn't know or didn't favor, she blew a goodbye kiss.

Now, a couple of weeks later, they were seldom disturbed during the evening hours when they were all sitting in the library reading.

Althea continued to teach Lottie and Hester, to give them more refinement. But she couldn't teach them forever. Soon she was going to have to determine a path for herself.

Althea missed all the nights when it had been only she and Benedict, when they'd been able to share personal stories, hurts, aches, and joys. The tulip glass of sherry still waited for her on the table. They still sat across from each other. No one else ever sought to claim those chairs as though they had been designed and constructed to hold only the two of them.

But with others in the room, the atmosphere had changed, the way the air did when a storm was threatening. Pages in books crackled as they were turned, sighs sounded, clothing rustled with the shifting of a backside, a stretching of shoulders, the bending of a neck.

At ten they would bid each other good-night with a punctuality that had not existed when she would become lost in stories Benedict shared or he would ask questions of her, when time held no sway over them.

After Hester assisted her in readying for bed and sought out her own slumber, after the building itself had settled in and gone quiet, she would sit on the bed with the counterpane folded back and wait. Wait for the quiet knock that invariably came.

She would open the door, welcome him in, and it was those moments she'd begun to live for.

She watched him now as he removed the timepiece from his waistcoat pocket and glanced at the time—as though the watch was more accurate than the clock ticking away on the mantelpiece. "Is that *the one*?" she asked quietly, knowing he'd need no further identifiers, not certain why she'd not thought to ask him before.

He leaned forward to show it to her nestled against his palm. She inclined toward him to see it better. A stag was intricately carved on the cover. "Lessened my guilt," he said, his voice low, the words meant for only her, "because it had no coat of arms or inscription to indicate it had any sentimental value. Just something a wealthy bloke purchased so he'd always know the time."

She almost asked if he'd be passing it on to his firstborn son, but that would mean shining a light on a future they both seemed reticent to discuss.

Every night he brought her pleasure—sometimes in a different way, sometimes in a familiar way, but never in a way that completely claimed her as his, that changed the status of her virginity. Often it felt as though her body was screaming for him to take her fully, to plunge into her, to ride her. It was an almost animalistic need.

She thought there were times when he was in need as well because he would utter guttural groans that echoed around them as though he was in pain. Even though he'd taught her how to bring him pleasure, she often felt bereft afterward, as though it wasn't enough for either of them.

"I probably give it more credit than it deserves in an attempt to justify my actions, but it changed the course of my life."

As he held her gaze, she thought perhaps he was referring to more than the watch, was applying the same influence to her. What she did know for certain was that he had changed the course of her life. That she seldom thought about returning to Society, that she no longer was certain that if she did, she would find that for which she'd been searching.

She'd begun to believe that what she'd been searching for was right here. Within the walls of this residence with him.

"Look at that," Jewel said, "it's past time for us all to be abed. You're falling down on the job, Beast."

Althea glanced at the mantel clock. Two minutes past the hour. It made her smile to have a reminder of the many nights when they'd looked at neither watch nor clock, so lost in each other they'd become.

He unfolded his body and stood, and the more recent nightly tradition of traipsing off to ready themselves for bed at the same time began. When it was completed, she sat on the bed and waited, setting free the buttons on her nightdress that she'd secured while Hester was helping to prepare her for slumber. She loosened her hair that Hester had patiently plaited.

The knock came. She opened the door. He closed it. They were together, alone at last.

As he did every night, he doused the lights, leaving only the fire on the hearth to hold the shadows at bay, and it did a very poor job of it. She wanted to do what they did in sunlight, with the sunbeams caressing him so she could see every one of his movements in exquisite detail.

She slipped off her nightdress. He tossed his shirt and trousers

aside. They crashed into each other in the center of the space between door and bed, and hungrily joined mouths as though he'd
returned from an odyssey that had spanned years instead of only
an hour.

She lifted her hand, and he threaded his fingers through hers
before tucking her hand behind her back, arching her so her
breasts were offered up for a feast that he devoured with such
skill she almost came completely undone then and there.

Since Christmas Eve, he had learned her body so well, had en-
couraged her to share what she liked, what she didn't, when she
needed him to be soft, when she required that he increase the
pressure. When slowness would better suit the purpose. When
speed was of the essence.

She loved this aspect of him. That he was so comfortable with
the act, made her comfortable with it, with something the upper
crust preferred to pretend never occurred. It was certainly not to
be discussed.

The naughty words he uttered didn't seem naughty at all, just
sensual and erotic. At first, she'd only shyly muttered them, but
now she used them when it suited her, when she wanted to drive
him a little more wild with desire.

He backed her up until she hit the bed. As though she was little
more than a child's rag doll, he lifted her and tossed her onto the
duvet-covered mattress. Followed her down, taking possession of
her mouth once more before leaving it to take his mouth on a lan-
guid journey down her throat, over her breasts, along her stomach
to the heart of her core where he began licking her, and her limbs
went lax.

"I'm not going to become a courtesan."

He stilled, waited a heartbeat, lifted his gaze to hers. In spite
of the shadows, the absence of enough light, she could still make
out his beautiful features, see the fire burning in his eyes. "Why?"

One word. A simple word. Yet, it contained myriad questions.

She reached for him. He took her hands, knotted their fingers
together, pushed himself up, placed their hands on either side of

her head, and gazed down on her. "Why?" he repeated, and in his voice, she heard doubt and hope.

"Because it's no longer what I want. It's not what I need. Because I'm happy here. With you. Because I love you."

With a groan that sounded as though his heart had been ripped from his chest, he lowered his head to the swell of her breasts, kissed one and then the other. Then he just lingered there, breathing in and breathing out, and she feared she'd made a terrible mistake in uttering the words.

"It's too big, Thea," he said quietly, "to have your love. It makes me feel as though my heart will explode through my chest."

He shifted until he was once again gazing down on her. "Do you know when I first started falling in love with you?"

Since she didn't know he had, she could only shake her head, even as her own heart soared with the knowledge that this remarkable man loved her.

"When you told me that you were none of my bleedin' business. The first fall wasn't much of a drop, but every day I learned something else about you that made me fall just a little bit further. I'm still falling. I suspect I'll keep falling until I draw my last breath."

"Ben," she whispered, too overcome by his admission to say much else. What they felt for each other *was* too big, yet not big enough.

"As small as you are, it is inconceivable to me how when I am with you, I don't feel as though I'm a great hulking beast."

She tried to break free of his hold so she could run her fingers through his hair, over his face, but he held tight. He always held tight.

"Make love to me. Fully, completely. I don't want to retain my virginity. I want to feel you moving inside me. I want to be only yours. I want you to be mine."

With a growl, he moved her hands to the small of his back before spreading his fingers over her throat, beneath her chin, and lowering his mouth to hers, his tongue sweeping along the contours. She scored her fingers up his back, outlining the defined delineations that flexed with his movements. So much strength. Such power. How could he consider himself hulking when he possessed an incredible elegance? Yes, he was taller than most and broad shouldered, but there was a sleekness about him, like a panther she'd seen at the zoological gardens.

He nipped at her collarbone, soothed it with his tongue.

She brought her hands around. He laced their fingers together. She stilled. Her brow furrowed. "Why do you do that?"

He stilled as well, although if it was possible, he was more still than she. "Do what?"

"Take hold of my hands—" No, it wasn't hands, not always. But it was always the left one. "You won't let me touch the right side of your face, your head." It was an area he seemed to shelter. Never had she seen him without his hair covering it. "Why?"

She heard his swallow more than saw it. "Because I didn't want you to discover why they first began calling me Beast."

HE SHOVED HIMSELF off the bed more with a sense of resignation than anger or frustration. Before they went any further, she had the right to know, to know everything about him. With the truth of him, she might decide she wanted to become another man's mistress, might return to her original plans.

The bed creaked with whatever movements she was making.

He wished he had with him the match safe his mum had given him, that he had those matches available because they could ward off the darkness now threatening. Instead, he tapped his fingers over the bedside table until he found the matches he knew rested nearby, struck one, and lit the oil lamp, bringing forth a light that chased all the shadows away from the bed, away from her, away from him.

She was sitting with her back to the headboard, the sheet clutched in her hands just below her chin, covering what she'd bared when he'd first walked into the room. A thousand times he'd yearned to see her unveiled in the brightest of lit rooms or in a field dappled with sunshine, had even considered not dousing the lamps, but he couldn't shine light on her without shining it on himself.

He sat on the bed, his hip resting next to hers. She'd yet to take her eyes from him. "Go ahead," he said quietly, "touch what I've not let you touch, see what I've not let you see."

She continued to stare, to press her lips together, and to draw in one unsteady breath after another. It was as though this woman whom he'd seen demonstrate courage countless times was unable to find it now.

"It won't hurt you."

She opened her hand, fisted it back up. "That's not my worry. Will it hurt you?"

He wouldn't experience any physical pain, but depending on her reaction there could still be hurt. "No."

Very slowly, she placed the flat of her hand where his shoulder curved into his neck and glided it up, stopping at the spot where his pulse thudded in his throat. For a moment she just waited as though counting the beats of his heart, and he wondered if she realized each one was for her. Tentatively, she slid her fingers up, the strands of his hair brushing over them. Another minute of stillness, looking into his eyes, before directing her attention back to where her fingers trembled slightly. A deep breath from her. None from him. She slipped her hand beneath the fall of his hair, raised—

A tiny pleat formed between her brows. She lifted higher. She released her hold on the sheet and it dropped down to reveal the magnificent breasts that he'd denied himself the sight of in light, but his gaze only darted down for a second because he was too mesmerized watching her expression. It had yet to reveal horror. The hand no longer clutching the sheet cradled his other cheek, and she shifted her eyes over to hold his gaze. "You haven't an ear."

"No."

"What happened?"

"I was born without it."

"Can you hear?"

"Not on that side. Sometimes I cock my head so nothing escapes my good ear. I've learned if I watch the movement of people's mouths, I can discern the words I might not have heard clearly."

"You always sit me to your left."

"I don't want to miss hearing a single word you utter."

"And they cruelly called you Beast because of this, something over which you had no control, something nature inflicted upon you?" A spark of anger hardened her voice.

"Children, yes. Beast, monster, devil. Mum would keep our hair short to decrease the likelihood of lice. Eventually, I wouldn't let her cut it. But even then, if I got into a scrap, it would be uncovered. And the taunts would begin. I can't tell you how many noses my brothers bloodied trying to get them to stop. Or how often I ran off because I didn't want anyone to see how I hurt, to witness any tears I couldn't hold back. I don't think they meant to be cruel. I was different, and I think the difference frightened them, because they feared it could have been them. Then one day I decided if I called myself Beast, if I pretended that it was of no consequence to me if I wasn't exactly like them, I would take away their power to hurt me."

"You thought I would taunt you?"

"No, I thought you would look at me as you are now—as though I'm to be pitied."

"I don't pity you. I feel sorrow that others were cruel to you, especially when you were just a lad. If you'll give me their names, I'll arrange to best them at four-card brag."

The last thing he'd expected was to smile, to release a small laugh, to feel such a lightening of his heart.

Leaning in, she brushed a kiss just above the spot where his pulse beat, and her tenderness caused his chest to tighten.

"In my eyes, you are no less perfect, Benedict Trewlove."

Ah, Christ. All the tension flowed out of him like a river rushing to the sea. He claimed her mouth. He was far from perfect. She, on the other hand, was all goodness and light.

Placing her hands on either side of his head, she drew him back, held his gaze. "I love you all the more for the way you have faced the challenges of your life. Douse the lamp and make love to me."

With a grin, he pushed her back down onto the bed. "No, this time I think we'll keep the lamp burning."

SHE LOVED THE freedom of plowing her fingers through the thick strands of his hair, cradling his face between her palms. The first time she'd done it, he'd stiffened, and at that moment she'd disliked every person who had ever made him feel . . . less. And she'd realized with sudden clarity that one of the reasons he understood her so well, had known what she had needed when it came to retribution with Chadbourne, was because for most of his life people had been metaphorically turning their back on him.

She took his mouth, slowly, sensually, until with a low moan he relaxed into her arms. She reminded him that she loved him.

When he had lifted himself up onto his elbows to look down on her, the heat smoldering in his eyes nearly unraveled her.

So much had been lost when he'd pleasured her within the shadows, and now they gloried in the sight of each other, fully revealed. They traveled over each other, examining dips, curves, ridges, and mounds.

"Your nipples are rosier than I thought," he said, and she suspected her cheeks had gone rosy as well.

"Your scar looks angrier than I thought."

"I like the pink hue that rushes over your skin when passion takes hold."

"I like the intensity with which you watch me."

And the way in which he caressed her, kissed her, licked her. She especially liked the attention his mouth gave to the valley between her legs. She liked that she could now knot her fingers in his hair and connect with him as he feasted.

After she cried out with her release, he moved up, her legs hooked over his shoulders. She felt the nudge as he tested her readiness.

"Are you sure?" he asked.

"I love you with all that I am, with all I ever shall be."

With a groan, he closed his eyes, opened them. "You humble me, Thea, that you should want me . . . Beauty to my beast."

"*Want* is too tame a word. Desire. Yearn. Crave. And you're not a beast. Not in action, deed, or looks. You're one of the most handsome men I've ever known. Become mine completely." In so doing, she would become his. Nothing would have the power to separate them.

With an almost feral groan, he began pushing his way into her, entering, withdrawing, over and over, a little deeper each time, giving her a chance to become accustomed to him. When he sank fully into her, stretching her, filling her, he stilled.

"Are you all right?" he asked.

"Yes. I like how it feels . . . having you inside me."

He buried his face in the curve of her shoulder. "You slay me, Thea, so easily."

He began moving within her, slowly at first, his tempo increasing as she mastered the rhythm of his thrusts, as they parted and met. He was strength, power, and purpose.

Hands caressed, sighs sounded, moans rippled through them. Her name was a litany on his lips, a benediction that caused molten heat to flow through her. Never in her life had she felt such a part of someone, had she felt that she was precisely where she belonged. The world in which she'd grown up lacked magic, depth, satisfaction. Only now did she realize it, only now did she understand that without him, her world had been an arid place where she never would have truly come into herself.

The pleasure built until she was writhing beneath him, digging her fingers into his back, his shoulders, taking her hands wherever she wanted, no longer being denied access to any part of him. Instinctually, she knew he'd never shared so much of himself with anyone else, had never trusted anyone as he trusted her. Knowing the truth of that served to heighten the sensations, caused her to surrender completely, to hold nothing back, because trust was a precious thing. She had his, and he had hers.

So many nights he'd brought her pleasure, but it had never been as all-consuming as this, cocooning her in so many various sensations. Anywhere he touched, her skin rippled with joy, her nerve endings tingled with appreciation.

The entire world floated away until it was only them, their breaths, the slap of their slick flesh, the scent of carnal lust they created. The ecstasy increased until she thought she would die of it. When her release washed through her, he captured her cry with a kiss that enhanced and consumed. She'd never known such bliss, such fulfillment.

He never took his mouth from hers, not even as harsh shudders cascaded through him, racking his body. She tightened her arms around his shoulders, dragged her hands up and down his glistening back. He groaned, bucked, stilled. Slid his mouth from hers, along her throat, settling it within the curve of her neck. Their breaths echoed around them, a sawing that hinted at unbearable pleasure experienced.

Carefully, as though she'd turned into glass that could easily shatter, he slid her legs from his shoulders, eased off her slightly so she was only half-covered, reached a long arm down to snag the sheet and brought it up over her. His hand rested heavily against her breast. She didn't know how he'd managed so many movements when she wasn't certain she'd ever move again.

They lay there replete, she in wonder that she might have never had this, might have never had him if not for bad decisions made by others.

"As I won't have a protector, will be no lord's mistress, can't teach Lottie and Hester forever, I shall have to find other employment," she said after a time. "I'm not certain what I shall do."

With a groan, he raised himself slightly, wedged himself between her thighs, and to her surprise, pushed into her once more, held still. She brushed his hair back from his face. He was studying her as though she was a treasure he'd unexpectedly found, hadn't even known he was searching for. "You could have my children."

Her heart stuttered. "I beg your pardon?"

He withdrew, entered her again. "Have my children, be my partner in the shipping business, handle Thorne every time he wants us to make a detour for something he needs that no one else does." He kissed one corner of her mouth, then the other. "Marry me, Thea."

A little cry escaped her lips, tears burned her eyes. "Do you mean it?"

"It nearly killed me every time I thought of you going to another man. Be mine, only mine. My wife, my love. We'll purchase a residence, where only the two of us will live so you'll no longer have to hold back those cries that carry my name. Marry me."

If he wasn't resting on top of her, hard and thick inside her, she might have floated out through the window, the joy coursing through her making her feel as though she could fly. "Yes. I want you to be my husband. You're already my love."

He kissed her deeply, soundly, began gently rocking against her. He slid his mouth to the sensitive spot beneath her ear, dragged his tongue over it.

"But you'll have to propose again elsewhere."

He shifted so he could once again hold her gaze. "Why?"

"Because ladies always ask each other to describe the proposal in detail, and I can't very well say he proposed while his magnificent cock was nestled deep inside me."

If he didn't already hold her heart, the grin he bestowed upon her would have stolen it. "Just tell me where and when."

Chapter 24

"I think the butler did it."

Beast looked up from his writing to the rosewood writing desk he'd moved out of one of the bedchambers not yet in use two days earlier—the morning following the night when she had accepted his proposal of marriage—because he'd wanted her near. Always wanted her near. He liked being able to get up and kiss her whenever he wanted. He especially enjoyed when she would get up and come over to kiss him. But he enjoyed most when she locked the door on her way over.

They had yet to discuss the details of their wedding because he had yet to give her the second proposal. He wanted to do it in a memorable way that would make her smile whenever she relayed the details of it. And she had yet to tell him when and where.

Now she was looking quite pleased with her deductive skills. While she usually spent her time at the desk determining what remained for her to teach Lottie and Hester, today she'd begun reading his manuscript. "The butler," he repeated.

"Yes. I know your inspector suspects Lord Chadburn of killing his best friend—after determining it wasn't the grieving widow—I like her by the way."

As did he. She very much resembled the woman sitting in his study.

"But I think it's the butler. He's so unassuming, always in the background. Always so quiet. He could easily sneak up on people."

"Possibly, you're correct."

"You're not going to confirm it?"

"No. I want you to read it without knowing who the murderer is so you can let me know if I've provided enough information so you can believe he's the murderer."

She tapped her pencil on the edge of the desk. "How much longer before you're finished?"

"A few more days."

She didn't seem happy about that, which served to assuage his worries that it wasn't holding her attention. "Another matter. Your Lord Chadburn. His name very much resembles that of an earl I know."

"Does it?" He feigned surprise, which only caused her to narrow her eyes at him.

"Why would you use a name similar to that of someone you loathe?"

Because he was going to take great pleasure in writing the scene where the man was hanged. Or he might become a victim. He hadn't really decided yet. Either way, gruesome ending for the bloke.

"Oh, my God, he's the murderer," she suddenly blurted.

He shrugged. "Maybe."

"I think it would be a great twist if it was the inspector."

Only he liked the inspector. The man was methodical, unemotional, and skilled at deduction. He wanted him to solve the murder in the next book as well. It was strange how he thought of these characters as though they truly existed.

A rap sounded on his door.

"Come in."

Jewel opened it and peered in. "Beast, a fancy gent is here to see you. His name is Ewan Campbell."

The name wasn't familiar. "Did he say what he needed with me?"

"No, but I think you're probably going to want to talk with him."

With a question in his eyes, he glanced over at Thea, who looked at him, studied him, slowly shook her head. "I don't know him."

"Well then, I guess I need to see what he's about."

Shoving back his chair, he stood. Since he was on his feet, he decided to take advantage of it, walked over to where Thea worked, bent over, and captured the mouth she'd tilted up to him. He'd never get enough of her kisses. Never get enough of her.

When he lifted his mouth from hers, she gave him a seductive smile. "Don't be too long. And lock the door on your way back in."

Chuckling, he strode into the hallway. Life had never been so sweet, so full of promise. His visit with the gent was going to be the shortest he'd ever experienced because he was already primed to return to the study and lock that door.

He quickened his steps as he went down the stairs to the front parlor. He'd barely crossed the threshold before coming to an abrupt stop at the sight of the man standing with his back to the doorway, his head bent as he studied either his shining boots or the fire dancing on the hearth. His visitor was large, as tall as himself, with shoulders just as broad. His black hair streaked lightly with silver brushed across his shoulders.

"Mr. Campbell, you wished to have a word with me?"

The man turned around slowly, and Beast had the sensation of his world tilting precariously, making it a challenge to retain his balance. It was like looking at his reflection in a mirror. Everything within him went still, quiet, hushed, his mind devoid of thought, his lungs battling to draw in air. He didn't know what to make of this man who reminded him so much of himself, the man staring at him as though he'd just encountered an apparition recently risen from the grave.

"You'd be Benedict Trewlove, then," Mr. Campbell said with a thick Scottish brogue. In his large hand, based on the shade of the cloth covering the hard binding, he was holding a copy of *Murder at Ten Bells.*

"I would be, yes. Are you in want of my signature in your book?"

Campbell looked down at his hand, seemingly surprised to find himself grasping the novel, as though he'd forgotten he had it. But he clutched it so tightly his knuckles had turned white. "Nae. I brought it as an excuse in case my Mara wasnae correct. But I'm thinking she has the right of it."

Beast couldn't make any sense of what the man was saying. "I'm sorry, Mr. Campbell, but I'm not certain why you're here."

"Do you know when you were handed over to Mrs. Trewlove?"

A cold shiver of dread skittered down his spine. "November." The tenth, to be exact, but he didn't see how it was any of this man's business.

"The year?"

"I don't see—"

"The year."

Suddenly, he didn't like that the man's hair was as black as his, his eyes as dark. That he had such a strong jaw, a broad brow. "Campbell, I don't know what the hell—"

"Have you seen three and thirty years?"

The man might as well have thrown a bucket of cold water on him, the shock might have been less. He wasn't one to go about giving people his age, so how the devil did Campbell know it? "The particulars of my life are none of your business."

"You'd be wrong, lad. I'm thinking I'm your da."

If Beast wasn't composed of such sturdy stock, he might have staggered back under the weight of the anger that ratcheted forcefully through him. For the man to show up after all these years and deliver such a striking blow with such calmness as though simply announcing that it might rain. A knife going in his side had hurt less. "Why the devil would you think that?"

"By just looking at you. I see myself when I was younger. Your ma would agree."

An anticipated rage burst through him at the casual mention of his mother by this man who had not done right by her, who had put her in the unenviable position of giving birth to a bastard and then having to give him away.

Balling his hands into fists at his sides, he took a menacing step forward. If duels weren't against the law, he'd be meeting the man at dawn. Perhaps he would anyway. "What was she to you? Your mistress? Someone you used and abandoned when she no longer suited you, when you grew bored with her? A servant you took advantage of?"

He saw the anger flare in Ewan Campbell's dark eyes, and just as quickly it was tamped down. "The love of my life."

"You loved her so much you left her alone to bring your bastard into the world. I assume she was alone, with no means, and that's the reason she gave me up."

"I didn't know about you at the time."

He wouldn't accept the excuse. If this man had truly loved his mother, how could he have not known she was with child? As hard as the words were to utter, he spit them out. "You can forget you know about me now."

He turned on his heel—

"You're my firstborn, my only son, my only child, my heir."

He froze, then barked out his laughter before once more facing a man he wanted to know everything about while having no desire to know anything at all about. "I'm a bastard. Bastards can't inherit."

"Not in England, no. But we're Scottish. Perthshire is where you were born, and in Scotland if the father of the bastard marries the mother of the bastard—it doesnae matter if it's years after the bairn is born—the child is entitled to inherit all he would have if his parents had been married when the babe came into the world."

Most of the words were of no importance to him, but some felt like slices of ice pelting him. "You married my mother?"

"I did, lad, as soon as I found her, but it took me a while to locate her." He shook his head. "Your granddad, my da, he was a right bastard."

"Born out of wedlock?"

The laughter was deep but caustic, and Beast didn't like realizing how familiar it sounded, how much it reminded him of his own laugh.

"Nae. But most likely spawned by Satan all the same. He didnae approve of the woman I loved. Her father was his sworn enemy, though God alone knows why. He didnae want her blood tainting the bloodline he was so damned proud of. He knew how desperately I wished to marry her. When he learned she'd brought my wee bairn into the world, he wanted to make sure you never inherited. He was consumed with hatred for her family. Don't know if he would have seen you killed, but she wasnae willing to chance it. Shortly after she saw you safely delivered into the arms of another, they found her and had her committed to an asylum for the criminally insane."

Beast felt another punch to his gut. He'd never considered her fate would be so horrid, and he had an urge to strike out and smash something.

Sadness and anger that mirrored his own marred Campbell's handsome features. "The cruelty she suffered. Took me five years to find her and when I did, I wanted to kill every cursed one of them who had ever touched her. But what good would I be to her, dancing in the wind? Though I took pleasure in leaving some of them bloodied. Even took my fists to my da. Wasn't much they could do to fix his jaw when I was done with him. No tears were shed when he drew his last."

Beast was thinking he might have inherited the man's temper. But the story he'd told sickened him, made him feel guilty for all the times he'd questioned why his mother had broken her promise and not returned for him.

"Your ma wants to see you."

He glanced quickly around as though expecting her to emerge from the wallpaper or step out from behind the draperies. "She's here?"

"Nae. She wanted to come, but I didnae want her disappointed if you turned out not to be our boy."

"You don't know that I am. You're just guessing."

He gave a quick nod. "What are you hiding beneath all that hair? The same as me, I suspect. Your ma told me you'd taken after me for certain in that one regard." With a smooth, efficient flick of his fingers, he brushed back the strands on the right side of his head. "'Tis the Campbell curse. Legend has it that one of our ancestors was always pressing his ear to the door, spying on witches. They cast a spell on him and his descendants. Some escape it. You and I weren't so fortunate. Although there are worse things to befall a person."

It was an unlikely tale, but what caught Beast's attention more was the reference to *our ancestors*. He had his family, bastards Ettie Trewlove had cobbled together into a unit that loved each other fiercely and fought just as fiercely for each other. But that family came with no ancestors—none that could be claimed or acknowledged anyway. Yet, now he was learning he had ancestors, ones who would be proud to claim him, ones with whom he sometimes shared the anomaly with which he'd been born. A heritage. A birthright—although he'd always viewed it as something wrong, not right. A legacy. If he was this man's son . . .

How could he doubt it when he was gazing into eyes as black as his own, when he possessed the same square cut of his jaw, the same sleek nose, the same high sharp cheekbones?

What had he inherited from his mum? No, Ettie Trewlove was his mum, would always be so. This other woman was his mother, his ma, the word pronounced with a brogue that he wasn't certain would ever feel natural on his tongue. He wasn't who—what—he'd always believed himself to be: a babe abandoned, forgotten, unwanted.

He'd been wanted, loved, protected. He wondered if that instinct to protect had been passed from his ma to him, if she was responsible for his nature more than his looks.

"Why didn't you come for me after you found her?"

"She couldnae remember where she left you. Sometimes, I'd think she made herself forget so she wouldn't be able to tell them where you were. I don't know if it's possible to do such a thing. To look at your ma, you might not realize how strong she is. I've never known anyone stronger, man or woman. So all these years, the one thing I did know was that wherever she left you, you were safe."

He had been that, at least while he was under the care of Ettie Trewlove. His encounter with Three-Fingered Bill had been his doing. But even then, it had been his family who had sent for the surgeon, his family who had nursed him back to health.

"After all this time, all of a sudden, she just remembered?"

"Nae. It was your book. I bought it for her when I was in London a couple of weeks ago. She likes mysteries, and I thought she'd enjoy reading one written by an author who carried the same first name as our son—only it was the Trewlove that caught her attention. Her memory of that night was that the woman with whom she'd left you had promised to love you true. But seeing Benedict Trewlove on the book . . . it unlocked something within her. When she slept, unlike all the other times she'd dreamed of that night, this time it wasn't so blurry, she saw the details of it. She thought maybe the woman's name was Trewlove. She convinced me to come have a word with you. I went to your publisher to find out where you lived, and here I am. And glad of it."

He was still struggling with it all, taking apart what he'd known of his life and reassembling it to include what he was now learning.

"Will you come with me to meet your ma?" Ewan Campbell—his father—asked.

Beast could do little more than nod.

Then the man whom he'd spent a good many years wondering about strode forward and held out his hand. A hand the size of ham hocks, a hand Beast could clearly see working the docks, lifting and hauling cargo. He knew if he placed his own against it, he'd be recognizing the man's place in his life, would be acknowledging his acceptance of who he himself was.

Yet, when their palms touched, he had the sense that he'd come home.

When his da drew him in close, wrapped an arm around his shoulders, and gave his back a thump, all he could do was blink back the tears suddenly burning his eyes.

"Welcome back into the family, lad. And I apologize because I don't recall giving you a proper introduction when we met. I was stunned by seeing you, seeing myself in you. I'd be the Duke of Glasford."

HIS FATHER WAS a bloody duke. Did that mean his inheritance included a dukedom? Christ, he had noble blood running through his veins.

He recognized Mayfair when the coach bearing the ducal crest in which he was riding entered the area. Since climbing into the conveyance, he and the duke hadn't spoken a word as though all the emotions that had swept through them with the handshake and embrace were simply too large and grand. Yet, in the silence they'd been assessing each other. He felt like he was moving about in a dream comprised of thick treacle that caused every action to be slow and difficult to navigate. At any moment he was going to wake up to discover it was all simply a bad and elaborate jest, perpetrated in cruelty.

Then the vehicle turned the corner and passed through wrought-iron gates, and he glanced out the window to see a massive manor, the sort in which he'd dreamed of living when he was a lad, crowded in a bed with his brothers. The kind of house that his years of hard work had put within reach, but he hadn't wanted to walk through it alone. Now he would walk through it with Thea.

"You should know you carry one of my titles as a courtesy," his father said quietly. "You're the Earl of Tewksbury."

A blasted earl. A blasted lord. What did he know about being a lord? "It doesn't seem real."

"I suspect it won't for a while. I'm having a hard time believing it myself. We searched for you for years."

Every time the duke revealed something, his chest tightened a little bit more. To have been wanted to such an extent they'd searched for years. A part of him wanted to simply say no to all this, hop out of the carriage, and make his way back to Thea. He'd left without talking to her, without telling her anything. The shock of it all, he supposed. Or perhaps he simply needed more confirmation that it was true before he told her. What words would he use to explain all this? "I assume you have a ducal estate."

"Aye. Lovely place, but the manor house there makes this one look like a doll's house."

He couldn't imagine it. Hadn't earned it, wasn't certain he wanted any of it. The title, the estate, being heir to a dukedom. Shouldn't he have had to do something to be worthy of it other than being born and surviving?

The coach came to a stop and a footman immediately appeared to open the door. With ease, the duke leapt out and Beast imagined him riding and striding over his lands, keeping himself fit. He followed him out and up the steps. Once more a door was opened. This time by a butler who bowed slightly. "Your Grace."

"Bentley, is the duchess in the gardens?"

"Yes, sir."

"This way, lad."

They strode down a long corridor with portraits dotting the walls. So many portraits, and Beast imagined he saw himself in many of the faces. He wanted to stop and study each one, learn their names and history. "How many dukes have there been?"

"You'll be the ninth."

He felt it like a punch to the gut. The words were said with no doubt, simply absolute conviction. Yet, he couldn't envision himself as a duke, as a lord of the realm. A man welcomed and respected simply because of his birth. He'd spent his entire life defending his birth as a bastard—and now he was legitimate. His skin suddenly seemed too tight, as though he no longer belonged in it, as though he no longer knew who he was.

What hadn't changed was his desire, his need, to protect women. "It's too cold for her to be outside."

"Aye, but that matters not one whit to her. She spent years without feeling the sun on her face or the breeze riffling through her hair. The day I married her, we spent that night sleeping beneath the stars. She comes indoors when she must but would rather be outside."

"I don't even know her name." He thought the duke might have mentioned it earlier, but he hadn't really noted it.

"Mara. She was a Stuart before she became a Campbell."

Journeying through the house was like making one's way through the warrens in the rookeries, easy to get lost if one didn't pay attention. He'd lived his life paying attention to the smallest of details. He could make his way back to the entryway and beyond if he had to. He'd never considered himself a coward, but at that moment his heart was thudding so hard he wouldn't have been surprised to learn the duke could hear it.

What would the woman think of him, of the man he'd become? What would he think of her? His mother, the woman who had brought him into this world and then given him away? He'd spent a lifetime believing she hadn't loved him. It was an adjustment to realize everything he'd once taken as fact was wrong. That she had loved him so much she'd fairly sacrificed herself for him.

Finally, they stepped through a doorway onto a terrace, and he was struck by how cold he suddenly felt. How off-kilter, how—

They'd stopped at the edge of the black marble, and it was then that he saw the woman sitting in the chair, a chair with wheels.

"They broke her body," the duke said, "but not her spirit. She was always stronger than anyone ever gave her credit for being. It's only one of the reasons I love her."

Beast was barely aware of the fact that he was moving forward, toward her. She was younger than he'd expected. Save for a wide streak of white that began at the center of her forehead and was swept back into a bun, her hair was black. But it was her eyes, the rich shade of cocoa, that drew him in. And her smile of gladness that tightened his chest.

At a loss for words, he knelt before her.

With a hand that was unexpectedly warm, she reached out and

cradled his cheek. "Look at you, my dear lad, all grown up. And me, not around to see you changing from a bairn into a man."

Placing his hand over hers, he turned his face and pressed a kiss against her palm. "I thought you didn't want me."

"I wanted you so badly I ached for the wanting of you, but it was the only way I knew to keep you safe. Give you to another. Was she good to you?"

She was a blur through the tears that had gathered in his eyes. "I couldn't have asked for a better mum."

"I'm so glad." Teardrops rolled down her cheeks. "I couldnae remember where I took you."

"I was well cared for. I have a family." He gave her a gentle smile. "It seems I have two."

"We want you to tell us everything." Then, as though she had no more strength, could no longer appear to be brave, she began weeping in earnest.

Slowly, gingerly, ensuring he caused her no pain, he eased her from the chair and onto his lap, folded his arms around her, and held her close. Although he knew it was impossible, as tears filled his eyes, he thought he remembered being held by her, the feel of her arms around him, the sweetness of her fragrance. Her warmth.

Everything about her seemed so familiar. Yet thirty-three years had passed, and he'd been a mere babe. It wasn't possible he could have any memories of her, but he couldn't deny he felt a connection, as though a corner of his heart recognized her, bloomed only for her.

"Don't cry," he whispered. "I'm here now."

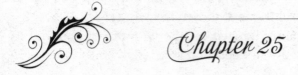

$\mathcal{S}$triving not to worry, and having very little success at it, Althea sat on her bed in her nightdress, staring at the mantel clock that was close to striking midnight. She'd not seen Benedict since he'd left his study to go speak with Ewan Campbell. Jewel thought she'd seen them leave together but couldn't be certain.

Why hadn't he come to tell her he was going out? Why hadn't he returned? If he wasn't back by the time the hour struck midnight in two minutes, she was going to send word to his brothers. Something was amiss. She felt it in the depths of her bones.

When the rap came at her door a minute later, she fairly flew off the bed to the door and jerked it open. Benedict looked as though he'd been battling demons and had quite possibly lost. "What happened? Where have you been?"

He stepped into the room, slammed the door shut. "Walking through Whitechapel. I need you, Thea. God, I need you."

The buttons on her nightdress scattered over the floor as he tore it off her, his own clothes quickly following. His arms came around her like bands, pressing their bodies close, her breasts flattening against his chest as he took possession of her mouth, his tongue delving, his hands frantically stroking as though he couldn't get enough of her, might never be able to get enough of her.

Tearing her mouth from his, she cradled his face, studied his eyes, and what she saw terrified her. He looked to be a man who had lost his way, and she was the North Star that would guide him home.

She leaped up and he caught her, his hands cupping her bottom as she wrapped her legs around him and reclaimed his mouth. Whatever was wrong, he would tell her. For now, in order to bring him back to her, she would be what he needed, wanted.

With long strides, he carried her to the bed, lowered her to its edge, and plunged into her. His groan was savage and raw as he pounded into her, lowering his head to her breast, licking it before drawing it into his mouth, his fingers kneading before he moved to the other.

Meeting him thrust for thrust, she stroked his chest, his shoulders. The pleasure came fast, hit hard like a runaway horse that never again wanted to feel the bit. When it broke free, he lowered his shoulder and she closed her mouth over it to silence the scream that would have woken everyone.

He followed her into the realm of ecstasy with a growl that sounded feral in its intensity. Breathing harshly, sweating, he collapsed on top of her.

Wrapping her arms around him, she simply held on.

"DID I HURT you?" He knew it was a little late to ask. He had probably frightened the devil out of her, taking her like he was riding a tempest.

He'd moved her farther up on the bed, and now he was on his back, with her sprawled halfway over his body, his arm protectively circling her, while his free hand skimmed lazily over flesh not hidden away by the sheet. He couldn't seem to stop touching her.

"No."

She combed her fingers through his hair. He loved when she did that, had been a fool to have stopped her from doing it sooner.

"Tell me."

If there was anyone he could tell, it was her, but he didn't even know where to begin, how to begin. He'd spent the evening dining and talking with his parents—his parents. He still couldn't get used to that. His mind stuttered every time he thought the words.

They'd told him about themselves, their estates, their families. Had asked questions of him. He'd told them about his mum, his brothers, his sisters. He hadn't told them about Thea. He didn't know why. She seemed too new, too private, too special. He'd told them about his ships, his writing, some tales from his youth—not about Three-Fingered Bill or Sally Greene or the brothel. He didn't want them feeling guilty because he'd been attacked. He didn't think they'd look favorably on the rest of it, and none of it mattered anymore anyway. They'd begun moving his building into the realm of respectability.

He knew he should be able to tell his parents everything, had never felt a need to hide anything about himself from his mum. But his relationship with the duke and duchess was too fragile. He'd felt as though he'd been striving to walk over eggs without breaking any. Occasionally, he'd hear a crack and he'd revert to the part of himself that relished privacy, that seldom revealed much. It had always amazed him that Thea had been an exception, that he'd given more words to her than he'd given anyone.

When the hour had drawn late, the duke had sent him back in the coach, but when he'd arrived, he couldn't bring himself to go in just yet. He'd felt raw, untethered, not himself. Therefore, he'd walked through the streets that were familiar, that had shaped him. But only now with Thea in his arms was he beginning to feel a bit more like himself again, like someone he knew and recognized. She was the way home.

"Was it that Ewan Campbell? Who is he? What did he want?" she asked into the silence. Normally, she wouldn't rush him; he knew that, but the clock had ticked for far too long since she'd issued those two simple words: tell me.

"He's my father."

She shot up so fast, the bed rocked. "Your father? How can you be sure?"

"I inherited a good deal of my features from him. My height, my hair, my eyes. Looking at him was like seeing a reflection of my older self in the mirror. He took me to meet my mother."

"Is she his mistress?"

"No, they're married."

"Why did they come to you now?"

She was incensed on his behalf that so many years had passed without them making an appearance. He heard the anger in her tone. "Apparently, they've been searching for me for some time. It's a long story. They only recently determined where to find me." He told her all he knew, all they'd shared, the story of their love.

When he was done, she tucked in her legs, scooted close so they rested against his side, and slowly trailed her fingers over his chest. "You don't seem very happy that they found you."

"I don't know how you did it, Thea. You were a lady and then you were not. How did you reconcile the difference between the two? For thirty-three years I was a bastard. Scorned, ridiculed, avoided. Thought to be the embodiment of sin." He shook his head, skimmed his fingers along the side of her lovely face. "Now I'm to inherit a dukedom, and I no longer know who I am."

She went still, so still, she didn't even blink. "I beg your pardon? A dukedom?"

"Did I forget to mention that little tidbit? He's the Duke of Glasford. Perhaps you know him by his title?"

"No. But then it's not as though I knew every titled lord. So they were married when you were born, yet still they gave you away?"

Again, she was infuriated, and it made him smile just a little. To have such a fierce warrior at his side. "No, I was born a bastard. But they later married, and under Scottish law, I inherit."

"They're from Scotland?"

He almost laughed with her continually repeating what he was saying. It seemed she was having as difficult a time believing and adjusting to all this as he was. He wrapped strands of her hair around his finger. "Somewhere in Perthshire."

"My God, that's an incredible change in circumstances."

"It was the oddest thing tonight. The servants kept calling me *my lord*. It always took me a moment to realize they were speaking to me."

"What's your courtesy title?"

"Earl of Tewksbury."

She released a sound that wasn't quite a laugh or scoff, but something in between that seemed to have a sad ring to it. "You're an earl."

"Apparently so."

"To inherit a dukedom."

He didn't quite understand her forlorn expression or the manner in which she looked past him as though striving to see into the future. He had to admit it was unsettling to be stepping into something he barely knew, but she was intimately familiar with that world and could help guide him.

Grazing his finger from her temple to her chin, he nudged her face back into his direction, captured and held her gaze. "On my arm, you'll be returning to Society."

A small pleat appeared between her brows. Using his thumb, he gently smoothed it out.

"How does all that happen?" she asked. "Do they just take out an advert in the *Times*?"

"The duke and I will be visiting with his solicitor tomorrow, to determine what all has to be done to ensure I am recognized as his heir and inherit. I'll have dinner with them tomorrow evening. Join me. I'd like to introduce you. Let you come to know them, them to know you. I think you're going to like them. I know they'll adore you."

A sweet blush dusted up her throat and over her cheeks, giving him cause to regret all the nights he'd had her in the dark and all the blushes he'd missed.

"It's too soon, don't you think? Your relationship with them needs to be on a more solid footing before you begin introducing surprises. You have no history together to have formed a foundation that can sustain the trials and tribulations that family members encounter. No memories of the better times to help you get through the worst."

He comprehended the wisdom of her words, of what she was explaining. He wanted to love Ewan and Mara Campbell, did love them because they were responsible for his existence, but his family remained the Trewloves. His letter had been L. He'd painted it in red. The first letter of *love*. Suddenly, it seemed significant. A letter tying him to a name, to a family, to an emotion.

They'd done it for Robin, but it was still part of him. He was still part of them.

Turning onto his side, facing her, he threaded his fingers through her hair. "Surely, you don't think you fall into the category of worst?"

"I think you don't yet know how they'll react to you marrying a woman whose father was a traitor. At Christmas, you knew your siblings would accept me because you had a history with them, knew how they had handled other situations. Did you tell your parents about me?"

He pressed a kiss to her forehead, avoiding her gaze. "The moment never seemed right. God, Thea, I don't know why I didn't. You're the first thing I should have mentioned."

Cradling his jaw, she pulled back and held his gaze. "I suspect right now you're all treading very lightly as you come to know each other."

She had the right of that. They still had so much to learn about each other. It wasn't enough to share the stories. He had fewer than a dozen hours of memories with them.

Tonight had involved a few awkward moments of silence as they'd searched for stories to be shared, as he'd mined his memories for the kinder, gentler ones that wouldn't leave them feeling guilty.

"Another time, then," he said, and felt her go lax in his arms, hadn't realized how tense she'd been. Was she dreading meeting them, learning their opinion of her? If they didn't accept her, he'd be unable to accept them. He needed to pave the way, so it wouldn't be difficult for her. He also knew none of the past would matter if his parents weren't part of the aristocracy. Perhaps, more than anything, that was what Thea was striving to make him understand. So much more mattered now.

He skimmed his fingers over her bare shoulder. "I don't know how to do it, Thea. How to be a lord."

She offered him a small smile. "For one thing, you're going to have to become a great deal more arrogant."

He returned her smile in equal measure. "Will you still fancy me if I'm arrogant?"

"I will fancy you however you are."

Yet, he was left with the distinct impression that something had shifted between them, and not necessarily for the good.

Chapter 26

*S*itting in the library, having poured her own sherry, listening as the mantelpiece clock ticked away, Althea glanced over at it to see that only a minute had passed since she'd last looked. It was nearing the hour of ten, and Benedict had yet to return since leaving that morning.

He might not know how to be a lord but certainly knew how to dress like one. She didn't know where he'd acquired the fine clothing—not the evening wear he'd worn for Christmas—but jacket, trousers, and waistcoat almost as posh. Possibly what he wore when meeting with the merchants or anytime he represented his shipping business. But he had most certainly given the impression of being a man comfortable in his own skin, a man who knew what he was about. A man upon whose shoulders a dukedom could securely rest.

She was relatively certain his parents would have been pleased by his appearance, by the knowledge their son displayed such confidence. The solicitor wouldn't doubt his place among the aristocracy.

Whereas Althea had spent most of her day questioning her place in his life. She'd come to understand who she would be with Benedict Trewlove, that she belonged with him, would be his wife. But what was to be her role in the life of Benedict Campbell? Did she even have a part to play upon the stage that would now encompass his world?

She wondered if she would ever wake up one morning confident that everything would be the same as it had been the day before. It seemed every time she came to understand who she was, fate laughed at her confidence as it tossed an obstacle in her path.

The empty chair across from her creaked as it became occupied.

"He shouldn't be much longer, I shouldn't think," Jewel said quietly.

She wondered if she'd ever have another night with him in this library. "They have years to catch up on."

He'd told Jewel of his change in circumstance but hadn't yet told Hester and Lottie. She didn't think he'd told his family, either. How would Mrs. Trewlove feel, after all these years, to see him with the couple responsible for his existence? Would she be happy for him? Or would she feel a tinge of sadness that he was no longer completely hers, that others loved him, sought to make him happy?

"I've been thinking I shall need to find an occupation and should like to let a room here."

"He's not going to leave you behind, Althea."

He might not want to, but eventually he would have to accept the reality as she had—he could no longer marry her, they were no longer of the same world, no longer . . . fit together as easily as they had. "I have learned through hard lessons that it is always wise to have alternative plans at the ready, just in case they are needed."

Jewel nodded, no doubt because she had also learned the advantage to having choices available. "If it's an occupation you're looking for, you could help me manage the boardinghouse. Your presence would add a bit of polish to it and perhaps we'd have fancier occupants."

"That's very kind of you, but I don't need your charity."

"It's far from charity. Beast"—she released a quick burst of air—"I suppose I should call him the earl now. Anyway, he's taught me a good bit about business. I know an asset when I see one."

Who would have thought one of her dearest friends would be a former doxy? "I appreciate the opportunity to prove my worth."

"Posh." Jewel slapped her hand at the air as though an irritating fly had suddenly made an appearance. "You've nothing to prove to me."

"Caw," Hester said, "look at the time. We all lose track of it when Beast isn't around to remind us."

Althea glanced at the clock. A mere five minutes past ten, and yet those minutes seemed significant. She could fairly hear them shouting, "He's not coming home."

But if he did, she wanted, needed, a night they would both long remember.

CHRIST, HE WAS tired. Who knew being a lord could be so bloody exhausting? Meeting with solicitors, the registrar at the College of Arms, answering questions, completing paperwork—

It had all seemed to go on and on and on.

Then dinner with his parents. More questions, more inquiries. A request. "Call us Mother and Father or Ma and Da." Only he couldn't, not yet. It still didn't seem real. He was going through the motions as though it was, but he kept expecting to discover he was in a dream. One not much to his liking because it was keeping him away from Thea for long stretches of time.

As he stepped into the residence, he looked at his watch. A little past eleven.

Near the stairs, he hung his hat and coat on the waiting empty coat stand. He was still unaccustomed to not finding men in the parlor at this hour, to not hearing Jewel's throaty laugh, or inhaling the fragrance of her cheroots. But the changes were good. Another couple of weeks and they would open to boarders. Not they. Jewel would open the establishment to boarders. He wouldn't be here.

A lightness came over him as he ascended the stairs. Thea was near. Hopefully awake, waiting for him.

He should have made his excuses, left earlier, but following dinner his father had begun taking him on a journey through the history of his ancestors and he'd been enthralled. Each had been captured in oils, portraits hanging throughout the manor, and he'd seen something of himself in each of them. He'd wished more than ever that Thea had been with him to hear of the tales of bravery, love, challenges, sorrows, victories . . . and, yes, even outlaws, criminals, and family members hanged. It seemed a long lineage included all sorts. Rebels, heroes, heroines, and sacrifices. An older brother who had willingly walked to the gallows so a younger one wouldn't have to. Women who married men they didn't love in order to save the family. The storyteller in him had lapped up every word. It seemed his father had come from a long line of bards and could weave a tale that entranced.

After they were married, he'd have the duke tell Thea all the stories just so Beast could watch the delight wash over her features.

Tonight, however, he wanted to watch a different sort of delight make its way over her entire body. He shouldn't have taken her so roughly and quickly the night before. He would make it up to her tonight. If she was still awake. If not, he'd slip into her bed and just hold her.

When he reached the top floor, he glanced into the library. The room was dark, no fire upon the hearth to warm it. He missed the hours when they simply sat there and talked. Missed her.

At her door, he knocked softly. Waited. Heard no sounds from within, not even the creak of the bed as she rolled over. Another gentle rapping, the light touch he'd learned in his youth that woke no one other than the person who needed to wake. But still all was quiet on the other side, and her door remained closed. He flattened his palm against the mahogany as he considered going inside but didn't want to disturb her unnecessarily, especially if she was sleeping soundly.

Turning for his bedchamber, he decided to prepare for bed, stripping down to his trousers and shirt, ridding himself of his boots, so he would barely make a sound as he joined her beneath the covers.

After opening his door, he stepped through and froze at the

sight of her lounging on his bed like a contented cat, her hair loose and cascading down her back. She wore naught but a red corset that shoved up her breasts where black lace teased. Its length was such that the laced hem dipped down in the front to cover the blond curls that brought him such delight, but the way she'd positioned herself revealed the back of the corset riding high on her right cheek—no doubt on her left as well, although he couldn't see it. The black piping running down the front accentuated her curves.

"Christ." Was that rough rasp his voice?

"You might want to shut the door," she said calmly as though he'd retained the ability to move at all.

Still, he somehow managed to do as she suggested without slamming it, without disturbing the rest of the household. "Is that the outfit for seduction I asked Beth to make for you?"

"I believe you *ordered* she make it." In a sinewy move, she rolled off the bed, giving him a good view of all that it didn't cover, and his body reacted as though his hands were already skimming over that bare flesh. "I told you she could have used a bit more fabric."

"It's only a corset."

Stopping in front of him, she glanced up into his eyes. "It does come with a skirt, but I thought why make you go to all the bother of removing it when I could simply not put it on." Reaching up, she curled her fingers along his jaw. "I wasn't certain you were coming back tonight."

"I'll always come back." If she wasn't standing there looking so delectable, he would have shared with her all that had delayed him, but it now seemed insignificant. He most certainly wouldn't be tardy again. He started to shrug out of his jacket. She flattened a hand against his chest.

"I want to do it. I want to remove everything from your person."

"You'll be the death of me."

"But won't it be a lovely way to go?"

With a growl he took possession of the mouth with the power to utter words that had the capability of dropping him to his knees. He would never get enough of the taste of her, the feel of her, the fragrance of her. The boldness of her. Ah, yes, especially the boldness of her.

Without separating her lips from his, she shoved his jacket off his shoulders, down his arms. It landed with a soft thud on the floor.

Cradling her head between his hands, he adjusted the angle of her mouth slightly and took the kiss deeper, their tongues twisting and twining as her fingers skimmed over his waistcoat buttons, setting them all free. He admired her patience. He'd have been content to hear the buttons pinging across the room as they were sent flying with the force of the fabric being torn.

The satin garment landed against his jacket with merely a whisper. His neck cloth quickly followed. When she began unfastening the buttons on his shirt, he went to work on the cuffs, even though he hated that he had to take his hands from her to do it. Ah, but what he was going to do to her with his hands once he was free of all the blasted clothing.

He had to separate himself from her completely in order to pull the shirt over his head.

"Let me see to my boots." He dropped into the nearby chair, grabbed a boot, stopped as his gaze fell on that little bit of pointed cloth that so effectively covered the sight of heaven. But if he was to dip his head just a little bit more . . .

"You're only wearing the corset, aren't you?"

"I am."

He lifted his gaze to hers. "How can a bit of frippery drive me mad?"

"Does it?" Her innocent tone only served to increase the madness.

"You know it does."

She pressed her lips together, smacked them, ran her tongue around them. Lord help him, he was going to spill his seed before he ever got out of his trousers. He jerked off his boots, his stockings. Stood. Reached for the buttons on his trousers—

Her hands landed on his. "I want to do it."

"Do it quickly."

She peered up at him with a saucy smile. "I'll do it as I want."

"Why are you torturing me?"

"Am I?"

"You know you are, you little witch."

One button freed. Thank God.

"You always lead, and I follow," she said quietly, studying the fall of his trousers. Surely, she could see that his swollen cock was about to cause the remaining secured buttons to pop off. "I want to lead tonight."

He hadn't realized he always led. Often, to him, it felt as though they were taking direction from each other. Except for last night, when he'd needed her so desperately and had set the pace, the frenzy. Not that she'd objected. Still, perhaps tonight was his punishment. As far as punishments went, it was one of the more pleasant ones.

Another button. Another, another until they were all freed.

With her nails, she lightly scored his buttocks as she drew down his trousers. The tremor that fissured deliciously through him with the scrape of her nails was nearly his undoing, and he almost didn't notice that she'd gone to her knees in order to lower his trousers all the way. After stepping out of them and kicking them aside, he reached down to help her to her feet, but when his hands curled around her shoulders—

"No."

He froze, waited.

She trailed her fingers up and down his thighs. "You have such firm legs."

She pressed a kiss to his knee. His knee, for God's sake. It very nearly buckled. Then an inch above his knee. The inside of his thigh.

"You often do very wicked things between my thighs with

your mouth," she said solemnly. She bent back her head, met his gaze. "Why did you never teach me that I could do something very similar to you?"

Was she insinuating what he thought she was? "Because I didn't think you'd enjoy it."

"Do you taste like Brussels sprouts, then?"

He furrowed his brow. "I very much doubt it."

Her lids half-lowered; her mouth pouted prettily. "That's the only taste I abhor."

His groan came up from the soles of his feet. "Thea—"

"I want to taste you." Her hands were clasping the backs of his legs, her mouth once again pressed to the inside of his thigh. "Would you like me to?"

How could she sound so innocent and yet so worldly at the same time?

"Yes." It came out as more a croak than a word.

She nipped at the sensitive skin where her mouth rested. His stomach tightened. His hands fisted. He couldn't take his gaze off the sight of her fair head so near to his cock. The unruly thing strained toward her. He had no luck whatsoever making it behave, no doubt because he had no desire for it to.

Her hands came around, and she closed her fingers around the base of his shaft, and now it had no choice except to do as she commanded. She licked her lips, then kissed the head, and the pleasure that shot through him caused every muscle to tighten. He threaded his fingers through her soft hair because he couldn't not touch her when she was touching him so intimately.

"No Brussels sprout flavor," she said, and took her tongue on a tour that left no part of that throbbing member overlooked. With a low groan, he dropped his head back with the exquisiteness of the sensations riffling through him.

A little death. That was what the French called it. He was going to die, here and now.

Then he felt her mouth—heat, dampness, softness—closing around him and every inch of him tensed. Glancing down, he watched as her head bobbed while she worked those plump lips and her velvety tongue over his sensitive flesh. "Thea . . . God . . . uh . . . do you know how beautiful you are?"

She didn't answer, simply took him deeper, and he honestly didn't know if he was going to survive her enthusiastic ministrations.

Chapter 27

*A*lthea wondered if he could feel her smile. His groans and moans and occasional curses only incited her to torment him further. His fingers kept jerking, his thighs quaked, his stomach quavered.

It made her happy to realize how much he was enjoying this. Not in a giddy, laughing, twirling-in-the-snow sort of way. But in a darkly, delicious, sweet-agony sort of way. She was incredibly familiar with the madness all those contradicting sensations could create. He'd put her through them often enough. It pleased her greatly to be returning the favor.

"Thea . . . sweetheart . . . I can't take much more." Gently, he cradled her jaw and eased away from her. "Let me take you to bed now."

She lifted her gaze to his. "Did you like it?"

"I loved it." Bringing her to her feet, he swept her up into his arms. "Kiss me, so I know what I taste like."

Plastering her mouth onto his with an enthusiasm indicating she'd die if she didn't, she swept her tongue over his, sighed as he sucked on her tongue as she'd sucked him. Their fall onto the bed broke the kiss but did little else to separate them as he took his mouth on a journey over the swells of her breasts.

"I'm torn between keeping this damn thing on you and taking it off," he declared with vehemence.

"Leave it on."

"It drives me mad. But now it's my turn." He scooted down until he was nestled between her thighs. The first stroke along her cleft was with his forefinger. "My God, but you're wet. You liked what you were doing."

"I did. Do you like what you're about to do down there?"

His lids were half-lowered, his gaze sultry. "I wouldn't be down here if I didn't."

Then his tongue replaced his finger, the caress slow and long, and she very nearly saw stars. She was so ready for him. Her little nubbin swollen and throbbing and so very sensitive to his touch. When he tugged on it, she jerked up, almost sitting, cradling his head between her hands. "I think I'm a wanton."

"I love wantons."

A suckle, a swirl of his tongue, and her entire body tensed, crying out for release. "I can't hold on."

"Then fly."

"Not without you. Not tonight. I want you inside me."

With a growl, he moved swiftly, rolling away from her, landing on his back. "Straddle me so I can appreciate this maddening corset."

Placing her knees on either side of his hips, she rose up. He positioned himself, and she began slowly pushing down until he was completely seated inside her. He filled her entirely, felt so wonderful. She blinked back the tears that threatened. She waited, simply absorbing all the wonderful sensations she experienced when they were joined.

"Can you breathe with this thing on?" he asked.

"Not well."

"We can't have that. Besides, I think it's done its job. It and your mouth. I don't think I've ever been this hard in my entire life."

She released a small laugh, partly because he sounded so disgruntled, partly because he sounded so satisfied and pleased.

He flicked the hooks free of their mooring, and breath rushed into her lungs. She hadn't realized how much she'd needed it.

After pulling the corset away from her, he dropped it over

the side of the bed. He filled his hands with her breasts, began kneading.

She moaned. "That feels so damned good."

"Did you just use profanity?"

With a smile, she lowered herself, kissed him. "I think my breasts were going to sleep. You've woken them up. It feels marvelous."

Placing his hands at her back, he held her in place as he rolled his shoulders off the bed and closed his mouth around her nipple, suckling and soothing. That felt even better.

He gave the same attention to her other breast, before dropping back down. "You have the reins, sweetheart. Ride me. Fast, slow, gentle, hard. I'll follow your lead."

At that moment she didn't know if it was possible to love him any more than she did. She rose up the length of him, slid back down. It was a different angle from what she'd ever experienced. She liked it. She liked it a lot. Then she began rocking, creating pressure where she needed it.

"Oh, you're enjoying that," he said.

"How do you know?"

"Because you look like you've found heaven."

She had. With him. But she didn't want to think about that now. Those thoughts were for later.

As his hands returned to her breasts, she rode him, increasing the tempo, sliding, rocking. They began panting in earnest; the pleasure began building. But the peak eluded her.

"I can't . . ." She shook her head. How could she explain it? "I don't . . ."

He cradled her hips between his hands. She slid up, and he guided her down with more force. The pleasure intensified. She gasped.

"Is that what you need?" he asked.

"Yes. Yes."

Because his hands were occupied, she used her own to knead her breasts, to tease her nipples, her joy increasing as his eyes darkened, his jaw clenched. All her nerve endings began tingling. The most exquisite sensations rushed through her.

When they exploded, she had to bite her fist to keep her scream contained. The vibrations were still erupting through her when he dug his fingers into her hips, groaned, and thrust deeply into her one last time.

She collapsed on top of him, not certain she'd ever again move.

BEAST DIDN'T KNOW why he'd never thought to bring her to his chamber. His bed was larger than hers. They had plenty of room to sprawl over it. Not that they needed it. As always, afterward, she snuggled against his side, one of her legs draped over his hip, while he held her close.

"I like when you lead," he said. "I like it very much. I think you should lead every time."

Her head was resting in the crook of his shoulder. Turning slightly, she pressed a kiss against his skin. "Not every time, but occasionally, because I like when you lead, too."

He'd enjoyed every minute of what had transpired after he'd walked into the room, but sometimes it had felt as though there was almost a desperation to it, as though everything needed to happen because it would never happen again. Which made no sense whatsoever.

"What you did earlier . . . your mouth . . . my cock . . . did Jewel teach you that?"

She lifted up until she could gaze down on him. "In a way." She blushed. "But not really. I've been thinking about it, wondering if it's what people did, because more and more of late, I've been wondering what it might be like to . . . taste you. So tonight I asked her about it."

"She taught you what to do?"

She shook her head. "Not really. She told me to just do whatever I thought I'd enjoy doing."

He threaded his fingers through her hair near her temple. "You thought you would enjoy doing that?"

Bobbing her head, she smiled. "And I did."

"Lucky me." He skimmed his thumb over her cheek. "In the future, you can always ask me if there is something you want to try. It doesn't matter if other people do it. It only matters that you want to."

Averting her gaze, she placed her head back against his shoulder. "I'll keep that in mind."

But he was left with the impression he'd said something wrong. "Thea, is everything all right?"

"Of course it is. Did everything work out for you today?"

He wished he could rid himself of the sensation that something was amiss. "It seems my father is a very powerful man, which I suppose explains how my grandfather was able to do all the damage he did. Whenever we walked into a building, an office, a room, everyone jumped to do his bidding. It was extraordinary. My siblings and I are formidable, but this was something more."

"He's nobility. It's not only his character or his temperament or his disposition. His title carries weight. The more revered his title, the more revered he is, even if it's undeserving. Like your brothers' father, Lord Elverton. He always made my skin crawl, but people bowed down to him as though he were a saint. Now that you're a lord, you'll exert more power than you do now."

"I've always known the nobility was treated differently. I suppose I never noticed it with Thornley or Rosemont because they regarded me as an equal. Although to be honest, I've never seen them outside of the family. My father didn't demand that anyone treat him differently. They simply did."

"You'll get used to it. Eventually, you won't even notice that everyone offers you such reverence. I never did. I just accepted it as my due."

He didn't know if he'd ever get used to the bowing and curtsying, the servants coming in to stir the fire, someone always on hand to take his coat, hat, and gloves. "I don't know if I'll ever feel completely comfortable with it all."

"You will."

What he did know was that it would all be easier with her at his side. He skimmed his fingers up and down her arm. "They want me to go back to Scotland with them. For a few weeks, so they can show me around and introduce me to my other family." He still wasn't accustomed to the fact that he had another family. Uncles, aunts, and cousins who were anxious to meet him. "You need to tell me when and where you want that second proposal because I want us to be officially betrothed when you go with me."

She went still, so very still. It was uncanny, the way he could detect the smallest of changes in her, especially when something was amiss. "Thea?"

She unfurled herself from around him and pushed herself up, bringing the sheet with her so the most delectable parts of her were covered. "I can't marry you now."

As his heart slammed almost painfully against his ribs, he shoved himself up to a sitting position. "What do you mean you can't marry me *now*?"

"You are part of the aristocracy."

"Which you wanted to return to. You will return to it with me."

Tears welled in her eyes. She gave her head a small shake. "I can't. It wouldn't be fair to you. It wouldn't be fair to your parents."

He slapped his hand against the headboard. The sting assured him that he was awake, hadn't fallen asleep and succumbed to some nightmare. "Explain how marrying the woman I love— more than life—would be unfair to me."

She dashed at the tears that rolled onto her cheeks. Blinked, blinked, blinked. Cleared her throat. When she once again looked at him, not a tear was to be found. "You're going to have a difficult enough time being accepted because people know you as a Trewlove, not a Campbell. Ben, I'd just be a liability. No one would look favorably on you if you married the daughter of a traitor."

"I don't give a bloody damn. I love you, Thea."

"I love you. And that's the reason I can't marry you."

He shot out of the bed, crossed over to where his trousers rested on the floor, and jerked them on. He couldn't have this conversation in the nude. Grabbing his shirt, he tossed it at her. "Put that on."

Because neither could he have this conversation with her in the nude or in that bloody corset.

Pacing, he fought to gather his thoughts. He heard the bed creak. Glancing over, he saw her sitting on the edge of it and refused to acknowledge how adorable she looked with his shirt swallowing her. "We can make this work."

"We can't. You don't know Society. I do."

"I'm not going to have a bunch of bloody nobs determine whom I marry."

She stood up and the hem of his shirt fell to her knees. "What of our children?"

"What of them?" Other than the fact he wanted every one of them to look like her.

"Did you not hear what Chadbourne said the night we bested him? How our children would have suffered because their grandfather was a traitor? As much as I'm loath to admit it, he was correct. I hated him for turning his back on me, but I would have hated him all the more if he hadn't, if we'd had children and they had to grow up with taunts and unkind barbs. You know what that's like. You experienced it. You know how much it hurts. I can't do that to my children. *Our* children."

He squeezed his eyes shut. With an almost unbearable ache, he wanted those blonde, blue-eyed girls and those black-haired, dark-eyed boys. He wanted to put them on his shoulders so they could place the star on top of the Christmas tree. He wanted them to have adventures with his nieces and nephew. And any others that came along. He wanted to see his mum cradling one of them in her arms. He wanted them to hear the stories his father had told him tonight. He wanted them to sit on his strong and protective mother's lap.

Swallowing hard, he opened his eyes, held her gaze, and forced out the words through the knot in his throat. "Then we won't have children."

"You're breaking my heart, Ben."

"It's only fair. You're breaking mine."

She turned away from him. He heard her release a shaky breath. When she again faced him, he saw standing before him the haughty, arrogant lady who had appeared in the dressmaker's shop and confronted Lady Jocelyn what seemed eons ago.

"You are a lord. Your first order of business is to provide an heir to inherit the titles and properties you will inherit. Your parents will expect it of you. The Crown will expect it of you. Society will expect it of you. I will expect it of you. Not having children is not a choice you have."

Bloody damned hell. Bollocks. Through his mind, he ran a few other choice words he'd learned from men working the docks. "We'll figure something out."

"We already have," she said as though she were a queen laying down an edict. "I will not marry you."

He thought he actually heard his heart crack. He knew he felt it. "When did you make this decision?"

Some of the haughtiness left her. "Last night, while I watched you sleeping."

He swung his arm out to encompass the entirety of the room. "And all this?"

"Was goodbye."

Chapter 28

*S*tanding by the fire burning brightly in his mum's small house, as he waited for his siblings to greet each other, hug their mum, pour themselves a drink, and settle into their favorite spots around the room, Beast reflected on the irony of his life.

For a good long while, as the Beast of Whitechapel, he'd not thought himself deserving of a woman's love, of a wife and children. He'd worried about the shame he'd bring them because he knew nothing at all about from whence he'd come, a bit self-conscious regarding what he viewed as an imperfection. Because he never expected to marry, it had never bothered him to own a brothel. Through it, he was able to help some attain better lives. Although he'd also known it wouldn't give a wife cause to boast about her husband's undertakings. But again, it hadn't mattered, because he'd envisioned himself with no wife.

Then Thea had come into his life with the strength of a storm that could so easily leave destruction in its wake, and she'd managed to blow away all the reasons he'd thought he wasn't worthy of her until he'd finally realized that he was. He'd asked for her hand, she'd said yes. He'd never known such satisfaction, such joy.

Now he was heir to a dukedom. He had obtained the power to grant her dream. Marriage to him would return her to Society, first as a countess, in time as a duchess. But now she wouldn't marry him because of the shame she thought she'd bring him—

and more important, their children. That her presence in their life would make it more difficult for him and them to be accepted.

Bollocks.

How could he ask his parents not to publicly recognize him as their son? How could he break their hearts when they'd already been broken once before because of him? How could he turn aside the inheritance they were proud and overjoyed to pass on to him? He wasn't even certain the law would allow it.

He felt the way he'd assumed he would have if he'd stayed on the ship heading out to sea—untethered, unmoored, desperately searching for a safe harbor. He didn't seem to know who he was any longer. The path he was on was full of brambles, and he didn't know how to navigate his way around them without first encountering the bite of their thorns.

The ache in his heart was nearly unbearable. And he knew of no way to keep others from tumbling into the brambles with him.

It was the clearing of Mick's throat that stirred him from the uneasy musings. His family was gathered around him, the ladies sitting in cushioned chairs, their husbands perched on the arms. Except for his mum, who had never remarried, had no interest in doing so, had devoted her life to raising the children of others.

His heart squeezed so tightly that it caused an ache to spread through his chest. He loved these people with every fiber of his being. For thirty-three years, until Thea, they had been the best part of his life. Shoving, arguing, taking a switch to his backside. Sharing confidences, protecting his back, standing firm at his side. Giving him a difficult time on occasion—especially Aiden— but always ensuring he knew they'd never let him down, they were all on this journey together. They would never leave him behind.

His siblings' faces were a combination of anxiousness in their eyes or smiles they were fighting to hold back. All day he'd practiced what he was going to say, and now the words scattered like dead leaves blown by the wind.

"We all know you're going to marry Althea," Aiden finally said into the quiet. "You don't have to be nervous about telling us. We approve of her."

If only that was it. He sighed. Shook his head. "Actually, it appears I won't be marrying her, but that's not why I asked you all to come. I've recently learned who I am."

At the widening of their eyes, he shifted his stance. That wasn't right. He knew who he was. He was Beast Trewlove—only he wasn't. He was supposed to be Benedict Campbell. He appreciated that everyone held their tongues, didn't bombard him with questions, gave him time to realign his thoughts.

"I'll try to make a long story short. My parents are Ewan and Mara Campbell, the Duke and Duchess of Glasford. I'm their only son"—he shook his head—"their only child. Heir to the dukedom."

"Bloody hell," Finn said quietly. "You're nobility. Legitimate."

"Apparently so, yes."

"How do you *know* they're your parents?" Gillie asked.

He felt as though he was abandoning her, leaving her as the only one who knew nothing at all about how she'd come to be.

"I'm the spitting image of him, and the duke and I"—Beast waved his fingers by the right side of his head—"it seems this is a common trait in the family."

"You don't seem very happy about all this," his mum said gently.

"To be honest, it's an upheaval in my life. It's like a storm that comes in and changes the shoreline. Some of it is the same, some is gone, and some is just different. I haven't quite sorted it all. They want to visit with you. They want me to return to Scotland with them for a few weeks, until they come back to London for the Season."

"You're a Scot?" Aiden blurted.

He'd intended to be methodical in the telling, giving them all the important details. Instead, he was omitting things. "Born in Perthshire."

"Why did they give you away?" Fancy asked.

He gave up on keeping the long story short and shared with them all the duke and duchess had told him.

"Christ," Aiden muttered when he was done.

"Your language," Mum admonished.

"Sorry, Mum, but Christ. I thought this sort of intrigue only happened in books."

"I wish that were the case."

"You're going to make a wonderful duke," Gillie said.

"I know Glasford," Thorne said. "Not well, but we have crossed paths. As I recall he has other titles. I assume he'll give you one as a courtesy."

"Earl of Tewksbury."

"So now we have to call you my lord?" Aiden asked.

"Only if you want me to hit you. I don't want anything here to change."

But even as he said it, he knew everything would.

THE FOLLOWING AFTERNOON Beast sat at his desk while Jewel read over the document he'd handed her.

Earlier, he'd taken the duke and duchess to visit with his mum. The camaraderie between them was instantaneous, perhaps because they'd showered his mum with gratitude for keeping him safe, and she had expressed appreciation that he'd been one of her lads. They'd wanted to hear tales from his childhood, and she'd been only too happy to accommodate their wishes.

As he knew all the tales, he'd bid them a farewell in order to see to some business that needed to be tended to before they left on the morrow. Tonight his mum and siblings would be dining at the duke and duchess's residence.

With confusion in her eyes, Jewel shook her head. "It says the building is mine. Why are you giving it to me?"

"I'd always intended to when it was time for me to move out. That time has arrived."

"But why?"

"Do I need a reason?"

"I'd feel better about accepting the gift."

"Because you've taken care of things here. You deserve your dream of having a boardinghouse."

She scooted up to the edge of her chair. "I don't want a boardinghouse. I only chose it because it sounded respectable. I want this place to be for other women what it was for me: a haven. But they'll have to understand that if they're staying here, they can't be spreading their legs anymore. So many women don't have a choice. I did. I chose to do it. I chose when to stop. But that second choice—I had it because you'd given me a place." She held up the document. "Now you've given me another."

"I like your idea of not having a boardinghouse. I'll designate all the profits from one of my ships to always come to you so you have the means to run it."

"You don't have to do that."

"Jewel, you're carrying on what I started. I'll do whatever I can to help."

"What if we call it the Sally Greene Refuge for Tarnished Ladies? Within these walls we'll polish them up."

He gave her a tender smile. "I like that."

AFTER HE AND Jewel completed their business, he went to his room and stuffed what little clothing he had into a cloth traveling bag he'd purchased before returning here. He tossed in his shaving items and his brush. Glancing around, he saw nothing else he needed. His most precious items, the timepiece, the miniature of Thea nestled in its cover, and the match safe, he always carried with him. All else could stay. He was going to miss the place, miss the people. But an earl could hardly reside in a former brothel.

He couldn't imagine living with his parents, although their residence was large enough that he could go days without seeing them. Perhaps he'd purchase or lease his own. He hadn't yet decided. He knew only that he could no longer reside within these walls.

He'd asked Jewel where he'd find Thea, so it was with certainty that he knocked on her bedchamber door.

When she opened it, he was surprised to see the blue shadows beneath her eyes as though she'd gone without sleep, the slight swelling of her lids as though she'd wept. He didn't want what he had to say to her to echo down the hallway. "May I come in?"

She moved back. He set his bag down in the corridor before striding in and closing the door behind him. She stood only three feet away, but she might as well have been in France for the distance that stretched between them. He held a package toward her. "The remainder of your salary and the extra for reaching the three-month deadline."

When she opened it, she'd find the additional thousand for his not teaching her to be a temptress. If he told her now, she'd object, and he didn't want to argue about it.

"Why give it to me now?"

"I wanted things settled between us before I leave for Scotland tomorrow. We'll return in early March, just before Parliament begins its session."

"I'll move out."

"No need. I'll no longer be residing here."

"Where will you live?"

He shrugged. "I don't yet know. I just know it can't be here."

He hated this stiffness between them, as though they'd never been intimate, as though he didn't know how wonderful it felt to have her muscles throbbing around his cock.

"If you're ever in want of a mistress . . ."

The words started out light in tone, growing quieter until they trailed off, no doubt because of the anger coursing through him that he couldn't hold in check. It had to be visible in his eyes. "Is that what the other night was? An audition?"

She blanched. He grimaced.

"You know it wasn't."

"I know. You didn't deserve that. But I don't want you to be my bloody mistress. I want you as my wife."

"I told you why I can't marry you."

"Do you think I give a bloody damn if someone turns his back on me? Do you think we can't teach our children how to handle the arses of the world? I began my life being bullied, Thea. It's not pleasant, can be incredibly hurtful. I don't know how many times I went off alone to a corner and wept. Then felt shame that I was crying. But I survived it, and I learned that I never wanted to do anything to make another person feel the despair I felt at that moment. It is survivable, and because of it, perhaps I'm a better person than I might have been otherwise."

"Proper Society is nothing like the streets of Whitechapel or the rookeries. You've not been a lord long enough to understand how very different it is. I think you'll find your opinion on the matter will change in time."

What he felt for her, what he wanted with her, was not going to change, but he didn't know how to convince her of that.

He also understood it was very different to be betrayed and bullied by those you once loved and thought loved you. Those who had treated him poorly had never meant anything to him, so he'd been able to brush off the taunts like so much lint. She couldn't claim the same. People who had mattered to her had been unkind.

"Because I thought we were going to marry, I took no precautions to ensure I didn't get you with child."

"I did."

Those two words crushed his chest because her being with child was his last hope to have her.

Her cheeks flushed. "I assumed you had Jewel teach me how to avoid pregnancy for a reason."

He nodded. "Only abstinence is a hundred percent. If you find yourself with child, you're to send word. Inside the packet, you'll find my parents' address in London and Scotland. You can always reach me through them."

"I know you don't understand that my decision is truly for the best, but a time will come when you will."

"Perhaps you have the right of it. But what I can tell you at this very moment, with absolute certainty, is that I will never stop loving you."

Her face crumpled, and that he could not bear to watch. "Goodbye, Thea."

He strode out of the room, snatched up his bag, and headed off into the unknown.

Chapter 29

*B*east stood at the large window in the front parlor and gazed out at the rain cascading from the heavens.

He'd been at the Scottish estate a little over a month, and during that time, he'd met aunts, uncles, and cousins. He'd galloped over verdant hills of green. Acres and acres and acres of it. So much land. One day it would be his. His father had taken him to a loch, and they'd fished. An abundance of activities to catch up on. An entire youth's worth.

He'd gone for a walk in the forest and caught sight of a stag. He'd thought of Robin and the delight the sight would have brought the lad.

Thank goodness he no longer got lost in this massive residence that was more castle than manor. Lamps and candles provided the light. When dusk arrived, he used a match from the match safe his mum had given him to light the lamp in his bedchamber to ward off the darkness. He didn't fear the absence of light. It was the pain of Thea's absence he was striving to ward off and having a devil of a time doing. In spite of all he was attaining, he'd lost what he most treasured, and when he thought of the future, it seemed bleak indeed.

Especially after reading the missive from her that had arrived that morning. She had been succinct and to the point. She was not with child.

Pulling his watch from his waistcoat pocket, he flipped open the cover and looked down at her portrait. He wondered if a time would come when the ache in his chest wouldn't increase with the reminder of her. Not that he needed the reminder. She was never far from his thoughts. Everything he saw or experienced he wanted to show her, share with her. Even the rain.

He wanted her opinions on matters. Was his cousin Angus as much of an arse as Beast thought he was? Did Beast look ridiculous in a kilt? He'd worn it only once. It was going to take some getting used to.

Would she like living here? Would she marry him if he could promise her that they would never return to London, would avoid Society, wouldn't need it? Although even as he had the thought, he knew she would argue that the children would need London and Society in order to be accepted. They couldn't hide.

With a sigh, he snapped his watch closed, tucked it away.

"You seem to spend a good bit of time checking the hour," a soft voice said, and he closed his eyes.

It wasn't the first time he'd been unaware of his mother watching him, that he'd been so lost in thought he hadn't heard her arrive. The servant who saw to her needs, helped her navigate the residence, kept that contraption of hers well oiled so it seldom made a creak or a moan. Opening his eyes, he glanced back over his shoulder at her, gave her a small smile. It was an odd thing, but after such a short time, he felt as though she'd always been in his life. "It seems to rain often in Scotland."

"Often enough." She moved herself closer. "Tell me about the watch."

"I stole it . . . when I was a lad of eight."

She seemed neither surprised nor horrified. "But it's not the hour you're checking."

So maybe she hadn't been asking about the origins of the timepiece. Maybe he'd known that, had thought if he shocked her, she wouldn't ask anything else about it.

"May I see it?" she asked.

Removing the watch from his pocket, he opened the lid and held it out to her, displaying it in the palm of his hand, not certain why he didn't detach the fob, why he wouldn't relinquish his hold on it.

"She's pretty," his mother said. "What's her name?"

"Thea. Althea, but to me, she's always been Thea."

"Have you known her long?"

He glanced at the portrait before once again snapping the lid closed and slipping the timepiece into its place. "Sometimes it seems like forever. Sometimes not long enough."

"You've never mentioned her."

"I'd only declared my feelings for her a couple of days before the duke came to call." For some reason he found it easier to view the duchess as his mother than the duke as his father. Perhaps because the duke was almost larger than life, and he knew at some point he'd be called upon to fill his boots.

"Is she a commoner?"

He nodded. "But she was born and raised in the aristocracy. Her fortunes changed when her father was found guilty of plotting to assassinate the Queen."

"Her father was the Duke of Wolfford?"

"You know of him?"

"Your father was called to London when the misdeed was thwarted. He serves in the House of Lords, you know."

"I'm still striving to get used to that. Do you go to London for the Season?"

"Usually, although we don't attend many balls. I'm not very skilled at the waltz."

There were times when she broke his heart. Not intentionally. She accepted her limitations, but he couldn't help feeling a bit responsible for them. If he hadn't been born, if she hadn't needed to hide him . . .

"Are you going to marry the lass?"

He turned his attention back to the rain, remembering how it had fallen the day he'd taken Thea to the dressmaker. He wondered if every aspect of his life would remind him of her. How could she have made such an impact in such a short time? "She thinks her father's actions make her an unsuitable wife for a lord."

"What do you think?"

"Bollocks." With a grimace, he swung around to face her. "My apologies—"

"Benedict Campbell, never apologize to your mother for being who you are. Besides, do you not think I've heard your father use worse language?"

Crossing his arms over his chest, he leaned against the window ledge. "It's a man's way, I suppose."

She smiled at that. He liked making her smile but had quickly learned that no one could make her smile as the duke did. Her entire face lit up when he walked into the room.

"Tell me about her."

He sighed. Where to even begin?

"She's strong. You remind me of her, with all the strength you've had to exhibit over the years." He gave her a gentle smile. "People fear me because of my size. That fear can be useful at times. But she was never afraid of me. Not from the first moment our paths crossed. She fairly told me to bugger off.

"I made her a proposition—it had to do with teaching some ladies I was striving to help find a better life. I laid out terms. She came back with a counter term. I agreed to it, even knowing I would never honor it. But I didn't want her going elsewhere. I convinced myself I did it for the sake of the ladies, that they would benefit from her knowledge. But I did it for myself because I thought I'd benefit from her presence."

"And you did."

He nodded. "She's clever, generous, and kind. She makes her decisions based on what she believes is better for someone else rather than herself." She'd done it for her brothers, done it for him.

"When she laughs, my world is brighter. When she smiles, it is more colorful."

"You miss her. You're lonely here," she said softly.

"Not lonely." Yes, lonely. Not only was Thea not here, but neither were his siblings, his mum. How many times had he felt an urge to speak with one of them? To have a pint at the Mermaid and Unicorn? To purchase a book from the Fancy Book Emporium? "I'm accustomed to the noise and the bustling crowds. Sometimes it's so quiet."

Especially at night when he lay in his bed, without Thea in his arms, her breathing a soothing lullaby. He couldn't sleep for the lack of noise.

"I rather enjoy the quiet. I spent years listening to the screams of the tormented day and night."

"If my grandfather weren't already dead, I'd kill him for his role in what happened to you."

"But not for his role in what your life was. That brings me comfort. The night we had dinner with your family, I so enjoyed watching the easy way you are with each other. I can't imagine you without them."

Neither could he. What a strange journey he'd taken through life.

"You don't have to live here, you know. Even when you're duke. You simply have to ensure the estate is properly maintained and see to your duties. You're a lord. You can live wherever you like. But then I suppose you could do that anyway with the success you've had." She studied him as thunder rumbled in the distance. "Do you wish we hadn't found you?"

With no hesitation, he shoved himself forward, knelt beside her, and took her hand. "No, of course not. It's just taking me a bit of time to become accustomed to this change in my life."

With the hand he wasn't holding, she brushed her fingers through his hair. "I hope you realize how very much we love you."

Bringing her hand to his lips, he pressed a kiss against her knuckles. "I love you."

"When we return to London, we're going to host a ball, ensure your place among the *ton* is understood and accepted. You should invite your lass."

London
March 1874

*F*ebruary was the shortest month of the year, yet had been the very longest of Althea's life.

She was glad March had finally arrived. Not that it would make any difference. It wouldn't return Benedict to her.

She missed him with a physical ache so painful that sometimes she wondered if her heart had stopped, only for a second or two, because stopping briefly was better than shattering altogether. She'd hurt him with her refusal to marry him. She understood that, but also knew he didn't have a clear understanding of how things worked among the aristocracy. Reputation did not begin and end with a person. It came with tentacles that wrapped around those closest to you, linking you to their disgraces, linking them to yours.

As she sat at what had once been his desk in what had once been his study, organizing the lessons she would begin teaching the first set of women who had arrived, she wondered if a time would come when so much stopped reminding her of him. When she lay in bed at night wearing his shirt, the one he'd tossed to her, that carried his sandalwood and cinnamon scent, she thought of him. When she was out shopping and saw a gentleman glance at his pocket watch, she thought of Benedict. When the winds blew cold, she thought of him. When it rained, when it didn't, she thought of him.

When she sat in the library in the evening, memories of the hours she'd spent with him tormented her. No sherry glass now waited for her. When he'd asked her to marry him, she'd envisioned a lifetime of sitting in a library, sharing moments with him.

When she'd had Benedict in her arms, she'd not needed a protector or Society. She'd felt fully capable of taking care of herself. All she'd needed was him. She'd given up what she needed in order for him to have an easier time adjusting to life among the aristocracy. He didn't understand now, but in time he would.

He would have hurts. It was the way of those she'd once walked among to be unkind, not as accepting as they might be. Perhaps he'd receive a cut direct, or a lady would refuse to dance with him, or a gentleman would not invite him to sit with him at the club. But the hurts would be pinpricks instead of the knife wounds being with her would have caused him. Pins didn't leave scars. Knives did.

Pulling on the chain around her neck, she pulled out the locket tucked behind her bodice, opened it, and looked at the portrait of Benedict. She did this at least half a dozen time every hour. Oh, she missed him so much. There were times when she could barely move for how much she missed him.

When Jewel walked in, Althea barely stirred. She never closed the door. Jewel wouldn't have knocked anyway. Jewel handled the books, Althea the education of those who came here, preparing them for a different life.

"You have a visitor," Jewel said, "in the parlor."

A parlor that now displayed not a single breast, buttock, or cock.

Other than her brothers, no one from Althea's past knew she was here, would visit her. Only one person would, and her stomach felt as though a thousand butterflies had suddenly escaped their cocoons to flutter around it. "Is it him?"

That was all that was needed. Jewel had been quite blunt one night in telling Althea she'd been a fool to turn him away.

"In a way."

What the deuce did that mean?

She rose, patting her hair, seeking loose strands, tucking them back into place. Her frock was a mauve that gave a bit of color to her when of late, she'd been far too pale. Lack of sleep did that. Staring at the ceiling instead, reliving every touch, caress, and kiss.

She swept out of the study and down the stairs, forcing her steps to slow so she didn't rush into the parlor with such haste that he would know she'd missed him dreadfully, was grateful he'd come, that to see him one more time was the wish she made upon the first star that appeared each night. In the foyer, she stopped, took two ragged breaths—that failed to calm her racing heart—pulled back her shoulders, lifted her chin, and glided in gracefully as though she'd placed a book on top of her head and didn't want it to topple off.

The sight of him stole her breath. It required stillness to take in all of him, to take note of all the subtle changes, and Jewel's words made sense now. *In a way.*

His clothing had always been well tailored, but the black trousers, gray shirt, dark gray waistcoat, black knotted neck cloth, black jacket he wore now was more so. It looked as though he'd been melted down and poured into the attire. His hair, still long, had been styled in such a way that it provided a frame for his face. In one hand, he held a walking stick and beaver top hat. But it was more than the outer trimmings.

Confidence, power, and strength had always shimmered around him, but now they seemed sleeker, yet more potent. She remembered Danny saying the Trewloves were royalty within Whitechapel. Now Benedict gave the impression of being royalty anywhere he appeared, even among the aristocracy. People would sense his presence when he walked into a room. Ladies would desire and men would envy. He'd never looked more gorgeous . . . or more alone.

"How was Scotland?" she finally managed to ask.

"I didnae expect it to be so beautiful."

She couldn't stop her smile from forming at the slightest hint of a brogue.

"But I have difficulty understanding half of what they say. I'm not familiar with some of the words they use and most Scots have such a thick brogue . . . you ken?"

She gave a quick laugh. "I do understand. But in time you'll become accustomed to it, and you'll sound as though you grew up there."

"I doubt that." She heard no Scot at all now, just the English accent that had marked his words before he left. "How have you been?"

Awful, terrible. "Busy. We have several ladies living here now."

"That doesn't tell me how *you* are."

She wanted to look away from him, afraid he was seeing into her too deeply, but didn't want to lose a second of having him in her sight, because she might never see him again. It would be a mistake to say it, but she said it anyway. "I miss you. More than I thought it possible to miss a person."

He studied her. *Say something, say something, say something.*

"You were right about the aristocracy. It's nothing like living in the rookeries. You told me about servants lighting the fires. I didn't know they were called to stir the blasted thing. You have two dukes. One is more important than the other. You better make certain you sit them at the correct place at the table." He shook his head. "Relatively quickly I'm going to have to take a wife—someone who grew up among the aristocracy and knows all the finer details to help me navigate my way through Society."

Certain he was going to ask her once more, she began lining up her arguments for why it couldn't be her, but they sounded hollow now in light of how much she'd missed him.

"My father assures me I'll have no trouble a'tall finding a lady willing to marry me."

Her heart thudded with the realization that another woman would be the recipient of his proposal. All for the best. With a great deal of effort, she managed to say, "I'm sure you won't."

He held her gaze with such intensity, she thought it would be impossible for them to ever separate. "Thea, if he had another son, I'd find a way to pass off this obligation that's been thrust on me. But when I think of what they went through, especially my mother, when I see how much they love me, even though I wasn't part of their lives all these years—their pride, their joy—I can't not be the son they'd hoped I'd be."

Of course he'd be a loyal son who'd make them proud because that was the sort of man he was. It was one of the reasons she loved him so much. "I know."

"They're hosting a ball next week in order to introduce their son around." Reaching into his jacket, he walked up to her and held out the vellum. "I would like for you to attend."

"It'll ruin things for them, for you."

"I think you're wrong." He tossed it onto the low table in front of the sofa. "I'll leave it in case you change your mind."

"I won't. Please don't hope that I will. You'll only be disappointed."

"I'd rather risk disappointment than take no risk at all."

With that, the Earl of Tewksbury strode out of the room, leaving her wishing that he'd at least kissed her before he left.

"YOU HAVE A visitor in the parlor."

Althea gave a start at Jewel's voice coming to her unexpectedly. She'd been reading the invitation Benedict had left with her five days earlier, not the first time she'd done so, and it probably wouldn't be the last. Every time she did, she envisioned him taking her in his arms and sweeping her over the dance floor. It was a beautiful dream, one that also visited when she slept. Except then, when they circled the room, as they passed by, people gave them their backs. She would awaken in a sweat, heart thundering, guilt gnawing at her because she brought him such shame.

"Is it him?" Had he come to ask her again?

"It's a woman. Says she's the Duchess of Glasford."

His mother. Why would she come here? She shot to her feet, patted her hair.

"Do I look all right?" She shook her head before Jewel could answer. "Never mind. It doesn't matter." What did she care what the duchess thought of her?

She dashed down the stairs and into the parlor, stumbling to a stop at the sight of the woman in the wheelchair. She needed to talk to Jewel about communicating more information so she wasn't taken by surprise. Hell, she needed to have a word with Benedict. Why hadn't he mentioned his mother's situation? She curtsied. "Your Grace."

"Miss Stanwick?"

She nodded. "Yes."

The woman tilted her head up to the man standing beside her. "John, please wait in the foyer until I'm ready to depart."

"Yes, Your Grace."

The man walked out, a servant, no doubt, who saw to her needs.

"I'll see about having some tea brought in," Althea said. She should have thought to tell Jewel to fetch it.

"Don't go to the trouble. I won't be staying that long." The woman contained a calmness, a gentleness, that seemed too soft for this world. She tilted her head toward the sofa. "Please, sit."

When a duchess asked, you did it, even when you didn't want to. Althea sat. "How may I be of service, Duchess?"

"You may come to our ball tomorrow evening."

Her stomach dropped to her toes; her fingers knotted in her lap. "I'm not sure how much you know about my relationship with Benedict—"

"Oh, I suspect I know nearly everything, Miss Stanwick. Our son spoke about you with a great deal of fondness while we were in Scotland."

"Then you know my father is a traitor." She was expecting her not to know, to see shock make its way over her face.

"I do, yes. He was involved in a plot to see the Queen murdered as I'm given to understand."

Her fingers were going numb. "As a result, you know I am not welcomed in Society. If I attend, it will be quite awkward, not only for me but for you and, more important, for Benedict. I will receive cuts direct. People will turn their backs. They will whisper ugly things about me, my father, you, Benedict. They'll wonder why you invited the daughter of a man who was hanged for being a traitor, a man whose children were denied their birthright. Your standing could suffer. It won't at all assist Benedict in finding a proper wife, one who will be proud to be at his side, who will love him. I've tried to explain all this to him, to make him see, but he hasn't been part of the aristocracy long enough to know how this will play out. He simply doesn't understand."

"But you do. You understand perfectly. Have the courage to show him. Only then will he truly understand the sacrifices that must be made."

Her entire body, mind, and soul rebelled at the notion. The humiliation she would suffer, the shame, the chill that would settle in her bones. It had nearly killed her before. The months since had toughened her, but was it enough to withstand the bludgeoning she would receive?

The duchess clasped Althea's hands. "If you truly love my son, you must attend the ball. You must force him to see the repercussions of your presence. Otherwise, I fear he will cling to the possibility of having you, and will never seek out another, will never know happiness. I love him far too much not to do what is best for him. I am in this wheelchair because of my love for him and his father, and yet I have never regretted a day of it. Knowing what I would suffer, I would do it all again in a heartbeat. How much do you truly love my son, Miss Stanwick? What would you endure to ensure his future happiness?"

Chapter 30

*A*s the coach the duchess had sent for her made its way hastily through the streets, Althea fought her nerves, strived for calm. She'd almost instructed the driver to return to the duke's residence without her, but eventually, she'd climbed inside.

She had considered the green gown, but in the end went with the red. To ensure Benedict understood fully all the ramifications of her presence, she had to be as visible as possible. In a small secret pocket, she'd slipped the match safe he'd given her because she knew on the journey home, which would begin shortly after she arrived, she would need the reminder that even in darkness she could find light.

Hester had fixed her hair into an elaborate coiffure, using the pearl combs Althea had purchased that afternoon. Thanks to Benedict's generosity, she could indulge herself every now and then. She'd also purchased a pearl necklace and earbobs. If she was going to face the ghosts of her past, she intended to do it with all the dignity and aplomb she could muster. She had no intention of letting them see how harsh they'd made her life.

She'd deliberately delayed her arrival an hour to ensure a more full ballroom, even though it meant a greater humiliation—more backs turned, more cuts.

But his eventual happiness was paramount, and he couldn't have it if he was lonely, if he didn't take a wife. She didn't want to consider how deeply the lacerations to her heart would be when she read of his betrothal in the newspaper. She would survive it.

The coach slowed, turned down a drive, and slowed even further as other vehicles made their way to the front of the residence where steps led into the massive manor. People were not lingering about, thank goodness, so she might make it inside without too many cuts directed her way.

She did notice one man not heading for the steps but standing only a little bit back from the curb. People were giving him a wide berth, not that she blamed them. His arms were crossed over his chest, and he greeted no one. Simply waited.

The coach finally came to a complete stop. A footman stepped forward, opened the door, and handed her down. Her feet had barely hit the brick when Aiden Trewlove was standing before her, having left the spot that it had appeared he was guarding. He offered his hand.

"Beast wasn't certain you'd show. He asked me to escort you in if you did."

She placed her hand in his. "You were waiting for me, not knowing if I'd make an appearance?"

Tucking her hand in the crook of his elbow, he began leading her toward the entrance. "He didn't want you to have to go in alone, and he's occupied being introduced to all the toffs. I'm sure he'd have rather been out here. Until tonight, he's never been to one of these things."

She hadn't been able to remember seeing him at a ball, but had thought that perhaps she'd simply overlooked him, although he was impossible not to see. "He's never been to a ball, ever?"

"No. Avoided them like the plague. No ball, no dinner, no fancy affair."

An earl and countess she knew were about to go through the doorway. It was obvious the countess caught sight of her. Her eyes widened just before the woman wrinkled her nose as though she'd smelled something foul and hurried into the manor.

As far as cuts direct went, it wasn't one of the worst. At the moment she was less concerned with how people were treating her and more concerned with how they were treating Benedict. A ball, especially one that it appeared most of London would be attending, could be overwhelming at the best of times. She'd been prepared for her first ball and still had found it unsettling as she'd struggled to find people she knew, to become comfortable with all the strangers she'd yet to meet. Almost everyone in attendance, except for his family, would be strangers.

And here was his brother, someone he truly needed inside that room, showing him a familiar face, a mischievous grin, helping to put him at ease with his surroundings.

Although the evening was cool, she hadn't bothered with a wrap so had nothing to leave with the waiting footman as they crossed the threshold into the grand and beautiful foyer. Another footman was directing people down a hallway that no doubt led to the ballroom.

But Aiden didn't follow the others. He directed her toward the sweeping staircase. At the bottom, standing about, was every other Trewlove sibling and their spouses. Benedict was alone in there, facing all these people for the first time. She was horrified by the realization.

Gillie smiled at her. "You came."

"Why aren't you all in the ballroom?"

"Because Beast asked us to wait out here for you."

Idiot man. He truly didn't understand what it was like to circulate through the aristocracy, how hard it would be if he knew no one else in the room. Although his parents would be with him, the people he truly needed were out here—waiting for her.

"Let's go, shall we?" Mick asked.

Yes, quickly. She needed to get them into the ballroom, so they could be there for him and demonstrate their support for him.

Selena approached, and Aiden released his hold on Althea in order to tuck his wife in close.

"Lead the way," Aiden said to Althea, "and know we're here if you need us."

Only she didn't need them watching out for her. She needed them standing at Benedict's back. She needed him to know he wasn't alone.

WHILE HIS SIBLINGS had attended balls, even hosted a couple, Beast had managed to avoid them. He'd never felt as though he belonged. His heritage said that he did, yet still he felt out of place, like a sprawling weed in a flower garden. He kept expecting someone to come along, pluck him out, and send him on his way.

He stood beside his parents, greeting the guests who were announced and ambled down the stairs. Fancy had gone through something similar the year before when she'd been introduced into Society and had advised him not to keep count of the introductions because it would only make the night seem longer.

What made it seem longer was the manner in which all the young ladies gazed at him as though he was a newly discovered dessert they were looking forward to sampling. He met pretty ladies, plain ones, short ones, tall ones. Some appeared bolder than others. Some shyer. He was certain many of them were delightful.

But none snagged his attention the way Thea had when he'd first laid eyes on her.

He'd promised himself he wouldn't think about her tonight. He'd kept the promise for all of two minutes. He wasn't certain how much longer he could live with the hope that she might show. That her presence would make this night bearable.

They were more than an hour in, and the ballroom packed with the glamorous, the elegant, and the arrogant. It seemed the duke and duchess were favorites among the *ton*. Which he fully understood. Even if they weren't his parents, he'd have liked them. They were kind, generous, and thoughtful. Once he'd wondered how different he might be if he'd been raised by them, but it was pointless to speculate. He couldn't imagine a life any better than the one he'd had, in spite of its hardships. His life would have been absent his brothers and sisters and his mum. He wouldn't have wanted that.

"Miss Althea Stanwick!" The majordomo's booming voice rang out, and it was like the pealing of a thousand bells at Christmas.

She'd come. His heart soared, everything within him came alive, even as he told himself that her presence made no difference, that she would not marry him. That tonight might be the last time she was in his life.

She stood at the top of the stairs in the red gown that flattered her, when she needed no flattery. Elegantly, with his siblings and their spouses forming a phalanx behind her—he'd never loved them more—she began descending. He wanted to take her to his bedchamber and peel that gown off her. He wanted to kiss every inch of her, make love to her until dawn. Maybe then he could forget her. *Give me one more night, Thea. We'll make it last.*

Except he didn't want only one more night. He didn't want to forget her.

He turned to his parents. "I love you both, but this is not my world."

She was his world.

His father simply gave him a stoic, brisk nod—and in that action Beast saw himself as a boy holding firm and strong when he'd been teased or ridiculed for things not his fault: his bastardy, his height, his bulk, his imperfections.

His mother took his gloved hand, squeezed it, pressed it to her lips, and looked at him through luminous eyes filled with so much love, a powerful love, a love strong enough to place her child, a product of her heart, into another's keeping, and she would do it again, bearing the burden of it without remorse or grief because protecting him, keeping him safe, was more important to her than anything she might suffer as a result.

And he realized he might have inherited none of his features from her, but he had inherited her heart.

While they'd told him he was their son, and he'd taken them

at their word, believed them, it wasn't until that moment that he truly felt he was their son.

What had she told him on that dreary rainy afternoon when missing Althea had brought him such sadness and loneliness? Never apologize to your mother for being who you are.

Who was he? He finally knew. He was a man who would find a way to honor their love and his birthright, but he would do it following the dictates of his heart, not Society.

He became aware of dancers stopping, people murmuring. He spotted Chadbourne making his way to the stairs. He recognized a man intent on revenge when he spotted him, a man who hadn't liked being bested at cards. Beast hadn't looked at the guest list, hadn't known who'd been invited until they arrived. He'd have struck this bloke's name right off the list. "Please, excuse me," he said to his parents.

His long strides soon carried him to Chadbourne's side. "Turn your back on her, and I'll snap your weak little spine in two." He didn't bother to moderate his voice, to keep his temper from flaring.

"You cannot allow her to fully descend these stairs. You cannot welcome her."

"I can and I will. What I cannot do is allow you to remain so much as one minute longer. So either carry yourself out of here or I shall take great pleasure in dragging you out."

The earl sneered at him. "You didn't grow up in Society. You don't understand its rules."

"Thank God."

"When other lords and ladies, dukes, duchesses, earls, viscounts, turn their backs on her—"

He didn't give him time to finish what was likely to ramble into an obnoxious question. "I will not tolerate anyone being unkind to her."

People had come closer and he wondered if they'd done so with the same purpose as Chadbourne. If so, a lot of dragging out of the room was going to happen, but he had three brothers and two brothers-by-marriage descending those stairs who would help him accomplish it. Aware of murmurings, he had the distinct impression his words were being repeated, repeated, repeated so they reached the farthest corners of the room.

"Go. Now," he said to Chadbourne. "And if you say one word to her to make her doubt her welcome here, you'll feel the weight of my fist against your jaw so fast you'll swear I have the ability to fly."

The man's glare wouldn't frighten a child. He turned. "Jocelyn, we're leaving."

"But it's a ball. I want to dance. Won't you send the carriage back for me?"

He seemed at a loss, but finally began stalking up the stairs. Beast watched him until he passed Thea on her way down. As far as he could tell the earl said not one word to her. Smart man.

He looked over at Lady Jocelyn. She held up her hands. "I shan't give her a cut direct." Then she began walking backward farther into the ballroom as though she feared if she turned around, he'd take offense.

Preparing to jog up the stairs, he turned back to them and froze. She was already there, in front of him, so close he could smell the gardenias. Based on how far back his siblings were, she must have dashed down.

He didn't know what to say to her. *You came* seemed rather trite when compared to all the deep emotions bombarding him. *You're beautiful. I'm so glad you're here. I've missed you dreadfully* were a little closer to expressing his feelings but still fell short.

"Here. Now."

Her words came quietly but clearly.

He studied every line and curve of her face, searching for a clue that she was implying what he dearly hoped she was, that she was telling him what he'd instructed her to do the night they'd lain in bed and bared their souls to each other, admitted their love for each other. Her eyes contained hope and doubt. If he was misreading what she was striving to communicate, he would appear a fool before all the lords and ladies crammed into the ballroom. His mistake would be expounded upon, described in detail, and used to fill columns in the gossip sheets.

Then he realized it would only be a mistake if he let the moment pass without taking a chance that he had the right of it.

It had never been a mistake to kiss her, to bare her breasts in a rumbling carriage. It hadn't been a mistake to take her to his bed, to make love to her.

Very slowly, he lowered himself to one knee. "I told you that when I was in Scotland, a lot of words were used that I didn't know. But there was a phrase I heard, and when I learned what it meant, I thought of you. *Mo chridhe*. My heart. You're my heart, Thea. You always will be. Please, for the love of God, honor me by becoming my wife."

SHE COULD BARELY see him through the blur of her tears.

He was correct. He didn't know the small, subtle aspects of life among the aristocracy. He did not know that one didn't use a booming voice when threatening a lord, that the words should be spoken quietly, just for the two of them. That they shouldn't travel up the stairs to circle around a woman and melt her heart.

And he certainly didn't threaten to do something barbaric like snap a spine in two. Not that she didn't think for one moment that he couldn't do it or that Chadbourne's spine wasn't weak. But a gentleman called for pistols at dawn.

And he didn't threaten to drag a man out of a room. A gentleman signaled to the footmen to do the dragging.

And he should have had his siblings in here with him, supporting him, not asked them to wait in the foyer for a woman who might not have found the courage to come.

So he did indeed need a wife to guide him through the quagmire of etiquette and to ensure he never again sacrificed his happiness for another's.

"Benedict Trewlove Campbell, Earl of Tewksbury, you have so much to learn about the aristocracy, but it seems you know all one needs to know about love. You're my heart as well. It will be my deepest honor to become your wife."

He stood, clasped her in his embrace, and claimed her mouth with a fervent passion that was normally reserved for bedchambers. An aristocratic gentleman would have simply brushed his lips lightly over hers—but on this matter, as she wound her arms around his neck, she was ever so glad he didn't know how it was done among the aristocracy.

Chapter 31

"*I* want to introduce you to my parents," he said some minutes later, threading his gloved fingers through hers. "I think you're going to like them."

She already knew she liked his mother.

As he walked over to where his father stood and his mother sat in her chair, she saw no backs turned, had yet to receive a cut direct within this room, but she wouldn't have cared if either happened. She would bear what she must to be with him. He would protect their children, as would his parents and his siblings.

"Mother, Father, I'd like to introduce Althea Stanwick, my heart and future wife."

She curtsied deeply. "Your Graces."

"It's a pleasure to meet such a courageous lass," the duke said. "We look forward to welcoming you into the family."

"Thank you." Before the duchess, she lowered herself, her gown blossoming out around her. "When you asked me to come tonight, it wasn't so he would see the way of things and understand. You asked me to come so *I* would see the way of things and understand."

The Duchess of Glasford smiled, and it was the most beautiful smile Althea had ever seen. "I wasnae there to comfort him when he was a wee lad and had hurts. When we were in Scotland, I could see that he was hurting without you, but now I could do something to try and stop the hurt. So, yes, I goaded you into coming, hoping it would go as I expected it would. So forgive me for that, Miss Stanwick, but know this. I have had the love of a Campbell man since I was fifteen years old. I know the lengths to which such a man will go for the woman he loves. I would not wish it upon any woman to be denied the sort of love that runs so deep."

"I will work to be the best daughter-by-marriage you could ever hope for."

"As long as you love my son and make him happy, you will be."

"That's an easy enough task you're asking of me."

When they walked away from his parents, they soon found themselves surrounded by his family, all except for Ettie Trewlove, who didn't attend affairs such as this. So many hugs, so many smiles. Funny how life could take a detour that could seem so wrong at the time but eventually would turn out to be right.

"Althea?"

Pivoting around, she smiled. "Hello, Kat."

"I wanted to offer my congratulations on your betrothal."

"Thank you. You were, of course, introduced to the earl."

"Yes, when we arrived."

Althea glanced over at the silent sentinel with his hand resting reassuringly against her lower back. "Lady Kathryn is a dear friend, who recently offered some wise counsel."

"Lady Kathryn, it's a pleasure." He bowed slightly.

"My lord." Kat gave a small curtsy, before giving her attention back to Althea. "I was hoping you might come around for tea when you have time. In the parlor."

"I'd like that very much."

"Wonderful. I have to dash. My next dance is claimed. Do take care." With that, she was gone.

Althea couldn't help but believe that in time, she'd be welcomed into more parlors. But at the moment she had more pressing concerns. She looked up at the man she loved so deeply. "Will you waltz with me?"

He gave her the smile that made him so achingly beautiful. "I thought you would never ask."

She laughed as he swept her onto the dance floor with so much grace that she knew she was envied.

"What you were saying to my mother earlier . . . You've spoken with her before."

"Yesterday she came to see me. I don't know if I would have come if she hadn't, although I was seriously thinking about it. I've missed you so much."

"You'll never have to miss me again."

"She didn't tell you she'd visited with me?"

"No."

"But you had your family waiting, even though you didn't know if I would show. When you needed them to be with you in here."

"Did you honestly believe I would have you face these people alone? I will always protect you, however I must. And if I can't be there, my family will be."

She was not going to weep in the middle of a waltz. "I can almost forgive my father—not for the plot against the Crown—but for the role he had in changing the course of my life. I might have never met you otherwise."

"What a tragedy that would have been."

His words held no teasing, just an absolute conviction. He meant them. She couldn't imagine how unsatisfactory her life would have been without him to love. "We have each other now."

"Now and forever."

Chapter 32

*T*wo nights later, lying in her bed, she listened intently for any sound at her window. That morning she'd gone to the address Griffith had left with her, delivered the message he'd told her would bring them to her. She'd been on edge ever since, whenever a floorboard creaked, a door was closed, a bump echoed somewhere. She'd left a candle burning in the window so they'd know which room was hers.

Then she heard a click. A pebble against glass. She scrambled out of bed, rushed to the window as another click sounded, and looked out. Only darkness greeted her. She blew out the flame on the candle, snatched up her wrapper, and slipped into it as she headed out of the room. Quickly, but silently, she made her way down the back staircase to the kitchen.

Opening the door, she stepped out onto the stoop. "Marcus? Griff?"

Two large silhouettes emerged silently from the darkness like wraiths in the night. She might have screamed had she not been expecting them. "Come inside. No one is about to disturb us."

She'd learned only too well that voices could carry outside.

Returning inside, she waited. As noiselessly as fog rolling in, her brothers fairly crept over the threshold, Marcus closing the door in their wake.

She barely recognized them. Their features were the same, but they seemed more substantial than before. An alertness hovered around them as they took in their surroundings, a tight energy escaped them. They came off as powerful and dangerous, men to be reckoned with. Marcus, especially. He reminded her of a viper she'd seen at the zoological gardens, poised to strike at the smallest of provocations.

"Would you like some scotch?" She'd brought in a bottle earlier, set it on the table, in preparation of welcoming them.

Marcus met her gaze, his blue eyes icy, sending a shiver through her. His sable hair was long, almost as long as Benedict's. The shade made his eyes stand out all the more. "No, thank you. It dulls the senses, slows the reflexes."

She feared they were constantly in want of both. Their jackets did not flow smoothly over their torsos, and she suspected pistols, knives, and weapons with which she was not familiar were tucked away.

"What did you need of us, Althea?" Griffith asked, a fissure of irritation in his voice at the inconvenience.

No hug, then, no joyful reunion. He had changed in the months since she'd last seen him, and she suspected he no longer apologized for his actions. His hair was longer. Like Marcus, he was in need of a razor.

"I have something for you." She picked up the paper-wrapped packet she'd placed on the table earlier when she'd brought in the scotch and extended it to Marcus.

He peered into the package, riffled through the banknotes. "It looks to be about four thousand pounds." He pinned her with his gaze. "How did you come to have this?"

"I earned most of it tutoring the ladies." She blushed, not certain why she felt a need to confess the rest, perhaps because she wanted them to know she had changed as well. "A little over a thousand I earned at the gaming tables."

"You've been gambling?" Griffith asked, and for a heartbeat he reminded her of the brother with whom she'd lived for three months and she almost smiled.

"Only once. I thought the money might help you in your quest . . . or even make it unnecessary."

"It's a kind gesture, but you should keep it, Althea. You might have a need of it," Marcus said.

"I won't. I'm to marry. An announcement will appear in the papers in a couple of days, but I wanted to tell you before you read about it."

"I haven't given you permission to marry."

The words were so stern, so absolute, that she released a blunt laugh. "I don't need your permission, Marcus. I've lived on my own these few months and I shall do as I wish."

"Who negotiated the settlement? What are the terms?"

In spite of his callousness, it appeared he still cared about her. "No settlement. I'm not in need of one. I love him, and he loves me. I'll never be without."

"You're marrying Trewlove," Griffith stated with certainty.

She glanced at him, smiled. "Yes, although as it turns out he's the son and heir of the Duke of Glasford."

"Bloody hell."

Her smile grew. "Yes, I think he might have reacted the same way when he discovered the truth of things."

She gave her attention back to Marcus. "I know part of the reason behind whatever it is you're doing was to ensure I have a good match. I've acquired that." *On my own.* "So if you're putting yourself in danger on my account, please know there is no need."

His features softened, his eyes warmed, and she saw a flicker of the brother she'd once known. "There is no honor to be had for Father, but we can restore honor to the family. You'll want that for your children."

She took a step toward him. "What I want is for my children to know their uncles."

"But what have their uncles with no honor?"

Tears pricked her eyes. "I don't suppose you'll come to the wedding next month, give me away."

"I doubt matters will be settled by then. It's important that we keep to the shadows and not associate with the aristocracy. It might bring you danger to be seen with us. It's better if those with whom we're presently . . . associating believe we've cut all ties with our past. But I do wish you every happiness."

She couldn't help herself. She flung her arms around his neck, hugged him tightly. "Please be certain that you do nothing that will prevent my children from knowing you someday."

His arms were sure and strong as he enclosed her in his embrace. "Don't worry yourself. We'll be back in your life before you know it."

She certainly hoped so.

When he released her, Griffith clasped her to his strong, lean body. "Who'd have ever thought I'd miss you?"

Her arms closed securely around him. "Watch his back and yours. I love you both. Please take care not to break my heart."

He stepped back. "You take care as well. Let Trewlove know if he doesn't treat you well, he'll answer to us."

"That won't even be an issue."

"I know. I saw the way he looked at you that night, but still it had to be said."

"We have to go," Marcus stated, "but we'll take the funds. They'll prove useful."

"If you ever need anything of me—"

He gave her a nod. "We know."

He opened the door. She followed her brothers through it and watched with sadness as they disappeared into the darkness.

THEY WERE MARRIED in St. George's. So many people were in the church that Althea had told Beast she couldn't decide if they'd forgotten what her father had done, forgotten she was his daughter, or resolved that she shouldn't be made to suffer for grievous actions over which she'd had no say.

But the breakfast that followed at the Duke and Duchess of Glasford's residence was a more exclusive affair, only family and close friends, so his mum would feel comfortable attending.

Still, it was quite formal with white lace-covered tables spread throughout the large dining hall. Beast and Althea sat at a long table facing the room. They shared the table with his mum and his parents.

As the food was served, he leaned toward Althea and whispered, "I'd rather be nibbling on you."

Although she blushed, her eyes warmed. "Maybe we should eat quickly."

"Do you think anyone would notice if we just . . . disappeared?" He hadn't made love to her since she'd agreed to become his wife. He was quite looking forward to taking her slowly, then quickly, then slowly again.

"As we're the guests of honor, I think so."

A tapping on a glass caught his attention, and he realized his father had stood. When everyone grew silent, the duke said, "Before we get started, I have a few words I'd like to say.

"When I was a young lad of sixteen, one evening near dusk, I looked across the glen and caught sight of Mara frolicking in the stream . . . and that was it for me. I fell madly in love, wanted no one else. I imagined the children we would have, the weddings we'd attend, the grandchildren we would spoil." He shook his head. "But Fate, she is a fickle lass. The dreams Mara and I dreamed, the lovely future we whispered about beneath the moon whenever we snuck out through our bedchamber windows and met near the stream . . . well, they were not to be.

"Until today. We have our lad back. We attended his wedding. And, yes, we're once again dreaming of spoiling a grandbairn or two.

"But we wouldnae be here, wouldnae have our dreams returned to us, if not for Ettie Trewlove. You gave our lad the family we couldn't. You kept the promise you made to Mara, to love him as your own. Which I'm thinking, based on the name so many people call him, was no easy task."

Beast grinned as laughter echoed around him. When it grew quiet again, his father continued.

"We thank you from the depths of our hearts for that. And we thank his brothers and sisters. It's clear you have a special bond, which you all appear to be too smart to take for granted. And now Benedict has a lovely wife whom we're looking forward to getting to know.

"To that end, I'd like to bestow upon our son and our new daughter a Scottish blessing. Because there are so many English crowded into this room, I'll spare you the Scottish version and give you words you can understand." He lifted his flute of champagne.

"May the best you've ever seen

"Be the worst you'll ever see.

"May a mouse never leave your pantry

"With a teardrop in his eye.

"May you always keep hale and hearty

"'Til you're old enough to die.

"May you always be just as happy

"As your ma and I'd wish you always to be."

He raised his glass higher. *"Slàinte."*

"Slàinte," echoed around the room as glasses were lifted and champagne sipped.

When Beast kissed his wife, cheers erupted.

Scotland
One week later

"I think I'm falling in love with Scotland."

Sitting in the bed, with one hand behind his head, Beast smiled at his wife's words, spoken as she stood nude before the window, gazing out at the early-morning mist blanketing the glen. His parents had stayed in London, giving him and Thea some time alone at the estate before joining them.

"I'm rather fond of the view myself."

With a laugh, she swung around. "I thought by now you'd have

grown tired of it. We've hardly worn any clothing since we arrived."

Because they'd seldom left this chamber. The second day he
had taken her riding to see the lochs, hills, and forests. In the early
evening they often strolled through the gardens. But he seldom
wore more than trousers and a shirt. She didn't bother with a
corset.

It made it easier to divest their clothing quickly when they returned to the room. They had weeks of abstinence to make up for.

"Will we live here, do you think?"

"Part of the year, but we'll take over another wing. Can't have
my parents hearing your screams of ecstasy."

Screams that drove him wild. Here they didn't have to be quiet,
and they weren't.

After the first hasty coming together, they'd gone more slowly
with the others, exploring each other as though every aspect was
new and unfamiliar. In a way it was. Now there was a certainty to
things. She was his wife, would always be so.

With slow, sensual movements, she strolled over, clambered
onto the bed, climbed onto him, and straddled his hips. "My fire
needs stirring."

Laughing, he threaded his fingers through her hair and brought
her mouth to his, claiming it with a thrust of his tongue. He still
couldn't keep his bloody mouth off her, which suited her just fine
as she seemed unable to keep hers off him. They were perfect
together. Their needs equal, their wants similar. Their desire to
please the other identical.

With a moan, she lifted her hips and lowered herself onto his
hard shaft. He groaned as she sank deep. He would never grow
weary of feeling her muscles clutching him.

Then she was riding him with the Scottish sun filtering in
through the windows, and he wondered briefly if it might kiss
her backside and leave freckles there for *him* to kiss.

Her gasps began in earnest and he knew pleasure was taking
hold of her just as it was him. They were so attuned.

When her cries began echoing around him, his grunts joined in, creating a melody he hoped to hear until the end of his days.

She melted over him, and he held her close while their breaths slowed and their bodies cooled.

It was several minutes before he was able to move and then it was only his voice. "Do you know what I thought the first time I saw you?"

Lifting herself up slightly, she captured his gaze and shook her head.

"She doesn't belong here. But I was wrong, *mo chridhe*. You belong wherever I am."

When she took possession of his mouth with a fervor that matched her love for him, he realized he belonged wherever she was.

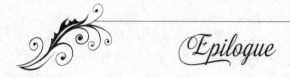

Epilogue

Scotland
November 1910

*W*ith his arms crossed over his chest, the Duke of Glasford stood against a wall in the great hall and watched as his duchess began gathering the crowd of nearly fifty children, spouses, and grandchildren into some sort of order in front of the massive fireplace that had warmed the arses of kings. Thea was a miracle worker when it came to organizing the Trewlove clan for a family portrait.

Beast had been duke for close to two decades. His mother had grown weaker and more frail through the years. He couldn't help but believe that all she'd endured to protect him had continued to take a toll on her and been responsible for giving him fewer years with her. Wearing a gentle smile, she had passed away with the two men who loved her each holding one of her hands. Beast had watched as his father's heart broke. So he hadn't been at all surprised when his father had passed away quietly in his sleep not more than six weeks later. His parents' love was such that it bound them not only in life but also in death.

His chest swelling with love and pride at the sight of his first-born son cradling within his arms *his* recently arrived firstborn son, Beast did wish his parents had lived long enough to see that the Campbell line was secure for at least two more generations. They'd met his son but not his grandson.

"I donnae know how she does it, arranging everyone and keeping them in place," Beast said. These days he sounded more Scottish than English.

"By terrorizing my grandchildren," Aiden said.

"I see nothing wrong with that. They're terrors, your grandchildren."

"They are not. They're little angels. Every last one of them."

With a soft laugh, Gillie shook her head. "Can you believe there are so many of us now?"

Not all their children had married, but those who had were quick to fill cradles.

"Does anyone have an accurate count?" Finn asked.

"Don't see the point," Mick said. "By the time you get your tally, someone either gets married or has a babe."

"Mum looks like she's in heaven," Fancy said, "with all her grandchildren and great-grandchildren surrounding her. She has such a lovely blush in her cheeks."

Thea had placed her in a white brocade winged-back chair, the newest babe in her arms, the other wee ones gathered at her feet, the older ones standing behind her.

"I'm not certain it's the children causing the blush," Gillie mused. "I think it might be Mick's gardener. Of late, I've gone to see her a few mornings, quite early, and he's there having a cuppa."

Years ago, when Mick had built himself a manor on land just outside London, he'd also built a lovely cottage for their mum so she could still have her independence but be near. Beast and his siblings contributed toward the upkeep, the servants, and anything else she required. It was going to be a blow when the day came that she was no longer with them.

"Gil, she has nine decades on her," Beast reminded his sister.

"And you have seven. Are you telling me you've become a monk?"

"Well, no, but . . ." He glared at Mick. "He a good man, your gardener?"

Mick shrugged. "Apparently so if he's putting a blush in Mum's cheeks."

"How long has this been going on?" Finn asked.

Mick sighed. "Years?"

"You bloody well knew and didn't tell us?" Aiden asked, his tone incensed.

"I suspected. He spends more time in her garden than he does in mine, and mine is ten times the size of hers."

"She's not alone or lonely. She has someone." Fancy smiled brightly. "I think it's wonderful."

"Because you've always fancied romantic stories," Aiden said. "When I get back to London, I'll be having a word with the bloke."

"No, you won't," Mick said.

"I'm not going to have him taking advantage of my mum."

"Aiden, when I said years . . . I'm talking possibly twenty-five."

"That long," Gillie said. "I wonder why she didn't tell us."

"You know, Mum. She has her secrets."

"Maybe she likes feeling a little bit naughty," Beast said. "But perhaps it wouldn't be unwarranted for us to let her know that we'd welcome him into the fold."

That suggestion was met with a series of serious nods. He glanced over at Robin. He'd been right about the lad's height. When he was finally done growing, he was only an inch or so shorter than Beast. "You've been unusually quiet."

The lad shrugged his slender shoulders, although he wasn't much of a lad any longer. He'd traveled the world capturing animals with his camera. He'd been twelve when he'd told Thorne he thought they should start leaving the animals in their original homes. "I'm just surprised so many of you didn't know about Gran and the gardener."

"You knew?" Aiden asked.

Robin grinned broadly. "Asked him some years back if he'd kissed her, and he admitted to doing so."

Soft laughter sounded among them.

"You ask that question of everyone?" Aiden asked.

Robin wiggled his eyebrows. "Want to know who your younger son is kissing these days?"

Beast could see that Aiden was tempted to ask, but instead he simply shoved playfully on the young man's shoulder. "Maybe you should focus on kissing your wife."

"I kiss Angela more than enough, thank you very much." Few knew that Angela was Finn's daughter, taken without his knowledge and raised by another couple. They'd all felt a bit of poetic justice had occurred the day she married Robin and became a Trewlove.

"No such thing," Mick told him. "You can always work in another kiss."

"All right!" Thea called out, motioning at them. "I'm ready to arrange you lot."

As they walked toward the fireplace, Beast glanced at the space above the mantelpiece where the framed canvas that bore the word TREWLOVE in a multitude of colors, the same canvas they'd all painted on a long-ago Christmas Eve, hung. When Robin had left to attend Eton, he'd given it to Beast.

"Since your last name is no longer Trewlove, I thought you might need the reminder more than I do."

He hadn't needed the reminder. At heart, he would always be and remain a Trewlove, but the lad's generosity had touched him deeply and so, just as he had with Sally Greene's coins, he'd accepted the gift graciously.

He'd continued to publish his novels as Benedict Trewlove. Over the years, he'd written thirty, and while Thea always guessed the butler was the culprit, he'd never had a butler commit a murder until his last book. It was his gift to her. When he had decided to put away his pen, in his final book, at last his detective had married the widow he'd once suspected of killing her husband.

He and his siblings stepped up onto the deep stone hearth that extended beyond the portion where a fire normally burned and arranged themselves in the order in which Ettie Trewlove had come into their life.

Mick, Aiden, Finn, Benedict, Gillian, Fancy, Robin.

Their spouses joined them. He placed his arms around Thea,

intertwining his fingers just below her ribs, where her hands joined his. The hearth was tall enough that it gave them enough height, so she'd be seen over the head of their son's wife.

Thea's hair had gone lighter, paler, over the years, was almost silver now. His hair was streaked with white but most of it remained the shade of midnight.

"All right," the photographer said, holding up a hand, "look at my finger. Say *slàinte!*"

"Slàinte!" echoed through the room five times as five photographs were taken.

"We're finished," he finally declared, and the crowd dispersed with hallelujahs and efficiency.

Within his arms, Thea turned to face him and sighed. "Well, that's done for another year."

The photograph, yes, but the portraits of the immediate family members that were to be painted in oils remained to be done. He doubted any other generation of Campbells had been documented as well as this one.

"You're so skilled at managing things," he said.

"I've gained a lot of experience from managing you over the years."

He scoffed, laughed. "You do keep me from becoming too arrogant."

With a great deal of tenderness, he tucked his forefinger beneath her chin and stroked his thumb over her bottom lip. She was still as beautiful to him as she'd been when she'd first approached his table and asked what she could bring him. She still managed to steal his breath. She still owned his heart.

"Do you have any idea how very much I love you, how grateful I am you've been at my side all these years, how much you brighten my world?"

"As though a thousand tapers had been lit?"

He'd forgotten how he'd once described to her Sally's smile in those terms. "So many more than a thousand. Robin once asked me what kissing you was like. I told him it was as vast as the oceans, as infinite as the stars. Even that is a paltry description. Of all the moments in my life, the one for which I am most grateful is the one that first allowed me to catch sight of you."

Smiling broadly, with all the love she felt for him shining in her eyes, she wound her arms around his neck. "At our age, I think people will understand if we go upstairs for a wee nap."

Which would result in no nap at all, at least not before he made love to her.

"Knowing how much I adore you, Beauty, and that we're a good five minutes from our chambers, I think they'll understand if it's impossible for me to wait that long to at least have a taste of you."

Drawing her in close, he lowered his mouth to hers. As his wife returned his kiss with an enthusiasm that guaranteed they would be heading upstairs in a very short amount of time, he recalled the blessing his father had given them on the day they married. He couldn't help but believe, through the passing years, that he had always been as happy as his parents had wished him to be.

Author's Note

$\mathcal{M}$y dear reader,

In 1869, the law changed so titles and properties of peers who committed treason would still pass on to their heirs, rather than be reclaimed by the Crown. Unfortunately, I did not discover this law until after the story had already taken hold of me. Altering the timetable made the story clunky, and so since I write fiction and have created a fictional world, I applied literary license. In my world, either the law didn't exist, it was ignored, or Parliament voted to make an exception for a duke who wanted to kill a queen. You may choose.

The condition that Beast and his father shared is microtia. There are several variations of it, and it can have an impact on hearing. In approximately 5% of cases, the condition is hereditary.

Harriette Wilson was an infamous courtesan during the Regency era, who did indeed publish her memoirs, which are now in the public domain and can be downloaded from several sources.

The Ten Bells pub exists to this day. At least two of Jack the Ripper's victims frequented the pub and are thought to have been seen leaving it the night they were killed.

Most of the working class couldn't afford clocks, and alarm clocks had yet to be invented. Therefore, people hired a knocker-up or knocker-upper to wake them. Beast's tale of running across a murdered woman is based on an actual account of a knocker-upper who ran across one of Jack the Ripper's victims.

If you're wondering why Finn and Lavinia didn't simply adopt Robin to give him their name— In Britain, child adoption didn't become legal until 1926. Prior to that it was informal, usually done in secret, and not legally binding.

The blessing that the Duke of Glasford bestowed on Beast and Althea is an ancient Scottish blessing that I once heard a dear Scottish friend give as a toast, and I fell in love with it.

I hope you've enjoyed reading about and getting to know the Trewloves. They are bound to make cameos in the next two books as Thea's brothers search for their own happily-ever-after.

Happy reading!
Lorraine

Coming next
The first book in the
Once Upon a Dukedom duology.

Scoundrel of My Heart

The second son of a duke, Griffith Stanwick was the spoiled spare for whom everything came easily. Until his family lost everything, and he lost the woman he loved. Now he will pay any price to have her back in his arms.